2015

To remember what you've read, write your initials in a square!

faculties of Harvard Medical School and the Salk Institute for Biological Studies. He is best-known for his research and writings on the biological basis of sexual orientation.

	DATE DUE	8/15

W9-CKJ-726

Also by Simon LeVay

NON-FICTION

The Sexual Brain

City of Friends
(with Elisabeth Nonas)

Queer Science

The Earth in Turmoil
(with Kerry Sieh)

Here Be Dragons
(with David Koerner)

Human Sexuality
(with Janice Baldwin)

Discovering Human Sexuality
(with Janice and John Baldwin)

Healing the Brain
(with Curt Fried)

When Science Goes Wrong

Gay, Straight, and the Reason Why

FICTION

Albrick's Gold

THE DONATION OF CONSTANTINE

A Novel

Simon LeVay

LAMBOURN BOOKS

LAMBOURN BOOKS

LOS ANGELES CALIFORNIA

www.lambournbooks.com

Cover: Pope Sylvester receives the imperial tiara from the Emperor Constantine. Detail of fresco in the Oratory of Sylvester, Basilica dei Quattro Santi Coronati, Rome (public domain image). *Cover background:* Latin text of the Donation of Constantine.

The song *Seven Days Since I Saw My Beloved* (Chapter 19) is adapted from a translation of Papyrus Chester Beatty 1 by the late Miriam Lichtheim. (in *Ancient Egyptian Literature—A Book of Readings, Vol. II: The New Kingdom,* University of California Press, 1976).

ISBN: 147013215X
ISBN-13: 978-1470132156

ACKNOWLEDGMENTS

For their comments on earlier versions of this book, I am greatly indebted to Sara Maitland, Judith Herrin, Susan Merzbach, Laurie Saunders, Julian Le Vay, Jo Dobry, and Benedict Le Vay.

My partner Mike Patel provided unfailing support and encouragement, without which the book could never have been started or completed.

Ahi, Costantin, di quanto mal fu matre,
non la tua conversion, ma quella dote
che da te prese il primo ricco patre!

*Ah Constantine, how many evils did your deed
give birth to—not your conversion, but the gift
that the first rich Pope received from you!*

Dante, *Inferno*, Canto XIX: 115-117

LIST OF CHARACTERS
(in order of appearance)

AISTULF (d. 756): King of the Lombards
EUTYCHIUS (d. 751): Imperial Governor of Ravenna
STEPHEN II (715-757): Pope, 752-757
AMBROSE (d. 752): First Notary to Pope Stephen
THEOPHYLACT: Archdeacon to Pope Stephen
PAUL (?720-767): Pope Stephen's brother, a Deacon
*ZAID: Teenage son of Omar
*LENORA: Teenage daughter of Sibylla and Marcus
*ANTONIUS: A seller of pastries
*OMAR: A trader in relics
*SIBYLLA: A spell-caster
*MARCUS: Sibylla's husband, a miller
*LEO: Commander of the Papal Militia
*MARCELLUS: Papal Treasurer
*PHILIP: Papal Paymaster
*TULLIUS: Papal Librarian
LEOBA (d. 782): An English nun and missionary
*GAIUS: Grain-master
*VALERIUS: Grain-master, successor to Gaius
AUTCHAR: A Frankish Duke
CHRISTOPHER (d. 771): A Papal Notary
ALDEBERT: A roving heretic
CHARLES (Charlemagne) (742-814): Son of Pepin
PEPIN III ("the Short") (?714 – 768): King of the Franks

(* Fictional character)

1

In the seven hundred and fifty-first year of our Lord's Incarnation

The end came at night.

Shouts and screams and the clash of metal flung the news across the sleeping city: another assault from the south! Bells rang, torches flared. Soldiers and priests, men and women, children and greybeards—all were torn from their dreams of fatness and feasting. Famine-thinned arms clutched for sword or staff or spear. Those who could do so ran or hobbled to the Cesarean Gate. There, at the parapets, the night guards were struggling to fend off dozens of men—how many, it was impossible to tell—who had already succeeded in scaling the walls. They must have come from the direction of Classe, easily crossing the spit of sandy ground that formed a weak link in the city's watery defenses. And the moat, filled with the debris of a year-long siege, no longer offered any hindrance to the assault.

The gate itself held firm. Gradually, the increasing numbers of defenders gained the upper hand. They hurled many of the attackers—living or dead—over the parapets. The tumbling bodies dislodged those still clambering upward, sending a human cascade into the abyss. Those below hesitated. The city might once more be saved; the end might yet be postponed.

But as the battle continued on the southern wall, disaster struck on the other side of the city. Although it seemed impossible, contingents of heavily armed men had dragged themselves, their weapons, and their scaling ladders through the marsh and mud and salt ponds that protected the city's inland flanks. Unnoticed in the general tumult, they had scaled the wall at its lowest and least defended point. Already they leapt from house-top to house-top, and from there down to the narrow streets. Some stopped to light torches, using them to fire the wooden upper stories of the buildings they passed. Others overpowered the few defenders left at Hadrian's gate, and threw it open.

"To the palace!" was the cry, "To the palace!" But where was the palace? In this maze of streets it could be anywhere. Women, hurrying their children to the uncertain safety of the Basilica of St. Vitalis, shrieked and shrank back into the brickwork as the armed invaders loomed up in the darkness. It took only a moment's wave of a sword under a neck to get the answer: "That way, that way, but spare my children, in the name of the Mother of God!" The men raced eastward.

Six months ago, this assault could have been repelled with ease. But since then the granaries had emptied, what with all the hungry peasants and refugees who had crowded into the city. The last lines of supply, from Rimini and from the sea, were cut off in the spring. The animals—scrawny sheep and goats and chickens, dogs and cats—had been slaughtered, and even the rats had been trapped and eaten. The stores of cheese and wine and oil had been emptied. Then there remained only the few miserable tubers and herbs that could be grown within the walls, and now there was just grass and weeds.

Many had died already, of hunger or the plague, and the living were so weak that they could barely raise a sword or stretch a bow. The rocks that once lay in piles on the parapets, ready to hurl down on the heads of attackers— those now filled the moat, and no one had the strength to replenish them. Of the soldiers, many had died in combat. Eighty brave men were lost in just one sortie—a quickly-hatched plan at a moment when the besieging forces seemed to have let down their guard. They had not.

Now hundreds of attackers roamed the city, striking down whoever blocked their way. The screams of the dying fueled their fury, and soldiering yielded to savagery. Murder, rape, looting, and arson—the routine accompaniments of a siege successfully concluded—replaced ordered discipline. These acts compensated the men for the months of hardship they had endured, for they had suffered almost as much as the defenders.

Still, the palace was the goal, and the men who made it there, more disciplined than the rest, engaged the guards in the toughest fighting of the night. But at last the guards were forced back and the men surged into the palace, while another group waited impatiently outside.

Twenty men returned, dragging a struggling prisoner with them. He was as gaunt as any of the city's inhabitants, but he wore a robe that betrayed his office, and his swarthy complexion marked him as a foreigner.

"Your name?" asked the tallest of the attackers, whose armor, though soiled with soot and blood, still flashed in the light of the torches and the blazing buildings.

"My name?" the man prevaricated.

"Your name, or your life!"

"Eu—Eutychius."

"Eutychius—governor of Ravenna?"

"Yes, by—by the Emperor's favor."

"The Emperor's favor?" The soldier laughed. "What kind of favor, leaving you to die in this rat's-hole?"

Yes, what kind of favor, Eutychius thought. Leo, His Most Christian Majesty, bestowed a great honor on him, or so he had imagined. Take care of Ravenna, my dear Eutychius, he murmured, as he sipped the pressings of the autumn's earliest pomegranates. Take care of the Exarchate. Remind the Italians of their duty to us—to Constantinople. Collect taxes. Get rid of those blasphemous images. It all seemed so easy.

But that was two dozen years ago, and a thousand sea-miles away. Leo died. His son cared only for Asia. Then the enemy came, and the Emperor did nothing, month after desperate month, plea after desperate plea. So many dead, and now the survivors were being cut to pieces.

"*What kind of favor?*" the soldier insisted, gesticulating in the governor's face.

Eutychius could hear the screams and smell the stench of death through the smoky darkness. A mindless rage got the better of his fear. "A great and noble favor," he replied. "And I'm ordering you in his name—leave Ravenna!" The men who were holding him tightened their grip, twisting his arms painfully behind his back, but he was working himself into a reckless passion. "Get out of Ravenna," he yelled. "Get out of the Five Cities, get out of Pavia!"

The tall soldier laughed again. "Really? Out of my capital? And where to then, may I ask?"

"Out of Italy. To wherever your people came from—across the mountains."

"Across the mountains?"

"To Francia—Germany—who cares?" Eutychius tried to raise himself to the same height as his questioner. "I'm Eutychius—imperial governor of the Exarchate of Ravenna! The Emperor orders you to leave. And take your filthy barbarians with you."

The soldier's amusement gave way to annoyance. "And I'm Aistulf, king of the Lombards," he says. "The Christian Lombards, whose home is Italy—now and forever." He drew his sword. "Tell your Emperor—I obey his orders like *this!* and *this!*"

2

———

Two footmen swung open a pair of heavy oaken doors— doors carved with scenes from the life and death of St. Peter—and bowed low as the apostle's ninety-first successor swept into the papal chambers, along with a dozen counselors. The faint sound of music and voices accompanied them into the room, for a choir in the adjacent basilica was still rendering thanks to God, and the crowd that had followed the new pope on his procession around the city was preparing for an afternoon of merrymaking.

"May we help with these, Your Holiness?" asked a deacon. With Pope Stephen's murmured assent he and another attendant lifted the tiara from his head, unpinned the scarf-like pallium and removed it from his shoulders, and then helped him off with the fanon and chasuble and other vestments.

"Be sure to dry them out," said Stephen with a wry smile. "They shouldn't be put away damp."

Sensing a rebuke, the First Notary interceded: "Forgive us for our failure to shelter Your Holiness," he said.

"It's nothing to apologize for, Ambrose, no harm's done. The rain and wind came out of nowhere."

"The pages were trying—"

"They couldn't hold the canopy upright—it wasn't their fault, or yours. I hope it wasn't a bad omen."

Theophylact, the Archdeacon, hastened to offer his reassurance. "Certainly not, Your Holiness. These sudden rain-squalls are normal for this time of year—they're a sign of good things to come—and warmer weather."

"I hope so. After this last week, we've had enough of bad things *and* bad weather."

The group fell silent for a moment as attendants gathered the vestments and took them out of the chamber. A deacon tried to relieve the mood. "The passing of our beloved Zachary was a cause of great sadness, Your Holiness," he said. "But we rejoice that he's with God. The memory of his good works will live forever."

"Indeed."

The deacon went on: "As regards Stephen—the other Stephen—we have to count his death a blessing." The new pope frowned, and the deacon hurried to offer some explanation. "We wanted to find a successor to Zachary as quickly as possible, as Your Holiness knows, given the danger we're in. But we acted too hastily."

A second official joined in. "Stephen—Stephen the priest—he wasn't the right person, Your Holiness. That's obvious now—why else would God have struck him down just two days after his election, and before he could be consecrated?"

"And there was a confusion of names, Your Holiness," added another voice. "I've heard of several who voted for the priest, thinking they were voting for Your Holiness. What happened has corrected an injustice."

Stephen, the new Pope, sensed the note of sycophancy creeping into the men's remarks, and he tried to close the discussion. "We pray for Zachary's soul, and that of Stephen equally, that they may find peace in God's bosom."

But there was something about the other Stephen's death—so recent, so unexpected, and so horrible in its details—that prevented the men from letting go of the topic. For there were several who had seen the Pope-elect keel over as he rose from breakfast, smashing his head against the marble floor. And many had witnessed the groaning that went on for hour after long hour, his struggle to rise from the bed where they had carried him, his futile attempts at speech and gesture, the vomiting and bloody diarrhea, and his final agony. All this seemed to demand some explanation, some clarification. "Your Holiness," asked Ambrose, "Was that man Pope?"

"No, he was not," the new Pope declared firmly. "Election is the work of men—guided by God's Word, for sure, but still fallible, if we close our ears to what He tells us. To be called Pope, a man must be consecrated as Bishop of Rome and anointed by the Holy Unction."

"So Your Holiness is the second Pope of your name, not the third?"

"The second, yes, after Stephen the blessed martyr, successor to Lucius. Now, Ambrose, you have a document for me?"

"Yes, Your Holiness, it's the Profession." Ambrose handed Stephen a parchment, and Stephen looked once more over the document from which, three hours earlier, he had read aloud in the echoing spaces of the Lateran Basilica. *'In nomine Domini Dei—In the name of the Lord God, Jesus Christ our Savior, and the Holy Spirit, in the fifth Indiction, and the fifth day before the Nones of April, being the seven hundred and fifty-second year of our Lord's Incarnation, I, Stephen, by God's mercy and grace elected to humbly occupy the Apostolic Seat, profess to you, blessed Peter—'* Stephen scanned down through the verbiage that some unfortunate scribe had spent all night copying from the procedural handbook of the papal chancellery. The document revisited the Council of Nicaea, the First Council of Constantinople, the Council of Ephesus, and others that followed—the sources of all the great promulgations that had saved Christendom from arianism, nestorianism, monophytism, and many other pernicious heresies. Stephen skipped through the doctrinal discourse, finally reaching the meat of it all. *'I promise not to change or lessen one word of what has been handed down from my most worthy predecessors, nor to add anything new, but rather, as their disciple, to fervently and with all my strength protect and revere what I have received from them. And if I presume to stray from this undertaking, or allow anyone else so to presume, may it count for ill against me in that terrible day of Divine Judgment. This Profession I, Stephen, sign with my own hand and offer with pure mind and conscience to you, blessed Peter, Prince of the Apostles.'* Stephen took the document to a desk, dipped a quill in an inkhorn, and wrote his name as elegantly as he could manage.

After drying the ink with a scattering of sand, he handed the Profession back to Ambrose. "Place this at the tomb of the blessed Peter, alongside the Profession of Zachary and those who went before him."

Ambrose bowed: "I shall, Your Holiness," he said. "And may I remind Your Holiness that the dinner in honor of your consecration will take place an hour from now. We'll return to dress you shortly." With that, he signaled the assembled officials to leave.

"Deacon Paul, please stay behind," Stephen murmured, as the others filed out. Paul closed the door, and the atmosphere immediately lost its oppressive formality. Paul picked a fig from a bowl of dried fruit and began chewing on it. "Your Holiness must be tired," he said with a smile.

"'Your Holiness, Your Holiness'—leave me alone with 'Your Holiness,'" Stephen muttered. "My name's still Stephen, isn't it? And you're still my brother, aren't you?"

Paul grasped the Pope's hands in his. "Yes, Stephen, my dear brother. But—I don't know—suddenly I'm so much your junior again, like when we were children."

"Junior? In years, maybe. But we did this together."

"With the Lord's blessing."

"With the Lord's blessing, yes. But I mean, you worked so hard for this. Have you had any rest since the other Stephen passed?"

"Not much," Paul replied, as he took several more figs and placed them in a pocket in his robe. "But to do God's work is its own reward. He chose you. All I did was help the electors understand that."

"Your time will come. When the Lord calls me, you'll wear this ring."

"That's in God's hands," said Paul, walking over to the window. "Who knows which of us will live longer, except the Lord? In any case, I'm not eager to take your place."

Stephen joined his brother at the window. "Look, you can see where we lived from here," he said. He pointed to a half-ruined tenement that loomed up from the slopes of the Esquiline Hill, a mile or so to the north. "That's where she brought us, after our father died, and she lost the mansion on Broad Street. What it must have been like for her to live in that squalor!"

"They're with God," said Paul. "And since that time, the Church has been our mother and father."

For a while, as the light faded, the two men stood silently at the window. That they were brothers was clear: they had the same aquiline nose, the same arched eyebrows, and the same dark eyes. But beyond those family traits, they could hardly have been less alike. Stephen was on the short side, and heavy-set; what was left of his hair was white, what were left of his teeth were dark, and the skin sagged in jowly folds from his skull. At sixty years of age, he was very obviously an old man.

Paul, at fifty-five, was far better preserved than his brother. When the Lateran Palace took in the pair of orphans, Paul was only three years old; the effects of malnutrition could still be reversed. He quickly outgrew Stephen, ending up a head taller, as well as stronger and healthier. Now, though no longer young, he was a fine-looking middle-aged man, with a full head of hair, some of it still black, a neatly-trimmed beard, and presentable teeth. He looked like he might still be capable of running up the long winding staircase that led to the papal chambers, and then sliding down the polished balustrade. He did not attempt such a feat, of course. In fact, the last time he had done so, forty-six years previously, on a dare from his brother, he earned himself a beating from one of his schoolmasters.

The two men also differed in their dress. Stephen's ceremonial vestments were gorgeous, of course—the silk, the lace, the gold, the lamb's wool, the finest embroidered linens—but they seemed to have been designed for a taller man—there had been no time to make alterations. And after taking off the vestments, he was left in a plain robe that made him look more like a monk than the Supreme Pontiff.

Paul had winced to see his brother so abase himself—as he saw it—in the presence of the assembled officials. Paul never let himself be seen in anything less than the finest attire permitted to his office. Sometimes, he even crossed that line, inventing new accessories that displayed to advantage a piece of damask silk or gold brocade that some visitor or pilgrim had given him.

"There'll be resentment, you know," said Stephen. "A deacon who dresses more finely than the Archdeacon? Than the First Notary? Men will say: 'This is the Pope's younger brother—the Pope-in-waiting.' That's dangerous."

"You may be right," said Paul—a turn of phrase that he instantly regretted. "You *are* right, Stephen. I'll keep that in mind. But I don't dress this way out of pride or—"

"Of course not—"

"I do it out of reverence for my office and for the Church." Paul looked across the room to the gem-encrusted tiara that still sat on the form where Ambrose had placed it. "These vestments, these baubles—they speak to the unlettered of the glory of God, and the respect due to God's servants on Earth."

"Yes, very well, Paul, I agree, but a little less ostentation might—"

"I understand. Anyway, Stephen, I have to say again how happy I am for you, and for Rome. Finally a Roman Pope again, after all those Easterners. Perhaps we'll hear a little more Latin spoken around here."

"Zachary was a Greek," said Stephen, "but he loved Rome."

"He did, and he was a worthy Pope."

"Worthy? More than worthy!"

"Well, he loved peace," said Paul, "and his peaceful style worked—with Luitprand, and with Ratchis. But they were gentlemen, compared with this Aistulf. Aistulf wears the Iron Crown, but at heart he's a thug, a common cutthroat. Negotiation, diplomacy, treaties—the things Zachary was good at—they mean nothing to him."

"We must make them mean something, or—"

"Since the moment he took the throne he's thought only of making himself master of Italy—by force of arms, by treachery, whatever it takes. And now, three years later, he's most of the way there. Aistulf—Duke of Rome? Aistulf—King of Italy? Aistulf—Emperor of the West? Where will it end?"

"Paul—"

"*Where will it end, Stephen?* Ravenna is his—the Five Cities—Perugia. The Dukes of Tuscany and Spoleto and Benevento bow to him. Only Rome is left."

"Thanks to Zachary—"

"Rome—and Sicily. Zachary never knew how to deal with such a man—a man who killed the governor of Ravenna—a prisoner—with his own sword."

"Eutychius?" said Stephen. "That eunuch was the Emperor's right arm—he tried to destroy the holy images, his death was just pun—"

"And Aistulf let his soldiers commit unspeakable crimes within Ravenna's holiest sanctuaries—good Christian matrons raped and butchered in front of their children."

Paul was working himself up into a froth of indignation. "Those saints and martyrs who looked down from the walls—they wept! Yes, live tears welled up and stained the mosaics—I have it on good authority! And—"

"Paul, Paul, enough! The Council will meet tomorrow, and we'll decide on a course of action. If Zachary's policies were wrong, we'll adopt better ones, I promise you." There was a discreet knock at the doors. "Here come the dressers, Paul. Enough of our troubles, for a few hours at least—let's be in good spirits for the feast."

3

"By day it's too hot, so we'll cross the desert by moonlight, and at dawn we'll pass the Pink Cliffs and come down to the oasis of Dakhla. We'll rest our camels in the shade of mulberry trees. We'll wash and pray—me toward Mecca, you toward Jerusalem—and then we'll go to the market—"

"I don't pray toward Jerusalem, Zaid, I pray to God, who's in Heaven, and to Mary the mother of God, who's also in Heaven."

"And where is that, Lenora?"

"Up in the sky."

"All right, you'll pray toward the sky. And then we'll go to the market, where we'll eat dates and pistachio nuts, and drink kefir with honey. Then we'll trade some of the daggers we brought from Damascus, the ones inlaid with stones of Lazhward, and you'll pick out the silks to sell when we get home."

"Must we sell them all?"

"No, the most beautiful will be for you to keep. They'll be blue like the desert sky at noon, shimmering like a mirage, with white almond blossoms all around the borders. You and our daughters will wear them at Eid ul-Fitr or at the festival of—"

"Our daughters? How many daughters will we have, then?"

"Two: Lenora, of course, and Naomi. Beautiful daughters, as beautiful as their mother. And three sons: Zaid, Aarif, and Aashif. Zaid will be a sailor, because he was conceived as we lay together on the felucca that brought us up the Nile."

"Zaid—stop! Don't talk of such scandalous things, such nonsense!" Lenora pulled her hand away from Zaid's.

"Well, Lenora, if you want children, that's how they're made."

"I don't believe you. I don't know what you're talking about, and I don't want to hear it. Tell me about the rest of our journey. How will we get back to Rome?"

The two teenagers—Zaid was fourteen, Lenora a year or so younger—lounged in front of a small store on Silversmiths' Street, in Rome's Transtiber district. This district came into being five hundred years before Stephen's accession to the papacy, at a time when Rome was similarly threatened by invaders from the north. To protect the city, the emperor Aurelian ordered the construction of a massive encircling wall. Although Rome lay on the east bank of the Tiber, Aurelian's wall also encompassed a small triangular area on the western bank: this area, called Transtiber, included a stretch of marshy floodplain along the river, as well as the slopes of the Janiculum hill, where Trajan's aqueduct descended into the city.

The original purpose of this western extension had been to protect the many mills that were powered by the cascading waters of the aqueduct: these mills produced flour enough to supply a quarter million Romans with bread. The aqueduct was breached during the Gothic War, and the Janiculum mills fell into disuse: they were replaced by ship-mills on the river. In spite of that, Transtiber flourished. A new embankment provided some modest protection against floods, and a skein of streets behind it became the home of fishermen, craftsmen, and foreigners. And for the thousands of pilgrims who visited the Basilica of St. Peter, on the Vatican Hill just outside the walls, Transtiber offered food, rest, and entertainment, as well as the opportunity to purchase relics, or little souvenirs of Rome that they could show their priests to prove that they had completed their penitential journeys.

Zaid waved to his friend Antonius, who was pushing a tiny handcart loaded with pastries down the street. "We head back to Rome by boat," he went on. "We board a grain-ship at Alexandria, but it's blown off course in a storm and we end up in Crete, where—"

"Zaid, get in here!" The shout came from a small open-front store next to the one where they were standing.

"—in Crete, whose people are amazed at your beauty. Men make eyes at you, but Cretan men are ugly and mean, and you realize how lucky you are to have such a handsome and wealthy husband as myself—"

"You've been to Crete?"

"Yes—well, no, not yet, but I've heard all about it."

"*Zaid!!*"

"Your father's calling you," said Lenora.

"Let him call. If he really needs me he'll come get me. But anyway, in Crete—"

"This journey, it would take us ten years or more, wouldn't it?"

"One year, maybe two."

"Maybe we should go somewhere closer by. I'd like to visit Lucca, where we come from. My grandparents still live there, but I haven't been there since I was six."

"Well, Lucca is easy, I'll gladly take you. In three weeks we could be there, once the roads are safe. Maybe your grandparents would come for our wedding, and we could go back with them."

"Our wedding? You have it all planned out, don't you?"

"Lenora, don't you want—"

"I do, I do! But it's not going to happen any time soon."

"The sooner the better. I need to get away from—speak of the devil!"

Zaid's father, Omar, had stormed out onto the street. With a limp and a scowl, he marched up to Zaid. "You're supposed to be bringing in pilgrims, not chatting with that floozy," he said angrily. He grabbed his son by one arm and sling-shotted him back toward his store. Zaid protested loudly but disappeared inside, while Omar called into the store where the young couple had been chatting. "Sibylla— get your daughter off the street before she's picked up as a whore!"

Sibylla—a pale woman in her early thirties, whose raven hair matched her all-black attire—came to the front of the store carrying a small covered pot, which she gave to Lenora. "Take your father his lunch," she said. As Lenora headed off down the street, Sibylla turned to Omar. "How's business, you old rascal?" she asked.

"Good."

"Good? I'm glad to hear that."

"While Rome burns, Omar gets rich."

"Well, it hasn't burned yet."

"No, but it will before long, everyone knows that. So everyone wants protection. Either a relic from me, if they're Christian, or a charm from you, if they're not. Times are good, aren't they?"

Sibylla laughed. "My magic is stronger than a bunch of fake relics."

"They're not all fake, not all of them! Many are from the East—from Syria or Palestine—"

"Hah! You're asking me to—"

"Constantinople is good right now: Ever since the Emperor renewed the ban on images, all kinds of things are coming this way."

"So a relic faked in the East is more powerful than one faked in your workshop?"

"Definitely. And then Zachary's death, and that business with the Pope-elect—that has got everyone in a fright. They need something. You have a customer right now, by the looks of it." Omar left Sibylla to her business and returned to his store.

A thin, elderly man approached the store front, dodging a woman who was hurrying by with a basket of charcoal. "I'm looking for Sibylla, the spell-caster," he said. He looked as if he came from across the river.

"I'm Sibylla, what can I do for you?"

"I need a curse. I'm the defendant in a lawsuit—a property case—I'm losing."

"I can help you. Come inside." Sibylla and her customer disappeared behind the curtain that separated her store from the street.

Meanwhile, Omar had set Zaid to work fastening colored beads to an ancient-looking crucifix. Omar had attached a splinter of bone to the center of the crucifix, and protected it with a small glass panel. The boy was now fastening the beads with a tiny hammer and even tinier nails, but he was making a clumsy job of it, and Omar swore or cuffed his son when he dropped or broke a bead, which happened frequently. Although Zaid was working near the front of the store, the light was poor.

Omar had the weather-beaten appearance of a man who had lived most of his forty-odd years out of doors. He was born in Damascus, but spent his early life in various parts of North Africa, where his father collected taxes for a succession of Umayyad caliphs. Omar himself entered the same profession, but the Berber Revolt changed everything: his father was killed during the massacre that followed the disastrous Battle of the Nobles near Tangier. Omar himself was wounded in the hip, but he was able to flee the city southward by boat, along with his wife and two-year-old son. After an arduous overland trek, during which his wife died, Omar and Zaid came to the Mediterranean once more, and were finally able to reach the relative safety of Alexandria.

Omar now embarked on a new life as a trader. He specialized in relics, where his literacy was a particular asset: he could read their inscriptions. Was a splinter of wood from the True Cross, or from the wheel on which St. Catherine was broken? Did a sword blade decapitate John the Baptist, or did it disembowel St. Erasmus? Was a dried-up finger the one with which St. Thomas probed the wounds of the risen Christ, or was it one of the digits hacked from the hands of

James the Persian before his final dismemberment? Omar made himself an expert in deciphering, restoring, embellishing, and even creating from scratch the little brass plaques or squares of faded parchment that documented each relic's grisly provenance. As he did so, he became more familiar with Christian martyrology than with the bloody history of his own, much younger religion.

After crisscrossing the Levant for several years, Omar's interest in relics brought him more frequently to Constantinople and to Rome, the two cities where relics were especially sought after. On his visits to Rome he would set up a store for a few weeks in Transtiber, where he could market his wares to pilgrims. But as his hip injury made travel more difficult, he stayed in Rome for longer periods: his current visit had lasted for over a year. He replenished his supply of relics from other traders, or by manufacturing them himself. Either option was far less burdensome than journeying to Tyre or Tarsus. What's more, the recent seizure of power by As-Saffah, the Slaughterer, made it inadvisable for a former protégé of the Umayyads to be seen in the Caliphate.

For Zaid, though, staying in Rome was a torture. Zaid had been brought up on the open road, or in the roadless wildernesses of the Maghreb. To move on was in his nature. He loved the animals—the camels, mules, and horses—who had been his companions on those journeys, more than he loved the society of his peers. The cramped store where he and his father now worked, and the sleeping quarters above it, felt like a prison. And although Zaid was still a slim and beardless boy, a rebellious adolescence had begun to animate him, provoking him into collision with a father who, on

21

account of his painful injury, often gave vent to an ungovernable temper. Only Zaid's increasing attachment to Lenora kept him on Silversmiths' Street.

Zaid allowed his attention to wander from his handiwork. "If Lenora and her parents go to Lucca, can I take them there?" he asked.

Omar was firing up his little charcoal furnace in preparation for some metalwork. "Certainly, after you marry her," he replied. "Which is never, because there's not a priest in Rome will marry you to a Christian woman—nor in Lucca neither."

A couple of pilgrims entered the store and began looking over Omar's wares. Omar greeted them politely. "Welcome, reverend sirs," he said. "You've come from far away?"

"From Francia, yes," replied one of the visitors, whose heavy Gallic-Latin dialect confirmed his statement.

"From Francia? From across the mountains? What a long and dangerous journey!"

"God's grace protected us." The visitors took the cups of water that Zaid offered them. "The Lombard militias were everywhere. We saw fields laid waste, vines torn up, even some villages burned. Many people are fleeing to the cities—they're terrified."

"Where was this?"

"Well, near Falerii, for example, and even south of there."

"So within the Roman Duchy?"

"On the border. We had to take side roads—the Flaminian Way was blocked by the Lombards. And with all the rain we've had, the lanes were nothing but mud."

"Well, all the travelers from the north tell the same story," said Omar. "It's a bad time to be on the roads, that's for sure."

"We give thanks to God that we've been able to reach Rome and pray at the tomb of the blessed Apostle. What can we take with us from here?"

"I have many relics, as you can see—relics from all corners of Christendom. But you're looking for something related to the blessed Peter, probably?"

"Yes. We've already touched linens to his tomb, and we've collected dust from around it. But we need something more powerful."

"This is my most precious and powerful relic," Omar said, as he showed his guests a tiny amber-glass ampoule that was fastened to a worm-eaten fragment of wood. The ampoule contained a drop of liquid. "This is a tear shed by the blessed Peter's daughter Petronilla—herself a blessed martyr—as her father was crucified."

"Didn't Petronilla die before her father?" asked one of the pilgrims.

This was news to Omar, but he didn't lose his composure. "Yes indeed," he replied, "and that was the miracle. Her body remained uncorrupted, and her eyes shed tears at the very moment of her father's passing. It was observed by many, as this paper attests." He held the inscription up to the pilgrim's face, confident that he would not be able to read it. "Several people have been cured of the plague by this extraordinary relic, including a bishop."

"What else do you have?"

Omar showed them some chips of rock, which he said were taken from the boulder that the angel rolled aside from the entrance to Jesus' sepulcher. When the pilgrims repeated that they wanted something connected with St. Peter, he pointed out a couple of thimble-sized pots, whose tops were sealed with wax. "This one has dust from inside the Apostle's tomb, which was collected by the blessed Sylvester himself, four hundred years ago. And this one has filings from the chain that bound the Apostle as he lay in the Tullianum. Look, here's the inscription. Their small size makes them very convenient for travelers like yourselves."

"They must be very costly," said one of the travelers doubtfully.

"Well, yes, I'll have to ask two solidi for each, which is what I paid for them. Or three for both."

"We don't have that kind of money. The few pennies we still have were given to us by the monks at Soracte—what else can you offer us?"

Omar showed his visitors a few other items. Eventually they settled for two little flasks of water from the Sea of Galilee, where Peter had plied his boat before he became a fisher of men. After seeing the pilgrims out, Omar continued working on the furnace. Then Sibylla came into the store, carrying a piece of broken pottery. "Omar," she said, "can you write down a name for me?"

"Who's the victim today?" asked Omar, as he took the potsherd and an awl.

"Vegetius," said Sibylla.

"Vegetius the landowner? What have you got in mind for him?"

"Nothing serious. A temporary skin problem, maybe. Something that will encourage him to take the waters at Tivoli for a few weeks."

"Very well. If I hear that anything worse happens to him, I'll report you." Omar scratched Vegetius's name into the potsherd. "Here, don't tell your client I had anything to do with this."

"Thank you, thank you." Sibylla hurried back to her fortune-telling parlor, and a few minutes later her client left with a small box. The litigious land-owner, who was sitting in a courtroom on the other side of the city, was already noticing a slight itch above his left ear.

Zaid continued working on his crucifix. "That was a good one with the miracle of Petronilla," he said sarcastically. "And speaking of miracles, isn't it amazing how the clear water of Galilee, when it's brought to Rome, takes on the exact same brown color as the Tiber River?"

"Close your mouth, you brat," said Omar. "People get what they want. Wherever the relics come from, they work—that I'm sure of."

"Yes? Then what about that man who gave you three solidi for a lock of Mary Magdalene's hair, and less than ten paces from our door he was knocked—*God dammit!*" Distracted by his own wit, Zaid had carelessly mis-aimed his hammer. He had smashed the glass plate in the center of the crucifix, along with the fragment of bone that it had been protecting.

In an instant rage, Omar flung the bellows he was using at Zaid; the heavy instrument struck his son full in the face and knocked him sideways. Dazed and enraged in his turn, Zaid seized the bellows and used it to smash the crucifix into hundreds of pieces; then he hurled the bellows to the other side of the shop, where it destroyed several more relics that had been hanging from the wall, including Petronilla's tear. This roused Omar to an even greater passion. "I'm going to kill you," he shouted. He seized a heavy leather strap, grabbed Zaid by his hair, and began thrashing him on whatever part of his body he could reach.

Screaming, Zaid tore himself away from his father's grasp and ran to the front of the shop. "You bastard!" he shouted. "You think you can beat me for no reason—for breaking a stupid little piece of bone—which you got from the charnel house just yesterday?"

"I'll break your stupid bones if you don't—"

"No, I've had it, I'm leaving, you won't ever see me again! *La'anatullah alaykum! La'anatullah alaykum!*" As he ran off down the street, Zaid continued to call down the curse of Allah on his father. Omar made to go after him, but his painful gait was no match for the boy's speed. He cursed his son in turn, and then limped back to his shop, where Sibylla and several others had gathered to find out what the racket was all about.

4

After taking the pot of food from her mother, Lenora walked down Silversmiths' Street to the Aurelian Way. The main road was busy. Besides the usual ox-carts laden with flour or firewood, some families seemed to be transporting all their household possessions. These included refugees entering the city as well as Romans leaving it. As she looked to the left, Lenora saw that a cart lay wrecked at the side of the street. Its owners must have lost control of it during the steep descent of the Janiculum—a common mishap. The cart had careened down the rain-slicked cobbles and smashed into a well-placed row of stone posts at the curve where the Aurelian Way turned toward the Aemilian Bridge. A small crowd of people were milling around the cart, some assisting its dazed owners, and some helping themselves to its scattered contents. The accident was holding up the traffic, and a couple of watchmen were trying to bring order to the situation.

Lenora turned to the right, working her way through the impatient mass of cart-drivers and horsemen. She trod carefully to avoid the animals' steamy droppings. In spite of these obstacles, a couple of minutes' walk took her to the river. Instead of crossing the Aemilian Bridge, she turned left along the embankment. Here, traffic was lighter, and Lenora was able to take in the more distant scenery. Clouds driven by a stiff sea-breeze hurried eastward; sometimes they shed a few raindrops, and sometimes they parted, allowing a sunbeam to bathe the ruined Temple of Aesculapius on Tiber Island. The river itself was unusually high and fast-flowing; it carried a freight of mud and vegetation that the rain had loosened from hillsides in Umbria or the Appenines, and the water lapped near the topmost steps of the fishermen's landings.

Lenora passed Gratian's Bridge, which connected Transtiber to Tiber Island. Beyond the bridge, four ship-mills were moored in a line along the curving western bank of the river. Each mill resembled a small house, with a thatched roof and wooden walls, that rested on a flat-bottomed barge scarcely larger than the house itself. Long ropes connected the prow and stern of each barge to bollards on the embankment. On the far side of each mill, facing toward the center of the stream, a much smaller and narrower barge was connected by beams to the first, forming a kind of outrigger. Between the two, a large paddle-wheel was suspended, its lowest vanes dipping a foot or so into the stream. Under the influence of the river current, the wheels of all the mills were turning at a respectable pace.

Lenora walked along the line of mills until she reached the one moored farthest upstream, which lay just beyond the end of Tiber Island. She turned and walked across the gangway that ran from the shore to the deck of the mill: she noticed that, on account of the high water, she had to walk slightly upward to the mill's deck, rather than downward as was usual.

Her father was occupied pulling some greenery out of the grillwork that protected the paddle-wheel from floating debris. At the sound of her voice he turned to greet her. To a stranger, his appearance would have been quite a shock: he was covered from head to foot in a uniform coating of flour, so that he resembled a ghost more than a mortal being. "Hello, sweetest," he said with a broad smile. Then father and daughter enacted a daily ritual, which involved his attempting to give her a bear hug while she shrank from the floury imprint that it would have left on her. "Don't touch me—I'll drop your lunch," she shrieked as she backed off.

"Come inside, it's cold," he said, and the two of them entered the mill itself. The interior was a single space, lit by small unglazed windows. It wasn't much warmer than outside, but it offered protection from the wind. Two other men, equally ghost-like, were tending the millstones.

The working mechanism of the mill lay in plain view. The axle of the paddle-wheel extended as a horizontal rotating shaft into the bottom of the millhouse. At its end it carried a toothed pit-wheel that engaged with a vertical shaft; this in turn carried another toothed wheel that engaged with a second vertical shaft. This second shaft passed upward through a hole in the center of the lower millstone, which remained stationary, and rotated the upper millstone against it. The gearing of these successive engagements transformed the lumbering rotation of the paddle-wheel into a spinning motion of the millstone that was too rapid for the eye to follow.

One of the men, standing in a kind of loft, was controlling a hopper that fed grain into the center of the upper millstone, while the other man stood on the lower floor and collected the emerging flour into sacks. Lenora's father—his name was Marcus—rubbed a sample of the flour between his thumb and forefinger; sensing that the texture was not quite right, he turned a wooden screw to adjust the gap between the stones. Then, seeing that the supply of grain in the hoppers was running low, he raised a grain-sack to the loft by means of a hoist that was also powered by the paddlewheel.

Marcus then took Lenora's pot, as well as a flagon of beer, and father and daughter sat down on a bench at the far end of the mill. It was a dusty and noisy environment, but they were used to it. "This current is making our work easy," Marcus said. "I should be done early today." He started eating the beans and bread that Sibylla had provided, along with a bunch of green onions.

"Since I moved up to this mill the work has really been easier," Marcus went on. "All the mills have the same daily quota, but the others sit in our wake—they don't get the full force of the stream."

"Will I start work at the bakery soon?" Lenore asked.

"Soon enough—why, are you impatient to start?"

"No, not really. Zaid stays at home, and he's a year older than me."

"They're foreigners," said Marcus. "And Zaid works for his father: he's learning a craft. You can't work in a mill."

"What about what mama does? I watch her—I could do that."

"Spells and magic can get you into trouble. The priests don't approve of it. Your mother has had to pay off the Pope's men more than once."

"Zaid wants to take me to Egypt and Africa—"

"Zaid, Zaid, always Zaid!" said Marcus, with his mouth half full of bread. "On which of his tall ships will he take you, let me ask you that?"

"—or to Lucca."

"Lucca? We'll go to Lucca, once we have money enough. And Zaid can come along, if his father lets him."

"Let me start at the bakery then, and I'll save the money."

"We'll see, we'll see. But don't get any ideas about you and Zaid. He and his father will leave Rome before long, and then it will be over. We'll find you a good Christian husband, when the time comes." Lenora tried to protest, but Marcus had finished his meal: he took a final draft of beer and handed the empty food pot to his daughter. "Better head back before it starts to rain again," he said. "I can hear the cart."

Lenora walked over to the doorway of the mill, taking care not to slip on the flour-slickened floor. Once outside, she saw that a man was leading a mule across the gangplank; the mule was laden with two grain sacks. She had to wait for the sure-footed animal to reach the deck, and then she headed off, pausing to say a brief hello to another man who was standing atop the delivery cart that was waiting at the quayside. The two men had already stopped at the other three mills, where they had exchanged most of their load of grain for flour; once they had finished at Marcus's mill they would head for one of the public bakeries.

As she walked back along the embankment, Lenora fell into a daydream of a kind that had been occupying her frequently over the last several weeks: it always involved herself, Zaid, and some dire predicament that he was extricating her from. On this occasion he was rescuing her from a castle where she was imprisoned, a feat required him to slay a couple of dragons and then scale the castle wall by moonlight. By the time she turned the corner onto the Aurelian Way, Zaid had earned the undying thanks of Lenora and her parents, and the ensuing nuptials were well under way. At that very moment, however, she practically collided with Zaid himself, who had been running down toward the river.

"Zaid, what's the matter with you? You look terrible— what happened?" Lenore cried.

Zaid was panting heavily. The right side of his face was marred by a bloody welt, stretching from his ear to his chin, where the bellows had struck him. Drops of blood trickled from the corner of his mouth, ran down his neck, and disappeared behind his tunic. The tunic itself was torn in a couple of places, revealing the marks where his father's strap had bitten into his chest and sides.

"Lenora!" was all he could say, but the expression on his face gave sufficient voice to the pain and anger that still held him in their grip.

"What happened? Who did this to you?"

"Who do you think? The one person I couldn't fight back against!" Zaid looked anxiously behind him to see if he was being pursued.

"Your father? Why?"

"Just because I messed up some cheap relic!"

"So where are you going?"

"I don't know—away. A long way away. Anywhere."

"Zaid, you can't! Let me wash your face."

Zaid looked up the street again. "I have to—he'll be after

me."

"What about us?"

"Us?" The word seemed to penetrate the fortress of anger that Zaid had raised around himself. It yielded at least briefly to a different emotion. "Lenora—my 'Nora!" He held her by the shoulders and then drew her to him.

"Zaid! What are you doing?"

"I love you—wait for me!" Zaid, for the first time ever, held her body close against his own and placed his lips on hers; she tasted his sweat and his blood.

For just an instant, Zaid and Lenore remained frozen in their embrace—long enough for some passers-by to stop and stare: a boy and girl locked in a public kiss, both black-haired, but he with the dark complexion of an Arab, and she with ivory skin and blue eyes, as if some northern blood ran in her Tuscan veins. It was a scandalous scene.

Zaid felt a passionate heat rising in his groin, but Lenora drew back. "I love you," she said.

As Zaid made to go, Lenora held him back for a moment. "Wait," she said. She reached for the knife that hung at Zaid's belt.

"What are you doing?" he asked in panic. But Lenora took the knife, reached to the hair that hung in abundance at the side of her face, and sliced off an inch of it. Then she took off a locket that hung at her neck, opened it, placed the hair inside, closed it again, and gave it to Zaid. He placed it around his own neck.

"Nora, wait for me!" he said again. And he was gone; she caught a glimpse of him running over the Aemilian Bridge, and then he disappeared from view.

5

Preceded by his herald, Stephen descended the grand stairway that, decades ago, he had dared his younger brother to run up and slide down. Since that time, the appearance of the Lateran Palace had changed greatly. The walls on either side of the stairway, which earlier had been bare stone, now carried mosaics commissioned by Gregory III. In bold defiance of the Emperor's iconoclastic edicts, the mosaics displayed many human and divine figures. These included a *Christos Pantokrator*—a Christ in oriental majesty—surrounded by other Greek-themed figures and labeled in Greek characters. A *Theotokos*—Mary as the mother of God—also graced the walls, even though, in Roman theology, Mary only gave birth to God's mortal Incarnation. Zachary too had left his mark on the Lateran, adding towers and porticos and screens, some of them adorned with the images of Eastern saints and martyrs. It was as if the succession of Greek-speaking Popes had sought to preserve in Old Rome the very traditions that New Rome was rapidly abandoning.

Stephen—who spoke little Greek and had never traveled outside the borders of the Roman Duchy—had been uncomfortable with this Hellenizing trend, and now planned to reverse it. In addition, he noted that his predecessors had been more interested in embellishing the centuries-old Palace than on keeping its structure in good order. As he descended the staircase, he had to sidestep several basins that had been placed to catch rainwater that was dripping from the leaking roof. And some side passages were closed off with crude brickwork: these led to areas of the Palace that were now threatening to collapse, or had actually done so.

Stephen's counselors were already assembled around a table in the papal reception hall, along with a notary whose duty was to take down the proceedings in shorthand. They all rose as the herald announced the Holy Father's entrance. After a brief prayer and some formal discussion relating to papal appointments, Stephen asked Ambrose to speak.

"Aistulf has no army in the field at the moment, Your Holiness," said the First Notary, "so there's no immediate threat to the city. But small detachments of Lombards and Tuscans have been marauding along our northern borders. Peasants in some areas have moved into the walled towns, and some have come to Rome. Many of the abandoned farms have been destroyed by the invaders. If this movement of the peasants continues, there'll be a significant impact on this year's harvest."

"What about Aistulf?"

"He's still at Pavia, Your Holiness. He does plan to advance on Rome, according to what our spies tell us. But the timing isn't settled—it could be either this summer or the next."

"And what means do we have to stop him?" Stephen asked.

"In terms of military forces, none at all. He can move his own army down the Tiber Valley any time he wants, and he can summon allied armies from Tuscany and Spoleto, and from Benevento too. He could assemble a hundred thousand men against us—four men for every man, woman, and child in Rome. So any kind of field engagement is out of the question. Everything depends on our walls."

"And how are our walls—Leo?"

"Your Holiness," replied Leo, the commander of the papal militia, "since Gregory's renovations, and those that Zachary commissioned, they've remained in good shape—we've got nothing to fear on that score. The militia is well trained and well supplied with weapons and defensive engines."

"I should think so, considering the amount of money that's been spent on them."

"But there aren't enough defenders. At the moment, there are less than ten thousand men of fighting age in Rome. We need at least twice that number to defend a twelve-mile wall. Unless we want to arm the slaves, we have to hope that there'll be enough men among the refugees entering the city. But they'll need weapons and training—and bread."

"Have you met with the grain-master?"

"Yes, Your Holiness. Unfortunately, the granaries are not as well stocked as I'd like. Since the Emperor confiscated our southern estates, it's been difficult to provide bread even for the usual population of the city, let alone for refugees. As we stand right now, the granaries would be exhausted after just six months of siege. That's if Aistulf is able to impose a complete blockade."

"Regarding that issue," said another voice, "Your Holiness will also recall that the previous Emperor deprived us of our legitimate tax revenues from Sicily and Calabria, as well as from Illyricum. An income of one hundred and fifty thousand solidi a year was stolen from us—money that would have been sufficient to buy any amount of grain."

Theophylact, the archdeacon, hastened to defend Constantinople. "The Emperor has to feed ten times as many mouths as we do, Your Holiness. Since Egypt fell to the Saracens, the grain ships lie idle, and—"

In spite of his junior rank, Paul interrupted the archdeacon. "The Emperor cares nothing for Italy, Your Holiness," he said. "What did he do to defend Ravenna? And since Ravenna fell, what has he done to regain it? Two ambassadors! He sent two ambassadors to lodge a complaint with Aistulf, and Aistulf turned them away unheard—that was the full extent of it. Where's the Emperor's fleet? Where's his army?"

Stephen interceded. "We're still subjects of the Emperor, after all. My worthy predecessors, Gregory and Zachary—they acknowledged as much. What authority do we have to take any path other than that of obedience?"

"Exactly so, Your Holiness," said Theophylact. "We can't hold out forever against a Lombard siege, no matter how much grain we lay up. We must send an appeal to the Emperor as his loyal subjects. And the Emperor must deliver us from the Lombards."

"That'll be futile, I can assure you," said Paul. "An Emperor who did nothing to save his own governor in Ravenna—the very heart of Imperial power in Italy? Why then should he do anything for this backwater?"

"Backwater?" challenged Theophylact angrily. "That's how you speak of the City of Peter?"

"Spiritually, yes, we're the center of Christendom, the hope of the world. But politically, militarily, we're nothing. The Emperor knows that. He even looks forward to our final eclipse—to the day when his Patriarch is recognized as Pope!"

"What blasphemous nonsense!" retorted Theophylact. "The Emperor and his predecessors have always acknowledged the primacy of the Roman Pontiff. If he lets Rome fall to the Lombards—well, that would be an everlasting stain on his name. He has armies and fleets enough—we must appeal to him."

"He has armies and fleets," said Paul, "but they're stretched to the breaking point as it is. He can barely defend his own territories. His forces are all in the field against the Saracens, the Bulgars, the Slavs." Paul waved an arm to three corners of the room, as if to point out the directions from which the hordes of unbelievers were threatening Constantinople. "He has far more enemies than we do."

"The Emperor's treasury is filled to overflowing," said Theophylact. "He can build another fleet whenever he wants."

"So let's just imagine he somehow conjured up a new fleet and a new army and they came to Italy and destroyed Aistulf. Let me tell you two things that would happen. First, he'd lay claim to all the lands of Italy: Ravenna and the Five Cities, Sicily and Calabria—"

"—Which are justly his."

"Perhaps—but also Perugia, all of Lombardy, Tuscany, Spoleto, Benevento, and yes, Rome. Imperial rule? Right now it's just a notion. Who actually pays any taxes to the Emperor? No one. Who obeys any Imperial edicts? No one. That would all change the moment the Emperor's general marched through the Salarian Gate like some new Alaric."

"That's just—"

"And the second thing—images," Paul went on, ignoring Theophylact's attempted interruption. "Since Artabasdos's revolt, this Emperor has become an even more fervent iconoclast—a more ruthless destroyer of sacred images than his father ever was. Haven't you heard of the bonfires in the streets of Constantinople? The thousands of holy images—of Jesus, of Mary—all gone up in flames? Can you imagine his enforcers running loose in *this* city? In the basilica of the blessed Apostle? In all the churches? Here in the Lateran Palace? Mosaics down, crucifixes burned—why, they'd rip the very ring off the Holy Father's finger! The—"

"Deacon Paul—!"

"—The people would rise up in fury, and the blessed martyrs would cry out in their graves!"

Paul paused long enough for Theophylact to get a word in. "Deacon Paul is letting himself be carried away by his own imagination," said the Archdeacon. "Did any of this happen in Ravenna, during all the years the Emperors ruled there? Go and see if any sacred images have been defaced in the baptisteries, or in St. Vitalis, or—"

"The people of Ravenna rebelled against the edict," Paul retorted, "That's how the previous governor lost his life, so that the Emperor had to send Eutychius. But here in Rome, everything would be different. And besides—"

"Your Holiness," said Theophylact emphatically, "no one here favors the destruction of sacred images, myself least of all. As many authors have affirmed, icons and relics and sacred images speak the Word of God to those who can't read the Holy Books. Images shouldn't be destroyed—but neither should they be worshipped. '*Non facietis—*'"

"No one's talking about *worshipping*, Theo, just—"

"*Non facietis vobis idolum—Ye shall make you no idols nor graven image, neither rear you up a standing image, neither shall you set up any image of stone in your land, to bow down unto it.*' Too many Romans bow down to icons and relics and pray to them in their own homes. Too many Romans believe that images have the power to cure disease or bring riches. They're turning our communal faith into some kind of private sorcery. They should be confessing their sins in church and following the instruction of their priests. This is the accusation that the Saracens bring against us—that we're breaking the Law of Moses—and this is what the Emperor is concerned about. Let's not prove the Saracens right. Your Holiness should lay out a firm policy on—"

"So we should let heathens dictate our theology?" asked Paul scathingly.

"My dear Theo, my dear Paul," said Stephen, "we've had many long discussions about images over the years. No doubt we'll have many more. And I greatly value your learning and wisdom, Theo, in this matter; and your opinions too, Paul. At this moment, though, we're discussing a more immediate issue—how to save our city from the Lombards." Paul and Theophylact muttered their apologies, and Stephen continued. "The issue is this: if we appeal to the Emperor, it'll be months before we hear from him. If he agrees to help us, it'll be a year or more before any forces arrive. And he may not be able or willing to help us, as Paul says. So are there any other steps we can take in the meantime?"

A new voice spoke up—that of Marcellus, the papal Treasurer. "Our beloved Zachary taught us what can be achieved by diplomacy, Your Holiness," he said. "Recall how he met with Liutprand at Terni, and the king yielded up the cities of Narni, Osimo, Ancona, and Humana to St. Peter, and returned a part of the Exarchate to the Emperor, along with Cesena, and released many hostages. They made a twenty-year peace, and Zachary was welcomed back to Rome like a victorious general in the age of Augustus, and he achieved all this without ever having to lift a sword."

Paul jumped in again. "Barely half of that twenty-year peace has run its course, and who controls those cities now?"

"Aistulf does," Marcellus admitted. "But Zachary was successful with Ratchis too: he persuaded Ratchis to give us back Perugia, and even to give up his own crown and enter the monastery of Cassino, where he sits today."

"I wish he had kept his crown—for who controls Perugia now?"

"Aistulf does," said Marcellus.

"And how much gold was spent by the Holy Father's predecessors to buy off the Lombards? Marcellus, you must know, tell us how much?"

"Many thousands of solidi, I don't know the exact amounts."

"Money thrown like chaff before the wind," Paul scoffed. "And do we even have such sums now in our Treasury, if we wanted to repeat that strategy?"

"Unfortunately not."

"Negotiation, treaties, bribes—none of these will work

with Aistulf," said Paul. "Nor even the threat of hell-fire. Your Holiness may hold the Keys to Heaven, but Aistulf thinks he can bludgeon his way in if he needs to."

"Your Holiness," said Philip, the paymaster, "Perhaps we should think of offering Aistulf an accommodation. We offer him sovereignty over the Roman Duchy in return for a pledge to respect the authority of the Papacy in spiritual matters, including ecclesiastical appointments. I know that's a hard idea to accept—having some puppet of Aistulf sitting in the Palatine Palace—but it would prevent a catastrophe like what happened at Ravenna. The Lombards are Catholic, after all, they're not barbarians or heretics. And they've been here in Italy for generations. Many Lombards are settled in Rome as it is, or have Roman spouses. Didn't Ratchis himself take a Roman woman as his wife? Must Lombards and Romans remain enemies forever?"

"The Lombards are Catholic in name only," said Paul. "If they were truly Catholic they would have more respect for St. Peter. Until recently they even denied that our Savior was of the same substance as the Heavenly Father—making them scarcely more Christian than the Saracens!"

"Well, actually, that's not quite—" began Theophylact.

"Theo, Paul," said Stephen, "Let's not get into any more doctrinal debates."

"Very well, Your Holiness," said Paul. "But my point is, if the Lombards are allowed temporal authority in Rome, they'll certainly seize spiritual authority too. Your Holiness would become their mouthpiece, their puppet, and if you refused, they'd do what the Emperor tried to do with our beloved Gregory, when he refused to burn the images." A brief silence ensued, as the counselors relived the night when the Emperor's assassins were arrested within the very walls of the Lateran Palace.

"Paul," said Stephen finally, "you say no to the Emperor, no to diplomacy, no to accommodation. So what do you recommend—that we simply do nothing?"

"That we seek help from the Franks."

Paul's suggestion triggered a general sucking-in of breath. "From the Franks?" asked Marcellus after a pause. "From so far away beyond the mountains? Why not from the Persians then, or the coal-dark Nubians?"

"Francia isn't so far away—it's closer than Constantinople, and you don't hesitate to seek aid from there."

"I doubt that," said Marcellus. "And even if you're right, no vast mountain range lies between us and the Emperor, that would stop him from sending his forces to Italy."

"Many armies have crossed the Alps, starting with the Carthaginians."

"So the Franks have a Hannibal?"

"Don't understimate the Frankish armies, or their leaders," said Paul. "Didn't Charles, whom they called the Hammer—didn't he earn that name by routing the Saracens, who've never shown their faces north of the Pyrenees since that day? Didn't he destroy the Frisians on the Middelsea, and kill Hrodbad their king, so that his son now pays tribute to the Franks? And Charles's son, Pepin, who now rules Francia—he outshines his father. He's seized the lands of Carloman and Grifo, his brothers. His territory stretches from the Western Ocean to the Danube, and from the Northern Sea to Burgundy and the borders of Aquitaine. The Frankish realm—not even the Emperor's lands compare with it. Believe me, Pepin's armies could drive every last Lombard out of Italy."

"The Frankish realm," echoed Theophylact mockingly. "Many trees—what else?"

"Many trees—and many Latin-speaking Christians who revere St. Peter. And who train with bow and sling and sword—every day from earliest childhood."

"Paul," interposed the Pope, "I don't doubt the strength of Pepin's army. But what would bring him to wage war on the Lombards? He's never had any designs on lands south of the Frankish passes. In fact, the Lombards are on good terms with the Franks. Didn't Liutprand send an army to help Charles against the Saracens? And our beloved Gregory already asked Charles for aid against the Lombards, when Liutprand was burning Roman cities. Begged him for aid, and Charles refused, on account of a treaty between those two nations. What can I offer Pepin that Gregory didn't offer a dozen years ago?"

"A crown."

"A crown—the Frankish crown?" asked Stephen. "He has one already. Didn't Archbishop Boniface anoint him king at Soissons, with Zachary's blessing, just this last year?"

"Yes he did, Your Holiness," said Paul, "but many of his own nobles dispute his legitimacy. So long as Childeric lives, they say, the Frankish crown belongs to the Merovings. Librarian Tullius, you've been quiet all this time, explain to the counselors why that is so."

Tullius was startled to hear his name called so abruptly. "Your Holiness, should I speak?" he began nervously.

"Of course, dear Tullius. Wasn't our beloved Gregory the Roman—wasn't that Gregory the papal Librarian before his election, or until his eyesight failed? It's a noble office. Speak freely."

Tullius blushed deeply. "He was indeed, Your Holiness. And what was it again that Your Holiness wished me to speak of?"

Stephen realized that Tullius had been asleep through the previous conversation. "As Deacon Paul requests, please explain to us why Pepin's kingship is in doubt."

"Pepin's kingship? Ah yes, indeed, Pepin's kingship—that's a long story, and a curious one. The Meroving dynasty was founded by Merovech the Salian, who, as we know by the authority of Fredegar, was conceived from the union of Pharamond's wife with a shape-changing sea-monster. That was three hundred and fifty years ago, when Innocent was Pope. After—"

"Perhaps just the more recent parts of the story, dear Tullius, such as are relevant to Deacon Paul's question."

"Yes, of course, Your Holiness—Deacon Paul's question. What was that question again, Deacon Paul?"

Paul began to regret having drawn Tullius into the discussion. "Briefly, why is the kingship of Pepin disputed?"

"Ah yes, well—I should have brought the histories with me, but in brief, it's this. Many great Merovings ruled over Francia, such as Childeric, the first of that name, and his son Clovis, who united Gaul under the Franks, and more recently Clotaire, and his son Dagobert. Those were kings indeed. But incessant warfare weakened the Meroving line, because the sons of each monarch—after his death—they divided their father's realm between them, and then they fought for each others' shares. What's more, they fought over women or chose their wives unwisely. I'm thinking for example of the evil Brunhilda, the Visigoth, whom Sigebert took for a wife. Over the course of her long life she caused the death of ten Meroving kings, according to Fredegar, and what is more shocking, she had Bishop Desiderius killed by three assassins, or perhaps stoned to death as other authorities attest, because the blessed martyr dared to preach against her wickedness. Only in her seventieth year did she receive her just punishment, when she was tied to four wild horses and torn limb from limb in the presence of—"

"The kingship, Tullius—"

"Yes, forgive me, Your Holiness. After Dagobert, the Meroving line degenerated. A succession of do-nothing kings sat on the throne. They bore illustrious names—Clovis, Chlothar, Theuderic, Childeric—but the real power was held by their chief ministers, who were called the Mayors of the Palace. Among them were Pepin, grandfather of the present Pepin, and his son Charles the Hammer, and others. It was a hereditary position, like a monarchy, except in name. The Merovings were now feeble in body—mostly they were children who died while they were still teenagers, to be replaced by some even younger and sicker child. When the Mayor of the Palace wanted to announce some edict, he hauled the poor king-child out on an ox-cart, and the people bowed down to him, and he mouthed whatever the Mayor told him to say, and then he was taken back to play with his toys. One of these do-nothing kings—I believe it was one of the Chlothars, or perhaps a Sigebert, if my memory serves me right—he actually led the Frankish army against the Thuringians, and was defeated, and afterwards he just sat on his horse and cried. He was ten years old."

"Tullius—"

"Why, yes, the kingship. So—"

"Your Holiness will excuse me, a call of nature," said Theophylact, and left the hall with a quick bow, as did Marcellus. While filling the piss-pot that was strategically placed in a side-office, Theophylact gave vent to his feelings. "That Deacon Paul," he muttered. "I could strangle him. Dressed up like a peacock, full of wild ideas—"

"And no respect for his seniors," added Marcellus.

"Exactly. A little would-be Pope, bathing himself in his brother's glory. But the Papacy is still an elected office, as I recall."

The two men returned to the reception hall, where the Librarian was continuing his history of the Frankish monarchy. "Two years ago, as Your Holiness knows, Pepin sent two ambassadors to our beloved Zachary—Burghard and Fulrad—and they asked 'Shall one who wields no power be called King?' and Zachary replied, 'No, let him be called King who wields the power.' And so it was that Childeric was deposed, and they gave him the monkish tonsure and sent him to the monastery at Sithiu, where he sits today. And Pepin was anointed by Boniface at Soissons, and calls himself King of the Franks. But there are many among his nobles who still say, 'Pepin is not descended from kings, his father was a bastard. By what authority is he called king?' And those nobles may refuse to bear arms for him, when they're summoned to the Marchfield."

"So how does this all relate to our crisis here?" asked Stephen.

"In this way," said Paul. "Pepin needs you to make him king."

"He was already anointed, by Boniface."

"Anointed, Your Holiness, yes, but not crowned. And by a bishop of the Franks, not by the Supreme Pontiff."

Theophylact broke in. "By what authority may the Holy Father crown a Frankish King? Is the Pope Emperor? Is Francia one of his vassal states? To give advice, as Zachary did—that's permissible, even praiseworthy. To allow a bishop to anoint Pepin, as Boniface did, that's permissible too—it's a spiritual act. It does nothing more than express the Church's approval of what the nobles did, when they raised Pepin on their shields. But to *crown* him, as the Deacon suggests—and with your Holiness's own hands?" Theophylact's voice rose almost to a shout, he glared around and banged his fist on the table. "Find me the passage in the Scriptures, show me the edict of any Council, or the words of Augustine or Jerome or any Doctor of the Church, or any of Your Holiness's predecessors in the Apostolic Succession—find me the words that authorize such an act! Spiritually, the Pope rules Christendom; temporally, he's a subject of the Emperor. If Pepin wants to be crowned, let him go to Constantinople." A general chorus of murmurs lent support to the Archdeacon's words.

"Theo is right, dear Paul," said Stephen. "What you suggest is not a proper function of my office. And even if I were to overcome my own scruples and make such an offer to Pepin, it would be rejected. The Franks know that I lack the authority."

"Very well, Holy Father," said the crestfallen Paul. "I thought that this could be a useful plan, but I see now that I was wrong. Even so, it may be worthwhile to approach Pepin once more, even if not with that offer."

"Maybe," said Stephen. "But there are other roads we

should follow first. Following Archdeacon Theophylact's wise suggestion, I'll send legates to Constantinople, to demand in the strongest terms that the Emperor come to our aid if he wishes us to remain his loyal subjects. And as Treasurer Marcellus says, we must also attempt to resolve the crisis through dialogue with Aistulf. Therefore I'll ask you, First Notary Ambrose, to go to Pavia with a letter from me. I'll send for a safe-conduct for you and your party. I choose you, Ambrose, because you worked together so closely with Zachary. Remind Aistulf of his obligations to St. Peter, and his father's treaty with Zachary, and the danger to his immortal soul if he should attack our Holy City."

"I'll do so, Your Holiness," said Ambrose.

"But, beyond all this, we must seek help from Him who founded his Church on the Rock that was called Peter. As one people we must confess our sins. In sincere penitence we must implore Almightly God, and Jesus our Redeemer, and the Holy Spirit, for the sake of the True Church, to deliver us from the great peril that faces us."

"Your Holiness has spoken wisely," said Theophylact. "And in humility I beg Your Holiness to allow me to make the arrangements for such a ceremony."

"We'll be most grateful for your efforts," said Stephen.

"And may I also make a suggestion," added Paul, "with the hope that it be received more favorably by Your Holiness and my fellow counselors than what I put forward before."

"Go ahead, Paul, what is it?" said Stephen.

"Your great predecessor, the blessed Sylvester, who baptized the Emperor Constantine, and who with Constantine's aid founded so many churches and palaces in this city, to the greater glory of God and of the blessed Peter—including the very palace in which we now sit—"

"Yes, Paul, Librarian Tullius can supply the details—what about Sylvester?"

"For four centuries and more," Paul went on, "Sylvester's holy remains have lain in the catacomb of Priscilla on the Salarian Way. It's a wonder that they haven't been stolen or destroyed during that time, and greater dangers face them now, with the Lombards threatening to invade the Duchy. So, if Your Holiness thinks well of it, let's take his sarcophagus—as one people, and with prayerful penitence and supplication for God's favor—let's carry his sarcophagus through the city, and lodge it where it truly belongs, in the Basilica of the Blessed Peter, next to the tomb of the Apostle himself."

Here finally was something that Theophylact could approve of, for the translation of saintly relics from the catacombs to St. Peter's was a time-honored tradition. What's more, making arrangements for the event would keep Paul's mind off other, more contentious issues for weeks, if not months. Perhaps Paul could even be given a permanent position as Translator of Relics, or some such fine-sounding title. "This is a noble idea, and I support Deacon Paul in this matter whole-heartedly," he said. Others also agreed, and Paul beamed.

"Very well then, Paul," said Stephen. "Please go ahead and plan for that, and the city will have your gratitude. So we will have Theo's ceremony in a few days, and Paul's translation of Sylvester a little later. We recall that penitence and supplication have often—over our city's long history— they have often moved the Lord, by the intercession of our

Savior and the blessed martyrs, to spare us from the retribution that our sinful lives so justly merited. By Christ's mercy, may it be so now. Let us pray. '*Pater noster, qui es in caelis, sanctificetur nomen tuum*—'"

6

———

A flash lit up the night sky over Rome. For the briefest instant, Zaid saw the city's churches, temples, and monuments illuminated in brilliant detail, before the scene vanished into darkness. Then came a deafening crack of thunder, followed by echoes that rumbled back and forth among the seven hills of the city and those beyond. And then it began to rain.

It rained with a suddenness and violence that took Zaid's breath away. It was as if the lightning bolt had opened a gash in the tent of the sky, through which water now cascaded in an unbroken stream. Within seconds, the Street of the Triple Gate became a churning lake mixed with mud that washed down from the Aventine Hill. Some of the resulting slurry ran between the warehouses lining the street's west side, crossed the narrow cobbled embankment, and emptied into the Tiber. Another muddy stream ran northward along the street, flooded the deserted cattle-market, and tumbled into the river above the Aemilian Bridge. On the backs of these torrents, all the debris of urban civilization—wooden crates, piles of rotting vegetables, and a dead dog or two—was freighted seaward.

Zaid and three other youths watched the storm from the doorway of an abandoned tenement on the east side of the street, where they had fashioned a crude habitation. In the two days since he ran away from Silversmiths' Street, Zaid had become acquainted with all the miseries of homelessness. He was cold. He was hungry. The pain from his cuts and bruises interfered with his sleep. He had a hard time knowing when or in which direction to pray, and he found few suitable places to do so. He had no plans or hopes for the future.

A part of him longed for reconciliation with his father. The thought that this would allow him to see Lenora again made the idea of taking that fifteen-minute walk back across the Tiber especially compelling. But he also still seethed with anger—an anger that the pain from his wounds helped keep alive—and he feared that his father would inflict more punishment on him for running away. So he resolved to stick it out.

After thirty minutes or so the storm moved to the east, and the rain tailed off. Eventually the sky cleared, unveiling a gibbous moon. Zaid and his new companions huddled up together and passed the time by recounting their life stories. The other three were Romans. Two were brought up in the city, the other, whose name was Nelius, came from a village ten miles to the north. Aside from the family difficulties and other problems that had left them on the streets, their lives had lacked much excitement. Thus Zaid, with his exotic background, was the chief story-teller, but he didn't get as much pleasure from recounting his adventures to these youths as he did with Lenora. Eventually, all four of them fell asleep.

When they awoke, it was light. Rain was falling again, but only lightly. The Street of the Triple Gate was now busy. Carts were lining up to enter the warehouses, and a boy was herding a flock of goats up the street. Zaid walked a few steps to a fountain, where he flicked a little water over his face and hands. The cold water stung his wounds. Then he found a quiet spot behind a building, faced in what he hoped was the direction of the Qiblah, and bowed his head. "*Allaahu Akbar, Allaahu Akbar, Allaahu Akbar, Allaahu Akbar; Ashhadu Allah ilaaha illa-Lah. God is great; I bear witness that there is none worthy of worship except God—*"

Having completed his prayers, Zaid rejoined his companions. Nelius suggested that they scout out the bakeries near the vegetable market to see if they could find something to eat. They agreed, and the four youths headed up to the Triple Gate and from there into the cattle market. The open space was streaked with mud from the previous night's downpour, and the river was so high that in places it had spread into the market itself. Workers were trying to clean up the mess. At the same time, farmers led their cows and goats and other animals into the wooden enclosures from which they would be sold off.

Zaid wanted to stop and play with some of the animals, but his companions hurried him on. They continued northward to the vegetable market. Several bakeries were located on a street behind the market. As they entered the street, Zaid recognized his friend Antonius with his little cart, and grabbed him from behind.

"What the—! Hey, Zaid!" cried the boy. "Where the hell have you been? And your face!"

"That's what my father did."

54

"Yes, Lenora told me, but I didn't know it was that bad."

"Tonius, can you get us something to eat? We're really hungry."

"Let me see," said Antonius. "I have to go load up." He disappeared with his cart into a bakery. He emerged a few minutes later, his cart laden with buns, biscuits, and small tarts. "You can have two each," he said. "That's about the most I can get away with—they figure out how many I've sold."

The four youths selected the largest-looking pieces and immediately began to eat, except for Zaid, who took time for a brief prayer: *"Bismillahi wa 'ala baraka-tillah—In the name of Allah and with his blessings."* Then he too started to eat. "This is great," he said between mouthfuls. "We've been eating stale stuff and garbage."

"Lenora is worried crazy," said Antonius. "She's been asking all over for you. She thought maybe you'd left the city."

"Maybe I will leave," Zaid said. "But I want to see her first. Can you tell her to meet me at the Aemilian Bridge at noon?"

"Sure," said Antonius. "But you should come home."

"There's nothing for me there."

"Well, your father is still mad at you, that's for sure, but you have a life there. What are you going to do otherwise?"

"I don't know—something."

"All right, I have to go. I'll tell her to meet you. This will make her day."

"Tell her not to tell her parents, or my father."

"I will." Antonius headed off, pushing his cart in front of him.

"Let's go back to the market," said one of Zaid's friends. "Let's see what else we can find." The four youths walked back to the vegetable market, which was becoming increasingly crowded. They were able to beg or purloin a few items off the stalls. A few stalls sold clothing, and at one of these Zaid pointed out a rack from which several woolen cloaks were hanging. "One of those would have kept me warm last night," he said enviously.

Zaid walked on further on, coming to a stall whose owner was trying to sell some puppies. As Zaid played with the animals, he heard an angry shout. Looking up, he saw Nelius running toward him, the woolen cloak under his arm. As he reached Zaid he handed off the cloak to him, saying "Run!" and he disappeared between the rows of stalls.

The stall-keeper was also running in Zaid's direction, shouting "Stop thief!" Zaid also dashed off among the stalls. He looked for a side street to escape the area, but several people tried to grab hold of him. After several frantic loops around the stalls he found himself trapped by a small mob. They pinned him down, and soon the stall-keeper and two watchmen arrived on the scene.

The stall-keeper retrieved his cloak. As onlookers muttered imprecations against the young law-breaker, the watchmen marched Zaid out of the market-place. Their destination, it turned out, was just a few steps away: the papal police had a lock-up in the partly-demolished Theater of Marcellus, which occupied a large site between the market and the east bank of the river. Once there, the watchmen threw Zaid into a small, dark cell. Then they slammed and locked the door.

7
——

Along the south side of the Lateran Palace, on the upper floor, was a row of small rooms, barely larger than cubicles. Each room was furnished with a simple bench and writing desk, or sometimes two. The only decorations were wooden crucifixes attached to the whitewashed walls, one to a room. What was unique about these rooms, however, was their large windows, which filled them with sunlight for much of the day. They also offered a view—only partially obscured by the thick glass—over the Lateran gardens, the Aurelian Wall, and the fields beyond the wall that rose toward distant hills.

These rooms seemed designed to encourage day-dreaming, but in reality they were hives of silent activity, for here labored the papal secretaries and scribes, for whom the bright light was essential. The secretaries worked for Ambrose, the First Notary: their responsibility was to deal with the Pope's voluminous correspondence, and also to write out the minutes of the Pope's meetings. The scribes worked for Tullius, the Librarian: their responsibility was to make copies of entire manuscripts—either because the existing manuscripts were wearing out, or because copies had to be supplied to other churches in Rome, in Italy, or elsewhere in the western half of Christendom.

The scribes and secretaries were men—usually younger men, whose eyesight was still capable of the close work that their jobs demanded. For the most part, they were the sons of patrician families who needed some gainful occupation before taking over their fathers' estates. Yet one of these little rooms, at the west end of the corridor, had been occupied for the past eighteen months by a woman, whose name was Leoba.

Leoba was in her late thirties. She had blond hair, blue eyes, and very fair and unlined skin that suggested a life spent indoors, but she came from a family of restless travelers, and she herself was no exception. She was born at Crediton, a small town in the southwest of Britain, and her parents placed her in the newly-founded double monastery at Wimborne. She of course lived in the female half of the monastery, where she never saw a man, but she corresponded with Boniface, whom she called her uncle, although actually he was a more distant relative. When she was barely out of her teens she suggested to Boniface that she come to Germany and help with the establishment of a convent there. Boniface did in fact call her, and thus began a new phase of her life.

On account of her remarkable intelligence and learning, Boniface authorized her to enter men's monasteries, which were normally closed to women. In addition, Boniface was favored by the Frankish rulers, including Charles Martel and later his son Pepin, because his missionary labors facilitated the eastward expansion of their realm. As a result, Leoba found herself frequently in the company of Boniface at the Frankish court, whose location shifted from one place to another every few months. In other words, Leoba became an unusually worldly and well-traveled woman, who conceded nothing to men in terms of education or independence of mind. And although she was strictly a nun, she wore the clothes of a modest laywoman more often than her religious habit.

When Mayor Pepin decided to asked Pope Zachary whether the do-nothing Merovings should still be called kings, Leoba begged her uncle for permission to go on the mission to Rome. Boniface's own first visit to that city had been a turning point in his life, so he agreed. Leoba traveled in the company of Burghard, a British missionary, and Fulrad, the abbot of the monastery of St. Denis near Paris. While in Rome, Leoba fell ill. Thus, when it came time for the ambassadors to return to Francia with Zachary's fateful answer, they had to leave her behind.

Leoba soon recovered, and over the ensuing months she occupied herself as a scribe, albeit an unpaid one. She also took every opportunity to meet Roman prelates or officials, or any learned visitors to the Holy See, who were willing to talk with her. She got on particularly well with Deacon Paul. They shared an interest in the arcane details of ecclesiastical history—details that were recorded in many a dusty manuscript in the papal library. From time to time, Boniface urged her to return to Francia, but a suitable opportunity never seemed to present itself.

On this particular morning, two days after Stephen's meeting with his counselors, Leoba was engaged in copying a psalter intended for a Frankish bishop. There came a knock on the door. Paul entered, carrying an old book.

"Am I interrupting your work, Sister?" he asked. Obviously he was, but Leoba was happy to lay down her reed pen and talk for a while. Her room had a spare bench, and she invited Paul to take it. She closed the door enough to allow some privacy, but not enough to suggest anything improper.

"I was re-reading this life of the blessed Pope Sylvester," he said. "You know I've taken on the planning for the translation of his remains?"

"Yes," said Leoba. "It's a wonderful idea."

"The Holy Father will deliver a sermon, and I have to write something for him about Sylvester."

"Well, that should be easy. There's so much that's known. And his life was so eventful."

"Yes, I'm going to start with the miracles of the ox and the dragon."

"Oh yes, how did those go?"

"Well, you remember," said Paul. "With the ox, there was a competition between a rabbi and Sylvester as to who could work the greater miracle. The rabbi spoke the word 'Jehovah' into the ox's ear, and the ox fell dead. Then Sylvester spoke the word 'Christ' into the ear of the dead ox, and it sprang back to life. And Sylvester was judged to have worked the greater miracle."

"Yes, I remember," said Leoba with a smile. "And the dragon?"

"The dragon lived in a cave under the Tarpeian Rock. His breath killed men by the score. Sylvester went down into the cave and bound the dragon's jaws with a thread, and placed the sign of the cross on him, and the dragon became tame and stopped harming people."

"Yes, those are good. The people love those stories. Do you think there were really dragons in those times?"

"I don't know," said Paul. "That was centuries ago, when many things were reported that no longer seem to happen today. But even if those stories aren't completely true, they help strengthen the faith of the common people."

"Yes," said Leoba. "And that's the important thing. And isn't there also a story about how he baptized the Emperor Constantine?"

"Oh, yes. This is what happened: Constantine was persecuting the Christians in Rome—this was before he moved the Imperial capital from Rome to Byzantium. Sylvester and his priests had to take refuge in the caves at Mount Soracte. But Constantine fell ill with the leprosy, and none of his doctors could cure him. So he asked the pagan priests what to do, and they said, 'You'll be cured if you bathe in the blood of newborn infants.' And Constantine ordered hundreds of mothers to be brought to the Capitol, with their infants—enough to supply the blood in which he could bathe."

"Don't go on!"

"But he couldn't bring himself to have the children killed. And that night he had a dream in which the blessed Peter and Paul told him to seek help from Sylvester, so he called Sylvester to Rome. Sylvester told him to repent of his sins and be baptized, and he agreed. So Sylvester baptized him, and he was immediately cured of his leprosy. After that he ended the persecution of Christians, because he had become a Christian himself. And he built many churches for Sylvester."

"Yes," said Leoba, "that's the story that I've heard. It should be in the sermon, for sure. Although I do have some doubt about that story too."

"Why—don't you believe in miracles?"

"I certainly do, especially those that happened in long-ago times. But I've read in Eusebius that he—Eusebius, I mean—he baptized Constantine at Nicomedia, when Constantine was on his deathbed. That was many years after Constantine left Rome. Why would Eusebius give a false account?"

"But why would Constantine wait until he was on his deathbed?" asked Paul. "Wasn't that risking his immortal soul, if he happened to die before he had the chance to get baptized?"

"In those days many people put off baptism until the end their life, from what I've read," said Leoba. "Baptism would wipe away all their previous sins, so they thought it was better to wait until they were finally done with sinning. Also, it may be that Constantine wasn't such a committed Christian as people think, for most of his life. I read that he also worshipped the sun-god at times—"

"Yes, or that he considered *himself* a sun-god," added Paul.

"Still, this is all beside the point," Leoba went on. "I think you should use the story of how Sylvester baptized him; it's what most people believe, and it's more fitting that Constantine was baptized in Rome by the Pope, rather than in Asia by some heretical bishop."

"Yes, I agree," said Paul.

There was a brief pause, and Leoba's eyes turned back to her work. Paul looked at the manuscript she was working on.

"You have beautiful writing," he said. "Where did you learn such a fine script?"

"At Wimborne," she replied with a slight blush. "Abbess Tetta placed a lot of emphasis on calligraphy. She used to say: 'With every letter we must convey the perfection of God's Word.'"

"Let me see if I can write like that," said Paul. He took a spare reed and Leoba's practice sheet, and tried to copy the last words that Leoba had written, which were *sub umbra alarum tuarum*—under the shade of your wings. Paul's effort was legible but not particularly graceful.

"Hold it more like this," Leoba suggested, demonstrating how she wrapped her hand around the reed. "And write from your shoulder, not from your wrist."

"Like this?" asked Paul, trying the new grip. He started to write the words again, but the reed's point caught on the sheet and sent a spattering of ink over what he had already written.

Leoba laughed. "Hold your thumb here, and then wrap the rest of your fingers around, like this." She guided Paul's hand around the reed. Paul tried again, but he was distracted by Leoba's closeness and the intimacy of her touch on his hand, and his next attempt was no better than his previous ones. "It's so frustrating," he said. "Your M's are perfect."

In Leoba's uncial script, each M was formed by two swelling curves that resembled nothing so much as a pair of ample female breasts. Paul and Leoba became conscious of this similarity at the same moment: they blushed, laughed nervously, and pulled apart from each other.

Leoba sought around for a change of topic. "You know," she said, "I heard about the discussions you had—how you wanted the Holy Father to seek help from the Franks."

"Yes, that wasn't well received," said Paul.

"But I actually agree with you. I've met Pepin, as you know, and many of his counselors. In fact, my uncle is one of them. There's a great reverence for the blessed Peter at the Frankish court—so they're very sympathetic to Peter's city. I think Pepin could be persuaded to move against Aistulf. But he needs something to strengthen the case, especially with his nobles."

"Like—"

"Well," said Leoba, "I think what you said about the Holy Father crowning Pepin was exactly right."

"You're very familiar with what we were talking about—were you listening at a key-hole?"

"No, no, certainly not," Leoba protested with a laugh. "The notary who took the record, you know, that tall man—Christopher, his name is—he showed me his transcript."

"He did?"

"Yes, he seems to be sensitive to a woman's charms—even women other than his wife." Paul's expression darkened, and Leoba went on quickly. "But you're right—Pepin's position would be greatly strengthened if he were crowned by the Holy Father. He'd do a great deal in return for that, I'm sure. The difficult issue is the one that the Archdeacon brought up—whether the Holy Father has the authority to crown him."

"Apparently he doesn't," said Paul. "That seemed to be the consensus at the meeting."

The sun had been shining for a while, but now a threatening bank of clouds was moving across the sky, and the room became noticeably darker and cooler. "No more storms, I hope," Paul commented. "The Tiber has already flooded in a couple of places."

"Yes, I feel sorry for travelers in this weather," said Leoba. "The roads must be terrible. At least this will keep Aistulf in Lombardy for a while."

Paul returned to the topic that Leoba had brought up. "Do you know of any authority that would allow the Holy Father to crown Pepin?"

"Not exactly. I've been trying to think of anything, without much success. But if Pope Sylvester worked a miracle to cure Emperor Constantine, then the Emperor would have been extremely grateful to the Pope, wouldn't he?"

"Yes, of course. And?"

Leoba's voice dropped just slightly, as if to ensure that no one in the corridor or the adjacent room could hear her. "And we know that, after that happened, he moved his capital from Rome to Byzantium?"

"Yes—so?"

"Leaving Rome without a resident Emperor, or any obvious source of authority over the city, or over Italy as a whole?"

"So—what are you saying?" asked Paul. "That he left Sylvester in charge?"

"It would make sense, wouldn't it? Who else could take over?"

"Well, there were still Consuls, and the Senate, weren't there? And was Sylvester really equipped to run the government—someone who'd been holed up in a cave for years?"

"Many of the senators moved East with Constantine,"

said Leoba. "And besides, Constantine might have given Sylvester the supreme authority, but Sylvester might have left the daily work of government to his underlings, just as many of the Emperors did."

"Let me think about this. You're saying that when Constantine left Rome he gave the Pope authority to rule in his place, and this authority is what would make it legitimate for the Holy Father to crown Pepin?"

"Yes, exactly. It would have given Sylvester temporal power over all the western territories that Constantine was leaving. It would be the logical thing for Constantine to do."

"And where's the authority for this?"

Leoba was silent for a moment. She gazed out over the city walls, then at the crucifix hanging from the wall, and then directly at Paul. "Well," she said finally, "what you've written so far, about the baptism of Constantine—that's the beginning of it. You'd have to add mention of what Constantine did to express his gratitude to Sylvester."

Paul was puzzled. "Just my writing it doesn't provide the authority for what Constantine did," he said. "We need something from Constantine himself—the deed or whatever it was he wrote—that spelled out the transfer of power. Where will we find that?"

"Well, you'd have to put that in whatever you write."

Paul paused a moment to digest what Leoba had said. "You mean, invent something?"

Leoba also paused. Then she said: "I wouldn't think of it that way. After all, it's our best guess that something like that actually happened. We can't supply the very document that Constantine wrote, but we can put down something as close as possible to what we think he did write."

"But you mean, as if written by Constantine himself?"

"Yes," said Leoba.

Paul thought about this for a while. "We'd be deceiving everyone, including my brother. I can't do that. He and I, we've always been—like this." Paul put his hands together with the fingers interlaced.

"You could tell him."

"No, no, no—that would be involving him in it—in the sin. Three sinners instead of two. And one of them the Pope, the Vicar of Christ. I can't do that, Leoba."

"Well then, we could leave him out of it. But is it a sin to write something that's our best effort to present the truth?" asked Leoba.

"But to deceive someone is to lie. And to lie to the Holy Father, my own brother, about such an important matter— no, I can't do it. What would your abbess—what was her name—?"

"Tetta."

"What would Abbess Tetta say about that?"

"She'd say that lying is no sin, if the purpose of lying is a godly one, such as saving an innocent life. In fact, it would be a virtuous deed. Holy Scripture says so."

"Where does it say that?"

"Don't you remember the two midwives, Shiphrah and Puah, and what they did after the Pharaoh ordered them to kill the male newborns?"

"Vaguely."

"Didn't they lie to the Pharaoh, saying that the Hebrew women gave birth without their help? So their lie saved the lives of those children. *Bene ergo fecit Deus obsetricibus—Therefore God dealt well with the midwives.*"

"I don't know if that's really—"

"And remember the harlot Rahab; didn't she lie to the king of Jericho, saying that the two Israelites had left the city, when in fact she'd hidden them under bundles of flax on her roof?"

"Yes, and her lie saved the lives of those two men, I remember. But—"

"Exactly, Paul—and how many more lives will be saved if our plan works and Rome is saved from the same fate as Ravenna? Thousands of men and women and children. And Paul, it's not just a matter of saving lives—it's a matter of saving the Papacy, perhaps even saving the Catholic faith itself. You call that a sin?"

"I—"

"And besides, you already deceived your brother—though for a good reason."

"I did? What are you talking about?"

"The second election—after Stephen the priest died. You told me what you did to win it, but you didn't tell your brother, did you?"

With a twinge of guilt Paul thought back to the hectic days after Zachary's death. The leading candidates to succeed him were the two Stephens. Stephen the priest was the presbyter of a titular church—one of the Roman churches that the Pope visited on a rotating basis to lead masses. He was an elderly member of a senatorial family, a fluent Greek-speaker, and conservative in every way. Archdeacon Theophylact worked tirelessly to generate support for him among the electors, most of whom were senators. Stephen the deacon, Paul's brother, was almost as conservative, and he had stood in great favor with Zachary, so Paul was able to win support for him among those electors who had been close to the deceased Pope. But the fact that he was not in holy orders counted against him, and Stephen the priest won the election.

The priest's sudden death a few days later triggered a renewed frenzy of activity. Theophylact's name was put forward by Marcellus, who promoted him as the natural replacement for the priest, and it quickly became clear that most of the electors who had voted for the priest would now vote for the Archdeacon. After all Theophylact, though younger than Stephen, was his superior in the Lateran hierarchy, so a simple respect for seniority favored him. Paul was able to bring a few more electors over to his brother's side, mostly by emphasizing what many already believed— that the priest's death was a sign of God's displeasure with the electors' previous choice. Nevertheless, as the election approached, it became clear that Stephen was going to lose once again.

Paul was in a quandary. He considered his brother a good and pious man who was a far more suitable choice for the Papacy than Theophylact. Certainly, Stephen had more traditional views on many issues than Paul himself did, but Paul would be in a good position to advise his brother and guide him toward more effective policies. After some heart-searching, he therefore developed an underhand strategy to influence the election.

Using funds that he had set aside over the years— income from distant estates that somehow didn't find its way into Marcellus's coffers—he secretly bribed several wavering senators to vote for Stephen. In addition, he bribed a member of the Notary's office to add a couple of dozen names to the roll of electors: these were mid-level officials at the Lateran Palace who were not from senatorial families and who were well acquainted with Stephen and Paul. His stratagem worked: Stephen won the election by a handful of votes.

The men who received Paul's money kept silent on the matter, of course, and neither Theophylact nor Marcellus, nor Stephen himself, learned of what Paul had done. Paul did tell Leoba, however. Perhaps he thought that bringing her into his confidence would increase the intimacy between them, but now he regretted it.

"I—I didn't tell him, no, but that wasn't lying," Paul said. "I just let him believe what he wanted to believe. My brother—I love him dearly, but I've always had to be the practical one, ever since we were children. Sometimes he has unrealistic ideas—or old-fashioned ones."

"Like, that the Papacy goes to the saintliest?"

"Well, something like that, maybe. He thinks Zachary was a great Pope, and he believed that he'd be chosen just by following Zachary's example."

"You did the right thing—that's what I'm trying to say. The right thing to ensure his election, and the right thing to deceive him about it."

"Deceive him?"

"Well, not to tell him."

"Leoba, what you're proposing—this isn't just not telling him something. It's weaving a whole net of lies and ensnaring my brother in it."

"It's what we believe is the truth—our recreation of the truth. If you can think of some other way to save Rome, tell me."

"Leoba," Paul pleaded, "my head's spinning. I'll think it over, but this can't be right." He rose to leave. "I'll think it over. In the meantime, let's keep this between you and me."

"Our secret," was Leoba's response.

8

———

Z aid remained in the lock-up at the Theater of Marcellus for the remainder of that day. He was even colder and hungrier than he had been before, and his loneliness was interrupted only once, when a watchman passed some dry bread through the slot in the door. His misery reached a climax around mid-day, when he thought of Lenora coming to meet him at the Aemilian Bridge, and how she would be waiting and waiting for him, and how she would finally have to give up and go home. She would assume that he had left town without bothering to see her. She would curse him and resolve to find a more loyal boyfriend. Once or twice he screamed out her name, as if his voice might carry the quarter-mile that separated them, but there was no response. The hours of daylight dragged by slowly, and those of darkness even slower.

Early the following morning, a narrow sunbeam illuminated the wall of Zaid's cell. He put his eye to the door-slot, through which the sun was shining. He saw the sun itself: it had just risen from behind the Tarpeian Rock— the cliff from whose summit countless miscreants were hurled in days of old, and at whose base Sylvester's dragon had incinerated men with its baleful breath. Zaid wondered what his own fate was going to be; part of him hoped that it would be something equally final.

An hour later, the same two watchmen arrived who had arrested him the day before. They took Zaid from the cell, shackled him, and walked him back through the market, then northward for a few minutes, until they reached the courthouse. Zaid was placed in a holding cell with several other miserable-looking characters. One by one over the following hour, the men were taken away. Finally it was Zaid's turn: the watchmen took him to a room where a papal magistrate sat, along with three bailiffs.

The proceedings were brief. The stall-keeper described how Nelius stole the cloak and gave it to Zaid, who then tried to run off with it. One of the watchmen described how Zaid was detained by the crowd, with the cloak in his hands.

The magistrate, an elderly man, turned to Zaid. "What's your name?"

"Zaid."

"How old are you, Zaid?"

"I don't know."

"Speak louder."

"I don't know."

"Do you confess to this crime?"

"It happened as the man said."

"Who's your father?"

Zaid paused. "I don't have one," he said finally.

"Your mother?"

"I don't have one."

"Where were you born?"

"In Africa."

"How did you come to Rome?"

"With traders."

"What's your religion?"

"I submit to the will of Allah, *Ar-Rahman*, the All-Merciful."

The magistrate turned and spoke briefly with one of the bailiffs, then he turned back to Zaid.

"The penalty for this crime is death, but you're too young. The God of the Christians can also be merciful." Zaid remained silent, and after a pause the magistrate went on. "Forswear your heathen gods and accept baptism into the Catholic faith, and you'll go free."

"There is only one God, *Ar-Rahim*, the Compassionate," said Zaid, "whose angel Jibril revealed the Qu'ran to the prophet Muhammad, may Allah bless him and grant him peace."

"We'll be compassionate with you, Zaid, if you accept baptism in the name of Jesus. If you refuse, you'll be taken as a slave."

"Jesus, the son of Mary, was only a messenger," said Zaid resolutely. "Many were the messengers who died before him."

"Here's a message for you, Zaid: If you don't—"

"There is only one God, *Al-Malik, Al-Quddus, As-Salam, Al-Mu'min*—" Zaid seemed determined to list all ninety-nine names of Allah, but the magistrate cut him off.

"Take him away, let him be enslaved," he said sharply, and the bailiffs hustled Zaid out of the courtroom, while the boy tried to continue with his recitation: "*Al-Muhaymin, Al-Aziz, Al-Jabbar*—"

The bailiffs took Zaid around to the back side of the

courthouse, where a man was lounging in a small office that was warmed by a charcoal brazier. One of the bailiffs spoke some words into the ear of the man, who looked at Zaid. "Come here, young fellow, I have something to show you," he said.

The bailiffs moved Zaid forward. Zaid noticed a strange-looking metal frame, and scarcely had he noticed it than he found himself trapped inside it: the framework held him around the chest. The man pulled on Zaid's left arm and attached a kind of clamp around his wrist. All this took no more than five or six seconds. Then the man bared Zaid's left shoulder and rubbed some oil on it.

"Look over there," the man said, pointing to the other side of the room. Zaid looked anxiously in the direction the man had indicated, and saw nothing, but at that moment he felt a searing pain in his shoulder as the brand bit into his skin. He screamed and tried to pull his arm away, but could not. The man applied some more oil, placed the brand back on the brazier, and released Zaid from the frame. "It's done," he said.

Zaid continued to scream. He looked at the source of the pain, and saw that the brand had burned a crude letter S, for *servus,* into his shoulder. His screams turned to sobs. "Father—Lenora—help me! Why is this happening to me? *Allah Al-Afuww*—take away my sins! *Allah Al-Mu'id*—give me back what I've lost!" He fell in a convulsing heap on the stone floor. At the same moment a violent crash of thunder announced the onset of yet another rainstorm.

"Take him to work in the Lateran stables," said the man to the bailiffs. "They're short of slaves."

9

At dawn on the following morning, Marcus, Sibyl, and Lenora were sitting down to breakfast—millet porridge and goat's milk, with a few greens—in their cramped living quarters above Sibyl's fortune-telling store. It had been a night of incessant rain—one of many over the last few weeks—and Marcus was concerned about the possibility of flooding.

"High water makes for fast work," he said, "but if we have to stop milling, I won't be paid," he said glumly.

"Well, let's hope it's not that bad," said Sibyl.

They fell awkwardly silent, aware that all was not well in the room. In the silence, a muffled sobbing could be heard. Marcus turned to his daughter. "Lenora, eat," he said, "You'll have to grow strong to work in the bakery."

"I don't want to work in the bakery," Lenora declared, and then buried her face in her hands.

"Listen, Nora," said Marcus, "Zaid, he was a good boy. But you're far too young to get involved with him—or any boy. And now he's gone. Your mother and I will find someone for you, someone better, when the time's right. A Christian, of course."

"He's not gone—I just need to know where he is."

"Well, he's probably far away from here by now. I expect he got himself hired with some family that was leaving town—there are plenty of them right now. They often need help. He hated being stuck in Rome. He probably left town the same day he ran away."

"He didn't," said Lenora.

"He didn't? How do you know he didn't?"

"He was going to meet me yesterday."

"What—how do you know? Did you see him?"

"Tonius saw him, yesterday morning."

"Tonius?"

"Antonius—the boy with the pastry-cart. He met Zaid, and Zaid said he would meet me at the Aemilian Bridge at noon."

"So that's where you were!" Sibyl broke in. "You disappeared for most of the afternoon."

"So what did he say," asked Marcus. "What's he doing?"

"I don't know—he never showed up!" Lenora broke into a wail. "I don't know what happened, or where he is."

"Nora," said Sibyl, "don't cry, there's probably—"

"He probably got hired by travelers yesterday morning," said Marcus, "And he had to set out right away—so he couldn't wait around until noon."

"He wouldn't have done that, not after he'd promised to meet me."

"Lenora, you're going to have to let Zaid go. I know it's painful, but you'll get over it. And before long—"

Their conversation was interrupted by the voice of a child shouting from the street: "Miller Marcus! Miller Marcus!"

"Uh-oh—that doesn't sound good," said Marcus. He

clambered down the rickety stairs.

A boy aged seven or eight was standing in front of Sibyl's parlor. "Miller Marcus," he said, "the grain-master needs you at the mill."

Marcus shouted up to Sibyl, "I have to go right away."

"Why, has something happened?"

"I don't know—I'll let you know later." Marcus gave the urchin a small coin and headed off down the street.

"That was strange," said Sibyl. "I hope he wasn't right about the flooding." She continued to eat her breakfast, while Lenora picked at hers. "Lenora, your father is right," she went on. "You're too young to get tangled up with any boy—there'll be plenty of time for that later."

"Mama, I love him," came Lenora's reply, and she started crying again.

"Nora, Zaid is a good boy, a good young man, but he shouldn't have run away like that."

"Did you see him—his face—what Omar did to him?"

"No, I didn't, but I heard."

"I've asked everywhere—no-one knows where he is. He probably did leave town, like Papa said."

"Well, he may come back."

"The journeys he goes on—they take years."

"Well then, you and he will be the right age, when he gets back."

"Oh Mama, don't joke about it! How can I wait years and not even know where he is or if he's still thinking about me?"

"Maybe we can help matters along."

"You mean, with magic?"

"We can try—I can't promise anything."

"You won't harm him?"

"No, no," said Sibyl with a laugh. She gathered the bowls and spoons and gave them to Lenora to wash at the street fountain. "Do you have anything of his?" she asked.

"No, nothing," said Lenora, and began to cry again.

"Then ask Omar for something. He should want his son back."

Lenora took the dishes down to the street and washed them. Two other women were there. One of them was saying: "Have you heard about the flooding?" So Lenora knew that her father had guessed right, and that he might be back home before long if they couldn't run the mill.

Before returning upstairs, she took a look next door. Although it was early, Omar was already working on a relic. Lenora took the plunge. "Omar," she said, "Mama wants to try and bring Zaid back," she said.

"Oh, with her spells?" Omar said, with a wry laugh.

"Yes, and she needs something of his."

"And why does she want him back? For your sake? You don't look too happy."

"Don't you want him back too, Omar?"

"Yes, to give him a good beating and set him to fixing everything he broke."

"He won't come back for a beating."

"That's his choice."

"Do you have anything—of Zaid's?"

"Go look upstairs, where he sleeps."

Lenora climbed up the stairs. The room above was similar to the one above Sibyl's store, but it was much less tidy. Besides some basic furniture—a simple bed, a table, and a bench—the room also held a motley collection of articles that seemed to be connected with Omar's work or travels: odd-shaped pieces of wood and metal, bundles of cloth, and saddle-bags. Lenora hadn't been in this room before, and she didn't immediately see where Zaid slept. Then she spied what looked like a bundle of rags in a dark corner. They were actually a couple of blankets covering a thin mat. Next to this bed was a small shelf, set low on the wall. It held a collection of wooden model animals: horses, mules, and goats, as well as a couple of birds.

Lenora felt a thrill of intimacy with her absent beloved. She took several of the animals from the shelf and looked them over, and then carefully replaced them. She cautiously touched the blankets. She lifted one of them off the mat and then, after a guilty look behind her, raised it to her face. Zaid's odor was unmistakable. Lenora buried her face in the blanket and held it there for a minute or two.

As she made to put the blanket down, she noticed that another carved animal had been lying on the mat, hidden under the bed-clothes. She picked it up: it was a camel, carved in a darker wood than the others, and more finely finished. Its surface was polished smooth by frequent handling. It was obviously Zaid's favorite.

Lenora noticed some strands of Zaid's hair on the mat, and she picked these up too. They reminded her of how she had given Zaid some of her own hair. She took the camel and the hairs downstairs, carefully holding the hairs between her thumb and forefinger.

"May I take this?" she asked Omar, showing him the camel.

"I don't see why not. And your mother will need this too." Omar took a thin sheet of lead, about the size of a hand. With a bronze stylus he scratched a couple of characters in Kufic script. "That's Zaid, in our writing," he said, giving it to Lenora.

"Thank you," she said. And then: "Will you forgive him, if he does come back?"

"We'll see. I need him. He's my son."

Back in the parlor, Sibyl was already preparing to cast a spell. She had placed a small table in the center of the parlor, and two stools. On the table she placed a lighted candle, an incense burner, and a variety of strange-looking stones, including a fragment of a geode encrusted with violet crystals, a sheet of creamy-green jade, a lump of drab rock in which several glistening cubes of pyrite were embedded, and a small glass cup that held a droplet of quicksilver.

Lenora showed her mother the camel and the hairs. "You're sure they're his?" Sibyl asked.

"Yes, they were on the mat where he sleeps."

Sibyl placed the lead sheet, the camel, and the hairs on the table. She sat her daughter on a stool, drew a black curtain around the scene, and sat down herself. The candle now provided almost the only light. On the inside of the curtain were embroidered a variety of signs and symbols, resembling the letters of some non-existent, fantastical alphabet. The fumes from the incense-burner, and the dim light, made the signs hard to discern.

Sibyl began her recitation in a chant-like voice. "*Mercuri trismegiste, liga Zaidum—Thrice-great Mercury, bind Zaid, hold him fast, wherever he may be, tie him with invisible threads.*" Sibyl paused to copy some of the signs from the curtain onto the lead sheet, using a stylus like the one Omar had used to inscribe Zaid's name. Then she went on: "*Thrice-great Mercury, bring*

Zaid to this place, whence he departed, draw him back, don't let him escape you, don't let him break your bonds, carry him back to his father—"

"—and to his betrothed," whispered the girl.

Sibyl was busy copying some more signs onto the lead sheet, and she pretended not to hear what her daughter had said. There was no point starting an argument and thus breaking the spell, so she went on: "Thrice-great Mercury, bring Zaid back uninjured, protect him from plague, and the miasma, and all disturbances of breath, blood, or bile."

After a few more rounds of chanting and inscribing, all eventualities had been accounted for, and Zaid's name was fully surrounded by magical signs. Sibyl then took Zaid's hairs, placed them in the middle of the sheet, and held them in place with her forefinger as she folded the sheet over them. Now neither the writing nor the hairs were visible.

"Take this back to Omar," she said. "Tell him to drive three nails through it. Then put it where you found the hairs, where Zaid sleeps."

"When will it work?" asked Lenora. "When will I see him again?"

"Within a month," said Sibyl.

"A month? So long?"

"Maybe sooner. But magic takes time to work, it doesn't happen at the snap of your fingers. Mercury has many things to attend to. You'll see Zaid within thirty days, if Mercury answers our prayers. Better not tell your father about this."

10

By the time Marcus was half-way to the Aemilian Bridge, his fears were confirmed: floodwaters extended for several hundred feet from the river. The water had not just inundated the Aurelian Way; it had also run down the side streets and invaded the little stores and workshops that lined them. Some of the owners of those establishments were trying to erect barricades against the flood, or to remove the water that had already entered. Others just stood around and commiserated with each other.

Although the floodwaters extended for a distance of several streets from the river, they were nowhere very deep. Marcus could see that ox-carts were still reaching the bridge and crossing it, and the water never rose more than half-way up to the carts' axles. Still, he decided that, rather than wade along the embankment, he would strike north along one of the side-streets that were still dry and then cut across to the embankment at the level of his mill. Thus, he only got his boots wet for the last few minutes of his journey.

When Marcus finally reached the embankment, an unfamiliar scene greeted him. Ordinarily a very modest river—one that ancient travelers could sometimes ford on horseback—the Tiber now aspired to the breadth and majesty of the Nile. The streets of Transtiber, and the grander avenues and squares of the Campus Martius on the other side of the river, had been transformed into a single, mile-wide expanse of muddy water. Out of this vast liquid plain, the churches, temples, palaces, and monuments of Rome ranged up in forlorn splendor.

Where they had spilled into the city streets, the floodwaters were placid, broken only by the ripples raised by a few trundling carts or wading pedestrians. But along the proper course of the river, which was marked by the tops of the bollards that lined the embankments, the water was moving at a threatening speed. This was particularly true at the level where Marcus stood, where most of the river's volume had to squeeze through the fifty-yard gap between Tiber Island and Transtiber. Here the racing waters were thrown into turbulent eddies: great brown waves crashed against each other, sending up sheets of spray that dazzled in the early-morning sunlight. The island itself resembled a gigantic ship that was bucking its way into a heavy sea.

Marcus spent little time taking in the larger scene: his attention quickly focused on the four mills tied up along the embankment. In normal times their location, opposite the northern end of Tiber Island, was ideal for catching the river's most productive current. Now, however, they were the target of the river's greatest fury. Although secured to the bollards, the mills were rolling and twisting, as if trying to escape from their moorings. Sometimes a mill succeeded in pulling a foot or so away from the embankment and then crashed back against it with an alarming thud.

A group of twenty or thirty men, along with a team of

twelve oxen, were standing in knee-deep water on the embankment, next to Marcus's mill. Marcus recognized the workers from his own and the other mills, as well as the grain-master, a short but muscular man named Gaius. With them were two Lateran officials on horseback—Paul and another deacon. They were sent by Stephen, who had heard about the flooding.

"It's your decision, grain-master," Paul was saying. "That's what you're paid for. Do whatever it takes to protect them. This is not a good time to lose a mill, with the Lombards not far off."

"Then we'll move them," said Gaius. "That's what I was planning to do anyway. Ah, Marcus, here you are. Get your mill ready—we're going to tow it up-river."

"What? Where to?" asked Marcus in surprise.

"To the Aurelian Bridge—where there's calm water."

Marcus looked upstream. The Aurelian Bridge, five hundred yards away, lay in a wider and straighter reach of the river, where the water was indeed flowing more smoothly than in the neighborhood of Tiber Island. What's more, he could see that the bridge's west abutment sheltered the area of the riverbank immediately below it, thus offering a safe haven for the ship-mills. But moving the mills in the present conditions would be a perilous undertaking. No oar- or sail-powered vessel could tow a mill against this current. Obviously the grain-master was planning to accomplish the task with the ox-team, and in fact his men were already attaching the team to Marcus's mill with a pair of long ropes. Because the tow-ropes would need to clear the bollards that were placed at intervals along the embankment, the men were securing the ropes high up on the mill structure itself, rather than to the barge on which it sat.

"This is very risky," Marcus said to the grain-master. "I think it would be safer to let the mills remain where they are. We could lash them more tightly to the bank, and maybe put mats around them."

"They won't last out the day if we leave them here," Gaius replies. "The city depends on the mills—we must bring them to safety."

"Do as the grain-master says," added Paul.

Marcus muttered an inaudible curse. What right did this dandy have to talk down to him like that, while he sat on his high horse and kept his dainty feet dry? What did he know about ship-mills? Out loud, he said to Gaius "Let me go look." He walked across the unsteady gangway onto his mill, with muddy water spilling out of his boots.

Marcus saw right away that the mill was in trouble: some of the beams that framed the mill were slightly out of place, presumably as a result of collisions with the embankment. A few inches of water had collected in the bottom of the barge, though Marcus couldn't see whether the water was coming through a leak or had washed over the side. Just trying to stand inside the rocking mill made Marcus queasy, and he realized that Gaius's dire prediction could easily come true.

"All right, let me fix things up here," he shouted to the grain-master, and he called one of his assistants to join him on the mill. The two men uncoupled the mill-wheel's axle from the gears that drove the millstone, and lowered the upper millstone so it sat directly on the lower one. They used ropes to immobilize the millstones and the gearing system. Then, using a ratchet system, they raised the entire mill-wheel far enough that its paddles were clear of the water.

Finally, they raised the sluice-board that blocked the river water's access to the mill-wheel when the mill was not in use. Water could now flow unimpeded between the main barge and the smaller outrigger, making the mill easier to tow against the current.

Marcus and his assistant returned to the embankment. The grain-master's men had the team of oxen lined up and ready to tow the mill. They tried to cast off the mill's moorings, but it proved impossible to loosen the mooring ropes from the bollards: the knots, now underwater, had swollen into concretions that refused to be disentangled and had to be cut with axes.

Ever so slowly, the laboring animals began to move the mill forward against the stream. The mill fishtailed from side to side under the influence of the turbulent current, but several men held on to the severed mooring ropes and thus prevented the mill from moving too far from the bank. Other men, equipped with poles and mats, did their best to prevent the mill from slamming into the masonry of the embankment. It was exhausting work.

Ten or fifteen minutes later, the strange procession had advanced about one hundred yards up the river, still under Paul's watchful eye. It seemed as if Gaius's plan might actually succeed. But then one of the men shouted "Look! There!" and he pointed to the water ahead of the mill. A huge half-submerged log—the trunk of some tree loosened by the rains from an upland forest—was bearing down on the mill like a battering ram. The men tried to pull the mill tightly into the bank, but within a few seconds the log struck the barge just to the right of its prow. From the sound of the concussion it was clear that the mill had suffered significant damage. More seriously, though, the sudden jerk on the tow-rope caused two of the oxen to lose their footing on the submerged cobblestones. They stumbled, and the remaining animals came to a halt.

The stern of the barge now swung uncontrollably toward the center of the stream, and the men holding the stern mooring rope had to release it. As the barge turned broadside to the current the force exerted on it increased dramatically. In spite of the men's urging, the oxen slipped backward, and two more animals fell.

"Tie her up!" yelled Gaius, and the men holding the front mooring rope tried to lash it to a bollard. But it was too late: the rope tore from the bollard and out of their grasp. The stumbling oxen were dragged backward at an increasing speed. Within moments, the rearmost pair was pulled right off the embankment and into the fast-flowing water of the river. There, still yoked to each other, they floundered in bellowing terror.

Aside from the two deacons, the entire group of men rushed to save the situation by grasping the tow-ropes and adding their efforts to those of the remaining oxen. It was a hopeless task, however, and to prevent more animals from being lost the grain-master gave orders to cut their traces.

Now all the men could do was watch as the mill, with the two flailing oxen attached, drifted with increasing speed away from them. As it was swept downriver, the barge spun slowly around. It stayed close to the west bank, and was heading for a collision with the second mill. Several men were on that mill, preparing it to be towed in its turn. Luckily, they saw the approaching danger and scurried to shore.

The drifting mill struck the second mill with a rending impact that tore that mill away from its moorings. Marcus's mill tilted over on its side, then popped upward like a cork as the millstones and other heavy machinery dropped to the riverbed. The combined wreckage of both mills quickly bore down on the third mill in line, which suffered a similar impact, as did the fourth and rearmost mill.

The resulting tangled mass of debris was carried swiftly downstream like the ruins of a floating castle. It didn't get far, however: within less than a minute it struck the arches of Gratian's Bridge. Planking, beams, ropes, machinery, and great wads of thatching piled up against the bridge, impeding the water's flow and worsening the flooding of the nearby streets. Of the two oxen there was no sign.

Marcus watched the destruction in paralyzed horror. These had been his workplaces for several years, and now they were gone, along with his livelihood. He tried to imagine his family surviving on Sibyl's erratic earnings. They might have to leave Rome, he thought.

And then Marcus realized that all Rome would suffer with them: there would be no more flour, and thus no more bread.

11

_____

"So what did you find?" asked Leoba.

"I couldn't find any letters by Constantine," replied Paul, "but I found several by Diocletian, his predecessor. I think these will give us a good idea of the style Constantine would have used." He placed several bound and unbound manuscripts on the table. "I've also got two lives of Sylvester and a collection of legends about him, including the ones we wanted to use."

Leoba looked over the manuscripts curiously. She and Paul were meeting in a room in the Lateran library. The room did not have as fine a view as the one offered by the scribal office where they met previously: its small window looked out over an interior courtyard. Still, it was more private, because this room housed a collection of seldom-read documents, and Leoba and Paul felt comfortable closing the door completely rather than leaving it ajar.

While Leoba was reading, Paul was trying to adjust to his conspiratorial role. After Leoba first laid out her proposal to him, he had made up his mind not to go along with it; he was determined not to take part in a scheme that seemed certain to damage his relationship to his brother. But soon his resolve began to weaken. With each passing day came fresh news of troop movements in Lombardy and Tuscany. Then an envoy arrived, bringing a letter from Aistulf. The Lombard king said nothing about Ambrose's visit—perhaps Ambrose had not arrived at Pavia by the time he wrote it. Instead, Aistulf reminded the Pope that Rome used to make annual payments to Ravenna in satisfaction of imperial taxes. He demanded that these payments now be directed to Ravenna's new master, himself.

In reality, Aistulf had little hope of receiving anything, for Rome had stopped making tax payments years ago, as the Emperor's authority in Italy had waned. Even if Stephen acceded to Aistulf's request, there was little or no money to be sent. Aistulf's actual motive was obviously to provoke Rome into an outright refusal, which he could then use to legitimize an attack on the city.

Stephen was deeply disturbed by this development. At meetings with his counselors he kept an optimistic face, speaking of the likely success of Ambrose's diplomacy, the arrival of help from the Emperor, or God's intercession on the city's behalf. When alone with Paul, however, his distress was obvious, and he seemed to be physically aging in front of Paul's eyes. On one occasion he broke down and cried, deeply paining his brother. Stephen seemed to expect Paul to find some way out of the crisis, but he continued to reject Paul's proposed deal with Pepin, repeating Theophylact's argument against it. Paul was desperate to help his brother, but how could he do so except by agreeing to Leoba's plan?

The deceit involved in the plan began to lose its significance as Paul mulled it over—it was readily justified by the promised benefit, just as she had argued. And agreeing to her plan would not make him Leoba's puppet or the instrument of her designs. The idea of a deal with Pepin was his own, after all; what Leoba proposed was merely a device to make his plan more likely to succeed.

There need be no poisoning of the relationship between himself and Stephen, Paul decided. In fact, if his scheme worked and Pepin did come to Rome's aid, the bond between the two brothers would become all the closer. And finally—although he wasn't fully conscious of this motive—entering into Leoba's plan would increase the intimacy between himself and her, something that seemed more and more desirable as time went by. So he agreed to pursue the scheme, volunteering to find ancient documents that might help them in their work. And as he involved himself in the project, solving its intellectual challenges became a reward in itself.

"These are very good," said Leoba finally. "Still, I think we should omit the legends about the ox and the dragon."

"Really? I like them," protested Paul.

"But think about it from Constantine's point of view. He's writing a deed that hands the western half of his empire to Sylvester—why would he write about an ox being raised from the dead? Or a dragon breathing fire under the Tarpeian Rock? Wouldn't he be more likely to focus on the miracle that he experienced directly—the one that cured him of leprosy? In fact, he might have written the deed just a day or two after his baptism, so the miracle would still be fresh in his mind."

"I suppose you're right. So we'll start with a formal greeting from Constantine to Sylvester, and a general profession of faith, like the one my brother gave at his consecration—"

"Yes," said Leoba, "but we must be sure not to mention the Councils that hadn't happened yet, when Constantine was writing this—"

"And then we'll have Constantine recount the whole baptism story, starting with the newborn children who were supposed to be killed."

"Exactly. At this point Constantine is extremely grateful to Sylvester, and he's also anxious to atone for the horrible things he did to the Christians earlier. So he'll go on and say, 'In gratitude I've decided to move my seat of government to Byzantium, and I leave the western territories under the command of Pope Sylvester and his successors,' or something like that."

"Well, wait a moment," said Paul, "What you just said will be in there, of course. It will be the climax. But we might want to put other things in there first. After all, this document will have great authority."

"What kind of things?"

"Well, for example, it could affirm the supremacy of the Pope—the bishop of Rome—over all other bishops and patriarchs. Those who challenge the Pope's supremacy always ask where that doctrine came from. There's a feeling that it was something negotiated in private at various Councils without any prior authority. This could supply the authority."

"But how would Constantine have the power to do that," asked Leoba, "if he only converted to Christianity a few days earlier?"

"Well, he had tremendous authority as Emperor. And it's not so much the authority of his position, it's having any kind of mention of the Pope's supremacy at that early time."

"All right, fine. Anything else?"

"Yes," Paul went on. "I'd like to have something on the rights and privileges of the Pope, and those of the various counselors and deacons and so forth. These are issues that people get very exercised about. Who can appoint who, and what insignia of office various people can wear—from the Pope down."

"Is that something that Constantine would be interested in?"

"Well, whether he would or not, I'd like to have it in there. So many privileges are based on tradition, not on actual authority, and that's why there have been so many disputes. You remember how the Milanese prelates started using the white saddlecloths last year?"

"The ones that were supposed to be reserved for our people?" Leoba asked.

"Exactly—but we couldn't provide chapter and verse to back that up, and they ended up thumbing their noses at us, which was very shameful. And actually Constantine could have been interested in these matters. After all, many of the rights and privileges of the Pope and his officials are based on Imperial traditions."

"So good, put that in too. But don't make it too long."

"I won't." said Paul. "After that, I'll get to the donation."

"And what will he donate, exactly?"

"Well, temporal power—imperial power."

"Yes, but over—?"

"Over Rome, Italy, Gaul, Spain, I'll list all the western provinces."

"Well, be careful, because you'll have to check which

provinces actually existed when Constantine was Emperor."

"Yes, so maybe it would be easier just to write 'all the western provinces' or something like that."

"It would be safer, yes."

"And then I'll have him sign the deed, using formulas from the Diocletian letters, or somewhere else. And he'll date it—how, by papacies?"

"No, no—I think he'd still be using consular years, or he'd date it from the foundation of the city. Look and see how Diocletian did it."

Paul checked one of the letters on the table. "This is by consular year," he said. "So let's go with that."

"Before you end up," said Leoba, "you'll need some kind of emphatic statement about the importance of the deed. Or what punishments will be dealt out to those who ignore it—in this world or the next. That kind of thing."

"I think I can find examples to copy," said Paul. "I've seen old decrees that end with language like that."

"Oh, and one other thing—what is Constantine going to say about what he is actually going to do with the deed? Is he going to simply hand it over to Sylvester?"

"Probably he would have placed it at the tomb of the blessed Peter, just as we do with other important documents. So I'll put in mention of that."

"Fine," said Leoba. "I think we've got the general outline. So why don't you go ahead and compose it, and then I'll check it over."

Paul was silent for a few moments. "I can't believe we're really doing this," he said at last.

"Are you having second thoughts?"

"No—well, maybe a little."

Leoba took Paul's hands in hers. "Listen," she said, "you and I are the only people doing anything useful—*anything*—to save Rome from the Lombards. To save the Papacy, actually. Which means to save Christendom—or the only part of it that matters. Those other ideas—appealing to the Emperor, negotiating with Aistulf—they have no chance of succeeding. You said so yourself. We have to bring the Franks to Italy, and this is the only way of doing it."

Paul wasn't listening to Leoba's words, he was gazing into her eyes. Never before had he been in such an intimate situation with a woman, and certainly not with a woman as attractive and forward as Leoba. "Are all your countrywomen like you?" he said finally.

Leoba smiled and let go of Paul's hands. "In what way? Having blond hair, you mean? There are plenty of—"

"Well, that, and—being so self-possessed, knowing what you want."

"There are plenty of blond-haired people in Britain. As to knowing what I want—I think it has to do with my parents."

"How do you mean?"

"They had me very late. They had hoped and prayed for a child, but none came. And finally, when my mother was in her late thirties, they prayed to God again. They promised that if He answered their prayer, they'd dedicate their child to the Church. And He did, and I was born. So later, they acted on their promise and put me in the monastery at Wimborne, even though they didn't want to. And *I* certainly didn't want to. I went kicking and screaming—I cried for days, weeks. I felt they betrayed me. They *did* betray me, actually." Leoba's eyes welled up.

"Leoba—how could you have thought about it like that?

Didn't you benefit from the monastery? Your education, your closeness to God? And the opportunities you've had?"

"That's true, absolutely, but that's not how I thought about it then. In all the years I was at Wimborne, I never saw my father once—he could have been dead, so far as I was concerned. My mother would visit sometimes, but not often—it was so far away. I felt abandoned, betrayed, by the two people I most loved."

"I can't believe I'm hearing this," said Paul. "You're the most accomplished woman I've ever met—Wimborne changed your life for the better, surely."

"I think the whole experience made me determined to make my own way in the world—not to rely on parents, a husband, an abbess, whoever. You know, before I left for Germany, I did go back to Crediton once, to my parents. It was a five days' journey, in the springtime. I remember how free I felt—all the possibilities of my new life. I was with a group of pilgrims who were returning from various places—from Winchester mostly, but some had been much further, to Rome even. One day we climbed to the top of the cliff they call the Golden Cap, and I could see far down the coast towards my home, and to the moors beyond, which I used to explore with other children. And the sea was shining and there was a breeze blowing up the cliff, and one of my companions was pointing out the directions—to Gaul, and Germany, and Spain, and Italy—just as if they were visible on the horizon. It was exciting. I thought of my cousin Willibald, who made a pilgrimage to Jerusalem—"

"To Jerusalem? Why, your family certainly likes to travel!"

"Yes, I suppose so. Anyway, at Exeter, I left my companions and followed the vale of the Creedy by myself, which wasn't entirely safe, but with each mile the country became more and more familiar—more loving, somehow. I longed to see my father and mother. But when I got home they had grown old, much older than their years. I realized what it had cost them, to give me up as they did. It broke them, I think. That pact they made with God—perhaps it was really with the Devil." Her eyes seemed to tear up slightly.

"Leoba, dear Sister Leoba, how can you say such a thing? Only God could have produced you. Only God could have brought you here." Paul now took her hands in his.

There was the sound of approaching footsteps. Paul and Leoba just had time to adopt more respectable positions before the door opened. It was Tullius, who was carrying a small pile of books. When he saw Paul and Leoba, the Librarian stopped dead in his tracks. He lunged forward to prevent the books from falling out of his arms, but a few escaped his grasp and scattered over the floor. "Oh, forgive me," he said in embarrassed confusion, as he squatted down to rescue them. "I had no—"

Paul helped pick up a couple of the books. "Tullius, Heaven has sent you," he said, a little too heartily. "We were discussing the persecutions of Diocletian." He indicated one of the emperor's letters that lay on the table. "And specifically, the question of the Sacrament of Penance, as it applied to the apostate bishops during that period."

"The Sacrament of—?" asked Tullius, as he checked the books for damage.

"If we reject the Donatist heresy, as indeed we must, then should we accept the validity of *every* sacrament celebrated by those bishops, no matter what the moral status of the bishop or of the person who received the Eucharist? What do you think, Tullius? Does the blessed Cyprian, or Augustine, have anything to say on this score? Perhaps you could help us by finding any relevant authorities?"

"I—well—on what score, exactly?"

Leoba intervened. "Perhaps you could be so kind as to bring us all the works of the blessed Cyprian that are in the Library," she said.

"The blessed Cyprian—yes, I could—I could do that, certainly. Let me look."

"We would be most grateful," said Paul, as Tullius closed the door behind him and hurried off.

Leoba and Paul waited until the sound of the Librarian's footsteps had faded away; then they broke into guilty laughter. "You're quite an actor," said Leoba, "have you considered a career in the theater?"

"I think the blessed Cyprian was looking out for us," said Paul.

"Anyway, I think we've agreed on the outline of the document. So you'll go ahead?"

"Yes, certainly, I'll put it together. But for the actual manuscript, your writing would probably be better, wouldn't it?"

"I'll make a fair copy. But we can't use that to show people—they would recognize my hand. And there's also the issue of how old it looks. You can't just write a manuscript and say it's a four-hundred-year-old deed written by the Emperor Constantine. It wouldn't look right."

"It might have been copied several times over the years—so it wouldn't have to look that old."

"Copied several times—and no-one realized how

significant it was?"

"You're right, that wouldn't work. So what do you suggest?"

Leoba thought for a while. "There are people in Rome—over in Transtiber—who know how to do this. For a solidus or two they could produce something very authentic, especially if we gave them a real manuscript from that period to look at—like one of these letters from Diocletian."

"But then they would know the truth."

"Yes, unfortunately, but we'd pay them a little extra to stay silent. They are used to this kind of deal. And we could choose a foreigner—someone who has nothing to do with our community, and who's likely to leave Rome before long. You can leave that to me."

"That's good," said Paul. "Because it would look odd if I was seen talking to strange people in Transtiber."

"And I can get the materials from Christopher, the notary."

"Christopher? Oh yes, your admirer—but you're not going to let him in on our plans, are you?"

"No, no, I'll tell him they're for something we're sending to the Emperor."

"Very good."

"There is one other matter that you do need to think about, though," Leoba went on. "How are you going to let people know about this deed? Are you just going to go to your brother and say, 'Look what I found while I was searching around in the Lateran library?'"

"That might be a bit suspicious."

"Yes, I think so too. Someone else has to discover it, or it has to discover itself, somehow."

"Let me think about this. Maybe there's some way that I can work it into the ceremony for Sylvester's translation."

Footsteps could again be heard in the passageway. "Is that Tullius back already?" whispered Paul. And then, more loudly, he went on: "The forty-nine martyrs of Abitene—didn't they break off communion with Mensurius over this matter, and his deacon Caecilian took it upon himself to—"

The footsteps passed by and faded into silence.

12

——

The morning after the loss of the ship-mills, Marcus got another early call from a messenger boy. This time the boy directed him, not to the river, but to St. Pancras Gate, at the top of the Janiculum Hill. He wondered what work might await him there, but chiefly he was glad that there was work at all: he faced the prospect of a lengthy lay-off while new mills were being constructed.

As he climbed the steep grade, Marcus paused every now and then to regain his breath, for he was carrying a heavy tool-kit in case anything in it should prove useful. He took the opportunity of these breaks to view the scene behind him. He saw that the flooding extended only a mile or so upstream and downstream from the city, and he wondered why the river had chosen to burst its banks precisely where it would do the most harm. It seemed as if some punishment were being inflicted on Rome for its people's sins—sins of the past, the present, or those yet to be committed.

At the gate, a crowd of men had gathered, among them many of those who had been involved in the previous day's disaster. Marcus recognized the deputy grain-master, Valerius, and went up to him. "Is the grain-master coming?"

he asked.

Valerius looked up. "*I'm* the grain-master," he said.

"You mean—what about Gaius?"

"Gaius is answering for what happened yesterday," said Valerius.

"He was arrested?"

"The city lost all of its mills."

Marcus was upset by the news. "It wasn't his fault," he said. "He had no choice but to move the mills—they were in great danger. That log could just as easily have destroyed my mill while it was moored at the bank."

"Well, I'm sure his lawyer will make that argument," said Valerius.

"I'd like to testify on his behalf. I agreed to his plan."

"You have a wife and children, don't you?"

"A wife and a daughter, yes."

"Well then, you might want to think about them."

"Meaning—?"

"Others will testify that you tried to dissuade Gaius from moving the mills. That makes you look innocent of any wrong-doing. Leave it that way. Be here to support your family."

Marcus frowned and fell silent. Meanwhile, other workers had arrived at the scene, and Valerius gathered them round himself.

"Men," he began, "we need to start milling again as soon as possible. We only have a few days' supply of flour, and some of that has been damaged by the floodwater. We're going to try and re-start the Janiculum mills."

A general look of puzzlement among the men triggered some further explanation. "There are at least twenty mills up here," Valerius went on. "All driven by Trajan's aqueduct. Or used to be driven."

"Used to be? When?" someone asked. "Not in my memory, I'm sure of that."

"Two hundred years ago," said Valerius, "before the Goths cut the aqueduct."

"Two hundred years? And you expect them to be here still, ready to start up again?"

"I've looked at a couple already. They're built of stone, not wood, and they're in pretty good shape. Some of the fittings have rotted, of course. You mill-masters are going to have to look them over and report back to me—whether they can be restarted, what it would take. That's what you need to do this morning."

"And what about the water?" asked Marcus. "Trajan's aqueduct is dry."

"There's plenty of water in the aqueduct, but it's not flowing into the city. After the aqueduct was restored the water was diverted to the Vatican Hill, to serve St. Peter's and the pilgrims' baths. The diversion is only about half a mile up the aqueduct from here. We can block the diversion channel and restore the original flow, I think. I have engineers looking into this right now. So, the four of you— Marcus, Flavius, Limping Lucius, and Old Man Lucius—take your assistants and check the mills. Let me know what the situation is. We need to get mills working again, otherwise Gaius won't be the only one in trouble. "

Marcus and his assistants went to the nearest mill, which was the uppermost one in the descending channel of the aqueduct. The mill was partially built into the structure of the Aurelian Wall, just south of St. Pancras Gate, where the aqueduct entered the city. The entrance had been bricked off a long time ago, but Valerius's men had already broken through enough of the brickwork to permit entry to the interior. Marcus walked down a winding flight of stone steps that took him to the basement of the mill, which was lit by some narrow window-slits high up on the walls.

The dry aqueduct ran as a broad channel across the floor; on the west side it emerged from a low archway next to the Aurelian Wall, and on the east side it exited the mill and headed further down the slope of the Janiculum, toward the other mills.

From the main channel of the aqueduct, two side channels were arranged so as to divert water into mill-races, one on each side of the aqueduct. The north race carried four mill-wheels that were suspended in a row over the race. The south race carried a single, larger wheel. All the wheels were in bad condition and would need to be completely rebuilt, Marcus could see. The same was true for the gearing that coupled the axles of the wheels to the vertical shafts. Still, the quality of the construction was impressive: Marcus particularly admired the marble bearing blocks from which the wheels were suspended: they looked far more efficient and robust than the wooden mounts that had been used at the ship-mills. Those ones had needed constant greasing, and even then only lasted a few months.

Marcus also saw that the channel of the aqueduct had been closed off with large blocks of masonry at the archway where it emerged from the Aurelian Wall. This had probably been done to prevent any besieging forces from getting into the city through the aqueduct. Those blocks would have to be moved, and the engineers would have to bring in hoists to accomplish the task—the blocks were much too heavy to be moved by hand. Marcus sent an assistant to tell Valerius about this.

Marcus then climbed back up to the milling chamber on the ground floor. There were a total of six pairs of millstones: one driven by each of the wheels on the north race, and two by the single, large wheel on the south race. The whole arrangement was far grander than that of Marcus's ship-mill, with its single pair of stones. There was even a separate store-room, as well as a work-room intended for carpentry or stone-dressing. The mill would have had at least a dozen men working at any one time, Marcus realized, and just this one mill could have supplied more flour than all the four ship-mills combined. Why then had Rome needed so many mills on the Janiculum—twenty, if Valerius was right? The population of the city must have been far, far greater than it was now, and Marcus reflected on the possible causes—plague and war especially—for the staggering decline in numbers.

On the wall behind each millstone was mounted a heavy oak beam, from the end of which there dangled a giant pair of iron tongs. This was the hoist used to lift the upper millstone—the running stone—away from the bedstone. The hoist appeared to be in good condition, and after testing it with his own weight he fitted the tongs into two sockets on the sides of the running stone. Then, while his assistants looked out for any weakening of the structure, Marcus gradually twisted the screwjack on the hoist, raising the stone inch by inch. Finally it was high enough that the stone could be rotated into an upside-down position and lowered back down onto the bedstone.

Marcus propped the stone in place with some wooden chocks, and then took a close look at the grinding surface. The furrows were still there—they were cut in a curving pattern that Marcus didn't recognize. The raised areas between the furrows were almost entirely smooth, however, whereas they needed to be scored with the hundreds of fine grooves that did the actual work of turning grain into flour. The fact that most of these grooves were missing or barely visible suggested to Marcus that the last users of the mill had been operating under desperate conditions—they had not been able to stop work and dress the stones, even though they must have been turning out something that resembled clay more than flour.

Marcus then went on to check the flatness of the stone surface with a paint-staff that he had brought with him. The surface was good—in fact, the original stone-dressers had put exactly the right curvature on the surface so that the grain, as it moved outward between the stones, would be ground to a progressively finer texture. Seeing that, Marcus felt an instant bond with his long-dead counterparts: he and they could appreciate something about the making of the stones whose significance would be lost on regular folk.

After finishing his inspection of the running stone, Marcus swung it aside and examined the bed-stone. After that, he moved on to the other pairs of stones in the mill. The work took a couple of hours, and before he was quite finished he and his assistants were called back to the place where they had assembled earlier.

Marcus soon saw why they had been summoned: The Pope and a large retinue were gathered there, and Stephen was speaking to Valerius and his workers, surrounded by a ring of curious locals. Stephen was on his way back into the city from a visit to the Church of St. Pancras, which was located a short distance outside of the Aurelian Wall. He had been there to venerate the hacked-off head of St. Pancras himself, a fourteen-year-old boy from Phrygia who converted to Christianity and then refused to give up his new faith, preferring martyrdom. That was four hundred and fifty years before, when Diocletian was Emperor. Stephen was fascinated by this saint—perhaps because Pancras, like Stephen himself, was an orphan—and he had ordered several images of him to be made for the church and for the Lateran Palace. The saint's head lay in the church in a silver cabinet; his other bones had been taken to Britain by Augustine of Canterbury and distributed as relics, except for one tooth, which ended up at the abbey of St. Denis near Paris, in a gilded reliquary, along with two walrus tusks and the left shoulder-blade of John the Baptist.

Stephen had been told about the loss of the ship-mills, so when he passed through St. Pancras Gate and saw a group of mill-workers talking with Valerius, his thoughts were torn away from the contemplation of ancient martyrdoms and directed toward the all-too-present crisis. In a departure from customary practice, he called for the procession to halt, stepped out of his carriage, and signaled for Valerius and his workers to approach.

By the time Marcus made his way through the onlookers, Stephen was finishing a prayer in which he asked God's blessing for the project the men were undertaking. Then he asked Valerius a series of detailed question about his plans, and how long it would take before milling could resume. Valerius, who had been grain-master for less than a day, was flustered by the Pope's unannounced visit to their work-site, and by his inability to provide exact answers to the Pope's questions. "Your High—Your Sir Holiness," he said, "We'll work as fast as humanly possible and with God's help—with God's help—"

"You must do so," said Stephen. "This is the worst time for a shortage of bread—with enemies on the horizon. We need the people's loyalty, and we won't get it if they're hungry. Do you need anything to make your work go faster? More men? Equipment? Speak to Leo or the Archdeacon if they can provide any help."

"Thank you, Your Holiness."

"And do any of you have any questions, or wish to say anything?"

There was a brief silence, then Marcus spoke up. Before he had time to judge the wisdom of his own words, he blurted out: "Your Holiness, the former grain-master, Gaius—"

Stephen's face darkened. "Gaius? What about him?" he said.

"He's a good servant to the city, Your Holiness. He did his best to—"

Stephen cut him off. "He will be judged fairly. You speak in the Tuscan fashion, don't you?"

"Yes, Your Holiness, I'm from Lucca."

"Tuscany is Lombard territory."

"Yes, Your Holiness, it is now. But the Tuscan people aren't happy about that. And I and my wife have lived in Rome for seven years—we have no reverence for Aistulf or for his puppet, Desiderius. We love Rome."

"Romans love Rome," said Stephen. With that, he

signaled his retinue to restart the procession, and they moved off down the hill into the city.

"You didn't listen to what I told you this morning," said Valerius to Marcus. Marcus remained silent, cursing himself for having said anything to the Pope. Valerius went on: "I got your message about the blockage. The engineers will come by later today to work on that. They're working on the diversion right now. It looks like they can fix that, so when the blockage in your mill is cleared they can run a test to see how well the water flows. How does your mill look otherwise?"

Mill-talk helped rescue Marcus's mood. "Well, we'll need the carpenters in to replace the wheels and some of the gearing. Two of the stones are good but they need dressing, which takes a couple of days. The others need to be completely refaced and recentered, which would take longer. What did the others find?"

"Most of the lower mills have been stripped," said Valerius. "The stones are gone. They must have moved them to the river when the mills up here were abandoned. But a few are usable."

"You could move those up here to replace the bad stones," Marcus suggested. "Then this mill by itself could produce enough flour for the city."

"Yes, either way we're going to be in good shape. Get on with the dressing of your two good stones, and I'll send the carpenters so you can explain what needs doing."

13

Leoba's exotic appearance—her blond hair especially—tended to draw attention on the streets of Rome, so she kept her head covered as she walked up Silversmiths' Street, a leather satchel under her arm. She inspected the storefronts carefully, and eventually entered Omar's establishment. Omar and an elderly man were haggling over the price of a torn piece of cloth that seemed to carry an ancient bloodstain; the cloth was mounted behind glass in an ornate gilt frame. While they talked, Leoba occupied herself examining some of Omar's other relics that were on display, along with their legends and inscriptions.

When the old man left without buying anything, Omar turned his attention to Leoba. "Welcome, reverend lady," he said. "Forgive me for making you wait. You've traveled from far away?"

"Yes, quite far," was her noncommittal reply.

"So you're visiting the tomb of the blessed Peter?"

"Do you have relics relating to the Apostle?"

"Why yes," said Omar. He produced a piece of wood onto which was fixed a glass ampoule, not very different from the one that Zaid had smashed two weeks earlier. "This is my most precious and powerful relic. It's a tear shed by the uncorrupted body of the blessed martyr Petronilla, three years after her death, as her father the blessed Apostle gave up the ghost. "

"That's remarkable," said Leoba. "I would hardly have believed such a thing, but I see that the inscription supports what you tell me."

"You're an educated lady. Yes, her body had been lying in the catacomb of Priscilla since her death, guarded the whole time by an angel with a lamp."

"Really? What else do you have?"

After reviewing the filings from St. Peter's chains and the dust from his tomb, Leoba changed the subject. "Is your business doing well?" she asked.

"Not really, I'm afraid. It was badly affected by the flooding, when people had difficulty coming here. And then there was the price of bread: people were spending so much for it that they had nothing left for this kind of thing. Now the new mills are working, I'm hoping that my business will pick up again."

"You work on your own, or do you have a family?"

"I have a son who worked with me, but he ran away a couple of weeks ago. Now I have to do everything myself. To be honest, I'm thinking of returning to the East, to find more relics. Whether I'll come back to Rome, or perhaps go to Constantinople instead, I don't know."

"Your name is Omar, I believe," she said.

"Yes, it is. How did you know, if I may ask?"

"Well, I've been told that you are a master scribe—that you're able to write in the style of our forefathers."

Omar tensed up. Had this woman come here to accuse

him of faking relics or their inscriptions? "I've taught myself to write the Latin language," he said. "The old texts have been my schoolbooks, so sometimes my writing may appear old-fashioned."

Leoba decided to plunge in. "I need someone to help me with a writing task, in confidence."

This sounded more positive to Omar. "I've never failed to keep a secret," he said. "What kind of task?"

Leoba took Paul's manuscript out of the satchel. "This document—I need a copy of it."

Omar looked it over. "Simply a copy, or something in an antique style?"

"In an antique style. It should look old—from the time of Pope Sylvester, four centuries ago. And not just the writing."

"No, I understand. Something that has sat on bookshelves for four centuries and has perhaps been read many times—such a manuscript doesn't look like this one, which was probably written in the last few days."

"Yes, it was," admitted Leoba, blushing slightly. "I have some other documents here, from that period. You can get an idea of how it should look."

Omar looked over the ancient manuscripts, and then back at the one Leoba had written. "May I ask, was this an important document, such as might be written on behalf of an emperor? I see the name of Constantine here."

"Yes, that's who wrote it—who we suppose wrote it."

"Because in that case it would have to be of the highest quality. It would be written on vellum from newborn calves, or even from those not yet born. And there would be vermilion and so forth."

"I can supply these."

"Very well. But it would be a week's unbroken labor to produce such a thing."

"It would only be four or five sheets."

"It's not just the writing. It takes a great deal of work afterwards—to make it look old."

"So how much would you need to do it?"

"I could do it for two solidi, if you supply the materials."

"That's a great deal of money."

"Believe me, I couldn't do it for less. I would lose a lot of other work during the time it would take me."

Leoba pondered the issue. It would be unfortunate at this point not to go with Omar, given that he now had some idea what was afoot. And Paul would have little difficulty getting the money. Still, she didn't want make herself seem too generous. "I'll tell you what," she said. "I can promise you one solidus, and another if the quality is what I am hoping for."

"Believe me, it will be," said Omar. "So it's a deal?"

"It's a deal," said Leoba with a relieved smile. "So please start on this right away. Here's an advance on the payment. And I will bring you the materials."

As Leoba left Omar's store and started down the street, she almost ran into Lenora, who had been standing outside her mother's fortune-telling studio. Leoba smiled at the girl. Emboldened by this, Lenora said, "Lady, may I ask you something?"

"Of course."

"Do you know of an Arab boy, named Zaid, who is a bit older than me? He has curly hair."

"I'm afraid I don't," said Leoba. "Why, who is he?"

"He's my—my friend. And he's the son of Omar, who

has the shop you were in."

"Oh yes, Omar told me that he ran away a couple of weeks ago."

"Yes," said Lenora. Then, lowering her voice slightly, she added: "Omar beat him." She looked as if she might start to cry.

"Do you know where he went?"

"No, he sent me a message to meet him, but he didn't show up. My parents think he left Rome, but I don't think so. I've asked everyone, but I can't find him."

"I hope he'll come back. Rome isn't a place for a young boy to be on his own. But I live over on the other side of the city, at the Lateran Palace, there's nothing for him there."

"But if—" Lenora began.

"Of course if I come across him, I'll tell him that he should return home, and that you want to see him. What's your name, anyway?"

"Lenora."

At this point Sibyl came out of her store, curious to know who her daughter was talking to. "Good afternoon, lady," she said. "What brings you to Silversmiths' Street?"

"I was visiting Omar's store, looking at his relics," Leoba said.

Sibyl saw that Leoba had not bought any. "Relics can be expensive," she said, "and they don't always work as well as you might like. If it's something of a personal nature—a dispute, or an affair of the heart—I may be able help you. I'm in communion with powerful spirits, who are able to—"

"Thank you and God bless you," said Leoba, "but my calling doesn't allow me to invoke magical powers." She went on her way.

14

_____

"So how are your plans going?" Stephen asked his brother one day, a few weeks after his consecration. The two men had just returned from mass in the eastern part of the city, and were now strolling through the garden of the Lateran Palace. Part of the garden was still warmed by the late afternoon sun, and part was cooling in the lengthening shadow of the Aurelian Wall.

"My plans?" replied Paul with a guilty start. Then he realized that Stephen's question was an innocent one. "Oh— for Sylvester's translation? I think everything's going well. I've been to view the sarcophagus with the engineers. They tell me that there'll be no difficulty with getting it up into the church."

"And then?"

"Then it will be carried by bearers to a carriage that will be waiting in the street. The order of the procession will be similar to the one that Theophylact organized—which everyone says was very successful. The only difference will be that the carriage with the sarcophagus will come immediately in front of your position in the procession."

"Will it be drawn by oxen or by horses?"

"By horses—that's more suitable, I think. The weight isn't so much."

"And the route?"

"We'll follow the Salarian Way into the city," explained Paul, "and then do a circuit of several important churches, starting of course with Sylvester's own church—the Basilica of the blessed Sylvester and Martin, as they call it. To be honest, I'm not sure why the blessed Symmachus chose to add Martin's name to that church—he had no obvious connection with it. Perhaps you might consider restoring its original name."

"That wouldn't be a good idea if you're interested in making an alliance with the Franks," said Stephen. "They revere the blessed Martin almost more than they revere Christ himself, I'm told. The cloak he divided with a beggar—that's their most precious relic. They carry it into every battle with them."

"Very well, let's forget about that. Anyway, after a brief prayer outside that church, the procession will go on to other churches, and then by the Bridge of the Blessed Angel to St. Peter's."

"The litany will be penitential, I assume?"

"Yes," said Paul, "just as with Theo's procession."

"So I'll have to carry the Acheiropoeiton again?"

"If you agree."

"I thought a painting made by angels would be weightless, but my back was aching by the time we got to St. Peter's."

"Well then, we can have someone else carry it from the cemetery, and you can just carry it into the church."

"And will we walk barefoot?"

"Some will walk the whole distance barefoot, and wearing sackcloth—perhaps even flagellating themselves, though we certainly don't approve of that. During Theophylact's procession we couldn't prevent it. However, the distance will be considerable—more than three miles. I'd suggest that you ride in the papal carriage except for brief stretches—perhaps before each of the stops?"

"That's a good idea. Please make sure that those stretches are swept!"

"I shall."

"Now what about the ceremony at the end?"

"During the mass, the sarcophagus will rest on a bier specially placed near the altar, and close to the permanent resting place that we've prepared for it," said Paul. "We had to move the relics of some lesser persons. The sermon that I'm writing tells the life of the blessed Sylvester, as we discussed. And in doing so, it will illustrate the central role of our city in the spiritual guidance of Christendom. Rome *is* Christendom—that is what the sermon will say. Hellfire will destroy those who seek to take the city of Peter from out of the hands of the Apostle's successors. We should send copies to the other Patriarchs, and even to Pepin."

"And to Aistulf," said Stephen. "Perhaps it will persuade him to hold back his army."

"I doubt it. Oh, and after the sarcophagus is moved to its resting place, it will be briefly opened, to be viewed by Your Holiness alone."

"You think that's necessary?"

"Yes, I do," said Paul. "It's the traditional practice, authorized by many of your predecessors. It assures people that the sarcophagus really does hold Sylvester's remains."

"Really? How should I recognize him?"

"Well, you could confirm that the sarcophagus contains a man's body, at least. And there are likely to be signs that it has been treated in a manner appropriate to such a holy personage. Perhaps he was buried in his papal vestments. And sometimes these bodies have been preserved in remarkably good condition, from what I have read."

"Very well," said Stephen. "But I hope no one has to open *my* sarcophagus, four hundred years from now."

The morbid turn of the conversation caused the men to fall silent for a while. They were walking on stone paths among raised beds of herbs—thyme, savory, basil, and hyssop. Stephen let his fingers trail through the greenery, stirring up the scented air and a host of flying insects. From beyond the garden wall came the sounds of activity in the courtyard—horsemen entering the palace, people shouting—but the noises were too muted to mar the serenity of the garden. The two brothers strolled on.

"In these weeks since I became Pope," said Stephen finally, "I've done nothing for men's souls."

"How can you say that?" said Paul in surprise. "You've led masses in churches all over the city, you've held—"

"Yes, yes, but so much of my time is spent on other things. The military situation, the flooding, the bread shortage, money problems—one crisis after another. Does it really take a successor of Peter to deal with all this? I'm the Holy Father, but what is holy about what I do?"

"Stephen, what are you suggesting?" said Paul.

"Nothing, nothing. Of course the Pope must tend his flock. And I have extraordinary assistance. How many people labor in this Palace? A thousand probably, don't you think, if we count up everybody. So many people supporting me."

"Including your brother."

"Including my dear brother, yes. I don't know what I'd do without you. But sometimes I wonder what the purpose of it all is. Why should the Pope have to deal with all these problems?"

"Stephen, this will change. Our beloved Zachary—I'm afraid he neglected many practical matters in his last years, so you are having to—"

Stephen went on with his lament without heeding Paul's words. "What has happened to this city? Where's the Emperor? Where's the Duke? Where are the Consuls—have there even been any in our lifetime? Where's the Senate? Yes, there are men who call themselves senators, but has the Senate actually met in this century, or the last one? There's no government, except for what we provide. And the people—where have *they* gone?"

"The people?"

"Yes, where have they gone? Look at this wall—it's twelve miles long. When Aurelian built it, he must have fit it to the size of the city that it protected, don't you think?"

"Of course."

"But now it fits like the tunic of a fat man after a year's starvation. Ruins, empty space, gardens, tombs—these are what the wall protects, more than the homes of living Romans."

"Well, at least we have space to grow some of our crops and vegetables inside the walls, which we may be thankful for, if Aistulf comes visiting."

"That's something, I suppose."

"Stephen, there'll be time for spiritual matters," said Paul. "But right now, our problems are worldly ones—war, hunger. We've been abandoned by the Emperor—Rome is an orphan, just as you and I were. We have to look out for ourselves, otherwise we'll be swallowed up. What Popes have always done—spiritual guidance—yes, you need to do that still, of course, but now you have to do so much more."

Stephen started to look uncomfortable, but Paul persisted. "This is a time of great danger, for sure, but also great opportunity, if we seize it. I mean—the opportunity to improve the Church's position in the world, so that we can look kings and emperors in the eye, like equals. I really—what's this?"

The Pope's herald had entered the garden; he approached the two men and bowed. "Forgive the interruption, Your Holiness," he said.

"What is it?" said Stephen.

"The First Notary has returned, and the other members of his legation. He awaits Your Holiness in the reception hall, along with your counselors."

Stephen was relieved by the excuse to terminate his brother's lecture. "Come along, Paul," he said. "We may learn something finally. Let's hope that he's had some influence on Aistulf."

The two men followed the herald back into the building, and along a marble corridor to the reception hall. As Stephen entered the room, with his brother a respectful distance behind, the assembled counselors rose.

"Be seated, please," said Stephen. "And welcome back, dear Ambrose. You must be exhausted from your long journey, which you've accomplished with commendable speed. We didn't expect you back so soon. What can you tell us?"

The First Notary rose again to respond, but Stephen signaled him to remain seated. He did not look well—not only had he had no chance to wash himself or change his mud-soiled clothes, he also appeared to have lost considerable weight on his journey.

"Your Holiness," he began, "we traveled to Pavia without hindrance from Aistulf's forces—our safe conduct was respected. But they didn't offer us any assistance either. The conditions on the roads were terrible, even on the Cassian Way, on account of the rains. We lost time on account of a river crossing that was impassable. When we finally reached Pavia, Aistulf at first declined to receive us, but after I reminded him of my dealings with his predecessors, he agreed."

"What courtesy!"

"We sat down on three occasions with him over the course of a week, and we had other meetings with his ministers. At first, Aistulf refused to enter into any serious negotiations. He said, 'Why should I speak with my tongue, when I can speak more eloquently with my sword?' So we talked about the past, about Zachary's dealings with Liutprand and Ratchis. In spite of his many unchristian deeds, Aistulf was anxious to affirm his Catholic faith. So I presented the issue of Rome as a religious matter that had no military or political significance. I assured him that Your Holiness is concerned only with the security of the Roman Duchy and its people, and that Your Holiness would freely acknowledge Aistulf's sovereignty over Spoleto and Beneventum, and the other territories he presently controls."

"Including Ravenna?" asked Stephen.

"Well, Your Holiness, we didn't specifically mention—"

Archdeacon Theophylact joined the discussion. "The Exarchate belongs to the Emperor, Your Holiness," he said. "How will it look in Constantinople, if it's reported that Your Holiness acknowledges Aistulf as the legitimate master of Ravenna? Won't it seem that we're in league with the murderer of Eutychius?"

"We'll deal with that issue if it arises," said Stephen. "Go on, Ambrose."

"We didn't specifically discuss Ravenna, Your Holiness. The point is, I expressed a willingness to recognize the situation that exists. We have no power to change it, so why not improve our own safety by acknowledging the present reality?"

"So what was the conclusion of your negotiations?"

"This, Your Holiness." Ambrose signaled an assistant to hand a document to the Pope.

Stephen spent a short while perusing the manuscript in silence. Then he looked up with a broad smile, as if weeks of anxiety had suddenly been lifted. "Ambrose—you've achieved the impossible!"

"*Apud homines hoc impossibile est—With men this is impossible, but with God all things are possible.*"

"This is a forty-year peace!" Stephen went on enthusiastically. "And he acknowledges the eternal sovereignty of the blessed Peter over the Roman Duchy. This is the best news we could have hoped for!"

"Does he offer hostages, Your Holiness?" asked Paul. "Does he send oxcarts laden with gold, as a token of his sincerity? Does he hand over the keys to the Five Cities?"

"No, he doesn't—and how could we expect such things? *We're* the ones who are powerless. Let's be grateful that we don't have to melt down our altar plates or send our sons to Pavia. And as for the Five Cities, or Ravenna—what are they to us? That is a matter between Aistulf and the Emperor."

Paul was not giving up easily. "Has Aistulf ever given his word and kept it? First Notary Ambrose has made a noble effort, and we should thank him a thousand times. But this treaty is worthless, because Aistulf's word is worthless."

"Deacon Paul, I understand your concern," said Stephen. "This peace may not last forty years. It may not last five years. But it's a reprieve. It gives us time to negotiate something better, or to make other arrangements. That is a cause for great celebration."

Several other counselors expressed their agreement with the Pope, and Ambrose was the recipient of general congratulations.

Stephen was struck by an idea. "The translation of the blessed Sylvester, which will take place shortly: it's been planned as a rite of supplication and penitence. But now it must be one of thanksgiving and rejoicing. This is so much more fitting a way to honor Sylvester, who was not a martyr, after all, but a great Pope. Is it too late to make the changes, Deacon Paul? And there should be some kind of distribution to the people, to memorialize the event."

Paul sighed inwardly. "This is such folly," he thought. Out loud, he said: "I'll be honored to reorganize the event in the fashion that Your Holiness indicates."

15

The Catacomb of Priscilla lay a mile or so north of the city, on the Salarian Way. Its entrance lay within a cemeterial church; this church was built by Pope Sylvester to protect the catacomb, on account of the many earlier popes, martyrs, and ordinary Christians who had been laid to rest there. Sylvester also chose the catacomb for his own resting place, preferring to await the Second Coming in the company of humble martyrs rather than in the grand but lonelier spaces of the overlying basilica.

Traditionally, the Christian dead were placed in *loculi*— shelf-like excavations in the walls of the catacomb's underground passageways. There was no need for coffins or any other receptacles: each body was placed in its loculus clad in its own clothes or in a simple shroud, and the loculus was then sealed off. Thus two able-bodied men, using a stretcher, could carry a body down the steep stairway and along the narrow tunnels to its final destination.

With Sylvester it was different. As with some of his predecessors, the pope's eminence demanded that he be entombed in a sarcophagus, and because of Sylvester's size—he was a large man who dined heartily in his later years—the sarcophagus could not be a small one. In fact, it had taken a considerable search through Rome's ancient cemeteries to find a sarcophagus that was sufficiently capacious and free of inappropriate pagan carvings. Finally, a suitable one was located—it was made of limestone and weighed well over half a ton—and its occupant was unceremoniously evicted.

A few years before his death, Sylvester laid himself out in this sarcophagus for half a day, in order to confirm the adequacy of its size and also as a reminder of his own mortality. Once satisfied on both counts, Sylvester had the original owner's name erased and replaced with his own. Other than that simple inscription, the sarcophagus bore only the strigillations—the simple patterns of wavy lines—that were favored by the Romans of imperial times.

To house Sylvester's sarcophagus, workers excavated a crypt out of the catacomb's easily-worked volcanic rock. This crypt was located a good thousand feet from the catacomb's entrance; the passageways leading to it were narrow and dark, and they featured several sharp turns. When Paul made plans for Sylvester's translation to St. Peter's, the papal engineers scouted these passageways. They were not able to determine exactly how the pope's body had originally been moved to its crypt, but they did notice, at the most abrupt bends along the route, that the projecting corners had been roughly hewn away, as if to ease the passage of the bulky sarcophagus. These cuts had encroached on pre-existing loculi, which now lay empty of human remains. Apparently, the earlier workers had moved them to other sites.

On the day before Sylvester's translation, Paul supervised

the work of a group of engineers who were preparing the sarcophagus for its move. The crypt normally lay in total darkness, but on this day it was lit by several oil lamps and torches that had been placed in brackets fixed to the walls. Thus it was possible to see, not only the sarcophagus, but also a fresco that had been painted on one of the crypt's side walls. This illustrated the biblical story of the feeding of the multitude. The scene had perhaps been chosen because it allowed for ample portrayal of fishes—representing Christ—as well as loaves and jugs of wine.

The workers set up two block-and-tackle hoists, one above each end of the sarcophagus. Because of the limited space between the sarcophagus and the ceiling of the crypt, the hoists could only raise the sarcophagus a foot or two from its stone bier, but this would be enough to swing it outward and lower it onto a small flat cart that had been placed on the floor of the crypt next to the sarcophagus. Riding on this, the sarcophagus would be pushed or pulled along the passageways; the engineers had already done a test run with a wooden box, laden with stones, that was the same size as the sarcophagus. They assured themselves it could be negotiated—albeit with some difficulty—round every corner along the way. As to the exit stairway, they had partially covered its steps with planking. Thus, with aid of another block-and-tackle hoist and a great deal of muscle-power, the sarcophagus would be hauled upward to street level.

To avoid any embarrassment on the following day, Paul asked the workers to do a test lift. Using crowbars, the men raised each end of the sarcophagus in turn by an inch or so—enough to slip an iron cradle underneath. They attached the ends of the cradles to the ropes, and hauled away. The sarcophagus rose a short distance from its bier. Then the workers lowered it gently back. Everything seemed to be in order.

"Thank you, your work's done for today," Paul said. "I'll remain here a while to pray." The workers filed out of the crypt, taking most of the torches with them in order to light their way back to the entrance of the catacomb.

Paul remained standing in the dimly lit crypt. After the men's footsteps died away, he became acutely aware of the silence. The only perceptible sound was that of his own heartbeat: in this city of the dead, it seemed to be counting down the moments toward the day when he would join them. Paul thought of Sylvester's bones lying concealed in the stone box before him, and then of the entire chain of ninety popes that linked Peter to Zachary, all now moldering in their graves. Before long, he knew, his brother Stephen would join them, and then he himself perhaps, and then others who at this moment were still ambitious young men working their way up through the papal hierarchy, or playful boys unaware of their destiny, or souls yet unborn or unconceived. How far into the dim distance stretched this procession of the future dead? How long would they linger thus, patiently awaiting the appointed day of resurrection and judgment? Paul thought of Christ's words to his disciples at the foot of Mount Hermon, "*Amen dico vobis—Verily I say unto you, there be some standing here, which shall not taste of death, till they see the Son of Man coming in his kingdom.*" Yet all had tasted of death, and none had yet beheld Christ's majesty.

Paul bowed his head in prayer: "*Domine, Jesu Christe, Rex gloriae—Lord, Jesus Christ, King of Glory, deliver the souls of the faithful departed from the pains of hell and the bottomless pit. Deliver them from the lion's jaws, lest hell engulf them, lest they fall into darkness, but let the blessed Michael, the standard-bearer, lead them into the holy light which you once promised to Abraham and to his seed."*

Although barely murmured, Paul's prayer filled the crypt with sound, leaving the ensuing silence even more oppressive. After a while, Paul opened his eyes and gazed at the sarcophagus in front of him. Then he stretched out his right arm and ran his fingers along its lid, a slab of limestone that had been smoothed by the touch of countless pilgrims.

Paul moved close to the sarcophagus, grasped the lid with both hands, and made as if to lift it, but the lid did not yield. Either it was too heavy, or it was sealed to the sarcophagus in some way. Paul looked around the crypt. The crowbars used by the workmen were still lying amongst a pile of their tools; Paul walked over and took one. He was able to work the end of the crowbar into the crack between the sarcophagus and its lid, near its left-hand end. Applying most of his weight to the handle of the crowbar, Paul was able to raise the lid slightly—enough to slip a dangling hook from the block and tackle under it. He repeated the process at the right-hand end of the sarcophagus. The front side of the lid was now raised by about half an inch.

Paul paused to regain his breath after his exertion. He listened for any sound from the outside world, but there was none. Then he cautiously began to pull on one of the hauling lines. Creakily, the rope moved on its pulleys, and the lid of the sarcophagus hinged slowly upward. After a few minutes of work, interrupted by pauses in which Paul listened for anyone who might be approaching, the front of the lid was raised about eight inches from its resting position. Paul fastened the lines, and then peered into the dimly lit interior of the sarcophagus.

At about the same time, a slender female figure, her head well covered, entered the church and approached the steps that led down to the catacomb. She stopped to light an oil lamp from one of the candles that were burning at the altar. Then she descended the stairway, picking her way carefully on account of the planking that covered most of the width of the steps.

The woman had visited Sylvester's tomb before, but always in the company of others. Now she was uncertain of the way and made several wrong turns. Twice, she had to retrace her steps to her starting point and try another passageway. Finally, after about fifteen minutes' wandering, she found herself on the correct route. Occasional air vents allowed some faint daylight to penetrate the catacomb, but mostly she had to rely on her lamp: this illuminated some memorial inscriptions that she remembered from previous visits.

So many of the dead were children—she had noticed hundreds of them, each an irreplaceable loss to someone. *VALENTIO FILIO BENEMERENTI QUI VIXIT ANNIS IIII FECIT MATER DOLENS*—*For her well-deserving son Valentius, who lived four years, his grieving mother made this.* A crudely carved dove, with an olive twig in its mouth, expressed her hope for the salvation of the youngster's soul. *SECUNDE BENEMERENTI QUAE VICXIT ANNU SEX MES OCTO DIES XXII FECIT FRATER IN PACE*—*For the well-deserving Secunda, who lived six years, eight months, and twenty-two days, her brother made this. In peace.*

Benemerenti, benemerenti—all these children were well-deserving, all deserved a chance at life, but that chance had been cruelly stolen from them. Her mood darkened as she made her way deeper into the labyrinth of the departed.

"Leoba!"

The sound of her name, spoken quietly but urgently out of a dark side-chamber, caused her to freeze and give vent to a barely stifled scream. Was this some spirit of the dead calling to her? Looking in the direction of the sound, she saw a lamp being uncovered.

"Leoba, it's me—Paul."

"Paul—what are you doing?" Leoba gasped. "I've never been so frightened in my life!"

Paul now removed his cloak from in front of his lamp, so that his face was more clearly visible. "I'm so sorry to have scared you," he said, and he gave her still-shaking form a reassuring embrace. "I was on my way back to the entrance. I heard someone coming, so I came in here and covered my lamp. I'm so sorry—come in here, sit down on this bench." Paul helped Leoba to the bench and sat down next to her. "I wasn't expecting that it would be you," he said.

"I wanted to know whether everything is in order for tomorrow," Leoba said, still breathing heavily.

"It is, it is."

"So you've completed your business—everything went according to plan?"

"It did," said Paul. "Tomorrow, everything will go as we expect."

"Good, good. Were you alone then?"

"No, the engineers were there, but they've finished their work and gone already."

"I see," said Leoba. "So shall we leave too?"

"Yes, in a moment, but rest a bit, you're still shaken up. I feel terrible for scaring you so."

"I'm all right now." Leoba managed a sheepish grin. "I thought you were a corpse that had come back to life."

The two sat quietly for a minute or two. The crypt they were in was a very cramped space. Like Sylvester's crypt, this one also housed a sarcophagus, but a much smaller one. Leoba could read the inscription: *AUR. PETRONILLAE FILIAE DULCISSIMAE*—*To Aurea Petronilla my sweetest daughter.* The inscription was surrounded by a frieze of carved dolphins.

"This is Petronilla, the daughter of the blessed Peter, isn't it?" asked Leoba.

"That's right," said Paul. "We're hoping to translate her remains to St. Peter's before long. She must long to be reunited with her father."

"Is it true that this inscription was carved by the hand of the Apostle himself, like people say, do you think?"

"I don't doubt it," said Paul. "He must have felt great sorrow at her death."

"It's strange," Leoba mused. "From what I've read, St. Peter brought many back to life, not just human beings but even an animal on one occasion—a fish, actually. It was a dried herring that hung from someone's balcony. He placed it in a pool and commanded it to swim, and it did so. Haven't you read something like that?"

"Yes, I have."

"So, having such powers, why didn't he raise his own daughter from the dead, after her martyrdom?"

"Not for lack of love, that's certain," said Paul.

"According to the holy books, Petronilla was afflicted with the palsy, so that one side of her body withered away, and she lay in a corner of their house and couldn't stand or walk. And people came to Peter and said, 'If you can work miracles, why don't you cure your own daughter of her palsy?' He answered, 'I *will* cure her, just to show you that it's possible.' He commanded his daughter to rise and walk, and she did so, and everyone was amazed. Then he commanded her to lie down and be paralyzed again, and she returned to her former state. Peter said, 'God made her thus, in order that she not be a temptation to men, so let her remain so.'"

"That seems so cruel," said Leoba. "What kind of love was that?"

"Not cruel, but obedient to God's will, and therefore loving. And it was also God's will that she suffer martyrdom for His sake."

"And beauty in a woman—that's just a snare, a temptation to be avoided? Should a beautiful woman pray to be palsied—or to receive some hideous disfigurement? Is beauty a sin?"

"The palsy was Petronilla's gift from God," said Paul. "Beauty is yours."

If Leoba blushed, it was too dark for Paul to notice. "Sometimes I wonder if parents are too concerned with their children's souls," she said. "Mine certainly were, putting me in a monastery as they did—depriving me of so many innocent earthly pleasures. They did it for themselves really—for the sake of their own souls and the promise they'd made to God. But what of me—they never thought of me, of my human needs."

"Leoba, my dear, I'll always be grateful that they did what

they did. Otherwise we would never have met."

"And the blessed Peter, when he made his daughter stand and walk, and then struck her down again—didn't he wonder what she would think, for the remainder of her days? Didn't he realize how she'd look back at that brief moment of perfect health, like a blind man granted one glimpse of the world? Didn't he think about how she'd curse her father and his godliness?"

Paul realized that Leoba had begun to sob, and he made to wrap his arm around her heaving shoulders. Leoba didn't resist the proffered comfort, but she continued to cry quietly.

"Petronilla was a blessed martyr," Paul said, "She wouldn't have cursed her own father, the blessed Apostle himself, whatever she thought about what he did."

"What he didn't do."

"What he didn't do. But I understand how you feel. I myself—my parents loved me, I'm sure of that; they did everything they could for me, and for Stephen. But they died, and to a toddler, that was the ultimate betrayal. You and I know what it's like to be abandoned."

Leoba reached for Paul's hand that was draped across her shoulder, and squeezed it, but said nothing. Paul went on. "But we're older now, we've learned how to understand—how to forgive. And we have the Church, which has been an ever-loving parent to both of us. And we have each other."

In some irresolvable blend of pastoral solicitude and carnal desire, Paul bent his head and touched his lips gently to Leoba's bare neck. The scent of her soft, pale skin filled his nostrils, arousing feelings that had lain dormant within him for decades. Leoba too felt the warmth of a long-

134

repressed passion. She turned her tearful face towards Paul's, and their lips met.

16

Like many of the residents of Transtiber, Marcus and his family decided to cross the river and join the procession that would escort Pope Sylvester's remains to the Basilica of St. Peter. It was a warm late-spring morning, the pope had declared the day a holiday, and there was a general mood of cheerfulness among the people streaming eastward into the city. The flood and the bread shortages were over, and the recently-announced peace with the Lombards had relieved Romans of their worst anxieties.

Marcus, Sibyl, and Lenora crossed the river by way of Gratian's bridge and Tiber Island. From the bridge, Marcus could see the now-empty western embankment where the old ship-mills were once moored. The renovated mills on the Janiculum were putting out enough flour to provide for Rome's needs, and the churches and hostels near St. Peter's, which lost their supply of water from Trajan's aqueduct, had been provided with a temporary supply from other sources. But the present arrangement was unsatisfactory: the location of the mills at the edge of the city, and at the top of a steep hill, made the transport of grain and the distribution of flour much more burdensome than before. The ship-mills were therefore being rebuilt, and Marcus looked forward to returning to his former work-site on the river, which was a shorter and easier walk from his home.

Marcus and Sibyl decided that they would meet the procession at its first stopping point, the church of St. Sylvester and St. Martin, which was located on the Esquiline Hill about a mile south of the Salarian Gate. It took them longer than expected to reach the church, not so much because of the climb from the river as because of the crowds of people who were gathering to watch the procession at various locations along the way. Marcus feared that they might miss the procession at the church, but in fact, once they had arrived there, they had to wait for over an hour, because it had taken longer than expected for Paul's workers to get Sylvester's sarcophagus out of the catacomb. Lenora used the waiting time to ask after Zaid, but no one she spoke to had seen him.

Eventually the spectators heard the distant noises of the approaching procession. Having passed through Aurelian's Wall at the Salarian Gate, the procession traversed the once-splendid Gardens of Sallust, which the Goths had long since reduced to a wasteland of rubble and weeds. Then, rather than passing through the old Servian Wall at the Colline Gate, it veered slightly eastward, taking the street that coursed along the wall's outer perimeter. Thus the procession stayed on the high ground, avoiding the need to negotiate the steep dips between the bluffs of the Quirinal, Viminal, and Esquiline Hills. Finally, having reached the Tiburtine Way, the procession turned right, passed under the central arch of the triple-spanned Esquiline Gate, and entered the inner city.

For the crowd at the church, the first portion of the procession to come into sight was a group of a dozen or so mounted militiamen, who moved children, animals, and other too-eager spectators out of the procession's path. There followed four chamberlains, who were carrying the pope's empty litter—he was to be carried in this chair after the celebrants entered St. Peter's. After the litter came the boys' and men's choirs of the Lateran Basilica, who sang familiar lines of praise and thanksgiving from the Gloria: *Laudamus te, benedicimus te—we praise thee, we bless thee, we worship thee, we glorify thee, we give thanks to thee on account of thy great glory.* Behind the choirs came the clergy of Rome's various district churches. Then came a group of young acolytes, who carried items to be used at the concluding mass, such as altar cloths, washbasins, communion bowls, flagons, and gold and silver candlesticks. Behind them in turn walked the deacons, two of whom carried locked books resting on cushions: Archdeacon Theophylact carried the gospel book, while a subdeacon carried the epistle book.

Compared with the onlooking citizens, most of whom were dressed in cloaks of coarse, undyed material, the deacons were more finely arrayed in their prescribed vestments—tunics, dalmatics, planets, and maniples—all of fine white linen or silk edged with red or gold. Still, there was considerable variation in the quality of their vestments. Those worn by Theophylact, for example, were quite badly worn and in need of cleaning. Paul, on the other hand, stood out. Not only was he taller than most of his colleagues, but his vestments looked newly-made, and he had added various accessories that had no specific authorization in the papal protocols. These included, for example, a scarf made of white silk onto which a lamb had been embroidered in golden thread. And whereas most of the deacons seemed already quite tired and footsore after two miles' walking, Paul was striding along energetically, and he smiled broadly at the onlookers. This may have been out of pride at the magnificence of the procession he had organized. Or, it may have had something to do with the illicit love affair that he had just embarked on.

After the deacons came three acolytes bearing two crosses of wood and a central cross of gold. These were followed by Sylvester's sarcophagus—the focus of most of the onlookers' attention. The ornate two-wheeled carriage on which it lay was drawn by a pair of draft horses, each guided by a groom, and the sarcophagus was draped with a silk cloth embroidered with christograms.

Looking up the road beyond the sarcophagus, Marcus and his family could see the approaching pope, who was on foot. He had dismounted from his horse at the Esquiline Gate and was walking the final hundred yards to the church behind the sarcophagus. This was an expression of humility, and not of the penitence that the original plans had called for, so he walked in his usual slippers rather than barefoot. Still, it would not be seemly if the Holy Father had to side-step any ordure deposited by the horses in front of him, and so a young groom walked between the sarcophagus and the pope; he was kept busy sweeping all offending material out of the pope's path with a birch-twig broom. Lenora's attention focused briefly on this slim, dark teenager.

"*Zaid!*" she screamed.

Zaid turned in the direction of the shout and recognized Lenora. A mixture of violent feelings warred within him: joy at seeing his beloved, pride at his better-than-usual dress and his position in front of the pope, and shame on account of the menial task he was engaged in. He smiled broadly at Lenora and made a reaching gesture toward her, but fearing punishment he said nothing and continued with his sweeping.

In spite of his silence, Lenora was overjoyed. Not only was Zaid here in front of her, but he was obviously healthy and well-fed, and the wounds on his face had healed without leaving any visible scars. She shouted again, "Zaid, Zaid!"

Zaid could not think what to do in response; then he twisted the left side of his body toward her and briefly raised the arm of his tunic, so that Lenora and her parents caught sight of the "S" branded into his shoulder. Lenora gasped and half fell, so that her mother had to support her.

At that moment the crowd became aware of a disturbance at the far end of the procession, near the Esquiline Gate. They heard shouts, more of alarm than celebration, and the choir that brought up the rear of the procession fell raggedly silent. Now a group of horsemen came into sight: they forced their way forward in the narrow gap between the procession and the onlookers, who had to press themselves against the sides of the buildings to avoid being trampled. Some angry words were exchanged between the riders and the onlookers.

Finally the riders reached the pope, who was standing in front of the church of St. Sylvester and St. Martin. The procession had halted, either because of the sudden alarm or because this was an appointed station for prayers. One of the riders leaped off his horse, approached Stephen, and bowed deeply. "Your Holiness, may I speak?" he said breathlessly.

Marcellus, the Treasurer, had been walking a few steps behind the pope. His usual role in papal processions was to deal with petitions presented to the pope by citizens, a practice that was strictly regulated—the petitioner could never approach the pope directly. Marcellus was angered by this gross violation of protocol, and at an event where petitions—even properly presented ones—were not to be entertained. He strode forward to intervene, but Stephen recognized the horseman as a papal messenger, and said "speak" before Marcellus could raise an objection.

"Your Holiness," said the messenger, "the Lombards have seized Ceccano."

Stephen's sense of shock was easily visible on his face. Aistulf had violated the peace treaty almost before the ink was dry on it. By taking a key fortified town on the Via Latina, just fifty miles from Rome, he had cut the city off from Naples and the Emperor's other territories to the south. Stephen wanted to ask the messenger for more details—had there been a massacre, who was leading the army, and where was it now stationed?—but the situation on the street started to get out of hand. The closest onlookers had heard the horseman's message, and they quickly passed it on to their neighbors, who spread it farther through the crowd. In the process, the news worsened: Aistulf was personally leading the Lombard army, he had taken Mentana and Fidenae, or he was approaching Rome itself with fifty thousand men and all his engines of war.

Panic seized the crowd. Men, women, and children pressed forward as if to seek the Pope's personal protection, and a general wailing broke out. Some of the militiamen tried to keep the crowd away from the procession, but the desperate citizens pushed more urgently. People west of the church, where the head of the procession was stopped, found their path toward the pope blocked by the carriage carrying the sarcophagus, which had turned obliquely sideways in the confusion. Masses of screaming spectators pressed against the two draft horses that were attached to the carriage. The horses, normally placid, became infected with the general panic and reared violently until the carriage tilted backward, and the sarcophagus slid off its runners and struck the cobbled road surface. Then it rolled over on its side, and its lid slid partway off. To the onlookers' horror, a skeletal arm came into view: it projected out of the sarcophagus and seemingly pointed toward the pope, who was standing twenty feet away.

Although the militiamen's efforts to hold the crowd back had failed completely, the appearance of Sylvester's arm had an almost magical effect. There was a general shrinking back; people gasped and crossed themselves. All eyes, including the pope's, were fixed on this ghastly and ill-boding apparition. A stunned silence fell over the scene, as if everyone was waiting for someone else to act.

One person did not cross himself—Zaid. He was still standing in the middle of the road, between the sarcophagus and the pope, the broom in his right hand. From his close vantage point, he could see that Sylvester's hand clutched what seemed to be a tattered, leather-bound document or book. Zaid stared at it, and then looked inquiringly at the pope, who gave him a slight nod. Zaid moved cautiously forward until he was within arm's length of Sylvester's hand. He reached down, loosened the document from Sylvester's bony grasp, and carried it over to Stephen. As the onlookers watched in transfixed amazement, Zaid bowed before the Holy Father, handed him the book, and retreated.

17

When Stephen entered the reception hall on the following morning, his counselors were already engaged in anxious and heated discussion about the events of the previous day. After a prayer and other formalities, the discussion resumed. Most pressingly, the counselors wanted to know more about the military situation.

"I've spoken further with the messengers who arrived yesterday," Stephen said in response to their queries, "and with others who came this morning. Aistulf has indeed broken his pledge, and that's a matter of great concern. Still, the situation isn't quite as dire as we feared. The forces that took Ceccano were just a small contingent of Aistulf's allies from Benevento. It's certainly not a force that could besiege Rome. Aistulf's main army remains at Pavia, and there's no sign of any planned movement. So we're not in any immediate danger. What's more, Ceccano fell without any major losses, and the citizens are safe. We must hope that the town will be restored to us before long.

"With regard to the translation of the blessed Sylvester," he went on, "we must accept what happened yesterday as a sign from God that our plan was mistaken. In fact, my beloved predecessor reached out his own arm in remonstrance and blame, pointing at me, and I accept responsibility for the grievous error we committed."

Paul inwardly thanked his brother for his effort to deflect responsibility from himself. Still, he knew that he would not easily live down the debacle. He wondered whether the failure of the translation was a punishment for his sinful behavior with Leoba in the catacomb. That thought provoked another one: would he be able to arrange another meeting with her today?

Stephen went on: "The clergy of St. Sylvester and St. Martin have restored the sarcophagus to order and moved it into their church, as that was the closest available refuge. I think now that we should make it Sylvester's final resting place. It is, after all, a church that he himself built, and thus a fitting place for him to lie. We'll organize a rite of purification to atone for the defilement he suffered yesterday, and I will ask you, Archdeacon, to make plans for his entombment there."

"I shall, Your Holiness," said Theophylact. Then he brought up the topic that everyone had been speculating about. "And may I also enquire," he said, "whether Your Holiness can tell us anything about what it was that you retrieved from Sylvester's hand."

"Yes, it's a letter of some kind," Stephen said. "One that Sylvester apparently received from the Emperor Constantine. Beyond that, I haven't examined it, but I'd like to ask you, Librarian Tullius, if you would kindly read it to us all." With that, Stephen produced the document and handed it to an aide, who conveyed it round the table to Tullius.

Paul watched the proceedings tensely. Although nothing

yesterday had gone according to plan, the letter had at least ended up in his brother's hands, as intended. Only, he was supposed to see it when the sarcophagus was opened for his sole inspection at the end of the mass at St. Peter's. That way, he would have taken possession of the letter in conditions of some privacy. As it turned out, everyone in Rome either witnessed or heard about the strange discovery and was wondering what it meant. This placed a great deal more importance on how it was received by the pope and his counselors.

Tullius stood and took cautious hold of the letter. He was nervous, but reading was what he did best, so he put on a good face and began.

"In nomine sanctae et individuae Trinitatis—In the name of the holy and indivisible Trinity, the Father, the Son and the Holy Spirit. From the emperor Caesar Flavius Constantine, the faithful, merciful, supreme, beneficent, pious, fortunate, victorious, triumphant, and august: to the most holy and blessed father of fathers Sylvester, bishop of the city of Rome and pope, and to all the succeeding pontiffs who shall sit upon the chair of Saint Peter until the end of time; also to all the most reverend and God-beloved catholic bishops throughout the whole world, subjected by this our imperial decree to this same holy Roman church, who have been established now or will be in all future times: grace, peace, charity, rejoicing, long-suffering, and mercy be with you all from God the Father Almighty and from Jesus Christ his Son and from the Holy Ghost. Our most gracious Serenity desires, through the pages of this our imperial decree, to bring to the knowledge of all the people in the whole world what things our Savior and Redeemer the Lord Jesus Christ, the Son of the most High Father, has most wonderfully seen fit to bring about through His holy Apostles Peter and Paul and by the intervention of our father Sylvester, the highest pontiff

and universal pope.'"

"So this is a decree, and not just a letter," commented First Notary Ambrose. "And a decree that relates to papal authority. How extraordinary that such a thing should come to light!"

"It is indeed," said Stephen. "I seem to hear the Emperor's voice speaking to us directly, from four centuries ago."

"Shall I go on, Your Holiness?" asked Tullius uncertainly.

"Yes, yes, don't mind our interruptions," said Stephen.

"'Nam dum valida squaloris lepra—Now at a time when a mighty and filthy leprosy had invaded all the flesh of my body, many physicians administered their care, but we did not achieve health by any one of them. Then there came hither the priests of the Capitol, telling us that a basin should be placed on the Capitol, and that we should fill this with the blood of innocent infants; and that, if we bathed in it while the blood was still warm, we might be cleansed. And very many innocent infants having been brought together, when the sacrilegious priests of the pagans wished them to be slaughtered and the font to be filled with their blood, Our Serenity, perceiving the tears of the mothers, straightway abhorred the deed. And, pitying them, we ordered their children to be restored to them; and, giving them gifts, we sent them off rejoicing to their homes.

"'Eadem igitur transacta die—That day having passed—the silence of night having come upon us—after we fell asleep, the blessed Apostles Peter and Paul appeared, saying to us: 'Since thou hast placed a limit on thy vices, and hast abhorred the pouring forth of innocent blood, we are sent by Christ the Lord our God, to give to thee a plan for recovering thy health. Hear, therefore, our warning, and do what we indicate to thee. Sylvester—the bishop of the city of Rome—on Mount Soracte, fleeing thy persecutions, lives in darkness with his clergy in the

caverns of the rocks. This man, when thou shalt have led him to thyself, will show thee a sacred pool; in which, when he shall have dipped thee for the third time, the leprosy will desert thee. And, when this shall have been done, do this in return for thy Savior, that by thy order through the whole world the Christian churches may be restored and legitimized. Purify thyself, moreover, in this way, that, leaving all the superstition of idols, thou do adore and cherish the living and true God and do His will.'"

"So it's true, what our people have always believed," said Marcellus, "that Constantine was baptized here in Rome, by the blessed Sylvester, and not in Asia at the end of his life, as some historians have claimed."

"Apparently so," said Stephen. "But let us see how the story proceeds. Continue, please, Tullius."

"Exsurgens igitur a somno—Rising therefore from sleep, straightway we did that which we had been advised to do by the holy apostles; and, having summoned that excellent and beneficent father and our enlightener—Sylvester, the universal pope—we told him all the words that had been taught us by the holy Apostles; and asked him who were those gods Peter and Paul. But he said that they were not really called gods, but Apostles of our Savior the Lord God Jesus Christ. And again we began to ask that same most blessed pope whether he had some image of those Apostles, so that, from their likeness, we might learn whether they were those whom revelation had shown to us. Then that same venerable father ordered the images of those Apostles to be shown by his deacon. And, when we had looked at them, and recognized, represented in those images, the countenances of those whom we had seen in our dream, then with a great acclamation, before all my satraps, we confessed that they were indeed those whom we had seen.

"'Ad haec beatissimus—Hereupon that same most blessed Sylvester

our father, bishop of the city of Rome, imposed upon us a time of penance—within our Lateran palace, in the chapel, in a hair garment—so that we might obtain pardon from our Lord God Jesus Christ our Savior by vigils, fasts, and tears and prayers, for all things that had been impiously done and unjustly ordered by us. Then through the imposition of the hands of the clergy, we came to the bishop himself; and there, renouncing the pomp of Satan and his works, and all idols made by hands, of our own will before all the people we confessed: that we believed in God the Father Almighty, Maker of Heaven and earth, and of all things visible and invisible; and in Jesus Christ, His only Son our Lord, who was born of the Holy Spirit and of the Virgin Mary. And, the font having been blessed, the wave of salvation purified us there with a triple immersion. And, being placed at the bottom of the font, we saw with our own eyes a hand from Heaven touching us; whence rising, clean, we saw that we were cleansed from all the squalor of leprosy.

"Et dum haec praedicante beato Silvestrio—And when, from the words preached by the blessed Sylvester, we learned that we had been restored to health by the kindness of Saint Peter himself, then we, along with our satraps and the whole Senate and the nobles and all the Roman people, who are subject to the glory of our rule—we considered it advisable that, as on earth Peter is recognized as vicar of the Son of God, so the pontiffs, who are the representatives of that same chief of the Apostles, should obtain from us and our Empire the power of a supremacy greater than what has been granted to Our Imperial Serenity. And, to the extent of our earthly imperial power, we decree that his holy Roman church shall be honored with veneration; and that, more than our empire and earthly throne, the most sacred seat of Saint Peter shall be gloriously exalted; we giving to it the imperial power, and dignity of glory, and vigor and honor.

"Atque decernentes sancimus—And we ordain and decree that he

shall have the supremacy as well over the four patriarchates of Antioch, Alexandria, Constantinople, and Jerusalem, as also over all the churches of God in the whole—"

Theophylact broke in. "Constantinople?" he asked sharply. "Constantinople didn't even exist then! How could he have spoken of a patriarchate of a city that had not yet been founded, nor even named or thought of? There was no patriarch in Constantinople until two hundred years after that time."

Paul cringed—he had made a gross and elementary blunder. Was he about to be exposed as a liar and a forger? But no one seemed to take Theophylact's objection very seriously. Marcellus said: "He probably had his move planned out already, and of course he expected that there would be a patriarch—maybe we'll learn more about this later."

Tullius was slightly flustered by the interruption, but he soldiered on. *"—as also over all the churches of God in the whole world. And whoever is pontiff of that holy Roman church shall be chief over all the priests of the whole world; and everything which is to be provided for the service of God or the stability of the Christian faith is to be administered according to his judgment."*

"The elders of the Council of Chalcedon made a wise decision, then," commented Stephen, "when they ruled that the patriarchate of Constantinople and the other patriarchates lay below Rome in precedence."

"Apparently so, Your Holiness," said Theophylact. "Still, isn't it strange that the order of precedence should have been set by a civil ruler and not a spiritual authority? And by a man who, just two or three days earlier, was an unbeliever and a persecutor of the Christians."

"Not really," said Stephen. "Many Ecumenical Councils have been presided over by Emperors, who have always concerned themselves with matters of faith. Go on, Tullius."

"*'Concedimus beato Silvestrio—We grant to the blessed Sylvester, the chief pontiff, and all his successors, our imperial Lateran Palace, which ranks above all the palaces in the whole world; and also a diadem—'*"

Theophylact jumped in again. "This Lateran Palace, where no Emperor ever lived or ruled, and which actually belonged to Constantine's wife—this palace ranked above the imperial palace on the Palatine, which was ten times larger and the residence of Constantine himself and countless preceding Emperors?"

Paul squirmed again—this was becoming more of an inquisition than he had expected. But Stephen stepped in once more. "I think he used that turn of phrase simply to gratify Sylvester—it was customary for rulers to overstate the value or magnificence of their gifts. Now perhaps we should let the Librarian read on without too many interruptions."

"Thank you, Your Holiness," said Tullius. "*'—and also a diadem, that is, the crown of our head, and at the same time the tiara, and also the shoulder-band, which is the collar that usually surrounds our imperial neck, and also the purple mantle, and crimson tunic, and all the imperial raiment; and we confer also the imperial scepters, and the spears and standards, as well as the banners and different imperial ornaments, and all the advantages of our high imperial position, and the glory of our power. And in order that the pontifical glory may shine forth more fully, we decree this also: that the clergy of this same holy Roman church may use saddle-cloths of linen of the whitest color; namely that their horses may be adorned and so ridden, and that, as our senate uses slippers of goats' hair, so they may be distinguished by*" *gleaming——'''*

"This will please you, Deacon Paul," commented Stephen, who had forgotten his own injunction of a moment before. There was general laughter, because Paul's interest in fine dress was often the subject of ridicule. Paul wondered whether he should have omitted that section, even though it was close to his heart.

"Your Holiness," said Theophylact, "your blessed predecessor Celestine—I recall his words: '*We must be distinguished from the common people by our learning and not by our clothes; by our mode of life, and not by our costume; by purity of mind, and not by elegance of dress.*'"

Paul felt obliged to weigh in. "None of us today dresses like the common people—not even you, Theo." The jibe at the Archdeacon's expense provoked some titters. "Apparently the blessed Celestine was mistaken in this matter, based on what Tullius has just read."

Theophylact was not amused. "So with regard to liturgical questions, the Deacon places less weight on the authority of a pope and a saint than on that of a civil ruler?" he asked scornfully.

"Let's not discuss this now," said Stephen hurriedly. "We have more urgent matters before us. Tullius, is there anything more of substance in the document?"

"I wouldn't presume to judge, Your Holiness," said the Librarian, "but I'll read on, with your permission. Let me see, where was I? '*—distinguished by gleaming linen.*' Wait, I think the next section will interest Your Holiness more. Let me start here: *Ipse vero beatissimus Papa—But since he himself, the most blessed Pope, did not at all allow that crown of gold to be used over the clerical crown which he wears to the glory of the Blessed Peter, we* *placed upon his most holy head, with our own hands, a glittering tiara of dazzling white representing the Lord's resurrection, and holding the bridle of his horse, out of reverence for the Blessed Peter, we performed for him the duty of groom, decreeing that all his successors, and they alone, use this same tiara in processions in imitation of our power.*

"'Unde ut non pontificalis apex vilescat—In order that the supreme pontificate may not deteriorate, behold, we give over to the most blessed pontiff, our father Sylvester, the universal pope, besides our palace, also the city of Rome and all the provinces, districts and cities of Italy and of the western regions, relinquishing them by this our inviolable gift to the power of the pontiff and his successors, and we declare that they shall lawfully remain with the holy Roman church.'"

There were some audible gasps from the counselors as they took in the significance of what they had just heard. "The Emperor certainly had a sense of the dramatic," said Ambrose. "From goats' hair slippers to the disposition of an Empire!"

Tullius read on. *"'Unde congruum prospeximus—Wherefore we have perceived it to be fitting that our empire and the power of our kingdom should be transferred to the regions of the East; and that, in the province of Byzantium, in a most fitting place, a city should be built in our name, and that our empire should there be established. For where the supremacy of priests and the head of the Christian religion has been established by a heavenly ruler, it is not just that an earthly ruler should have jurisdiction.'"*

"So Marcellus was right, Theo," said Stephen. "Constantine was already planning his new capital at the time he wrote this deed, and he had settled on the name of it. Go on, Tullius. I see we are near the end."

"'Haec vero omnia—We decree moreover, that all these things which we have established and confirmed shall remain uninjured and

unshaken until the end of the world. Wherefore, before the living God, and in the face of his terrible judgment, we conjure, through this our imperial decree, all the emperors our successors, and all our nobles and satraps and the most glorious Senate, and all the people in the whole world now and in all times, that none of them in any way allow himself to oppose or disregard these things which have been conceded to the holy Roman church and to all its pontiffs. If anyone, moreover, prove a scorner or despiser in this matter, he shall be subject and bound over to eternal damnation, and being burned in the nethermost hell, he shall perish with the devil and all the impious.

"'Huius vero imperialis decreti—The text of this our imperial decree we did place above the venerable body of Saint Peter chief of the Apostles, and there we did hand it over, to be enduringly and happily possessed, to our most blessed father Sylvester the supreme pontiff and universal pope, and through him to all the pontiffs that shall succeed him, with the consent of God our Lord, and our Savior Jesus Christ.

"'Datum Roma—Given at Rome on the third day before the Kalends of April, in the year of the fourth consulship of Flavius Constantinus, and that of Gallicanus, most illustrious men. '"

18

"Thank you, Tullius, for your excellent reading," said Stephen. Tullius beamed, bowed, and sat down. He carefully closed the ancient document and placed it on the table in front of him.

"And now, dear counselors, what should we make of this?" Stephen went on. "Ambrose, let's hear your opinion first."

"Holy Father," the First Notary began, "with your permission I'll comment first on the news from Ceccano. The seizure of that town was indeed a gross violation of the treaty that we agreed on so recently. Considering my long and arduous journey to Pavia, the rich gifts that I gave to the King with my own hands, and my extensive diplomatic efforts at the Lombard court, this news offends my ears as if it were a personal and degrading insult mouthed by Aistulf himself. But more importantly, it confirms what some of your wise counselors already expressed at our earlier meeting: Aistulf is a perfidious and despicable liar, a breaker of faith, not fit to be called a Christian, deserving rather to be denied communion and to burn in that same nethermost hell of which Tullius just spoke. We have the authority of

Ambrose, my blessed namesake, for that, for didn't Ambrose deny communion to the Emperor Theodosius himself, after the Emperor ordered the massacre of the seven thousand innocent citizens of Thessalonica? Didn't Ambrose stand in person at the door of the cathedral at Milan in order to bar the Emperor's entry? Surely what Aistulf did at Ravenna was an equally grave sin, not to speak of the many evil acts that he has committed since that time."

This is moving in a more positive direction, thought Paul.

"It's a great relief to hear from Your Holiness that Rome faces no imminent danger," Ambrose went on. "But still, we must expect Aistulf to advance against the city at some point, if not this season then the next. And any assistance from the Emperor is beginning to seem unlikely."

"It's still too early to be expecting a reply from Constantinople," put in Theophylact, "especially if the Emperor is raising an army to confront the Lombards."

Paul also broke in. "Raising an army to save us? That is fantasy. The Emperor has washed his hands of us, so let's not make any more plans that involve his assistance."

Ambrose went on. "Given the crisis we're in, this letter from Constantine—this deed or donation, however we should name it—it seems like a message sent from God Himself. Indeed, we must believe that our blessed and beloved Sylvester reached out to Your Holiness from beyond the grave, in order to give you this missive at the time of our greatest peril. Surely it holds the keys to our earthly salvation—as surely as St. Peter holds the keys to our salvation in the hereafter."

"And how will it save us?" asked Stephen.

"Well, it gives Your Holiness temporal authority over the

entire western Empire. So, to begin with, letting Aistulf know of this should cause him to acknowledge your authority and yield to St. Peter. But, we know that he is unlikely to do so. Therefore, we should give renewed consideration to the idea put forward by Deacon Paul previously—the idea that we did not view favorably at the time."

"You mean, to seek aid from Pepin?"

"Yes, Your Holiness," said Ambrose. "In view of the letter that Librarian Tullius just read, my own opinion on the matter has changed completely."

"Meaning—?"

"Meaning that, as made clear in the letter, the Supreme Pontiff does indeed have temporal authority over the western provinces, which would include Gaul. The King of the Franks rules by the grace of Your Holiness—at least with respect to the larger part of his realm that was once a province of the Roman Empire. So it's well within your authority to crown Pepin, just as Deacon Paul urged at our previous meeting. And, seeing this decree, the Frankish nobles will acknowledge your authority to do so. Thus it will be greatly to Pepin's advantage to be crowned by Your Holiness—it will secure the allegiance of his most powerful subjects. And he will be more strongly motivated to help us against the Lombards."

"Thank you, Ambrose. What about you, Marcellus?"

"Your Holiness," said the Treasurer, "I previously spoke in favor of negotiations with Aistulf. It's now clear that that approach has no merit. I can't see what is left except to appeal to Pepin, and this deed does seem to strengthen our bargaining position."

"And you, Librarian Tullius?"

"I? I—well, I agree with the views just expressed."

"Theophylact?"

Theophylact stood. He scanned the gathered counselors with the grim severity of an Old Testament prophet, fixing Paul in particular in a hostile glare. Everything so far had been going exactly as Paul had hoped, but he steeled himself for what was to come.

"This so-called letter, or decree, or donation, of the Emperor Constantine, Your Holiness," the Archdeacon began, "how excellent that it should come to light at this particular moment! Yes, it's as if Divine Providence guided the events of yesterday so as to offer us an unlooked-for salvation, just as the First Notary suggested. I've raised some trifling questions or objections, which doubtless have been well answered by Your Holiness or by others present here. That Constantine speaks of the patriarchate of Constantinople, two centuries before that patriarchate came into being—no doubt that reflects the Emperor's extraordinary power of foresight, as Treasurer Marcellus wisely indicated. That Constantine refers to the humble Lateran Palace, where we now sit, as if it outranked the Imperial Palace itself—yes, this was in all likelihood the customary hyperbole associated with an Emperor's munificence. And that a lay person—an unbeliever two days before—should be making rules about liturgical robes and tiaras and so forth, thus claiming some kind of ecclesiastical authority over a mere pope—"

"Well, this was just—"

"*Over a mere pope,*" repeated Theophylact, waving off Paul's attempted interjection. "Yes, that likely reflected the habit of imperial authority in all matters religious, as we see in the history of the Ecumenical Councils.

"No doubt I could also have remarked on other strange-seeming aspects of this document, if I had wished to raise any doubts about its authenticity. Is it not odd, for example, that the Emperor would devote more space to minute and—to be frank—absurdly trivial details of liturgical dress than to the disposition of his own Empire, or the better half of it, which he hands over in a mere brief sentence or two, not even troubling himself to delineate the regions that shall or shall not be included in the donation? Of course, it could be that he expected his meaning to be readily understood without detailed and tedious listing of cities and provinces, so let us pass over this objection as completely lacking in substance.

"More troubling, perhaps, to a person who might have concerns about the document, is this: The decree spelled out in it, by which Constantine suddenly gave away half his empire to a Troglodyte, had absolutely no—"

Paul jumped in again. "A Troglodyte? Our blessed and beloved Sylvester was some kind of daylight-shunning half-man? He lived in a cave, certainly, but only out of necessity—in order to keep the fragile light of the True Faith burning through the years of persecution. In no way did that—"

"Deacon Paul—please let the Archdeacon continue," said Stephen.

"Forgive me, Your Holiness."

Theophylact went on. "As I was saying—what's so troubling is that this alleged decree had *absolutely no effect*, as far as anyone is aware. What imperial edict was ever issued by Sylvester or his successors, such as this supposed donation would have justified or even demanded? I can't think of a single one. In truth, didn't Sylvester and those coming after him confine themselves to the spiritual guidance of their flocks, humbly and rightfully following the example of the blessed Apostle and first Pope? And did Constantine or his successors, by any action or inaction that we know of, ever acknowledge or imply any surrender of imperial authority in the west? Far from it, far from it! They repeatedly intervened in western affairs, set up western Emperors in Rome, sent their generals to invade Italy and governors to rule here as their representatives; in short, they did everything in their power to enforce their rule. If the present Emperor has given up his authority in Italy, as Deacon Paul is rash enough to believe, then he's the first in four centuries to do so, and he takes this action, or inaction, only out of military necessity, not because he has suddenly brought to mind this edict, Constantine's donation—a donation that had inexplicably been ignored by every one of his predecessors over the course of four hundred years.

"How can we explain that a decree of such importance was completely lacking in effect? Did Sylvester, having received the deed from the penitent Constantine—did he clutch it to his breast for all the remaining years of his life, not speaking of it or showing it to anyone, and did he finally take it with him to his much-deserved rest and entombment, so that it might never—as he must surely have thought— that it might never again see the light of day until the end of time? What reason could he have had for such a course of action? *What reason*, I ask you? Is it not possible, or indeed certain, that the donation had no effect because it *didn't exist*—because this so-called decree, this piece of raggedy rubbish in Tullius's hands, it's the creation of a malevolent trickster—a shameless and pernicious forgery!"

There was a general sucking-in of breath, followed by a silence as the assembled counselors absorbed the force of Theophylact's words. Paul knew that everything depended on his response. "If I may speak, Your Holiness," he said.

"Go ahead, Deacon Paul."

"Those smaller points that the Archdeacon brought up earlier, they are indeed without merit, as others have pointed out, including Your Holiness, and as the Archdeacon himself concedes. Now with regard to this other objection, that the decree had no effect, the Archdeacon's rhetoric makes this seem like evidence against the deed's authenticity, but it's not. There are many reasons why Sylvester might have hesitated to exercise the imperial power granted by the deed. He was a humble man, unused to the ways of the world, by temperament more given to persuasion than to command, like our beloved Zachary. And, even if he had commanded, who would have obeyed? Would the western legions have suddenly marched to the orders of a cleric, the leader of a religion that, up until that very moment, had been an outlawed and persecuted cult? Surely Sylvester realized that he would best preserve the Christian faith by confining himself to religious matters, rather than, as it were, stretching out his head to be struck off by the first centurion who desired to restore the pagan gods. And, given that Sylvester chose not take up the reins of imperial power, it's understandable that Constantine and the succeeding Emperors felt the need to continue some form of governance in Italy and the west, even after the establishment of the eastern capital.

"Now, the Archdeacon asks, Why would Sylvester have kept this document secret and taken it with him to his grave? But there is no reason to believe that he did keep it secret. What we have lying before us is doubtless the original deed, which Sylvester valued greatly as a personal letter from Constantine, even if he chose not to take advantage of the temporal powers that it conferred. But certainly he had a copy made and deposited at the tomb of St. Peter, for he no doubt foresaw that there would come a time—even if centuries in the future—when a Pope would need to act on it."

The Archdeacon broke in. "Where is that copy, then? Is there such a copy, Tullius?"

"I'm afraid to say there is not, at the tomb, Your Holiness, I'm confident of that," said the Librarian. "But space there is very limited. Most documents deposited there are moved later—to the archives here at the Lateran Palace."

"So is there a copy here?" asked Stephen.

"Not that I am aware, Your Holiness," said Tullius. "But as Your Holiness knows, the archives are extensive; they take up many chambers and hallways and store-rooms, and their contents are, I must confess, in some disorder, especially with regard to the older documents. A letter such as this one would be very difficult to find, unfortunately."

"Well, please make a search, when you are able."

"I shall, Your Holiness."

Paul went on. "The fact that Sylvester didn't immediately take up imperial command, and that the Emperors didn't immediately yield it—that fact doesn't in any way diminish the significance of this decree. What this decree means is that, over all these ensuing years, the Emperors' authority in the west has been illegitimate, their representatives have been usurpers, their edicts unenforceable, their armies traitorous. No, Archdeacon—let me finish! Now, finally, it's in our hands to restore the rightful patrimony of St. Peter, not just here in Rome, but in Italy and throughout the west. The decline and decay that we see all around us, this depopulation and impoverishment of our capital, the shameful treatment we've endured at the hands of the Lombards and so many other uncivilized peoples—it's in our hands to reverse all of this and to restore the power and pride of Rome as it was in the time of the great Caesars. Let's bring Pepin to Italy, let's drive the Lombards out of our rightful lands, so that we can regain our proper sources of taxation and raise the armies that we need to defend ourselves.

"And let me emphasize, none of this will be for the love of worldly power or for personal aggrandizement or enrichment. It will be for the love of the blessed Peter and the hearth of our faith that he established in this city. Only when the Roman Pontiff is supreme in his own land can he truly be the spiritual leader that his position as Apostolic Successor demands. In the matter of sacred images, for example, we'll no longer have to pay any attention to those misbegotten eastern doctrines. We'll no longer have to fear that imperial enforcers will come racing through our streets, tearing ancient paintings and mosaics from our walls and making bonfires of them in our public squares. We'll be free to venerate—not *worship*, Theo, but *venerate*—our beloved icons and relics as they should be venerated. And with regard to church appointments: finally, when a bishopric falls vacant in Italy or Francia or elsewhere, the pious candidate chosen by Your Holiness will be the one actually seated, rather than whichever rascal paid the largest bribe to the local duke. Worldly power—yes, but only in the service of spiritual power and godliness, for the benefit of Christians everywhere and to the greater glory of God."

"Thank you, Deacon Paul," said Stephen, "and thank you all for your sincere and well-expressed opinions. Now with regard to your arguments, Archdeacon: this document is not a forgery. Certainly there are oddities in it, such as you've rightly pointed out. But that is true of any writings from centuries ago. In those days, people reasoned and expressed themselves in ways that can seem peculiar to us. Their habits of mind were different from ours. By your arguments, how many of the holy books would we have to condemn as forgeries?"

"Your Holiness—" Theophylact began, but he was cut off.

"Let me continue, dear Archdeacon. Let me also remind you all that this deed wasn't slipped into to my hand by some scheming politician, or brought by traders from an unknown land; it came to me out of the very hand of our blessed and beloved Sylvester, who reached out from his sarcophagus to deliver it to me. Is Sylvester then a mischievous forger? No, the very idea comes close to blasphemy! And look at the document itself, Archdeacon—pass it to him, please. Feel the tattered binding, look at the faded ink. Handle it carefully, please; it's ready to fall apart into dust! Consider the ancient style of writing, such as no one employs today and few even know about. And look at the detailed information in it—who today, for example, could know that this person named Gallicanus was the other Consul during the fourth consulate of Constantine?"

"Do we in fact—"

"Peace, Archdeacon, peace! No, this document is an authentic decree of the Emperor Constantine. For us to believe otherwise would be to risk retribution from the very Providence that sent it to us in our hour of need. Let there be no more discussion of that matter, either here or elsewhere—I solemnly adjure every one of you to cease all further words and thoughts on that score."

Paul directed an expression of pained sympathy toward Theophylact.

"Now finally comes the question of what to do—what action to take on the basis of this remarkable document," Stephen continued. "Let me tell you, I've no desire for worldly power. I'd prefer to leave temporal affairs to those who are skilled in the ways of government. I've paid all too little attention to spiritual matters, in the few months that I've held this office. Would that we could return to those earlier days—when a pope was a spiritual shepherd first and last. But we have a military crisis on our hands, and it's for us alone to resolve it. This is how I propose to do so. First, I will personally go to Pavia, and demand from Aistulf face to face that he desist from his hostile actions against us and adhere to the treaty of peace that he signed so recently."

"Your Holiness—"

"No, let me speak. I'm well aware that this effort has some risk, and is unlikely to be successful. Still, it's possible that Aistulf, as a professed member of the Catholic faith, will be swayed by the leader of that faith. I'm obliged to give him that opportunity. If he doesn't give immediate and unambiguous token of a change of heart, I'll proceed to Francia, to the court of Pepin. I must pass through Lombardy on the way to Francia, in any case, unless I should go by sea, which is far too dangerous. So I'll need a safe conduct from Aistulf. And to Pepin, I'll make the offer that was proposed by Deacon Paul—to crown him King of the Franks, in return for his undertaking to lead his army against the Lombards. I will of course send him this donation of Constantine, or a copy of it that we'll have made. I'll request the company of several of you on this journey, while others must take over the responsibilities of leadership in Rome during my absence, which could be lengthy. But it will be many weeks before I can depart, given that we must await word from Aistulf and make many other arrangements. In that time I will also send secretly to Pepin, sounding out his willingness to enter into an agreement such as we have discussed."

"What about the situation here, Your Holiness," asked Marcellus. "The panic."

"We must let the people know that the danger from Aistulf isn't as bad as they think, and that the blessed Sylvester has provided the means to our city's salvation. We must reasssure them that peace and security will be restored before long. I've told you my plan. Now, speak your mind, whoever wishes."

19

" Seven days since I saw my beloved,
And sickness has invaded me;
I am heavy in all my limbs,
My body has forsaken me."

Zaid sang quietly to himself as he massaged the flank of a great grey draft horse, moving the curry comb in widening spirals, dislodging the dirt and grime that Rome's unpaved lanes had thrown up, and loosening matted clumps of hair. Then he took a stiff brush and swept out the loosened dirt, starting at the horse's mane and working toward his belly.

The Lateran stable, where Zaid was working, held a hundred or more horses of all sizes, builds, and colors. Some other stable-hands were working nearby; one called over: "Zaid, leave us alone with your misery-gut melodies! Is that how everyone sings in China?"

"China? I'm not from China, you baboon. In China they sing to the Moon-Princess, like this: *Wah-wah-weia-awah-wowa!* No, this is from Egypt, from long ago. Listen, Titus!

When the physicians come to me,

My heart rejects their remedies;
The spell-casters are quite helpless,
My sickness is not discerned."

"Sounds like *Wah-wah-weia-awah-wowa* to me!" Five or ten other nearby boys contributed a jangling refrain: "*Wah-wah-weia-awah-wowa!*"

"You're good, keep practicing!" said Zaid derisively, and he turned back to the horse he was working on. With a soft brush, he worked on the horse's face and legs.

"The words 'She is here' would revive me!
Her name would make me rise,
The coming of her messenger,
That would revive my heart!"

"Cantor Zaid, have you heard the news?" called Titus. "The pope and his counselors are going to Lombardy, to visit their king. And maybe to Francia too, to visit *their* king. Some of us will be taken along."

"I'd love to go," said Zaid, "except my girlfriend is here in Rome."

"Your girlfriend? You mean Esmeralda?" said Titus, slapping the haunches of the worn-out old nag he was grooming. "So that's why you've been sneaking in here at night?"

"Tell us about it, 'Meralda," shouted another boy, "was it good for you too?" Titus coaxed a whinny out of Esmeralda, which provoked gales of laughter.

"I'll go to Francia," said another stable-boy by the name of Sebastian. "I've heard that their war-horses wear shoes of iron."

"Shoes of iron?" asked Titus skeptically. "How can a horse wear shoes of iron?"

"That's what I've heard. The shoes strike fire from the ground, terrifying their enemies."

"What nonsense! And perhaps they have dragons that tiptoe about in lambswool slippers, so as not to interrupt the ladies' singing?"

"Another thing I've heard," said Sebastian, undaunted, "the riders put their feet in iron hoops that hang from their horses' saddles."

"Why would they do that?"

"So that they can stand up when they shoot arrows or throw spears."

"I've never heard of that," said Titus. "How can a rider mount or dismount if his feet are in iron hoops?"

Zaid turned to his horse's hooves. He placed himself next the horse's left shoulder, facing backward, and pushed the horse sideways to shift its balance to its right forefoot. Although the weight of such a large horse could hardly be shifted by a slender boy like Zaid, it did eventually lean over enough that Zaid could slide his hand down its left leg, grasp the hoof, and pull it backward off the ground. The horse protested and tried to move across the stall, but his halter prevented it.

"Easy, Hercules, easy!" said Zaid, following the horse's attempted movement. Then he took a pick from his belt and began cleaning dried mud out of the hoof.

The stable-master came into the yard. "Less talk and more work, please, unless you want to go to bed hungry tonight," he shouted to no one in particular. "Zaid, you're wanted out front."

The other hands stared curiously as Zaid walked toward to the courtyard in front of the stable. Even before he got there, he heard a familiar voice speaking in a familiar tone.

"He's my son," Omar was saying angrily. "Give him back to me, you've no right to hold him."

"We have every right—ah, here he is." The stable-master pointed to Zaid, who was approaching from out of the shadows.

"Zaid!" Omar shouted. "Come home, what are you doing here?"

Zaid said nothing.

"Is this man your father?" asked the stable-master, pointing to Omar.

A tangle of emotions seized the boy. In the weeks since he had been delivered to the Lateran Palace, Zaid had come to value his new life. His masters had treated him well, aside from a single beating that he had brought on himself when he had climbed onto the roof of the stable in the middle of the night. He loved working with the horses: he not only cared for them in the stables, but also exercised them in one of the large paddocks to the east of the palace. He got on well with his companions, even if they picked on him for his dark skin and his strange habit of frequent prayer. And now he was excited by the possibility of a long journey to unfamiliar lands. On the other hand, his father's presence in front of him aroused a sense of family and a connection to his mother—a mother he had heard so much about from his father's lips, but couldn't himself remember. On Silversmiths' Street, Zaid knew, he could learn his father's trade, perhaps start his own business, earn some money, and hope to travel again as he once had. Soon, he knew, he would be tall enough and strong enough that his father would think twice before beating him. Soon, he would be a free man.

More than anything, returning to his father would mean returning to Lenora. Seeing her briefly at the procession a week earlier had reminded him how much he missed her. What had happened to his dreams of marrying her, of their moonlit journeys through eastern deserts? What about the children she was to give him, their strong sons and beautiful daughters?"

"Yes," Zaid said finally, "he's my father."

"You see!" shouted Omar. "Give him back to me!"

"Who knows if you're lying, you and him too," said the stable-master. "And what does it matter? Look here." He grasped Zaid's arm and raised his sleeve, exposing the S-shaped scar.

Omar had already heard about the brand from Lenora and her parents, but it was still a shock to see it with his own eyes. He wanted to embrace and protect his son, but the stable-master kept the boy at arm's length.

"You had no right to do this," Omar said. "Zaid is the son of a free man, living legally in Rome."

"Zaid is no Christian, and he's a confessed and convicted thief, spared from strangulation on account of his young age. He was offered his freedom if he accepted baptism, but he refused."

"Zaid is no thief. Are you, Zaid?"

"I—I didn't mean to—I was cold. I needed a coat."

"You see, he's a thief, he says so himself," said the stable-master.

171

"You had no right to enslave him. Give him back, or I'll go to the papal court."

"Go to any court you want. It's once a slave, always a slave. Now leave us in peace, unless you fancy being enslaved yourself. And get back to your work, Zaid."

"Zaid, I will free you—I will free you!" shouted Omar to his son, who turned back toward the stables, both out of obedience to the stable-master and to hide the tears welling in his eyes.

"My curse on everyone in this shit-palace," Omar went on, as he turned and limped his way out of the courtyard. "*Zibl mufarrak! Nighif! Ragham allah anfu!* You bits of dung and snot! May Allah grind your noses in the sand!"

20

In her small writing room in the Lateran library, with its view out over the gardens and the Aurelian Wall, Leoba was preparing a copy of Constantine's letter. It was one of three copies she had been asked to make. One would be kept at the Lateran Palace, as a stand-in for the fragile original. One was intended for Aistulf, and the third would be sent to Pepin. It was a warm summer day, and the sunlight streaming into the room made Leoba sleepy. She jolted awake, however, when she heard a knock at the open door and saw Paul entering. After looking to make sure there was no one else in the corridor, he closed the door gently after him. They shared a brief embrace.

"Paul, it's not good to keep coming here," Leoba said. "The chamber where we meet, that's safe, but here I'm expected to work with the door open. If the other scribes see you coming and going, and they see that you and I are behind closed doors, that'll start their tongues wagging."

"Leoba, I'm sorry, but there's news that I wanted to share with you."

"Which is?"

"First, ambassadors arrived from the Emperor."

"Really? Is the Emperor going to help us? What does he say?"

"He says: 'Order Aistulf to hand back Ravenna.'"

"That's it?"

"That's it."

"What a brilliant suggestion," said Leoba sarcastically. "Aistulf, hand back Ravenna! Why didn't we think of that months ago?"

"Exactly. Now finally perhaps Theo will realize that we're on our own. But there's better news."

"Tell me."

"Stephen has decided on who he's going to take to Pavia, and to Francia if necessary. He's taking Archdeacon Theophylact, First Notary Ambrose, and several others—but not me."

"Not you? So—"

"I'll be his deputy here, during his absence."

"You'll be in charge—in the Pope's place? Why not the Duke—he usually stands in for the Holy Father, doesn't he?"

"I think Stephen has more trust in my judgment. He'll be away for several months—maybe a year or more."

"That's very good—you'll be able to do all the things that you wanted to, without interference from Theophylact."

"Yes," said Paul. "And I'd been thinking Stephen would want me to go with him. So this is wonderful."

"I'm actually a bit surprised that you don't want to go. I mean, wouldn't you like to meet Pepin? Don't you want to help your brother with his negotiations? It's your plan, isn't it? You don't want it to go wrong."

"I would have liked to go, very much—except for one

thing."

Leoba frowned slightly. "Which is what?"

"That we'd be separated."

Leoba was silent. Finally she said, "You shouldn't make this decision for my sake, Paul."

"Not for your sake or my sake—for our sake." Paul took Leoba's hands in his own, and looked her in the eyes. "There's this magic between us, Leoba—something I've never felt before." Then, in a hushed but melodious voice, he began to sing. *"Quam pulchri sunt gressus tui—How beautiful are thy feet with shoes, O prince's daughter! The joints of thy thighs are like jewels, the work of the hands of a cunning workman. Thy navel is like a round goblet, which wanteth not liquor; thy belly is like an heap of wheat set about with lilies. Thy breasts are like two young roes that are twins."*

Leoba, even more quietly, sang in her turn. *"Caput eius aurum—His head is as the most fine gold, his locks are bushy, and black as a raven. His eyes are as the eyes of doves by the rivers of waters, washed with milk, and fitly set."*

Paul took his turn: *"Pone me ut signaculum—Set me as a seal upon thine heart, as a seal upon thine arm; for love is strong as death."*

And Leona responded, *"Quia fortis est ut mors dilectio-- Jealousy is cruel as the grave; the coals thereof are coals of fire, which hath a most vehement flame."*

"Aquae multae non poterunt extinguere caritatem—Many waters cannot quench love, neither can the floods drown it."

"Si dederit homo omnem substantiam—If a man would give all the substance of his house for love, it would utterly be contemned."

The two sat hand in hand for several minutes, looking out of the window. Then Leoba said, "Paul, I'm going to ask your brother if I can go with him."

"What?" Paul let go Leoba's hand in consternation. "*You* want to go with him? Why?"

"I want to stay here with you, but I need to go. I'll come back, I promise you."

"Why do you need to go? I can't believe you're saying this. It's because of us, isn't it? You want to put an end to— to what we—"

"No—well, I—no, that's not the reason."

"What's the reason, then?"

"I—I have an obligation to Boniface. I came to Rome with Burghard and Fulrad, but they've long since returned to Francia, and I should have gone too—that was the understanding."

"If it's an obligation, it's one you've had ever since they left—when was that, two years ago? Why do you need to act on it now so suddenly?"

"I've received letters from my uncle—several letters. Bishop Chrodegang brought another one last week, and he spoke to me very strongly about my need to return. My uncle is an old man."

"But a healthy man, a strong man."

"People think he's strong. They remember how he felled Thor's Oak with his own hands, but that was thirty years ago. He's still strong in spirit—nothing could weaken that. But his body is weakening, Chrodegang tells me. This may be my last chance to go."

Chrodegang was Archbishop of Metz and a minister in the Frankish court—he was the second highest ecclesiastic in Francia, after Boniface. He had come to Rome, accompanied by Duke Autchar of Picardy, to bring Pepin's message to Stephen: The pope would be welcome to visit his court, and

Chrodegang and Autchar would accompany him on his journey. But the two ambassadors would need time to recuperate from their weeks on the road, so the pope's departure would have to be delayed somewhat.

"I need to go," Leoba repeated. "Then, once I've fulfilled that obligation, I can ask his permission to come back here. And he'll grant it, because he knows my interests—that my calling is that of a scholar, not a missionary."

"Then I'll come with you. I'll ask Stephen. Theo can be his deputy here instead of me."

"You want Theophylact to be his deputy? Go ahead and ask your brother, but he won't agree. First, Theophylact would make all the wrong decisions, as you very well know. He'd try to get us back under the control of Constantinople. He'd probably offer to smash every sacred image in Rome if that would please the Emperor—which it would. And second, I'm sure your brother wants you to be deputy so as to give you experience, raise your status—to improve your chances to be chosen—later—"

"As his successor? Leoba, if it's God's will that I survive my brother, and that I should be pope, then let it be so. But I won't scheme and plot to get there. There are things that are more important to me—like being with you."

"Paul, you speak of God's will—but didn't you scheme and plot to get your brother chosen? How was that God's will, tell me? So why shouldn't it be the same with you? Theophylact is already doing that—as if your brother were already on his deathbed. He's always sweet-talking some senator or other, as I've heard."

"Leoba, maybe I should forget about any ideas of becoming Pope. Right now I'm a deacon. I'm not a priest."

"So? Many deacons have become Pope—they're ordained bishops, just as your brother was."

"No, I mean, certain things are expected of priests. And of bishops, including the bishop of Rome. Things that are not expected of deacons."

"You mean—to be celibate?" asked Leoba.

"Well, yes."

"Paul, what are you thinking? That what's going on between us—between you, a deacon, the pope's brother and heir-apparent, and me, a nun—that this can be dragged out into the light of day, and sanctified by marriage, blessed perhaps by the pope himself, with choirs of angels singing hymns of praise?"

"It's not—"

"Or is your idea that we sneak out of the back door of the palace one night, dressed like peasants, and head for a village church, to be married by some yokel priest?"

"Leoba dearest, you're a nun in name, but—"

"Paul, what's between us is between us only, and must remain so. Believe me, you're precious to me, and always will be. But you have a path laid out for you that you have to follow, and duties to the Church and to Rome that no one else can fulfill. What you're thinking about—that would destroy your future and lead you to despair. And it would be impossible for me too. Let's remain as we are. Let's enjoy a freedom that has no name, that's known to no one. Stay in Rome, do good work, and wait for my return. The idea of separation is extremely painful to me, I'll miss you every hour of every day, but our love will be the stronger for it. And I *will* return, you can be sure of that."

21

Tap, tap, tap—Omar was working away with his little hammer, fixing fragments of colored glass to a crucifix, when two men, one lean and one fat, entered his workshop. "Good afternoon, reverend sirs," Omar said, rising to greet the strangers. He added: "You've come from far away?" although he realized that they hadn't.

"From the Lateran Palace, if you call that far away," said the lean man, who was dressed as a middle-tier member of the priestly hierarchy.

Omar stiffened. Were these men seeking redress for the language he had used at the papal stables? Or was this something to do with his work on Constantine's donation? Either way, it didn't bode well. But the men didn't seem to know anything about those matters.

"You're a relic-trader, we're told."

"I am. What can I do for you?"

"You may have heard that the Pope will soon be departing on a long journey."

"Yes, I have—everyone's very unhappy about it."

"They should be happy. He is going to seek peace and safety from the Lombards."

"People say he should send his ambassadors. If the Pope

leaves Rome, so will God's protection."

"That's nonsense, Rome will be well looked after—by God, and by the Pope's officials in his absence. Anyway, His Holiness needs many relics for the journey, and we need the help of fine craftsmen such as yourself."

Omar relaxed a bit—this was sounding more positive than he had feared. "What kind of relics?"

The fat man, who wore the dress of a subdeacon, opened a bag and pulled out several sheets of white linen. "These have been touched to the bones of the blessed Apostle Peter. We need you to cut them up into small pieces—this big—and mount them on crosses—like the one you're working on, but smaller—like that one over there." He pointed to a cross the size of a man's palm that was hanging from the wall. "And we need inscriptions for them."

"So you opened the martyr's sarcophagus? I heard nothing of that."

"No, there was a small hole in the lid, which pilgrims used in times past for this same purpose. It was closed with mortar. We reopened the hole, and we lowered the cloths down into the sarcophagus, so that they touched his bones. Then we closed the hole up again. This was all according to the Pope's instructions."

"Then these are powerful relics, certainly," said Omar, "and their power won't be diminished by cutting them smaller. So the pope will give these out on his journey?"

"Yes, to the lesser folk—innkeepers, ostlers, and so forth."

"Oh, instead of paying his bills?" Omar asked with a grin.

The subdeacon frowned. "Such people don't usually request payment from the Holy Father, but they are glad to receive some token of gratitude, especially when there are so many people in his retinue. Now for the people of quality, and for the clergy, we'll need something finer." The subdeacon looked around at Omar's display, and Omar began to envision a major deal.

"I have the best collection of authenticated relics in Rome," he said, "thanks to my many journeys in the East, and my contacts with trustworthy suppliers. Let me show you some things. Here, for example, is my most precious relic—the finger of the blessed Thomas, which he placed in the wound of Christ."

"That's very good," said the priest. "Now let me see what else you can provide." The men picked a number of different relics for purchase or manufacture. Finally they were satisfied, and a discussion over price began.

Omar had an idea. "My son was seized by your people—unjustly so—and now he's a slave and working in the Lateran stables. Do you think we could arrange a deal?"

"What kind of deal?" asked the subdeacon.

"His liberty—in exchange for all these relics we've agreed on?"

The two visitors looked at each other skeptically. Then the subdeacon said: "That wouldn't work. You can't just buy a slave's freedom. And we have no influence over the slave-master. Now it's possible, with the money that we pay you for these, that you could exercise some persuasion. However, I doubt that the money would be enough, frankly, because it is no small matter for the slave-master to let a slave go—he has to arrange for manumission."

"There's another possibility, though," said the priest. "You could petition the pope—especially if some injustice was involved, as you say. If he's sympathetic to your case, he might issue a manumission, and you'd have your son back, at no expense."

"How do I petition the pope?"

"Approach him during his daily procession to mass. Or his brother, who'll take his place after he leaves for Pavia. People will tell you which titular church he's going to that day."

"What should I—"

"The paymaster or another official will hear your request, and the pope or his brother will make a decision, either then or later, depending on whether he has to make inquiries."

"I'll take your advice, thank you. And now, we were discussing the payment for the relics you've requested."

22

O n the morning of the thirteenth of October, a large crowd gathered at the Flaminian Gate to witness the departure of the papal party. As ill luck would have it, Stephen had developed a cough a few days before, and his doctors had advised him to postpone his journey. But with winter not long ahead and a possible crossing of the Alps in the offing, Stephen was reluctant to delay any longer. He did his best to mask his ill-health and express an optimistic view of the journey and its likely outcome.

The party consisted of about thirty-five people. These included two high papal counselors, Archdeacon Theophylact and First Notary Ambrose, neither of whom were very happy with their selection. Theophylact was all too aware of the reason why he had been chosen for a mission that he didn't believe in—to keep him out of the halls of power during the Pope's absence. Thus he was in a sour mood. As for Ambrose, he resented the idea of having to negotiate with Aistulf again, after the ill-faith that Aistulf had shown toward him earlier. Besides, Ambrose was not in the best of health, and at sixty years of age he was well beyond the usual age of persons who undertook such journeys. Still, he could hardly complain on this score to the Pope, who was a few months older than himself. Nor could he complain at Stephen's decision to make the journey on horseback, in the interest of greater speed, rather than in carriages as Ambrose would have preferred.

In addition to these two high counselors, several other officials and clerics were members of the party. There was Ambrose's deputy, the Second Notary, as well as two bishops, Bishop George of Ostia and Bishop Wilchar of Mentana, who was a Frank by birth. Besides these, there were four papal priests and two district administrators. Then there were the two Frankish legates, Archbishop Chrodegang and Duke Autchar, several grooms and other attendants, as well as a small detachment of armed guards under the command of Leo, the chief officer of the Roman militia. Besides all these men, there was one woman—Leoba, who obtained Stephen's permission to join the party after Chrodegang undertook to watch over her.

Any lack of enthusiasm amongst the senior members of the party was more than made up for by the younger participants, particularly the grooms and other attendants, some of whom were skylarking around the crowded area just outside the gate. Even Zaid, who had been quite ambivalent about being chosen, was now chattering excitedly with his peers about the happenings that might lie ahead.

Large numbers of ordinary citizens were mingling with the papal party, in spite of militiamen's efforts to hold them back. The citizens were not in a good mood. Many were remonstrating with the pope or his fellow-travelers, urging them not to leave. Some were expressing their displeasure by wailing or groaning in loud voices. Clearly the Roman people believed, not that the Pope was going on a rescue mission, but that he was abandoning the city to its fate.

Among the onlookers was Lenora, who had walked over from Transtiber without her parents, in the hope of seeing Zaid. The young couple soon caught sight of each other. Because of the general disorganization of the scene, it was easy for them to meet and embrace—they were not the only young couple saying goodbye. They talked in the shade of the tower that guarded the west side of the gate.

"Zaid, I've missed you so much," said Lenora, as the two teenagers held each other close.

"I've missed you too, Lenora—I've missed you every day, every hour."

"Do you have to go on this journey? Can't you get out of it?"

"I've got no choice. But it won't be so bad, and hopefully I'll be back soon."

"Yes, but I'll miss you."

"Me too. But I miss you even when I'm at the stable. Isn't it better to be traveling?"

"I don't know why. Not if you're traveling without me."

"When I come back, and we meet again, I'll have so much to tell you. Hey, you have flour on you—are you working in the bakery already?"

"Yes, I'm trying to earn some money," said Lenora. Then she lowered her voice. "Zaid," she went on, "why don't you slip away with me now? No one will see you, no one's looking. We'll hide you. Let's go." She tried to pull him back through the arch of the Flaminian gate.

"Nora, I can't," said Zaid, resisting her tug. "They'll come after me—they know where to look. And I have this." Zaid touched his left shoulder to indicate the location of his brand.

"Your father told me that he's going to try and get you freed—because it wasn't legal, making you a slave. So you won't need to hide forever."

"Does he know I'm going with the Pope?"

"No, no one knows. I didn't even know—I came over here just in case."

"Who knows if he'll be successful getting me freed?" said Zaid. "Lenora—if I come with you, and they catch me, the least thing they'd do would be send me to a papal estate—where many slaves are worked to death, I've heard. I'd never see Rome again. And the worst they could do—" Zaid put his hands tightly around his throat by way of demonstration.

"Don't talk of such things. I love you so much, I can't bear to think of how long you'll be away, and the dangers you'll be in."

"Dangers—from what?"

"From the Lombards, from bandits, from wild animals—who knows?"

"Nora, my sweetest—nothing bad is going to happen. I'll be with the Pope—and we'll still be in Christendom, where everyone venerates him. Your God will look after him."

"I pray that He'll look after you too."

"He will. And if not, I have my own special protection, from the angel Lenora." Zaid showed Lenora her locket that still hung around his neck. "There's nothing to fear. Besides, I can look after myself. I've seen half the world already—now I'm going to see the other half."

"Zaid—you really want to go, don't you?"

"I'd rather be with you, Nora, but if I can't, then I'd

rather be going on this journey than shoveling muck in a stable all my life. Look, they're getting organized, I've got to go. Tell my father where I'm going, tell him that I'll see him before long, that I'll make him proud of his son—and, and—"

"And what?"

"That I love him in spite of everything."

"I will."

"And you, wait for me, please. I'll be back for you sometime, somehow."

"I will."

"I love you, Lenora."

"I love you, Zaid," said Lenora, as she ran her hand through his curly black hair.

After a quick kiss, Zaid ran back to where the travelers were assembling. But before they could depart, there were prayers to be said. The pope had held a special mass that morning at the Lateran church, but now he led more prayers for the safety of his own party, for the success of their mission, and for the safety of Rome in his absence. The travelers stood with bowed heads, their plain traveling clothes barely distinguishing them from the onlookers. Finally, Stephen blessed his brother and invoked God's guidance for Paul's stewardship of the papal government.

Paul himself was dressed in his usual finery—perhaps he was even more splendidly attired than usual. It looked as if he was the pope and Stephen one of his flock, particularly when Paul spoke a benediction for his brother. The role reversal was not lost on Theophylact or the onlookers. But Paul's gaudy appearance belied his mood. He had watched Zaid and Lenora's amorous embrace with gnawing envy. For his part, he had to avoid even an exchange of glances with Leoba, lest he should lose control of himself and the pain of their separation made itself apparent to all. It completed his misery to see that Ambrose had picked Christopher to accompany him: This was the junior notary on whom Leoba had used her charms to see the council records and to obtain vellum for Omar.

During the prayers, Zaid was standing next to his fellow stable-hand Titus, who had also been chosen for the journey. Titus whispered in Zaid's ear: "So you weren't lying about your girlfriend, you devil."

"No, I told you," Zaid whispered back.

"And she's not half good-looking, with those blue eyes."

"Yes, I told you."

"If I were you, I'd run for it. They'll never be able to follow you, what with the crowd. Live sweet for a day, then take what comes."

Zaid shook his head silently. At least he'd gained some credibility with his peers.

Finally, the Pope and his retinue began to move off. A couple of mounted guards led the way, followed by Stephen and the others. The riders were followed by a couple of wagons that carried the travelers' baggage.

It was a sunny, cool autumn day. It had not rained for several weeks, so the roads were dry. For the first two miles the party, still accompanied by wailing citizens, rode past ancient cemeteries. In places, old tombs formed almost solid walls along the sides of the road. The names of the deceased seemed to compete for the travelers' attention, as the deceased had intended.

The travelers soon reached the Milvian Bridge. Stephen

reminded his companions how, at this bridge four centuries previously, the God of the Christians had granted Constantine a great victory over Maxentius—his brother-in-law and rival for the imperial scepter. The Tiber had run red with the blood of the defeated forces, and Maxentius himself suffered an ignominious death by drowning. "With God's help, Aistulf will perish in the same way, if he dares attack Rome," Stephen said.

On this day, however, the river ran clear and placid, and willows along the bank stirred in the gentle breeze. The travelers crossed the bridge to reach the west bank of the Tiber, where they turned left onto the Cassian Way. They entered a rolling landscape dotted with market gardens, woods, and small homesteads. It might have been a pleasant enough ride, except for the onlookers who continued to walk or run along the pope's side, keeping up their supplications. Others joined them from the local villages, swelling the crowd. The guards were kept busy clearing the pope's way. This went on for hour after hour, and the travelers were glad to reach a monastery near the eighteenth milestone, where they stayed the night.

The next day, the travelers started early and made better time. There were fewer supplicants to delay them, so the travelers had more freedom to talk among themselves; Archbishop Chrodegang, for example, discussed with Leoba the deplorable state of the Frankish clergy and what he hoped to do about it.

At the summit of a long climb, the travelers paused. Ambrose, who was familiar with the road from his many diplomatic journeys, pointed out several landmarks. Below them, to the west of the road, lay the wide expanse of the Sabatine Lake, the origin of Trajan's aqueduct. Along the northeast horizon ran the ridge-like summit of Mount Soracte, where Sylvester hid from Constantine before the Emperor's conversion. Stephen expressed a wish to visit the place, but Ambrose said that it was too far off their route.

By early afternoon the travelers had already reached Sutri, where they had planned to spend the night. Not wanting to waste daylight, Stephen and his companions decided to take a quick lunch and push on. By the time they reached the fortieth milestone, however, darkness was falling, and there was no obvious habitation in sight. The riders stopped and Leo consulted his itinerary.

"The town of Vetralla is two miles ahead," he said. "It's just within Tuscany, so it's under Lombard control."

Stephen wasn't too happy about the idea of approaching the first Lombard town in the dark, but there was little choice, and the party began to move on again.

"Look, what's that?" shouted several of the travelers at the same moment. A great fiery globe was lighting up the sky; it shone so brightly that it cast shadows of the horses and their riders onto the road. The light was ahead of them, to the north, but it quickly and silently traversed the entire arc of the sky toward the south, while the men's shadows swung at equal speed toward the north. Finally, the light sank out of view below the southern horizon. After it had disappeared, the twilight seemed much darker than before.

Several of the horses shied or attempted to bolt, and their riders had trouble calming them. The travelers themselves were terrified. What was it that they saw? What did it signify? In their fear and perplexity, they turned to their spiritual leader. Stephen collected himself as best he could, and said: "It was a falling star."

"A falling star—an omen, then?" asked one or several voices.

"An omen, yes, by God's will."

"Meaning what?"

Stephen paused. "A great evil," he said finally. "A great evil is coming to Rome—from the north."

"What evil? What's going to happen?"

"It must be the Lombards," he said.

There was general consternation. "So they'll destroy us?"

"I'm not sure," Stephen responded.

Theophylact spoke up. "We should turn back immediately," he said, forgetting to add "Your Holiness." "The Lord is telling us that our journey will end badly if we enter Lombardy. Let's turn back now."

One of the priests joined in. "This is like what happened with Sylvester, Your Holiness. That was a sign to stop the procession. This is a sign to stop our journey, before something terrible happens." Several others in the party seemed to agree.

Stephen's mind was seized by anxiety and doubt, but he struggled to regain control of the situation. "What happened with Sylvester turned out to be a blessing," he said. "He gave us Constantine's deed, which will be the key to our salvation. And this sign—"

Theophylact spoke up again. "Your Holiness, regarding that deed, you ordered us to cease any further discussion about its origin, and we *have* kept silence, as you ordered. But in this moment, when it's so important, I beg leave—leave to—"

"Leave to what?"

"Leave to revisit this issue, Your Holiness. Because I have certain knowledge that the deed—that it wasn't—may I speak about this, Your Holiness?"

What a time to bring up this issue again, Stephen thought. Theophylact was clearly intent on undermining the whole justification for their journey. But if he cut off the Archdeacon, it wouldn't solve the problem. Others would pester him about what he knew until he told them, and Stephen himself would be the only person left in ignorance. "Speak, then," he said, "but keep it brief. It's getting dark— we can't spend the night here."

"Thank you, Your Holiness," said Theophylact, while the other travelers moved closer to hear his words. "So, Your Holiness will remember that the deed was signed by Constantine when he was Consul for the fourth time, and that the other Consul during that year was a man named Gallicanus, according to the deed?"

"Perhaps. Yes, I think so. What about it?"

"The historian Ammianus, who was living at the same time as Constantine, and who was most truthful in everything he wrote—I was reading his history, in connection with some other matter. And in the year that Constantine was Consul for the fourth time, he says that the other Consul was Licinius, not Gallicanus. The only year in which Gallicanus was Consul was two years after Constantine's fourth term, when the other Consul was a man named Bassus. So is it credible that Constantine put down the name of a man who wasn't Consul, and who never had been Consul up to that time? Could he have been mistaken about who his fellow Consul was at that very moment when he was writing, even though that Consul was surely appointed by himself? No, only someone writing long afterwards could have made such a blunder—when the names of the Consuls were no longer common knowledge. Only a forger, in other words."

Stephen felt a sickening dread rising in his stomach, as if his papal authority was draining away and the whole world was about to collapse around him. If only Paul were here—he would know what to say or do, he always had the right answer to Theo. He should have brought Paul on this journey. Perhaps it wasn't too late to send for him. But while Stephen was searching around for some way to rescue the situation, Leoba spoke up.

"Your Holiness, if I may make a comment on what we've just heard?"

"Go ahead, Sister Leoba," said Stephen, hoping for some relief.

"The Archdeacon is right about what Ammianus wrote," she said firmly. "But what Ammianus wrote was an error. When those events happened, he must have been an infant or a very young child—much too young to know anything about who the Consuls were. And he didn't write his history of those years until he was an old man. So he was writing about what had happened almost a lifetime—"

"Ammianus would have checked the—"

Leoba ignored Theophylact's interruption. "What's more," she went on, "he had every reason to be mistaken, because this Gallicanus was a nobody whose name was quickly forgotten by everyone, whereas Licinius was Constantine's great rival and co-emperor—before he was executed, that is. In fact, Ammianus may have suppressed

Gallicanus's name on purpose: Gallicanus was the first Christian Consul, but Ammianus was a pagan, and he worked for Julian, the cursed apostate. It would have pleased Julian to erase the memory of Gallicanus."

Theophylact finally got a word in. "I'm sure that Constantine and Licinius were Consuls together."

"That's true," Leoba went on, "But not in the year when Constantine was Consul for the fourth time. In that year it was Gallicanus, just as Constantine's deed states, and when we return to Rome I can show you unquestionable authority for this." And there must be *some* authority, Leoba thought to herself, because Paul wouldn't have just plucked a name out of the air, would he? Besides, most likely I'll be returning to Rome later than the others, by which time the whole issue will have been forgotten.

To Leoba's surprise, Notary Christopher weighed in on her side. "As I recall, your Holiness, what the sister says is correct—it was Gallicanus, not Licinius, in that year."

Leoba gave him a quick smile of gratitude, but Ambrose was annoyed by his subordinate's presumption in joining the debate. "Your Holiness," he broke in, "it's getting dark and cold. Whether we continue on or head back, we should do so soon. If we wait much longer, we may not be able to rouse the gatekeepers at Vetralla. And behind us, it's miles to the next decent habitation, as we've seen."

Archbishop Chrodegang also put in a word. "Duke Autchar and myself at least—we have to go on. We're obliged to return to Francia, Your Holiness."

"Thank you, Sister," said Stephen finally. In general, he had a poor opinion of Leoba, whom he considered unwomanly. And now it worried him a little that Leoba didn't give the name of her 'unquestionable authority.' But her words did allow him a much-needed breathing space, and they enabled him to suppress any doubts he might have had about the Donation. "Look, that boy there," he said, pointing to Zaid, who was standing a few paces away with Titus, holding the reins of two horses in his hands. "That boy took the deed directly from Sylvester's grasp. We all saw it. The deed is not a forgery, Theo. And that's enough on this subject—for now and forever."

The Archdeacon said nothing, and Bishop Wilchar filled the silence. "So be it, Your Holiness," he said. "But what about the falling star? If evil is coming to Rome—"

"Yes, it tells of Aistulf coming to Rome with a great army," said Stephen with more assurance. "But didn't you see—when it reached the south, the star was extinguished, leaving no trace. That's telling us that Aistulf will be destroyed, him and his army, if he dares to attack our city."

Some of the travelers remained unconvinced, and they continued to urge retreat, but Stephen wouldn't hear of it. "Let's pray for God's forgiveness for our sins," he said, "and He'll be merciful to us."

Those who were still on their horses dismounted, and Stephen led a prayer of penance and supplication. After a pause, the travelers remounted—in the absence of any convenient mounting blocks, Zaid and Titus had to help several of them get up. Then they continued on their northward journey, some of them reassured, and others still gripped by fear or despondency.

23

———

"Leo is back? So soon?" asked Paul.

"Yes, sir," said his chamberlain, a stocky man named Calvulus. "When the Holy Father reached Vetralla, the Lombards insisted that their militiamen should provide the escort to Pavia, rather than Leo's men. So Leo returned to Rome, but he left several men near the border, in case the Holy Father or one of his counselors should return unexpectedly."

The two men were talking in Stephen's chambers, which Paul had taken over for the duration of his brother's absence.

"I hope the Lombards treat the Holy Father with the proper respect, and keep him safe," Paul said. "I would have been much happier to hear that Leo had gone with him the entire way. When he has rested, please ask him to come by. I'd like to learn more about how their journey has gone so far."

"Yes, sir. And, sir, the man who petitioned you during yesterday's procession—the craftsman named Omar—he's arrived as you requested. He's waiting downstairs."

"Oh yes. Did you make the inquiries that I ask for?"

"Yes, sir. His son was enslaved, as he said—for the theft of a cloak at the vegetable market. He was enslaved after he refused baptism. He was put to work in the stables here, but now he has been sent as a groom with the Holy Father."

"Very well, thank you. Please bring the man in."

Calvulus left with a bow, and Paul went over what had happened at the procession the day before. It had halted briefly, as was usual when an onlooker presented a petition. Omar stated his case to Philip, the paymaster, and then Philip relayed it to Paul. After some discussion, Paul and Philip agreed that Omar's petition had no merit. Paul beckoned Omar to come forward, and briefly told him of the rejection. Then, instead of simply bowing and retreating, Omar said "I had hoped that Your Holiness would look favorably on my petition, especially because of the work I did on the document for the lady Leoba."

Paul had difficulty maintaining his demeanor. Leoba hadn't told him the name of the person who had produced the antique version of the Donation, but now he realized that it must have been Omar. So he was still in Rome, even though Leoba had given Paul to understand that he had been planning to leave the city. The fact that Omar would allude to the matter, even very obliquely, in this public setting made Paul uneasy. To cut off any further opportunity for embarrassment, he said: "Well, come to my chambers at the palace tomorrow and we'll listen more carefully, but I don't expect that we'll change our mind." With that, he signaled the procession to continue.

Paul's thoughts turned from Omar to Leoba. It was only five days since she had left, but his heart was already aching. The fact that he couldn't discuss their relationship with anyone made his loneliness even harder to deal with. At least it would be appropriate to ask Leo about her, so long as he didn't seem excessively concerned.

The chamberlain returned with Omar, interrupting Paul's daydreaming. "Come in," said Paul, and the two men entered. "You may leave us, Calvulus, he added."

"Shall I send a notary, sir?"

"No, won't be necessary, thank you."

"Very well, sir," said Calvulus, and he closed the door behind him as he left.

Paul and Omar stood facing each other—the tall Deacon in his ornate vestments, and the swarthy craftsman in his working clothes. Omar waited to be addressed.

"You were petitioning for manumission of your son, as I recall," said Paul.

"That's right, Your Holiness."

"Don't call me 'Your Holiness'—that's reserved for the Pope, whose place I am taking for a short time. Sir is sufficient."

"Very good—sir. Yes, his name's Zaid. Your magistrate enslaved him in the belief that he was an orphan or a vagabond, but that was a mistake—he's my son, and I'm a legal resident of Rome. I'm a trader and craftsman from Syria."

"You mentioned a document that you prepared. Which document was that?"

Omar trod carefully. Leoba hadn't told him who was party to the forgery. He had guessed that Paul was involved, and the fact that Paul had hurriedly offered him a private audience certainly suggested that he was in on the plot. Still, Omar wasn't certain. "The document given to me by the lady Leoba, sir, which needed to be written out in a special style."

Paul was now certain that Omar was referring to Constantine's Donation. "That assignment was supposed to be undertaken in completely confidence. I'm surprised that you brought it up yesterday when several people were present."

"I tried not to be too direct," said Omar. "But I felt that I needed to broach the subject, so that Your Holiness—that you might take my efforts on your behalf into consideration, sir."

"You were well recompensed for your work, weren't you?"

"Fairly recompensed, yes, sir," said Omar.

"Well then, we don't owe you anything more."

"No, sir, but it's not a matter of money owed. I was hoping for my son's release as a courtesy—considering the quality of my work, and my willingness to do the work secretly and to keep the strictest confidence about it since then. I realize that it would be extremely unfortunate for my role in this to become known, and so I haven't spoken a word about it to anyone. Doesn't that deserve some consideration, sir?"

Paul wondered whether this was a threat. "Wasn't it part of the agreement that you would leave Rome after the work was complete?"

"I did mention to the lady Leoba that I hoped to set out on my travels soon, but there have been some delays."

"Can you leave now?"

"If Zaid is returned to me, sir, then yes."

Paul thought for a moment. It didn't seem like he had any

other choice than agree to Omar's request. Doing so shouldn't arouse any particular suspicion, so long as it was done properly.

"Well, I'm sympathetic to your case. Your son would probably not have been enslaved if it were known at the time that he was living with his father in Rome, or was temporarily separated from him. My understanding is that he denied having a father, so the magistrate's sentence was justified based on what he knew at the time. Now I know the real situation, I'd like to help you."

"I'm very glad to hear that, sir," said Omar.

"In the normal way, I could issue a manumission in the name of the Pope, who is absent from Rome. However, your son is traveling with the Holy Father; therefore he's under the Holy Father's direct control—I can't send a letter of manumission to the very person who has the ultimate power in this matter, you understand?"

"I do, sir."

"But I can send an informal letter, laying out the reasons why I believe your son's sentence was in error, and recommending a manumission, which the Holy Father will then issue, I expect. Still, you must understand that this may take considerable time—the Holy Father may continue on from Pavia to Francia, and if so he'll be hurrying to cross the high passes before winter. A letter may not reach him until next year."

"I understand, sir."

"In the meantime, you must undertake to maintain complete secrecy in this matter. There'll be serious consequences for you if you don't. And you must leave Rome as soon as your son is returned to you."

"I'll speak of this to no one," Omar said, "and we'll leave Rome the moment Zaid returns. I'm extremely grateful to Your Holiness for your generous offer."

"Sir," said Paul.

"Excuse me—sir. They say that 'Your Holiness' will be the right phrase, one day."

"Enough of that. Now go. The letter will be written." Paul rang for the chamberlain, who escorted Omar down the staircase and out of the palace. Paul remained standing in his chamber, lost in a sea of anxious thoughts.

24

Ten days after leaving Vetralla, the papal party reached the Tuscan city of Lucca, where they planned to rest for two nights. Most of the travelers were already quite tired from their journey, even though it had been fairly easy going. Stephen's cough had worsened, and Ambrose was also looking unwell, so they looked forward to the short break. In addition, Stephen planned to participate in a special mass in honor of Lucca's celebrated relic, the Holy Face.

The Holy Face was a life-size wooden statue of Jesus on the Cross, which, according to the Luccans, was sculpted by the Pharisee Nicodemus—the man who assisted Joseph of Arimathea in preparing Jesus's body for burial. What made the sculpture especially worthy of veneration was this: when Nicodemus had completed the entire sculpture except for the face, he gave up on the project, fearing that he could not do justice to Jesus' visage. Then, while he was sleeping, an angel miraculously completed it. Thus, beyond any doubt, the face was an exact portrayal of the face of Jesus.

This sculpture had appeared in Lucca just eleven years before Stephen's visit. It had lain forgotten in a cave in the Holy Land for centuries, until a visiting pilgrim found it and placed in on a small ship, which he pushed off to sea without a human crew. This ship, on its own account, took the statue to Luni, on the Ligurian coast north of Lucca. Because it arrived in such a strange way, strapped to the mast of an unmanned vessel, the citizens of Luni and Lucca fought for ownership of it. Eventually, they decided to let the Divine Will decide between their competing claims. The statue was loaded onto an ox-cart, and the oxen were allowed to go on their way without human guidance. They headed straight for Lucca. Some inhabitants of Luni complained that their rivals had played a trick on them. Luccan oxen had been hitched to the cart, they asserted, so the animals followed their natural instinct and returned to their home city. To the Luccans, on the other hand, the oxen's choice proved that their city was the relic's intended home, and they gave it a place of honor in the cathedral of St. Martin.

The fame of the Holy Face and its miraculous journey had spread far and wide, and pilgrims came from distant lands to venerate it and to cut chips off of it for talismans. Already, a decade later, the Holy Face was barely recognizable as a face at all, but this only added to its holiness. Zachary had twice visited Lucca to see it, and he had led processions in which the statue was carried around the city on the same ox-cart on which it had arrived. Stephen and his retinue now participated enthusiastically in the same ceremony. Even Theophylact, whose Eastern sympathies made him suspicious of these kinds of doings, could find nothing to object to. After all, no human hand had been involved in the creation of the Holy Face.

The procession started at the cathedral, made its way northward to the ruined amphitheater—a miniature

Colosseum—and thence to the nearby church of St. Fridianus. After prayers there, the procession took a winding route back to the cathedral, a route that took in some other churches as well as many of the tiny city's back streets. The people greeted the Pope and his companions with unabashed enthusiasm, for Desiderius, the Duke of Tuscany, was a puppet installed by Aistulf and was not much loved by the Luccans; their sympathies lay more with Rome.

Leoba participated in the procession. She had her own personal reason to visit the church of St. Fridianus, however, for one of her uncles was buried there. This was Richard, her mother's older brother, who had been traveling on a pilgrimage to Rome with his two sons Willibald and Winnebald, Leoba's cousins. At Lucca he fell ill and died, and the two youths had to continue on without his guidance. Leoba took the opportunity to clean her uncle's gravestone and to pray for his soul.

While the pope and the other Roman officials were taking part in the ceremony, Zaid was left on his own. His experience of the journey so far had been much more positive than that of his elders. The fellowship of the road had broken down much of the formality and class-consciousness of Roman life. Stephen's companions often neglected to add "Your Holiness" to every utterance directed toward him, and he didn't correct them. Even the servants and slaves found themselves free to chat with the people of quality.

Because Zaid was the person who received Constantine's Donation from Sylvester's hand, Stephen had come to view him as a bringer of good fortune, in spite of his false religion. In addition, Stephen couldn't help identifying Zaid with St. Pancras, the martyr in whom he took a particular interest. After all, both of them were fourteen-year-old boys from the East. Stephen even toyed with the idea of commissioning a new wall-painting of the saint, using Zaid as the model, when they returned to Rome. He had the image already in his mind: With his slender frame, youthful smile, and curly back hair, and already stripped for execution, Zaid stood with his hand resting indolently on the hilt of the immense sword that would be the instrument of his martyrdom. Well, it couldn't be quite like that, Stephen realized—except in his private imagination.

For these reasons, Stephen picked Zaid out as the person to assist him on many occasions during their journey. Whenever the party had to make a difficult detour around a damaged stretch of road, for example, he would have Zaid lead his horse on foot. He made the same request when a thunderstorm struck, and Zaid was able to keep Stephen's horse calm when some of the other riders had difficulty controlling their mounts. Stephen was generous in allowing Zaid to take some time off for his prayers, even if that held up the group briefly. And from time to time he asked Zaid questions about himself and his family, or got him to recount stories from his travels—stories that seemed quite exotic to Stephen.

The procession honoring the Holy Face was to be made on foot, however, so Zaid was not needed, and after he had seen to the horses' needs he left the stables and wandered around the city, taking in the sights. He asked a few people whether they knew Lenora's grandparents, and by luck one woman did—she directed Zaid to their home, which was on one of the narrow alleys that had sprung up on the ruins of the ancient Forum. No one was at home, but Zaid waited, and eventually the elderly couple came back from the church of St. Michael, where they been watching the procession pass by.

Zaid introduced himself to them as Lenora's betrothed. They were surprised and skeptical.

"She's only a young girl," said the grandfather, who was a soap-boiler by trade. "Far too young for marriage—are you sure you mean our granddaughter?" But Zaid reminded them of how many years had passed since Lenora and her parents had left Lucca, and he explained that they were not intending to marry for several years yet.

Then Zaid showed them the locket that was hanging around his neck. "She gave me this to remember her—look, this is her hair!"

"That locket!" said Lenora's grandmother with a little shriek. "I gave it to her. I got it from *my* grandmother, *many* years ago. I hope you'll keep it safe. I'd like it to go to *her* granddaughter." And then she corrected herself with a smile: "—hers and yours."

The locket was the clincher. The old couple devoured Zaid with questions about Sibyl and her family, insisted that Zaid share a meal with them, and gave him a small amount of money. When Zaid departed, they wanted to load him with presents for Lenora and her parents, but Zaid explained that he was traveling north, perhaps to Francia. He promised to call in again on his return journey, if the pope should take the same route back, to pick up the presents then.

"It's dangerous in Rome," said the grandfather as Zaid left. "There's no future there—Rome is history. Here there's plenty of work, and it's safe. Tell them to come back to

Lucca. And come back yourself—bring Lenora." Zaid's race and religion didn't seem to concern them.

25

On the afternoon of the tenth of November, the pope and his retinue finally reached the city of Pavia. The travelers had mixed feelings about their arrival. They welcomed the prospect of another short break from traveling, because the weather had turned cold, and the hilly terrain on the route from Lucca had taken its toll on both the travelers and their horses. On the other hand, the meeting with Aistulf was not likely to be amicable, or to result in any resolution of the crisis. And with winter rapidly approaching, the thought of tackling the far higher and more difficult passes of the Alps weighed on everyone's mind.

The travelers had crossed the Po at Piacenza, so they approached Pavia from the east, and their destination was visible across the flat expanses of the Po Valley for a long time before they arrived under its walls. The city lay on the north bank of the little Ticino River, which was spanned by an ancient stone bridge.

Gazing at the pocket-sized city, Stephen wondered how it could possibly pose a threat to Rome. "Surely a dozen Pavias could fit inside our walls," he remarked to Ambrose.

"That's true," said the First Notary. "But this scene

would look very different if Aistulf had summoned his army to greet us. Their camp would stretch from the city walls to way over there." He gestured vaguely toward the northern horizon. "Pavia isn't a center of trade, there's no mining or manufacture here to speak of. Just Aistulf's court, a school of grammar, and a few churches. It's simply a meeting point for his army, and for the armies of his allies."

The pope called the party to a halt and sent Duke Autchar ahead to sound out the King. He returned an hour later. "The King bids Your Holiness welcome and promises you safety and hospitality in his city," Autchar reported. "He'll be pleased to meet you when you are rested, and he'll be honored if you will be willing to lead a mass at the Cathedral of St. Mary. But he commands you not to mention certain topics—Ravenna and the other cities and territories that are in dispute between him and Your Holiness."

"He commands me? What kind of greeting is that?"

"Forgive me, Your Holiness, but those were his words that I'm reporting to you."

"Why did we come from Rome then?" asked Stephen angrily. "To play a game of Nine Men's Morris? To go shad-fishing in the Ticino?"

Autchar couldn't think of anything to say in response, and Stephen went on. "Lead us into the city. We'll meet with Aistulf, and we'll bring up all the issues that need to be discussed, whether he likes it or not."

The party moved forward. The city, though very small, looked well-nigh impregnable: the wall was high enough to block any view of the buildings within, and it was well furnished with bastions from which defenders could harass any would-be attackers with arrows or rocks. Stephen recalled how the Goths, after they were defeated by the Lombard King Alboin in a pitched battle near the city, held out in Pavia for three years before starvation forced the survivors to surrender. Alboin made the city his new capital, and over the following two centuries the Lombards raised the wall higher and improved the city's defenses in other ways. Yet so far, these defenses had not been put to the test: as with Rome in its years of glory, the Lombard realm had expanded so widely that no hostile army had been able to come anywhere near to the capital.

The gate stood open, and the Lombard guards led the way into the city. A few people gazed curiously at the visitors from street corners or from the windows of buildings, but the bulk of the populace was either ignorant of the visitors' identity or had not been forewarned of their arrival. Thus in just a few minutes the Pope and his retinue reached Aistulf's palace. It was a large brick edifice in the center of the city; it had been built by the Ostrogoth King Theodoric for his use when traveling away from his capital at Ravenna. A middle-ranking official greeted the visitors and showed them to their quarters.

On the following morning Aistulf greeted the Pope briefly, and accompanied him to the cathedral, where he led a mass. Afterwards, Stephen handed Aistulf an ornately-bound gospel book and several other presents. Finally Stephen, Ambrose, and Theophylact sat down with Aistulf and some of his aides in a drafty hall of the palace.

To Stephen, Aistulf didn't look particularly regal. Certainly, the Lombard king was tall and finely dressed, and he was wearing the Iron Crown. But he had an uncomfortable, darting look, and squirmed on his throne, as if he was longing to scratch himself. In addition, he seemed consumed by anxiety that his crown—which was several sizes too small for him—would fall off his head, and he sometimes had to adjust its position.

Stephen cast about for an innocuous topic to start the dialogue, and he settled on the crown. "Your Most Catholic Majesty," he said, "the famous crown that you are wearing—I'm extremely happy to see it, because I have heard that it contains one of the most sacred relics in Christendom."

"Yes, Your Holiness," replied Aistulf. "I had it brought specially from Monza for this occasion, because I thought that you'd be interested in it." He seemed glad to take the thing off his head, and he offered it to Stephen for inspection.

Stephen took the crown, wondering momentarily whether this was an unexpected gesture of obeisance. The outer surface of the crown was gold and enamel, set with precious stones. "Look inside," said Aistulf.

The inner surface of the crown was gold too, except for a thin strip of rusty iron around the inner circumference. "This, as you know, was made from one of the Holy Nails used at Our Savior's crucifixion."

"Yes indeed," said Stephen. He closed his eyes and offered a short prayer of veneration, while Aistulf took the opportunity to relieve his itch. His prayer completed, Stephen went on. "And as I understand, the Lombard Queen Theodelinda received the crown from Gregory, the first pope of that name?"

"That's correct," said Aistulf. "The crown was for her son Adaloard."

"All Catholics honor Theodelinda, because she rejected

the Arian heresy and baptized her son in the Catholic faith."

"Yes, unfortunately Adaloard went mad and had to be put away."

If this was a hint at some connection between the baptism and the insanity, Stephen ignored it. "Another person for whom we have great reverence is the blessed Severinus Boethius," he went on, "who was imprisoned by Theodoric here in Pavia for twelve months, and then executed in the most inhumane manner. The work that he wrote during that time—*The Consolation of Philosophy*—it has been very instructive to me and others."

"I haven't read it," said Aistulf, "but Boethius is entombed here, in the church of St. Peter."

"Boethius was martyred for his Catholic faith by the Arian heretic, Theodoric."

"Is that so?" said Aistulf, who seemed to know little or nothing about the famous author or about Arianism.

"Yes, it's thanks to such people as Theodelinda and Boethius that the more recent Lombard monarchs, such as yourself, acknowledge the true Catholic faith and the spiritual supremacy of St. Peter and his successors."

Aistulf began to wonder if Stephen was leading him into some kind of trap. "There are no doctrinal differences between us, that I'm aware of," he said blandly.

"No, I am glad that that is so—such a happy change from former days!" Stephen paused momentarily, and then went on: "In Heaven, great rewards lie in store for monarchs who respect the patrimony of St. Peter, and great punishments for those who would harm it."

Aistulf realized that Stephen was trying to introduce the forbidden topic of conversation by a back door, and he was not happy. "Your Holiness is confusing two different matters, if I may say so," he said. "I and my people fully acknowledge the spiritual authority of Rome. But that doesn't mean that Rome is the rightful owner of the lands that are in dispute between us. Are you suggesting that Ravenna is part of the patrimony of St. Peter? When was that ever so? Would the Emperor agree with you on that? I don't think so. Aren't you just trying to get hold of a city that you never owned—by words instead of by arms?"

Theophylact inwardly agreed with Aistulf, but he was shocked by the Lombard's disrespectful tone, and he broke in. "Your Majesty, His Holiness is not addressed in that fashion," he said.

Stephen tried to calm the situation. "I never mentioned Ravenna, Your Majesty," he said. "With Ravenna, there's a complicated history. In the peace treaty that we signed, we agreed not to dispute the ownership of that city. But what about Ceccano? For hundreds of years that city has been part of our patrimony—no one has ever doubted it."

"Ceccano—a city?" said Aistulf scornfully. "Call it a village and you'd be exaggerating. A few barracks behind a broken-down wall, as I've been told, and a couple of goats."

"Ceccano is part of the patrimony of the Blessed Peter, and you seized it, in violation of the treaty."

"The Beneventans seized it."

"Under your orders," put in Ambrose. "We learned that directly from your messengers."

"You lie," said Aistulf, looking directly at Ambrose for the first time.

Ambrose got up from his chair, as if he was about to deliver a stinging rebuke, but Stephen headed him off.

"Gentlemen," he said, "this intemperate language must cease, so that we can discuss our dispute and find a peaceful solution."

"There *is* no discussion," said Aistulf. "No discussion! Why should I discuss these matters with you? God has ordained that the Lombards will be masters of Italy."

"Don't presume to tell the Holy Father what God has ordained," broke in Ambrose again. "You broke God's ordinance at Ravenna, when you allowed your men to violate and murder innocent women in the churches."

"Those women weren't innocent. They hurled down tiles and stones from the rooftops, killing my soldiers. When women become combatants, the Christian Law permits retribution."

"Your Majesty," said Stephen, still trying to maintain a modicum of civility, "you rightly distinguish between spiritual and temporal authority. '*Reddite ergo quae sunt Caesaris—Render therefore unto Caesar the things which are Caesar's, and unto God the things which are God's.*' But the Pope is not lacking in temporal authority—far from it. Recently, a deed written by the Emperor Constantine was miraculously revealed to us—it was given to us from the long-dead hand of the blessed Sylvester, who received it from the Emperor himself. We have a copy for you here—please give it to His Majesty, Ambrose. The deed was written when the Emperor was baptized and decided to move his capital to the East. It cedes all temporal authority over the Western Empire to Sylvester and his successors. So all the western kings and princes, including yourself, rule by our grace. Please look at the deed."

"Keep your deed," said Aistulf scornfully, pushing it back

across the table to Ambrose. "I've got no use for it. I'm a soldier, not a monk. Do you think I waste my time reading?"

"But I can tell you the meaning of it," said Stephen. "The deed states that—"

"I don't have to know anything about this so-called deed," said Aistulf. "You have temporal authority over me? What nonsense is that? My army is stronger than yours, therefore I have authority over you—it's that simple."

"Your Majesty misunderstands what—"

"This audience has gone on too long," said Aistulf, rising. "I've other matters to attend to."

"We'll leave," said Stephen, rising too. "But it'll be with a heavy heart if we accomplish nothing. Let's meet one more time, when passions have cooled, to see if we can find some points of agreement."

"There's no point—leave Pavia."

"Very well," said Stephen, "if nothing more can be done."

"Nothing. And by the way, let me ask you, why is Duke Autchar with you, and the Frankish cleric?"

"They came to Rome—they brought an invitation for me to visit the Frankish king."

"Are you planning to travel to Francia, then? Perhaps you imagine that King Pepin will come to your aid with his army? Your journey will be in vain, let me assure you. Save yourselves the trouble, because Pepin won't help you. The Franks and the Lombards are friends."

"We *are* planning to visit Pepin, yes," said Stephen. "But as to the purpose of our journey, that is our concern."

"By what road are you hoping to get there?"

"By the Frankish passes."

"Through Lombard territory, then? Well, you may not do so—I forbid it! My soldiers will stop you. Return the way you came—before I run out of patience."

Aistulf changed his mind the very next day. Early in the morning he received a visit from Duke Autchar, who told him that the Frankish king would be greatly distressed if the Pope was not permitted to travel to Francia. This gave Aistulf pause, because the friendship between the Lombards and the Franks, of which he had boasted to Stephen the day before, was really quite tenuous, and it related more to the Frankish nobles than to Pepin himself. In addition, Aistulf had recently learned that some Slavic tribes, who had been beaten back in their efforts to take Constantinople, were now threatening his Istrian territories. Faced with the possibility of having to campaign on his eastern frontier, Aistulf didn't want to disturb the relationship with his powerful northern neighbor. He therefore told Autchar that the pope and his retinue could depart for the Frankish passes after all.

They did so immediately, leaving Pavia through its western gate. Stephen and his companions traveled as fast as they could toward the mountains, and in just six days they reached the relative safety of Aosta, an outpost of the Frankish realm. Stephen and his companions therefore performed a litany of thanksgiving for their deliverance from Aistulf. The citizens of the town, who had no love for the Lombards, joined in the celebration and offered the travelers their finest accommodation as well as food and drink in abundance. The pope reciprocated with a generous distribution of relics.

On the following day, the going got harder as the travelers climbed out of the valley floor, but they still made it in good time to their intended resting place on the south side of the Mons Jovis pass, the village of St. Rhemy, which lay less than four thousand feet below the summit. Here they met several travelers who had just crossed the pass in the southward direction; they said that the pass was mostly free of snow, despite the season. But they complained bitterly about the state of the road: only near the summit, where the Roman engineers had cut the roadway into solid rock, was it in good condition. Elsewhere, they said, the road surface was badly broken, necessitating many awkward diversions. The papal travelers slept uneasily.

26

The next morning dawned clear but very cold. Stephen and his companions had exchanged their horses for mules, and hired a guide to see them over the pass. They started out at first light, because fifteen miles of difficult terrain lay ahead before the first resting place on the other side of the pass, the little village and hostelry of St. Peter. The first seven of these miles would be an unrelenting climb to the eight-thousand-foot pass known as Jove's Mountain. After a prayer for a safe crossing, they set out from St. Rhemy, well bundled in cloaks and blankets, their breath steaming in the frigid air.

Above them, the sun was already illuminating the alpine peaks, but the valley itself lay in deep shadow, and the travelers followed the course of a stream upward through a forest. After a mile, the road turned left and began to switchback up the side of the valley. Everyone looked forward to coming out of the shadows into the sunshine, but a bank of clouds rolled across the sun, leaving them as cold as ever.

The route continued through the trees, which allowed only occasional glimpses of the valley below or the slopes ahead. After about an hour, however, the forest began to thin out. Now the travelers faced a vast rocky amphitheater; in places they could see the road clinging to the slopes as it circled upward and to the right, leading to the pass.

The sky was now heavily overcast, and the guide urged them to keep up a good pace, in case conditions worsened. Stephen asked if they should turn back to St. Rhemy and wait for better weather. "You might have to wait until May," was his response, so they continued on.

After another hour, they came to the first serious obstacle: the road was blocked by a rockslide that couldn't be crossed, even with mules. The guide was familiar with this slide and led the group on a diversion, but it was very steep and difficult, and almost another hour had passed before they found themselves back on the road a quarter mile beyond the slide. At that point, it began to snow. The summit ahead of them, which had lain in clear view, was now sometimes obscured by scudding masses of fog that were blowing over the pass from the south.

Beset by increasing anxiety, Stephen and his party continued on their way. The farther they climbed, the worse the condition of the road, and there were several more diversions, some nearly as time-consuming as the first one. The snow began to fall more heavily and to accumulate on the road surface, sometimes concealing rocks and holes. The wind also picked up, and although it came mostly from behind them, there were frequent occasions when turns in the road brought the wind into their faces. At those times, the driving snow was almost unbearable, and the riders tried to mask themselves with their cloaks or whatever else was at hand. Now the summit had disappeared entirely from view, even though it was only about five hundred feet above them.

While they were taking a brief respite in the lee of a large rock, a group of Frankish pilgrims met them on their way down to St. Rhemy. They told the Romans that they started at the hostelry of St. Peter that morning; they said that the road had been clear of snow and in reasonably good condition until they approached the summit, where they had a great deal of difficulty on account of the snow and wind in their faces. They confirmed what Stephen's guide already knew, which was that there were no habitations at the summit or between the summit and St. Peter.

Stephen consulted with the guide. Without the sun, it was difficult to judge the hour, but the guide acknowledged that it was becoming less and less likely that they would make it to St. Peter before dark. Still, there were various shelters along the way, he said, which would serve to protect them in an emergency. They decided to press onward, if for no other reason than to avoid turning their faces back into the driving wind and snow.

Stephen asked Zaid to lead his mule for the final stretch to the summit, and Zaid was happy to do so. For one thing, walking would keep him warmer. Also, he had been riding one of the pack mules, and the combined weight of himself and the baggage had caused the mule to tire and lag behind the others. The guide had emphasized the importance of staying together, and Zaid had no desire to be cut off from the other riders. So he trudged along, leading Stephen's mule as well as the pack mule he had been riding, who was now able to keep up with the others without too much difficulty. Titus performed a similar service for First Notary Ambrose.

The going became even harder. About a half-mile from

the summit the road steepened and veered to the southeast, exposing the mules and their riders to the full force of the wind and snow. At least the wind blew most of the snow off the right side of the road, which faced downslope, so by walking along that edge the mules were able to avoid any significant drifts. This provided a vertiginous experience for the riders, however.

With less than a quarter-mile to go, the road turned directly toward the summit, and the riders felt the storm on their backs, propelling them forward. Finally, they reached the highest point of the road, and through the driving snow they could make out the frozen summit lake in front of them.

Although everyone was relieved to have completed the climb, Stephen noticed with dismay that the light was now fading rapidly. It seemed unbelievable, but somehow they had taken the entire day to reach the summit. Stephen had a shouted conference with the guide. Reaching St. Peter was now out of the question, the guide agreed. What's more, he could see that parts of the road ahead, where it skirted the lake, were covered by snowdrifts, which must have built up after the Frankish pilgrims passed through. If there were many such drifts on the road the mules would have a very hard time of it. They might not even be able to make it to one of the shelters along the way.

The guide pointed to a collection of stone ruins to the left of the road. These included what remained of a temple of Jupiter, erected by the emperor Claudius in the first century and torn down by another emperor, Theodosius, in the fourth. In slightly better condition were the remains of a hostelry, which had been used by those who traveled in the official service of the emperors. In particular, the stables at the back of the hostelry were in relatively good condition: the walls were still intact, but the roof had long since fallen in. These stables, the guide said, would have to be their refuge for the night. He led the travelers off the road to the tumbled-down buildings, and before they settled into their uncomfortable quarters he distributed some bread and cheese that he had packed for just such an emergency, as well as some grain and hay for their mules. Stephen led a brief prayer for God's protection, and then the travelers quickly downed the food and dispersed into separate stables.

Zaid knew that the smallest space was likely to be the warmest, so he picked out what had probably been a stall for a single horse. He led both his and Stephen's mules into this space. Then he rummaged through the baggage that his mule was carrying and found some baled cloth that was probably intended as a present for some Frankish noble. From this material he was able to fashion a simple awning that kept the worst of the snow off the animals. He used other items from the baggage to make resting places for Stephen and himself between the two mules. Then he invited the pope, who was standing shivering in the open, to enter this makeshift resting place.

As the travelers settled in for a long and uncomfortable night, the storm began to abate. Soon it stopped snowing, but the temperature dropped even further. Without the mules' body heat, neither the pope nor Zaid could have survived.

"It's better not to sleep," said Stephen. "If we sleep, we might not wake up."

Zaid was in any case too cold to sleep. "Well then," he

said, "may I ask you a question?"

"Of course."

"Why do you treat me so kindly? Almost like your son. But I'm not—I'm your slave."

"Because—well, because of what you told me about how you came to be arrested."

"How so?"

"I was homeless too, me and my brother, when we were even younger than you are."

"Really? That's hard to believe."

"It's true. I was eight years old. Our father died, and then our mother, and we had no relatives, even though we came from a noble family. So we lived on the streets. Paul was only three, so I had to look after him as well as myself."

"How did you survive?"

"By begging, mostly. And Paul being so young—barely more than a baby, really—that helped. People took pity on us. But even so, sometimes we were really hungry, and cold."

"I know what that's like."

"Yes. And sometimes, we had to steal, like you did."

"Did you get caught?"

"No. It nearly happened, but Paul helped again. He looked so innocent, but he grabbed things off stalls—pieces of bread, or a slice of meat pie, or fruit. I distracted the stall-keeper. Sometimes he'd see what Paul was doing, but you can't do much if it's a three-year-old, can you? I pretended to be angry with him. I cuffed him, and made him give the food back, and then we went on our way."

"What a story! The Holy Father!"

"I wasn't so holy then," said Stephen, and a weak smile flitted across his drawn face. "It was only for a few weeks.

Then a priest saw us and felt sorry for us. He was going to take us to the orphanage, but when I told him who our parents were, he took us to the Lateran Palace instead—my palace, as it now is. I remember the huge door, and I wondered how they could get it open. But a small wicket gate opened and I saw a man in black. The priest talked with him, and he beckoned us to come through, but it was so dark that I was afraid to go in—I thought we were in for some terrible punishment. I screamed and refused to move. The man disappeared and came back with some bread, and Paul saw it and ran through to get it, so I had to follow. They treated us kindly."

"Your brother must be very grateful to you."

"And me to him. He gave me a reason to live, and he helped us survive."

"You must be very close."

"We are."

After a pause, Zaid felt emboldened by Stephen's confessional to pose another question. "Can you tell me—why are you going to Francia?"

"To seek help from the King of the Franks against the Lombards."

"Why don't you have your own army?"

"Well, for many years we were subjects of the Emperor in Constantinople, and he was supposed to protect us. Some say that we're still his subjects, but we've received no protection from him, so we have to find help somewhere else."

"But can't you raise an army yourself, and protect your own people?"

"We have soldiers, but they're too few to face Aistulf. To

raise a larger army, we'd have to rule Italy, but we don't—Aistulf rules most of it. And, there's another reason. I'm the successor to the blessed Apostle Peter, and leader of the Christian religion. I'm a spiritual leader, not a king or a general."

"You can't be leader of the church and a king or a general?"

"No, that's never how it's been. Some think that should change."

"Then how did the Christians conquer so many nations?"

"They didn't conquer any nations. They preached the word of God, and people in many nations heard it and decided to become Christians themselves."

"Wasn't Jesus a king or a general?"

"A king in heaven. He said: '*Regnum meum non est de mundo hoc—My kingdom is not of this world.*'"

Zaid took some time to digest this. One of the mules shifted its position in the stall. The other stood stock still, with its left rear leg supported on the tip of its hoof. Zaid knew this meant it was sleeping. He wondered whether it was dreaming of some more pleasant lowland environment.

"May I ask you another question," Zaid went on.

"We have all night," said Stephen, "so keep asking." He pulled the bedding more tightly around himself.

"Your name—Stephen—that's the same name as the Pope before you, who died suddenly, isn't it?"

"That's right."

"So you took the name Stephen on account of him—to take his place, so to speak?"

"No," said Stephen. "Stephen was the name that my father gave me when I was baptized. I and Stephen the priest, who nearly became Pope—we happened to share the same name."

"Why did your parents give you that name, then?" asked Zaid.

"To honor the memory of Stephen, the blessed martyr, who lived in Jerusalem soon after the time of Our Savior. He was the first martyr of the Christian religion."

"Did he die in battle?"

"No, he told the Jews that he saw Jesus standing at the right hand of God, but they called him a liar and stoned him to death for saying so."

If Zaid had his own doubts about Jesus standing at the right hand of God, he didn't mention them. Instead he said: "I don't think he achieved very much, being martyred for that reason, do you?"

"Yes, I do," said Stephen. "But tell me about your own name—why did your parents call you Zaid?"

'They named me for Zaid ibn Harithah," Zaid said.

"Who was that?"

"Zaid ibn Harithah was the adopted son of the Prophet Muhammad, may Allah bless him and grant him peace."

"Do you know anything about that Zaid?"

"This is what my father told me about him. He was the son of Harithah and Su'dah. Su'dah went to visit her family in Bani Ma'n. While she was there, a neighboring tribe attacked Bani Ma'n and seized many prisoners to sell into slavery. Among them was Su'dah's young son, Zaid. He was taken to the slave market at Ukaz, where he was bought by Hakim ibn Huzam. Hakim gave Zaid to his aunt, Khadijah, who was the first wife of Muhammad. This was before Muhammad received his revelations. He freed Zaid and adopted him as his own son. Shall I go on?"

"Yes, go on, I'm listening. But keep yourself wrapped up, it's getting colder."

"Well, in the meantime Su'dah had returned home and told Harithah what had happened. They were both very sad, but they weren't able to find Zaid. Then, several years later, some relatives of Harithah met Zaid by accident in Mecca. They told Zaid how much Harithah and Su'dah missed him. Zaid told them to tell Harithah and Su'dah that he loved them, but that he lived with a new father who was very good to him. When he heard this, Harithah came to Mecca and asked Muhammad to give Zaid back. He said he would give Muhammad any sum of money that he thought right. Muhammad had Zaid brought to him, and told him to choose whether he wished Muhammad or Harithah to be his father. 'If he chooses you,' Muhammad said to Harithah, 'then you can take him with you, with no payment.'"

"What a fortunate boy," Stephen commented. "He had two fathers and two mothers, all of whom loved him. Many of us lacked even one father and one mother, or there was no love between parent and child. So which parents did he choose?"

"He chose to stay with Muhammad and Khadijah. But my father said that Harithah wasn't too sad, because he realized that Zaid was lucky to be brought up by a good man like Muhammad."

"That may be true," said Stephen. "But Harithah and—"

"Su'dah."

"Harithah and Su'dah—they had a strong claim to him, I'd say, seeing that they were the boy's birth parents and they never willingly gave him up. Anyway, go on."

"My father says that Zaid was the first convert to Islam, after Khadijah. Other people say it was Ali, or Abu Bakr, but my father says those people ignore Zaid because he had been a slave and therefore wasn't worthy of that honor, which is not a good reason. But Zaid became a great warrior. Muhammad chose him to lead his army in their first battle against the Christians, which was at the village called Mu'tah, near the Jordan River."

"Oh yes," said Stephen. "That was a battle fought by the Emperor Heraclius. The Moslems were defeated, weren't they?"

"No, they weren't," said Zaid. "They were three thousand men, with Zaid carrying the standard. They faced one hundred thousand Christians under Heraclius, and another hundred thousand Arabs of the north, who were in the pay of Heraclius. So they were outnumbered seventy to one. But even so, the Christians were not able to defeat Muhammad's army."

"What happened to Zaid?"

"He became a *shahid*, a martyr, early in the battle. After that, Jafar ibn Abi Talib took up the standard. Jafar's right hand was cut off by a sword, so he carried the standard with his left hand. Then his left hand was cut off, but Jafar continued to carry the standard between his arms. Then he in turn became a martyr. And then Abdullah ibn Rawahah took up the standard, and he too became a martyr. Their bodies were placed in a great mausoleum at Mu'tah, and they're still there today—I've seen the place. After Abdullah was martyred, Khalid ibn al-Walid took the standard, and the Christians had to retreat."

"How did Muhammad react when he was told that his

son had died in the battle?"

"He wasn't told—he knew. At the same time as the battle was going on at Mu'tah, Muhammad was describing it to his companions in Medina, which was more than three hundred miles to the south. When he announced Zaid's death, he cried bitterly."

"And was it worthwhile, do you think? The battle, I mean, and all those who died?"

"Those who attained martyrdom are in the Garden of Paradise. Allah gave Jafar two wings in place of his hands, so that he could fly in Paradise from one place to another."

"But did the battle gain anything?"

"Yes, of course. After the battle, all the Arabs in that region converted to Islam. And there were other victories after that. So each successor of Muhammad ruled over more land than the one before. And now the word of the Prophet has spread so widely that those who follow his teachings are more numerous than the Christians. That's what my father tells me, anyway."

The two were silent for a while, then Stephen said: "I should visit the others—come with me." This was the last thing that Zaid felt like doing, but he got up and obediently helped Stephen rise and bundle himself in whatever lay to hand. Then the old man and the youngster stepped out into the night. The cloudless sky shimmered with fixed and wandering stars. Zaid looked up at the five brilliant lights of *That-al-Korsi*—the Seated Lady—who ruled the constellations from her throne high in the northern sky. To the east of her he made out the fainter and more sinister cluster of *Hamil-Ra's-Al-Ghul*—the Bearer of the Demon's Head. Below them, *Ad-Dub Al-A'shgar* and *Ad-Dub Al-A'kbar*—the Lesser and the Greater Bears—tumbled toward the northern horizon and the hidden plains of Burgundy. Zaid thought of the long treks that he and his father made by night to escape the desert's heat, when the stars were their faithful guides.

Here, though, it was blisteringly cold, even though the wind had died down, and Stephen was anxious to complete his task. Helped by Zaid, he moved stiffly from stall to stall. He was relieved to see that everyone was still alive. A few had even managed to fall asleep, but most had not, and some were suffering badly, especially Ambrose. And Leoba, who had rejected an offer from Christopher to share his stall, had only her own meager heat to keep her alive: She sat shivering in the corner of a stall, wrapped like a mummy in the windings of some precious textile.

Zaid tried to rearrange the travelers' bedding to keep them warmer. Stephen exchanged a few words with them and uttered a brief prayer for God's mercy, mentioning each of them by name in his supplication.

By the time they returned to their own stall, Stephen was shivering violently. They lay down again, and Zaid gradually drifted off to sleep, but Stephen remained awake and in extreme discomfort. He began to wonder if any of them would survive the night. Dark thoughts chased each other in small circles in his mind. Was this the doom that the falling star warned them about? Should he have turned back? Was the whole journey a terrible error, as Theo had said? And was Theo right about the Donation after all?

Stephen gazed at Zaid's face, which was close enough for him to reach out and touch, though he did not do so. Instead he said: "Zaid—*Zaid!*"

The boy dragged himself back to the waking world and

opened his eyes partway. "Zaid," Stephen said again, more urgently. "Constantine's Donation—you took it from Sylvester's hand, didn't you?"

"Took what?" Zaid asked blearily.

"The Donation—you took it from Sylvester, didn't you?"

"The Donation? That book? Yes, he was holding it. I took it and gave it to you—you saw me. Why?"

"You didn't put it in his hand? Or did anyone else put it in his hand or give it you to put there, that you know of—or did you write it yourself?"

By now Zaid was wide awake. "Write it myself? No—how could I do such a thing? How could anyone do such a thing?" It briefly crossed his mind that his own father had the necessary skills, but he thought no more of that. "I thought you said the old Emperor wrote it—Constantine. You said he gave it to Sylvester."

"Yes, that's what happened, that's what happened," said Stephen. "I was dreaming or something." And then, talking mainly to himself, he went on: "Paul was in charge of the whole thing, no one could have opened the sarcophagus without his knowledge. Everything is as it should be."

"What do you mean?" asked Zaid.

"Oh—nothing. I'm rambling. I think I'm losing my mind in this cold."

There was a minute's silence, then Stephen began again in a more tremulous voice. "Zaid," he said, still shaking, his face ashen-gray, "It may be that the Lord will take us this very night."

Zaid ached with the cold, but he didn't feel as if he was going to die. "No, that won't happen, believe me," he said as confidently as he could manage. "Let me see if I can find something else to put over you."

"No, no," said Stephen, "stay there. But listen to me. I've told you already before—to be saved, to avoid hellfire, you must be baptized. You refused, but I'm asking you again, in the face of death—renounce your false religion. Receive eternal life through the mercy of Jesus Christ, our Lord and Savior."

"Baptized? But—"

"Yes. In this moment of urgent necessity I can baptize you here and now, without preparation. I'll say, 'Do you renounce all pagan and heretical beliefs and acknowledge our Lord Jesus Christ as your only true Savior?' and you'll say with a sincere heart, 'Yes, I do.' And I'll say, 'Are you willing to be baptized into the Holy Catholic Church?' and you'll say, 'Yes, I am.' And then I'll say, 'I baptize you in the name of the Father and of the Son and of the Holy Spirit,' and I'll baptize you with this, which I'll sanctify." He reached for a pot of water that sat nearby, but the water had frozen solid. Stephen wondered whether baptism with ice was acceptable.

"No, I don't want to," said Zaid. "It wouldn't be sincere."

"The blessed Pancras, who I've told you about—he was willing to convert."

"You told me that he refused."

"No, I mean earlier—he converted to Christianity. Later he refused to convert back to the pagan religion. The Emperor Diocletian was moved by his beauty; he offered the boy great wealth if he would do so."

"I don't want to convert," said Zaid again. "I have faith in the truth revealed to the prophet Muhammad, may Allah bless him and grant him peace."

"What has following that false religion done for you? It

got you enslaved, that's all. And that Christian girl you told me you love—"

"Lenora."

"Lenora. It's the reason that you can never marry her—besides the fact that you're a slave. Even if you had your liberty, you and she could only wander the world as you did with your father. You'd be outcasts—from Christendom, and from the Caliphate too. But if you accept baptism, and if the Lord has mercy on us this night, then I'll set you free, and I'll marry you and her at the Lateran church. I'll give you employment at the stables again, but as a freedman. Perhaps you'll become stable-master in due course—you'll be able to support your family. And if we don't survive, why then you'll stand with me tonight among the angels in Paradise. I promise you this as Christ's representative on Earth—as Holder of the Keys of the Kingdom of Heaven."

Zaid was silent for a long time. The situation seemed unreal. This holy man was offering him happiness in this world and the next. If he had happened to be born into a Christian family, he would never have questioned the Christian faith, so why shouldn't he accept it now? Why shouldn't it be just as true as his own faraway religion—or more so? And he was being offered this choice at the top of an icy mountain, in the middle of the night, by a Pope huddled under rags, in a broken-down stable with two mules for witnesses—so removed from his familiar surroundings that he felt, for one moment at least, released from all his former obligations and cleansed from the sins of his short life, free to remake himself in a new image and enter a new world.

"You're so kind to me—I can't thank you enough," he

said at last. "But I can't do it. It would dishonor the memory of my mother. God would cast her soul out of the Garden of Paradise. And my father, if I see him again in Rome, as I pray I will—how could we ever be reconciled? I can't do it."

"The blessed Pancras—"

"Allow me to imitate his refusal in the face of death— Your Holiness." The formality of the now-unfamiliar salutation gave Stephen pause, and in the silence Zaid closed his eyes and was soon lost to the world once more.

Stephen longed to draw the sleeping youth toward him, to enwrap and protect him in his embrace, and to draw something of the boy's youth and beauty into his own decrepit and careworn body. And it would be no sin to do so, he thought, if their mutual warmth helped to keep them both from freezing to death. But something held him back, and instead he whispered a short prayer. "Blessed Peter," he murmured, "if this boy should be called tonight to judgment, may you look kindly on his soul, as our Savior in His infinite mercy gathered the Holy Innocents to His bosom." Then he too drifted off to sleep.

27

The night seemed to go on forever, but eventually light glimmered in the east, and before long sunlight streamed across the lake into the broken-down hostelry. Stephen, who had been sleeping soundly for the later part of the night, opened his eyes. Although miserably uncomfortable, he was glad to find himself still alive. He noticed that Zaid was not in the stall, and his cloak was gone. With considerable difficulty he stood up and warmed himself by swinging his arms as vigorously as he could manage. The stall reeked of the mules' urine and droppings, so Stephen stepped out into the icy mountain air. Zaid sat a few paces away: he had cleared a small space in front of the hut and was praying in a direction to the right of the rising sun. He had just completed the *salat* prescribed for dawn, and now he was catching up on three *salawat* that he had had to skip on the previous day—those for the afternoon, sunset, and nightfall.

Other members of the party were also rising. Most seemed in reasonable shape, and they were able to warm themselves a little by jumping up and down in the early sunshine. Only Ambrose failed to join in the activity: he was slightly disoriented and his breathing was labored. Titus had to help him put on the cloak that had been covering him during the night.

There was no more food or water for the travelers or their mules. When the animals were led out, some of them started to eat the snow. The guide knew that this would sap their strength, so he and Titus went down to the lake, where they managed to break a hole in the ice with a large rock. After the travelers drank some of the icy water, the mules took their turn. Then the baggage was repacked.

In a heartfelt prayer, the travelers gave thanks to the Lord for watching over them during the night, and asked His protection for the remainder of the journey. Then they mounted the mules. Ambrose again had to be helped, and he asked repeatedly where they were going, even though their goal—the village of St. Peter—had just been mentioned in their prayers.

Already within a couple of hundred yards the travelers ran into a three-foot deep snowdrift. The guide knew that the mules would quickly become exhausted if they had to walk through such deep snow, particularly because they had been insufficiently fed. He had everyone except Stephen and Ambrose dismount and walk ahead of the animals, pushing the snow aside with their bodies. The travelers took turns in the tiring lead position. This particular drift lasted only to the end of the lake, but there were others further along the road. In a couple of places, the drifts were too deep even for the humans to walk through. Then they had to crawl across the snow on their bellies, making holes with their arms and legs which the mules could use to step in. It was very slow going, and everyone quickly became tired and cold.

Gradually, however, as they descended further from the summit, the drifts became shallower and less frequent. After four hours—by which time the party had traveled less than four miles—the going became easy. Two miles later, the guide pointed out a curl of smoke rising from the hostelry at St. Peter, and in another half hour they had arrived.

The inn-keeper was amazed to see anyone arriving from the direction of Jove's Mountain—least of all the Pope along with his counselors and retinue. As he hurried to organize food and lodging for the party, everyone else in the village joined the travelers in the tiny church of St. Peter, where they gave thanks both to God and to St. Peter himself for their safe passage of the mountain.

From St. Peter it was a two-day journey to the abbey of St. Maurice, at Agaunum in the upper Rhone valley. For the first day of the journey, the travelers had to continue on mule-back, because the innkeeper had already sent his horses down to the valley for the winter. He did provide a small cart for Ambrose, who was now too ill and confused to ride, but the reluctance of the pack animals to draw it, combined with the poor state of the road, slowed down the whole party. The next morning, the travelers obtained horses, including some used to drawing a carriage, and they made better progress.

The abbey was located next to the river, under a thousand-foot cliff. As the travelers approached the abbey, they could already hear the famous chanting that the monks had kept up without the slightest interruption since the abbey's foundation more than two centuries earlier. They saw a group of the 'Sleepless Singers' leaving the church, having just been replaced by a fresh relay of monks.

The abbot, who knew Stephen from a visit he had made to Rome some years before, greeted him with enthusiasm. "I'm so delighted to be able to call you 'Your Holiness' at last," he said, slapping Stephen on the back.

This struck Stephen as a little too familiar, but he was so happy to arrive at this safe haven that he ignored the breach of protocol. "You know of our mission?" he asked.

"Certainly," said the abbot. "And I'm afraid I have to disappoint you a little. I know you were hoping to meet King Pepin here, but there was an unexpected emergency—an invasion by the Saxons. Pepin had to lead an army to the East. We're hoping to hear shortly from him about his plans for meeting you—Your Holiness."

"So we should stay at St. Maurice until he sends word?"

"We'll be honored if you'll do so, Your Holiness. You and your people will be comfortable and well looked after, I can assure you."

"Well, in one way that's fortunate. First Notary Ambrose is quite ill, as you can see. He needs rest."

"Of course. And I'll bring our doctors to look at him. God willing, he'll be on his feet again in a few days." The abbot signed for some of his assistants to carry Ambrose to his quarters. Then he turned back to Stephen. "Let me show you the tomb of our blessed Maurice."

The abbot led Stephen and Theophylact into the church. "Are you familiar with his story, Your Holiness?" he asked.

"Not really," said Stephen, who would have preferred dinner and an early bed. "Tell me."

"Maurice was a Roman soldier, the leader of the Theban Legion, which had six thousand, six hundred and sixty-six men, all of them from Egypt, including Maurice himself.

This was at the time when Maximian was co-emperor with Diocletian, and the persecution of Christians was at its height. Here we are, by the way, this is the tomb—it's a fine piece of work, isn't it?"

The tomb carried an effigy of Maurice in full armor. "Maximian ordered the legion to root out Christians in this area," the abbot continued, "but the legionaries refused. They said, 'We've found them already, they are us.' Because they were Christians themselves, you know. So to punish them, Maximian ordered the legion to be decimated: every tenth man was killed. Then he asked the remainder if they would obey his orders, but they still refused, and Maximian ordered another decimation. And so it went until all six thousand, six hundred and sixty-six soldiers were dead. Their bodies are buried near here; only their leader Maurice lies here in the church."

"God grant them eternal rest," said Stephen, and Theophylact and the abbot said: "Amen."

"Many years later Maximian tried to kill Constantine, after Constantine became emperor," the abbot went on. Stephen tried to maintain an appearance of interest, but Theophylact was yawning audibly. "He crept into Constantine's bed-chamber at night and stabbed him through the heart with a dagger. But it wasn't Constantine who was sleeping there! The Emperor had been warned of the plot by his wife, so he slept in a different room and had a eunuch sleep in his own bed. Maximian was required to commit suicide, which was better than he deserved after all the innocent people he had killed over his lifetime, don't you think?"

"Yes, a merciful end," said Stephen.

"That was a good trick that Constantine played. Maybe

you should arrange something like that for your own safety, Your Holiness, now that Aistulf is out for your blood. Assassins have gotten into the Lateran palace before now, as I remember."

"If you'll excuse us, my dear Abbot, my companions and I are very tired, and I'm wondering—"

"Of course, of course, Your Holiness, forgive me—let me lead the way. By the way, Constantine ordered Maximian's name to be erased from all records and monuments, and no one was allowed to mention his name thereafter. But several years later he changed his mind: he declared that Maximian was a god and put his face on coins. So fickle is infamy!"

On the following day Duke Autchar and Archbishop Chrodengang set off northward, hoping to locate Pepin and tell him of Stephen's arrival at St. Maurice. They carried a letter from Stephen that outlined the pope's proposal, along with the copy of the Donation of Constantine that Leoba had prepared for him. Though couched in oblique hints, the meaning of Stephen's letter was clear: Stephen would crown Pepin, as authorized by the Donation, in exchange for a campaign by Pepin against Aistulf.

Stephen and the others remained at St. Maurice. Stephen penned letters to Paul and others at Rome, but there was little chance of the letters being delivered anytime soon, because the passes were now closed. Stephen also made short trips to churches in the upper Rhone valley and on the eastern shore of Lake Geneva.

Stephen's main preoccupation, though, was with Ambrose, whose condition grew steadily worse in spite of the recommended bed rest. In order that he could breathe at all, he had to be propped up with numerous pillows; even then, drawing each breath was a struggle for him. The doctors who put their ears to his chest heard such a cacophony of rales, crepitations, and bruits that they inwardly despaired for his life, although they maintained a façade of optimism and carried out a variety of treatments, especially the application of bleeding cups. Ambrose experienced no obvious benefit from the bleedings, however.

As the doctors ministered to Ambrose's body, Stephen ministered to his soul. Not that any meaningful discourse was possible between the two men, for Ambrose had little notion of what was going on around him; he spoke little, and when he did his words were hard to make out or didn't make sense. Mostly, Stephen prayed for Ambrose's recovery, and when that was no longer likely he prayed for his soul. After a week of this, Ambrose died peacefully. At his funeral, his body was placed in a sarcophagus in the abbey, not far from the tomb of St. Maurice, but the understanding was that his body would be returned to Rome when conditions allowed.

Finally, after three weeks at St. Maurice, a messenger arrived from Pepin. Leoba was delighted to see that it was Fulrad, the abbot of St. Denis, whom she had accompanied on her journey to Rome a couple of years before. Fulrad told Stephen that Pepin had met Chrodegang and Autchar; he was now heading for his palace at Ponthion, a hundred miles east of Paris, and Fulrad's mission was to escort the pope and his party there.

It was now mid-December, and the thought of spending another two or three weeks on the road was far from appealing. Still, Stephen had little choice: if Pepin would not come to Stephen, Stephen would have to go to Pepin. It might in any case be necessary to go to Paris, if a coronation was to take place. So the travelers geared up again and set out on what they hoped was the last leg of their journey. At least Fulrad had brought a sizable contingent of soldiers with him, so the travelers' safety was assured.

28

"The Commander of the Militia tells me that he's received news from the north," said Paul to the assembled counselors. "Leo, please go ahead."

"Yes, Deacon Paul," said Leo. "One of my men has returned from the border at Vetralla. He heard from a pilgrim who met with the Holy Father at Vercelli. The Holy Father told him to bring you this message: 'The meeting with Aistulf was fruitless, we're proceeding onward to Aosta and will meet with Pepin at St. Maurice, God willing.'"

"He didn't bring a letter?"

"No, the Holy Father thought that was too risky. The pilgrim was trustworthy. We told him to come to the Lateran when he reaches Rome, but my man brought the news ahead on horseback."

"Anything else?"

"Not from the Holy Father," said Leo. "But my man also heard that Slavs are threatening Istria, and that Aistulf is likely to campaign there."

"That's good news," said Paul. "Let's hope they keep Aistulf busy as long as possible—that could be our salvation."

Marcellus, the Treasurer, spoke up. "Respected Deacon," he said, "The policy I supported earlier—that we negotiate with Aistulf—that's failed. The Holy Father now pursues another strategy, which is to seek help from Pepin. Perhaps he'll be successful. But have you thought about what might happen if he does succeed? Once Pepin enters Italy with his army, won't he look around and say to himself: 'Look at these ancient cities, these splendid castles and churches! How much nobler to be King of Italy than of rough-hewn Francia!' It may be easier to welcome the Franks than to bid them farewell."

"Marcellus," said Paul, "you talk as if the Franks were homeless heretics, like the Vandals or the Goths. They're not. They're true Catholic Christians, and they have a home—in Francia. Pepin has a special reverence for the blessed Peter and his patrimony. If he comes to Italy, it'll be out of gratitude to the Holy Father, and for the sake of his own immortal soul. He'd never violate the faith that the Holy Father puts in him. Besides, what other path is open to us now?"

"Well, there's still the Emperor," Marcellus went on. "We could offer him Ravenna, the Five Cities—Lombardy, even."

"The Emperor will never help us," replied Paul sharply. "How many times do I have to tell you that? And besides, you want to give away all this land that Constantine deeded to us—just months after we found out that it's ours? In any case, the Holy Father has decided what we're going to do." Paul's peremptory tone put a damper on further discussion, and before long the meeting came to an end. Paul was glad to get back to the papal chambers.

As he sat at his desk, however, Paul found it difficult to

concentrate on the pile of documents that had been placed there for his perusal. An estate manager at Sutri had failed to provide the prescribed amount of corn. The bishop of Naples accused some priests of sorcery. The patriarch of Alexandria sought the Pope's opinion on the doctrine of metastoicheiosis.

Paul stared at the documents, but his thoughts turned to Leoba. Why had she left Rome, right at the moment when their relationship had become most intense? Was she really obliged to heed Boniface's call—when she'd ignored it several times before? Was it just her restless nature—a yearning for distant places that had to be satisfied once every couple of years? Or was it her way of saying 'It's over'? Would she come back, as she had promised? And if she did, would things be the same? What if—Heaven forbid— Stephen should die and he was elected Pope? Could he and Leoba continue their secret relationship in the full glare of attention that was directed at the Holy Father?

Paul recalled the physical and emotional intimacy between Leoba and himself—intimacy that he hadn't experienced since he was a small child. He revisited every curve and recess of her body, smelled once more her musky odor, listened again to her soft voice. He recalled every word, as it seemed, of their conversations; he re-enacted every scene of their love-making. How could all that be granted to him, and how could it then be so cruelly taken away?

Leoba had insisted that he not write to her, but Paul was aching to do so. If she didn't hear from him, wouldn't she think that his ardor had cooled? Wouldn't she seek consolation with some other man—who knows, with Theophylact even? He imagined the two of them doing what she and Paul had done, and the horror of it tortured him.

If he wrote to her, what would he say? Paul took a blank sheet and a pen, and poured out his yearning for her. He filled a page, then another. If only I could send it, he thought. But Leoba was right, it wasn't safe.

Then he thought: What if I seal it and send it inside a letter to Chrodegang—a letter about reforming the Frankish clergy or some such thing? That wouldn't draw any attention, and I could ask him to give it to Leoba. He'd just pass it on to her without unsealing it, and no one but him would know I'd written to her.

As Paul was playing out this fantasy, there was a knock at the door. It was the chamberlain. Paul pushed the letter out of sight. "What is it?" he asked.

"The man who petitioned you for manumission, sir—for his son. His name's Omar, from Transtiber—he's here again."

"Omar?"

"He says you asked him to come. Shall I send him away?"

"I didn't ask him to come," said Paul. Then he thought better of it. "Well, maybe I did, I can't remember. Bring him up."

The chamberlain disappeared, and came back a few minutes later with Omar. "Do you want a notary, sir?" he asked, but Paul waved him away.

"What is it?" Paul asked as soon as he and Omar were alone.

"I wanted to thank you again for the manumission for my son Zaid, sir," Omar said.

"That's why you came? Your gratitude is exemplary."

"Well, I also wanted to mention that I've lost my son's

services now for several months, because of his wrongful enslavement. Now I understand that he's on his way to Francia with the Holy Father's retinue, so he'll be away for a long time still. This has been a great loss to me, and it becomes more so with every month that goes by."

"Whether your son's enslavement was legitimate or not—I've no opinion on that matter," said Paul testily. "The manumission was issued as a personal kindness, not to rectify any wrongdoing."

"Very well, sir. But you still might consider recompensing me for the loss of income I've suffered. And for the faithfulness with which I've kept silent about the letter I wrote for you—Constantine's deed. This will continue of course, while I wait for my son's return, so we can both leave Rome forever."

"That sounds very much like—" Paul cut himself off. Yes, he was being blackmailed, but making accusations wouldn't help. "How much do you think you deserve for your—what did you call it—faithfulness?"

"I'd suggest one hundred solidi, sir."

"A hundred solidi!"

"As a down-payment," said Omar. "And then a monthly payment for as long as Zaid is absent—perhaps twenty solidi a month."

"Twenty solidi!"

"Surely these are trivial amounts for the Lateran Treasury, aren't they?"

"And if we don't pay you?"

"I sincerely hope that it won't come to that. My desire and intent is to remain silent. After all, it would be extremely damaging for the truth in this matter to come out, wouldn't it, sir?"

"No one would believe you," Paul replied. He started to pace the room.

"They might if they saw the version that the lady Leoba gave me, in her own hand. But of course, it won't come to that. My sincere wish is that this whole matter remains a secret between you and me."

What, Paul thought, *Leoba let him keep her original? What madness was that? As if I don't have enough problems on my hands, now this tawny-skinned unbeliever is threatening to expose the whole thing. That would make Theophylact happy, that's for sure—but it would be my total undoing. And it would destroy Stephen's chances of a deal with Pepin, which would likely mean Rome's destruction at the hands of Aistulf. What choice do I have? What choice do I have? But if I pay, won't he just come back for more, and even more?* Paul continued to pace the room.

"I can give you twenty solidi now," he said finally, reaching for a drawer in his desk. "The rest I'll need to requisition, it will come to you shortly. For this, I expect your complete silence, and I expect you to leave Rome for good the instant your son returns."

"That is promised, sir," said Omar. "I greatly appreciate your understanding of the situation, and I look forward to receiving the balance very soon." He took the proffered gold coins and turned to the door.

After Omar left, Paul sat down at his desk, sank his head into his hands, and remained there in silence. Then, after a minute or two, he muttered out loud: "That villain! That monstrous villain! How much I'd give to have him silenced forever!"

"Excuse me, sir, did you need something?" Paul started;

the chamberlain was standing in front of him.

"No, no," said Paul hurriedly. "I was day-dreaming. Nothing, thank you. That will be all."

29

———

Stephen and his companions circled the eastern shore of Lake Geneva and then struck north across the Jura Mountains, which turned out to present few obstacles. On the eighth day they reached Besançon. After this, the going became easy, but very tedious, because they rarely saw anything but thick forest. Theophylact drew some satisfaction from the realization that his earlier assessment of Pepin's realm—"many trees, what else?"—had been quite accurate. On the fourteenth day the travelers reach Langres, on a promontory overlooking the Marne Valley. Here the pope joined with the bishop of Langres to celebrate Christmas.

A few days later the travelers assembled at the north gate of Langres for the last ninety miles of their journey to Ponthion. From the gate they had a fine view over the valley and the low hills beyond. Once they had dropped down to the valley floor and crossed a mile or so of fields, however, they again found themselves in forest. The trees in these parts had shed their leaves for the winter. This, along with the overcast skies and occasional rain shower, made a somber impression. A few travelers passed them—pilgrims or traders heading for Langres—or an old woodcutter trundled by on a broken-down cart. For the most part, though, the travelers had the road to themselves, and the monotony of their journey was relieved only when they crossed streams or passed an occasional hamlet with its surrounding fields. Still, the thought of approaching their destination lifted their spirits, and there was much lively talk and banter, in which Zaid and Tito were able to join freely.

After a few hours, they saw ahead of them a crowd of peasants, perhaps two or three hundred in all, who were walking in the same direction as themselves. Coming closer, Stephen saw that the group consisted mostly of women, who were carrying crosses and singing some unfamiliar hymn. Unlike most of the common people that Stephen and his party met, these travelers did not seem particularly excited by the sight of the papal party; in fact, they ignored them and continued with their singing.

As Stephen passed the front of the group, he saw that it was led by a middle-aged, wild-looking man with unkempt hair and beard, a sackcloth robe, and bare feet. Yet he was surrounded by a half-dozen young women of unusual beauty, and these women treated him with fawning respect.

"This must be Aldebert—the heretic," said Fulrad to Stephen.

"Aldebert?" asked Stephen. "Who's that?"

But the man caught Fulrad's words. "Yes, I'm Aldebert," he said. "Aldebert, the Frankish Angel of Christ, and these are my disciples."

Stephen might have been annoyed by the man's failure to show any of the usual courtesies toward him, but he was curious to know more. "Where do you come from?" he asked.

"I issued from the right flank of my mother," Aldebert replied, "as Jesus issued from the right flank of the Virgin Mary."

"And where are you going?"

"To the next village, and the one after that, to set up a cross and preach."

"And what will you preach?"

"Whatever ministry Jesus instructs me in, by his letters, or through his angels," said Aldebert. "The ministry of universal forgiveness, without confession—for I see into the heart of every man and every woman, and I know their sins directly, and I forgive them. Look, I have letters, here, and here, written in Jesus Christ's own hand, which tell me to do this. And I'll heal the sick, as I've healed these women and many others who believe in me."

"How do you heal them?"

"With spells taught to me at midnight by the angel Uriel, or Raguel, or Tubuel, or with incantations that the angel Adinus whispered in my ear during storms of hail or thunder, or the angel Michael, or Tubuas, or Saboac, or Simiel the overseer of Heschwan!"

"How do you live?"

"By the Word of God, and by whatever I am given. I preach and found churches, and the people love me." Several of the women around him nodded enthusiastic agreement. "And I give them relics of myself, which they place in these churches and cherish."

"Relics? What relics, if you're still living?"

"Locks of my hair," Aldebert replied, "and to the most favored, the clippings of my fingernails."

Stephen began to remember about this Aldebert. Several years ago Boniface had complained about his activities, and Zachary had summoned a synod attended by twenty-four bishops, who decided that the man was mad. They therefore gave him a chance to change his ways or risk excommunication. But this leniency had no effect, Stephen realized, for here was Aldebert, pursuing the same old sinful activities.

"Repent of your heresies, or face hell-fire," said Stephen, as he moved on.

"Hell-fire is for rich people," Aldebert called after him. "For people who ride fine horses and wipe their arses with silken kerchiefs."

"This man has been a most pernicious thorn in the side of the Frankish church," Fulrad said to Stephen, once they were out of earshot. "And there are others like him. Unfortunately, there are not enough legitimate priests in Francia. Those men who are called to the religious life, they prefer to enter monasteries, where they contemplate the infinitude of God while gorging themselves on fat capons. In this region, outside of Langres, there are no priests, or if there are one or two, they lack the Holy Books and they've forgotten every Christian prayer beyond the Pater Noster. So Aldebert comes and preaches the universal salvation of the poor, without confession, and they flock to him, especially the women, and they build churches for him, and—I'm afraid to say—they also serve his carnal pleasure. He has fathered many children, it's said—did you notice the pregnant women in the crowd? Boniface has tried to make changes, over many years, without too much success. You might speak to Pepin about this."

"I intend to," said Stephen.

The travelers rode on for an hour or two. Around the middle of the afternoon their solitude was interrupted once more—this time by the sight of a dozen horsemen approaching from the north. As they came within thirty yards, the riders halted. Most of them seemed to be soldiers, but they deferred to a beardless youth who approached the pope's party by himself. Abbot Fulrad, who had been riding next to Stephen, hurriedly leaned over and whispered: "It's Charles—Pepin's eldest son."

The Frankish prince dismounted. He looked at the various members of Stephen's party, trying to identify the pope. Fulrad helped him out by pointing discreetly to Stephen. Then Charles knelt in the road directly in front of the pope, raised his hands in prayer, and said: "Your Holiness, in humility I seek your blessing."

"May the Lord's grace and mercy shine on you all the days of your life," Stephen said. "Now please rise, noble prince."

Charles stood, brushing the dust from his legs. Everyone in the pope's party was struck by his appearance and bearing, but no one more so than Zaid. To the dark-skinned slave, Charles seemed more like an apparition than a real human being: as young as himself—probably younger, to judge by his still child-like face—and yet almost as tall and powerful as the members of his bodyguard. With his fair skin, blue eyes, and unshorn blonde hair, he could have passed for a much younger brother to Leoba, but he carried himself with the confidence and authority appropriate to his station as heir to the Frankish realm. Zaid felt a twinge of envy. What had this boy done to earn his beauty or his position in life? And Zaid knew that, with Charles in their traveling party, his own position would be relegated to one of lowly servitude.

Zaid also looked with interest at Charles's horse. It was a magnificent grey warhorse, far superior to the packhorse that Zaid was riding, and its saddle and other accoutrements were finely tooled and decorated. In addition, he noticed that iron stirrups hung from the saddle, just as the stable-hand Sebastian had said. He looked to see if the horse was wearing iron shoes, as Sebastian had also asserted, but it was not, so far as Zaid could see. Still, the horse generated a metallic clatter as it walked, whose cause Zaid was eager to investigate.

Charles had prepared some more remarks. "My father, Pepin, King of the Franks, and the most noble ruler of Austrasia and Neustria and Burgundy, has charged me to convey his humble greetings to Your Holiness, and to request the honor of bringing Your Holiness and your companions to his residence at Ponthion, where he awaits you."

"We thank your most noble father and yourself," replied Stephen, falling into the same formal rhythms that Charles had established. "Your father's esteemed advisor, Abbot Fulrad, has through his wisdom conveyed us safely from St. Maurice to this point. We look forward to the opportunity to make acquaintance with you over the remaining few days of our journey."

Stephen introduced Charles to Theophylact, Notary Christopher, the bishops George and Wilchar, and several others in his party. He started to introduce Leoba, but

Charles greeted her before Stephen could mention her name. In doing so the formality of his speech began to dissipate. "Dear Sister Leoba," he said, "I'd almost lost hope that I'd see you again."

"Well, here I am," she said brightly. "I must say, you're hardly the same person that I knew! You're a head taller at least. And riding on such a fine horse! When I last saw you, you were a child trotting around on a little pony."

Charles was unoffended by Leoba's familiarity. "I've so much to tell you," he said, "and so much to ask you. But now, with the Holy Father's permission"—he turned back to Stephen—"let's continue on, so that we can reach Chaumont by evening. I told them to make preparations to receive you there, because we heard that Your Holiness intended to set out from Langres this morning."

The group—now enlarged to more than forty persons—moved off in the direction of Chaumont. Along the way there were lively conversations between Charles, Stephen, and his companions. Charles asked about their journey from Italy, and Stephen told him about their fruitless visit to Pavia, the difficult crossing of the Alps, and the death of Ambrose. Charles recounted recent happenings in Francia, including the successful conclusion of Pepin's campaign against the Saxons. He said that he was looking forward to leading men into battle himself before long. Charles conversed easily with the Romans in Latin, though with a heavy Gallic accent and some unfamiliar idioms. When speaking with the men in his own contingent he used a Germanic language that the southerners didn't understand.

After Chaumont, they continued northward for three days, leaving Burgundy and entering the Frankish heartland of Neustria. On the final day of their journey, Charles sent ahead to alert his father of their approach. Anticipating their meeting with Pepin, Stephen and his companions put off their drab traveling clothes and donned their appropriate vestments. It was as well that they did so, because they had barely come within three miles of the palace when Charles pointed out his father leading a large party on horseback toward them.

Many in both parties were curious to see how a King and a Pope—both of them accustomed to obsequious subservience from all-comers—would greet each other. In fact, as Pepin came forward, he outdid his son in the obeisance he showed to Stephen. Dismounting from his horse, he threw himself prostrate on the ground in front of the pope—though not before an aide had laid down a sheet. He remained lying there, resistant to all entreaties, until Stephen also dismounted and helped him to a standing position with a hand under his shoulder.

The King of the Franks offered a stark physical contrast to his son. For one thing, he was more than a head shorter—Charles must have outgrown him years ago. In fact he was even shorter than Stephen, who was himself of below-average height. His hair and eyes were dark above an unkempt beard, his skin was weather-beaten, and battle-scars were visible on his face, one of which had slightly deformed his nose. Yet he radiated a natural dignity and authority, which was striking in someone who had just been groveling on the ground. From under his dark eyebrows his eyes gazed out imperiously, demanding everyone's attention. He was wearing fine woolen and linen garments, but he bore no crown or other insignia of his office. Everyone recognized him, and that was sufficient.

There followed a series of exchanges in which the two men praised each other with the most effusive phraseology that their assistants had been able to dream up. Because the men were giving voice to previously rehearsed sentiments, and because the two men had difficulty understanding each other's dialects, their utterances did not always meld into a coherent dialogue. Still, they did label the meeting as historically significant.

After a few minutes of this, followed by further introductions on both sides, Pepin indicated the way to his palace. And then, instead of remounting his horse, he grasped the bridle of Stephen's horse and walked ahead while holding it, just as Zaid had done for the more difficult stretches of their northward journey.

Stephen was greatly encouraged by Pepin's words, and even more so by his actions. He recalled a sentence from Constantine's Donation: *Et tenentes frenum equi ipsius—And holding the bridle of his horse, out of reverence for the Blessed Peter, we performed for him the duty of groom.* Surely Pepin must have read this passage, and was now intentionally performing the very same service for Stephen as Constantine had done for Sylvester. It was a signal, no doubt about it—a signal that Pepin was well-disposed towards Stephen's proposal.

Pepin's residence at Ponthion was more of a well-appointed hunting lodge than a palace; it was just one of the many stops that Pepin's court made on its annual circuit of the Frankish realm. The wooden buildings included dining and reception halls, sleeping accommodations, an adjacent chapel and stables, barracks, and housing for servants and laborers.

The buildings were surrounded by military exercise grounds and fields, which quickly gave way to the royal forests that extended for miles in every direction.

The main reception hall was decorated with hunting trophies and weapons, and featured two large fireplaces that contributed a little heat and a great deal of smoke to the indoor environment. Here, Pepin introduced the visitors to the members of his household. His wife Bertrada was a tall, blonde, energetic woman who had obviously contributed more to the making of their son Charles than had her husband. She was the center of a circle of well-dressed noblewomen, most of whom were known to Leoba. Besides Charles, Pepin and Bertrada had another son, Carloman, who was only about three years old and rarely left his mother's side.

The introduction of Carloman reminded Stephen that Pepin had an older brother of that name, who inherited half of their father's realm but then quickly abdicated. He retired to Mount Soracte, where he built a shrine to venerate the memory of Sylvester. Finding even Soracte too worldly—he was plagued by visits from Rome-bound pilgrims—Carloman moved to the remote Benedictine monastery of Cassino, where he had been living for the last six years, in the company of Ratchis, Aistulf's predecessor on the Lombard throne. "I have it on good authority that your brother Carloman is in fine health and continues in God's favor," Stephen said.

Several bystanders cringed: it was never a good idea to bring up the subject of brothers with a Frankish monarch. Many suspected that Carloman's abdication had been engineered in some way by Pepin, who thereby obtained sole control of his father's realm without the usual necessity for bloodshed. Pepin didn't offer any comment, and Stephen, seeking another topic of conversation, deepened the embarrassment by continuing: "And don't you also have another brother, named Grifo?"

"No longer, since last month, Your Holiness," said Pepin cryptically. Then, feeling that some more explanation was called for, he added: "My good servant the Count of Vienne cut down the treacherous pretender as he was on his way to Lombardy, where he was hoping to find allies in his schemes against us."

This was interesting news to Stephen; it suggested that the friendship between the Franks and the Lombards might not be as robust as some of his advisors had suggested. He said: "The Count was an agent of God's will, for a false claim of kingship always earns divine retribution."

"Sadly, the Count also died in the battle," said Pepin. Not knowing exactly how to fit this into the Divine Plan, Stephen simply muttered "God rest his soul."

The next morning, Stephen and Pepin had arranged to meet in the chapel. Stephen knew that Pepin's display of self-abasement on the previous day demanded some reciprocal gesture. So, not to be outdone, he donned sackcloth and had himself liberally sprinkled with ashes; then, when they met, he threw himself prostrate on the floor of the chapel in front of Pepin. With tears welling from his eyes, he begged Pepin to come to the rescue of St. Peter and the Roman Republic.

Now it was the King's turn to raise the Pope from the ground. "For the sake of Christendom," he said, "and for the salvation of my own soul, I shall hasten to do your bidding—just as soon as I have obtained the agreement of my nobles. After all, it's they who must raise troops and money for this campaign."

This was Pepin's way of alluding to the issue of the coronation, whose purpose was to strengthen Pepin's hand with the nobles. Stephen didn't immediately respond to this; rather, he engaged Pepin in a lengthy prayer session, which was followed by a mass attended by the entire court. After that came an exchange of presents. Stephen gave Pepin a relic of unusual sanctity—the Holy Prepuce, which was the circumcised foreskin of Jesus, preserved in oil and contained in an ancient golden box encrusted with rare jewels. Pepin reciprocated with a bloodstained battle-ax. He explained that his father Charles the Hammer had used this very ax to decapitate the Saracen leader Abdul Rahman Al Ghafiqi during the battle of Tours, thus saving Gaul for Christianity. Stephen couldn't fail to grasp the relevance of such a gift to the purpose of his visit, and he thanked Pepin profusely.

Over the following few days, allusion and symbolism gave way to hard bargaining, as Stephen, Pepin, and their advisors negotiated the details of their agreement. In the final pact, Stephen would crown Pepin, as well as his two sons, in front of his assembled nobles at Fulrad's abbey of St. Denis, near Paris. In doing so he would make a clear statement that the divine right of kingship was being conferred on Pepin and his descendants. Pepin, for his part, would compel Aistulf to hand over a large swath of territory to the papacy, including Ravenna, the Five Cities, and other cities that Aistulf had seized in the region between Ravenna and Rome. There was no mention of restoring any of these cities to their previous ruler, the Emperor. Thus Pepin's and Stephen's agreement would, if carried out, establish a new order in Italy—one in which the pope would for the first time become the ruler of an extensive territory in central Italy, and thus would be capable of raising taxes, levying armies, and waging war on his own behalf, just as the Donation of Constantine entitled him to do. What's more, by crowning Pepin, he would be asserting his own right to make and unmake kings across the entire western half the old Roman Empire.

Certain things were left unsaid in the agreement. What if Pepin totally destroyed the Lombard kingdom? Would he then be free to extend the Frankish realm to include all the fertile lands of northern Italy that Aistulf now possessed—even perhaps the duchies of Tuscany, Spoleto, and Benevento that Aistulf ruled through proxies? No doubt Stephen would have to acquiesce in some southward expansion if Pepin demanded it. But Pepin was adamant that he would not seek land beyond the Frankish passes. He had enough troubles to deal with in the East and in Aquitaine, he said, without attempting to expand his current empire.

With the details of the agreement worked out, thoughts turned to the coronation. Pepin suggested that Stephen and his party move to the abbey of St. Denis, where the coronation would be held. Not only would this simplify the planning, the abbey would also offer a more comfortable residence, and its ecclesiastical environment was more suited to the visitors. Ponthion boasted only a few clerics, and these, Stephen found, exemplified what was wrong with so many of the Frankish clergy—they were unlettered and seemingly unconcerned with anyone's spiritual welfare, least of all their own. Stephen was determined to have some serious conversations with Chrodegang and Boniface on this score.

So the papal party, along with Pepin and most of his court, set out on the six-day journey to St. Denis. About the only people who regretted leaving Ponthion were Zaid and Tito, who had spent their free time there exploring the forest, hunting small game, and learning the fiery mysteries of horse-shoeing. Such a freewheeling existence was not likely to be possible at St. Denis.

30

——

Stepping cautiously to avoid waking her parents, Lenora made her way down from their sleeping quarters to the parlor where Sibyl practiced her black arts. She lit a candle at the remains of a small wood fire, and then she assembled on Sibyl's table the objects that she needed: the geode, the quicksilver, and the other minerals. She also placed Zaid's wooden camel among the minerals, as well as the lead tablet with Zaid's hair, which she had asked Omar to return to her. Then she lit the incense-burner and drew the black curtain with its embroidered symbols around the table.

Lenora was intent on renewing the spell that had worked, after a fashion, last year. She did indeed see Zaid, as her mother had promised, but it had only been a brief view at the procession and then a short conversation and hurried embrace before Zaid's departure with the papal delegation. Now Zaid had been gone for four months, and there was no word from him. Omar had told her about the manumission, but what good was that when Zaid was hundreds of miles away and wasn't even aware that he would be freed?

Surely her mother's magic could do better than that! But Sibyl had refused to repeat the spell, saying that it was bad luck to do so. It may also have been that she now agreed with Marcus—that it was time for Lenora to forget about Zaid. So Lenora had made up her mind to cast the spell on her own.

"*Mercuri trismegiste*—Thrice-great Mercury," she whispered. That much she remembered, because that was how her mother began most of her incantations. "*Liga Zaidum*—bind Zaid—" What came after that? Lenora couldn't remember, so she extemporized. "Mercury, please bring Zaid back to me, because he's been away for so long and I'm worried about him and I miss him so much." Then she tried to copy some of the symbols from the inside of the curtain onto the lead sheet. She wasn't very successful at it.

Lenora tensed as she heard footsteps in the street outside. But it was only the night watchman on his usual rounds— she saw a glimmer of light from his lantern that percolated under the curtain. After his steps disappeared into the distance, Lenora's attention began to wander away from the task at hand. She went over the past conversations between Zaid and herself, especially the last one. Then she imagined talking to him in the here and now. She asked him about his travels and adventures, and made up some fantastical replies. She in turn told him about her parents' doings, about her life at the bakery, and about the recent changes in her body that were announcing her arrival at womanhood.

Ten minutes passed in this reverie, and then Lenora was surprised to hear footsteps again. The night watchman never retraced his steps, she knew. She peeked out through the curtain. It was two men, rather than one, but it was difficult to make out anything about them, even in the moonlight, because they were darkly clad and carried no lanterns.

Lenora tiptoed to the front of Sibyl's parlor. She could see that the two men had stopped by Omar's doorway, and then they disappeared inside. Either Omar had left the door unsecured, or they had quietly forced the lock.

Lenora thought of waking her parents, but then they would see what she had been up to. So she crept out of the store and edged her way to the front of Omar's workshop. The door was ajar, but the men didn't seem to be in the workshop. She heard the sound of muffled movements, and wondered whether the men had climbed up the steps to Omar's bedchamber and were intent on robbing him.

Lenora took a few steps inside Omar's workshop, straining to hear what was going on. Then she heard Omar's voice, calling out: "What's that? Who's there? Who's—" His voice quickly became muffled, as if he was struggling to resist suffocation, and there was the noise of groaning and thumping and struggling limbs.

Lenora screamed at the top of her voice: "Help! Help! Murder! Help!" Her cries woke some of the neighbors: she heard shouts of "What's going on?" and "Who's there?" from several sides. But before any help could arrive, she heard the sounds of men descending the steps from Omar's bedroom. They were breathing heavily, and one of the men was trying to urge on the other, saying "Let's go! Let's go! Get out of here!" Lenora shrank back into a dark corner of the workshop, pressing herself back against an array of relics that were hanging from the walls.

Just a moment or two later, Lenora saw a figure enter the workshop from the street. It was her father, carrying a heavy staff. He entered the workshop, shouting "What's happening? Who's here?" He collided with the first of the two assailants, who were trying to make good their escape before the whole neighborhood was aroused. Marcus saw a glint of moonlight reflected off a bloodied dagger that the man was carrying. He tried to stab Marcus, but Marcus struck him on the head with his staff, and he fell to the floor. Now the second assailant, who was also holding a dagger, made a run at Marcus. Again Marcus swung with his staff, but this time the assailant was able to grasp the staff and force Marcus backward and downward.

Lenora could see that her father was in immediate danger of being stabbed. She reached instinctively behind her for something to use as a weapon. By chance, she touched on a sword. It was as rusty and blunt as would be expected for an ancient relic, but she pulled it from the wall, ran forward, and thrust at her father's assailant. The man heard her coming and turned partway toward her, so that the sword sliced into the side of his neck. He screamed and fell down, bleeding profusely. In the turmoil, the other man rose groggily to his feet, grasped the situation, and made a run for the door before Marcus could stop him.

Lenora's thoughts turned immediately to Omar, and she climbed the steps to his bedroom, closely followed by her father. The relic-maker was lying slantwise on his bed; his gasping breaths alternated with fits of choking. Even in the faint light, Lenora could see that blood was running from stab wounds in his chest and belly. His eyes were open but he didn't look toward Lenora or Marcus.

Already horrified by the events downstairs, Lenora was put into an ever greater state of terror by the sight of Omar's agony. She and Marcus tried to ease his breathing by raising up his head. Marcus said, "Omar, who did this?" Omar tried to form some words, but none came out. Then he was seized by a fit of choking and coughing, which momentarily cleared his airways, and he took a couple of decent breaths. "Omar! Who did this to you?" shouted Marcus once more.

Omar struggled to speak. He finally managed the word: "Paul." Then, after another fit of choking, he said again: "Paul—Deacon Paul! He sent them!"

"Deacon Paul? Why? Why would he do this to you?"

Omar seemed not to hear Marcus's question. He managed to utter a few more words that Marcus did not understand: *"La ilaha illa Allah—There is no God but Allah."* Then he fell back, no longer either breathing or choking. Blood continued to trickle from the corner of his mouth, and from his wounds, but he was obviously dead.

Lenora and Marcus heard a confusion of shouts from downstairs and saw the flickering light of torches. "Let's go," said Marcus, and they descended to Omar's workshop, where they found an ever-growing crowd of neighbors gathered around the body that lay in a pool of blood. Sibyl was among them. Marcus pulled Sibyl and Lenora out of the workshop and brushed away several people who tried to ask him what had happened.

Once they were back in their own home, Marcus gathered his wife and daughter in a huddle. "Omar was killed—by the Pope's men," he said.

"Omar's dead?" asked Sibyl in horror. "That body wasn't him though, was it?"

"That was one of the men who killed him. He tried to kill me too, but Lenora got him. Omar was upstairs."

Lenora was shaking violently, and then she was seized by a fit of retching. Sibyl tried to comfort her.

"How do you know who they were?" she asked her husband.

"Omar told me—before he died."

"Why? Why would they do that?" Sibyl asked. Then she turned her attention to her daughter and offered her a cloth. "Nora, here—wipe yourself."

"I don't know. I have no idea. He worked for them. Maybe he cheated them. Or maybe they didn't want to pay. It makes no sense. Nora, you saved my life."

Lenora now broke into unrestrained weeping, and Marcus joined his wife in hugging and comforting her. "I'm so sorry you had to see that," he said. "That you had to do that."

"Poor Omar," sobbed Lenora. Although she knew that Omar had sometimes been brutal to Zaid, she herself had always been treated well by him, and the thought of his struggle against the knife-wielding assassins tortured her. "And poor Zaid—when he comes back." She imagined Zaid returning home and finding his father's mutilated body, and being left alone in the world.

"Marcus," said Sibyl, "you say there was another man? He ran away?"

"Yes, there were two."

"So he knows what happened—who killed his partner?"

"Yes," said Marcus. "And they'll be back for revenge, there's no doubt about that. We have to leave."

"Leave?" asked Lenora. "Where to?"

"I don't know—anywhere—away from Rome."

"When?"

"Right now. Get your things—whatever you can carry."

The hubbub from next door was constantly increasing. "What about Omar? Who's going to bury him?" asked

Lenora.

"I don't know," said her father. "Come on, we have to go, right now. Get your things."

The three of them hurriedly gathered together their most necessary items, including their savings, a few other valuables, food, and some clothes. Lenora grabbed Zaid's wooden camel.

Sibyl pointed to her spell-casting items assembled on the table, and the still-burning candle. "What were you doing?" she asked her daughter.

"I was trying to bring Zaid back," said Lenora, amidst renewed tears.

"We've got to go," said Marcus impatiently.

The three of them, with their little packs, looked out into the street. A crowd had gathered around Omar's store. "This way," said Marcus, leading his wife and daughter in the other direction. No one seemed to notice their departure.

"We should head for Lucca," said Sibyl. "We'll be safe there."

"Yes," said Marcus, "that's what we'll do. But we can't leave until the gates are open. Let's go wait up at the old mill—no one will come there." The new ship-mills were now working, so the mills on the Janiculum had been abandoned once more.

The family made their way down Silversmiths' Street, and turned left up the Aurelian Way. Once or twice they had to dodge into side alleys to avoid being seen by watchmen. After about twenty minutes they reached the mill at the top of the Janiculum Hill. The moon was setting and it was very dark. They entered the mill and sat on a bench, waiting. The aqueduct had been diverted to St. Peter's again, so no water ran through the mill and the mill-wheels sat motionless and silent. Occasionally, mice or rats scurried about, looking for any grains that the millers might have left behind.

After about an hour it started to get light, and then they heard the sound of St. Pancras Gate being opened and a few travelers entering or leaving the city on carts or horseback. They waited until the sounds died away, then left the mill and walked through the gate, which was just a few paces from the mill. The gate-keeper knew Marcus and gave him a familiar nod.

Before leaving Rome, they turned and took a final look at the city. The river and the flatlands next to it were shrouded in mist, but the sun was about to rise behind the Caelian Hill on the other side of the valley, and below it they could see the Lateran palace and the neighboring basilica. The sight reminded Marcus of everything that had just happened. He was filled with rage against Deacon Paul and the entire papal hierarchy that had, for reasons he could only guess at, killed Omar and forced them to flee the city where they had lived for seven years.

After heading west for a short distance, the three refugees struck north on lanes that crossed the Vatican Hill above the basilica of St. Peter. Eventually they joined the Cassian Way a mile or so north of the Milvian Bridge. They continued northward, and after about an hour they were able to get a ride on a farmer's cart in exchange for a few coins.

31

The ladies of the court fussed around Bertrada like workers around a queen bee. Two of them stood on chairs, holding Bertrada's coronation robe above her, and then they gradually lowered it over her head until it rested on her shoulders. Other ladies grasped the edges of the robe and cautiously worked it downward, past her shoulders, bust, and hips, until the hem reached the floor. Another lady tied the robe around Bertrada's neck. They all stood back to look at their creation, then some darted forward and made adjustments here and there, until they were all satisfied.

Ever since they arrived at St. Denis, six weeks earlier, the ladies had labored almost without rest to embroider a multicolored pattern of flowers, birds, and fishes onto the white linen. Bertrada hadn't been so magnificently attired since the day of her wedding. She walked up and down, showing off the robe. The low cut of the hem hid her feet—one of which was slightly deformed—and made her seem to glide like a swan rather than walk on human legs.

The young Carloman was being kept at a distance from his mother. This, in addition to the stiff and unusual clothing he was wearing, made him fretful, and a couple of women tried to keep him distracted. He was the only male present in Bertrada's drawing room, until there was a knock at the door, and Pepin's voice could be heard: "Bertrada, are you ready?"

"Let them in," Bertrada said to one of her companions, who opened the door to Pepin and Charles. Both were dressed, like Bertrada, in white linen, but overlain with capes of blue silk and edged with ermine.

"Are you ready, my dear," Pepin asked again after he had been admitted. "The ceremony will begin shortly. You look more beautiful than I could have imagined," he added. Then he cuffed Carloman in a friendly way. "And are you ready, young man?" Carloman didn't seem particularly ready; he knew something was afoot but had no idea what it was.

In spite of Pepin's friendly demeanor towards his wife, he was actually thinking about divorce: he was wondering whether the coronation would complicate matters. Pepin's grandfather had two wives at the same time, and no one thought the worse of him for it. His father, Charles the Hammer, took a second wife only after his first wife died, but he kept a concubine who bore him several children. Bertrada was Pepin's second wife, but he married her only after divorcing his first wife and sending her off to a monastery. Now, with the increasing involvement of the papacy in Frankish affairs, monogamy would be expected, and divorce might require special permission from Stephen. He might not be willing to grant it, especially if Bertrada was leading an exemplary life. Pepin regretted not having divorced her some years ago, before Zachary had started to lay down the law about marital and sexual arrangements among the Franks.

While Pepin was mulling over these matters, Stephen talked with Abbot Fulrad and Bishop Chrodegang in a different part of the abbey. The two Frankish clerics would assist him at the coronation. Boniface would have been an obvious candidate to participate, but he decided not to travel from Mainz for the ceremony. In his mind, Pepin was already King of the Franks, having been anointed as such by Boniface himself at Soissons, with Zachary's blessing. Thus the coronation at St. Denis seemed to wrongfully diminish or deny the significance of the earlier event.

While Stephen was talking with the two prelates, a herald approached with some packages. "Your Holiness, a messenger arrived with letters from Rome," he said, handing one letter to Stephen and one to Chrodegang.

These were the first letters to reach Stephen and his party since they left Rome. "How timely—arriving on the day of the coronation," he commented.

"The messenger knew about the coronation, Your Holiness, and made haste to be here," said the herald.

Stephen saw that his letter was from Paul. He was anxious to know how things were going in Rome, and how Paul was faring as his proxy. Still, the coronation was about to begin, so he put the unopened letter in the inside pocket of his robe. Meanwhile, Chrodegang had opened his and perused it. "Deacon Paul is very interested in liturgical reform in Francia," he said. "I must read it later, but he may not understand that we have some different traditions here. Oh, what's this—he's also written a letter to Sister Leoba."

"Oh," said Stephen casually, "Give it to me, I'll be seeing her shortly." Chrodegang handed over the sealed letter, and

Stephen pocketed it. It seemed slightly odd to him that Paul would write to Leoba at all, and that he would enclose the letter within another letter to Chrodegang. Still, that was probably because Paul had little idea of Leoba's whereabouts, so he had thought best to let Chrodegang give it to her or forward it to her at her current location.

The three men walked over to the abbey's basilica. Fulrad apologized to Stephen for the small size of the church, and he mentioned that Pepin had ordered the construction of a larger one. As they entered the vestry they could hear a choir singing, as well as much talk and laughter. There was also the clanking of armor and weapons, for many of the nobles considered their military gear to be the most appropriate dress for Pepin's coronation. After all, Pepin first became the ruler of the Franks in traditional fashion—by being heaved skyward on a shield by heavily armed men. By coming to the coronation as if to a pitched battle, the nobles may have been signaling their preference for the old Frankish ways over new-fangled Italian ceremonial.

An acolyte entered the vestry and approached Stephen to say that the royal party was slightly delayed. So the three men sat in the vestry for a minute or two. Stephen pulled out his brother's letter, unsealed it, and began to read: "*Dilecta Leoba, dulcissima Leoba—Beloved Leoba, sweetest Leoba, I know you—*" Stephen stopped. He'd opened the wrong letter, obviously. He made as if to close it again, but it was too late. The first words shocked him deeply, and he had to read on. "*I know you told me not to write, but my heart is breaking with the pain of separation from you. Every hour of the day I think of your angelic face and sweet voice. Every hour of the night I dream of the warm pressure of your body and the gentle heaving of your breasts, and then I am cruelly woken to a cold, empty bed. Each day without you adds to the torture. When we were together, I didn't realize the intensity of my feelings. Oh, Leoba, there's a heavenly magic between us, let's not break the spell. You have promised to return, so do so as quickly as possible—as soon as the winter has passed. And in the meantime, write to me. Tell me where you are and everything you have done, and all the thoughts that are in your head. Do you still think of me as passionately as I think of you? Have you seen Boniface yet? Have you asked him whether you may return to Rome? What did he say? If he says yes, hurry back before he changes his mind. If he says no, don't accept it. Beg him, present all the arguments that we discussed. Tell him that Stephen values your work highly and wishes you to return. Write to me quickly, by the same messenger who brings this letter to you. Tell me how often you think about me. And when you think of me, are you filled with the pain of separation, as I am, or have you reconciled yourself to my absence? Tell me the truth, sweetest Leoba, but don't break my heart. Leoba, my dearest Leoba, hurry back, for sometimes I fear that I cannot go on without you. I need your hand in mine, your—"*

"Your Holiness—Your Holiness!" Stephen's attention was jerked away from the letter, and he looked up. "We're ready, Your Holiness," said Fulrad. "Pepin and his family are entering the church."

"Oh yes," said Stephen, stuffing the letter back into his pocket. "Then give the signal."

A subdeacon emerged from the sacristy into the basilica, which was crowded far beyond its limited capacity, and walked solemnly toward the altar. He was followed by an acolyte carrying an ornate gospel book and another carrying an epistle book. At the sight of the Holy Scriptures, everyone rose from their seats—the men on the south side of the church, the women on the north side, and the priests and bishops in the apse. Having reached the altar, the subdeacon took the books and placed them reverentially on the altar, then stepped aside.

The choir now began to chant the introit, and a splendid double procession entered the church: one consisting of Stephen, Fulrad, and Chrodegang, and the other of Pepin, Bertrada, and their two sons. Each of these groups was preceded by seven acolytes carrying candles and a deacon swinging a golden censer, whose fragrant smoke wafted through the basilica.

Pepin and his family took their seats on four thrones on the south side of the altar; thus Bertrada was the only woman on that side of the church. Stephen prayed silently at the altar, and then gave the kiss of peace to Chrodegang, Fulrad, and several other high ecclesiastics. The deacons walked two by two to the altar, and kissed the ends of it, and then Stephen kissed the gospel book and the center of the altar. Having done so, he walked to his throne, which was located in the center of the apse. It was noticeably higher and grander than Pepin's. He stood silently facing eastward during the Kyries, then he turned to face the congregation and intoned the Gloria, which was taken up by the choir.

Even at this early stage of the mass, the congregation noticed subtle changes from the Gallican rite to which they were accustomed: the Pope had insisted on use of the Roman rite throughout. Although elements of this rite had been creeping into the Frankish liturgy for years, this was the first fully Roman mass that they had witnessed, and it made some people uncomfortable—another sign, they thought, that southerners were trying to dictate how Franks practiced their religion. Others, though, welcomed this instruction in a liturgy that might be more pleasing to God than their home-grown version.

"*Pax vobis—peace unto you*," said the Pope, again disturbing those who had been expecting *pax vobiscum*. But there was a hearty "*Et cum spiritu tuo—and with thy spirit*" from the congregation. Stephen sat down on his throne, and signaled others to sit.

A deacon ascended the epistle pulpit and began to read the words of St. Paul. After he was done there was more chanting, and then another deacon ascended the other pulpit and began reading from the gospel of Matthew. Stephen had chosen a passage that led up to the question posed to Jesus about the tribute money, which led to his famously ambiguous reply, "*Reddite ergo quae sunt Caesaris Caesari— Render therefore unto Caesar the things which are Caesar's, and unto God the things that are God's.*"

This passage was very relevant to the day's proceedings, but it didn't hold Stephen's attention. In his mind he was obsessively rereading the words that he had just seen in Paul's letter. *How could this be?* he thought. Paul was his younger brother and loyal supporter, a lifelong and energetic servant of the Church. His trustworthiness had never come into question. His ideas on how to save Rome from the Lombards, though they initially struck Stephen as too radical, now seemed as if they had a good chance of succeeding. He was a strong candidate to be the next Pope—and a Pope who would save the Catholic faith from the backward-looking ideas of men like Theophylact. How then had he so demeaned and polluted himself, and put his future in such great danger, by writing a shameless love-letter to a nun? His letter hinted at—no, spoke outright of fornication. Surely he must have been aware of the depravity of it? Surely he realized how great was the likelihood of discovery, and how it would destroy him and leave Stephen deprived of his counsel and exposed to every kind of attack from Theophylact and his allies?

The deacon completed his reading, and there was more chanting, followed by a little procession, and then more reading, but Stephen neither heard nor saw any part of it. He thought only of Paul. How could he have been so deceived about the character of his brother—the one person on Earth he was close to, and this over a lifetime? And if Paul was a liar and a sinner, what else might he have lied and sinned about? Decades of memories passed before Stephen's eyes. Paul had always been the arranger, the fixer—as they struggled up the Lateran hierarchy from lowly orphans to deacons and trusted counselors of a succession of popes— popes who passed over any number of more likely comers in favor of the ambitious pair. Paul had organized Stephen's first, unsuccessful candidacy for the Papacy, and then his successful one. How he had relied on Paul at every turn, how he had trusted him and never inquired about anything! Was that a terrible mistake?

And what about Constantine's Donation, which had propelled Stephen on this long journey, and which at this very moment was turning Paul's far-fetched plans into reality? Stephen recalled how smoothly Paul had disposed of Theophylact's skeptical arguments. Could that all have been deceit, intented to cover up some devious plot? Was the whole foundation for his dealings with Pepin nothing but a monstrous lie?

Stephen couldn't permit himself to believe that this was

possible. No, Paul wasn't a liar or an evildoer: he was a victim. This gross lapse in his behavior had only one cause—Leoba. Stephen had never been comfortable with her presence in the Lateran palace. Yes, she was an unusually learned woman who had many productive and engaging dialogues with his counselors and visitors. She had done fine work in the scriptorium. But she was headstrong—she followed her own impulses rather than listening to the admonitions of her superiors. Her education, no doubt, had caused her to reject the natural modesty of womanhood. She rarely wore the veil within the palace, and thus drew men's eyes toward her. She was, Stephen now realized, little more than a harlot in the outward form of a nun. Seeking to satisfy her own carnal lust, she had worked ceaselessly to engender and satisfy that same lust in Paul.

From his throne in the apse, Stephen looked to his left, where the women were sitting. Yes, there she was, unveiled as usual, sitting among the ladies of the court rather than in her proper place among the sisters of the Abbey. She was even whispering into the ear of the woman next to her, who seemed to be smiling or laughing at her words. There was really nothing unusual about that—many quiet or not-so-quiet conversations were going on as the deacon read from the gospel book—but to Stephen it reflected more than mere boredom at the length of the proceedings; it signaled a satanic wantonness on Leoba's part. A misogynistic streak in Stephen's personality got the better of his judgment. Breaking with liturgical usage, he rose abruptly from his throne, and the deacon paused in his reading.

"*Mulieres in ecclesiis taceant,*" Stephen bellowed, glaring directly at Leoba. "*Let the women keep silence in the churches.*"

After the echoes of his words died away, there was a deathly hush in the basilica. Few members of the congregation understood Stephen's words, but the manner in which he delivered them made their meaning clear. No one knew how to proceed. Stephen sat down again and signaled the deacon to continue his reading, which he did in a more hesitant voice than before.

By framing his outburst in the words of St. Paul, Stephen had lent it a certain scriptural authority. It was also justified, to some extent, by the disrespectful chatter that had been going on—something that Stephen would never have had to listen to in Rome. Still, his action was a highly unusual interruption of the established liturgy. And besides, there had been audible conversations on both sides of the church, not just among the women.

Stephen instantly regretted what he had done. Leoba had to be punished, but in as private a way as possible. Any kind of public shaming would run the risk of drawing attention to the reason for it—the secret liaison between her and Paul. For the moment, Stephen tried to turn his attention away from Leoba and focus on the liturgical proceedings.

After the gospel reading, a deacon called for the unbaptized to leave the church, and a few youngsters did so. The liturgy of the Eucharist took over two hours, on account of the elaborate anthems sung during the offertory and the rites that followed, and because of the large number of communicants. Twenty priests assisted with the provision of the sacramental bread and wine to the assembled men and women. Only the most prominent among the congregation, such as Pepin and the bishops, tasted directly of the wine that was changed into the blood of Christ at the altar. The rest made do with ordinary wine that had been sanctified by addition of a few drops of the wine that had undergone transubstantiation.

With the Eucharist finally completed, the coronation itself began. Another procession entered the church, bringing the sacred oil and four golden, gem-encrusted crowns to the altar. Stephen blessed all of these, and touched them to the box that contained the Holy Prepuce. Then, preceded by acolytes and accompanied by Abbot Fulrad, Pepin came to the altar and knelt before the Pope, who anointed him on the head, chest, and hands while giving him God's blessing. Bishop Chrodegang then took the largest crown from the altar and handed it to Stephen, who placed it on Pepin's head and pronounced him both King of Francia and—to cement his ties to the papacy—a Patrician of Rome.

Pepin rose and received the kiss of peace from Stephen, and then stood aside while Bertrada and the two boys were similarly anointed and crowned. Carloman was well behaved during his own crowning, but started bawling when he was kissed, startled perhaps by the proximity of Stephen's unprepossessing face. The embarrassing noise was quickly drowned out, however, as the assembled nobles began a raucous and unholy shouting and clashing of their weapons by way of marking their assent to the four coronations.

Stephen turned to the assembled nobles and signaled for silence, and then offered a solemn declamation. *"Benedictio Dei omnipotentis*—May the blessing of Almighty God, the Father, the Son, and the Holy Spirit, descend on you and remain with you always. And we hereby bind each one of you, under our interdiction and penalty of excommunication, that you shall never, for all time to come, presume to elect a

King sprung from the loins of any other but of these persons whom the Divine Mercy—in accordance with the intercession of the holy Apostles—has deigned to exalt and confirm and consecrate by the hands of their Vicar the most blessed Pope."

After some concluding rites, Stephen and the other ecclesiastics left the basilica in solemn procession, to the accompaniment of anthems. The entire proceedings had lasted four hours, and Stephen was glad of the opportunity to use the urinals before the great mass of congregants descended on them. Having done so, he walked over to his quarters, accompanied by deacons and other attendants who would help remove his tiara and the outer layers of his vestments. He asked one of them, in as causal tone as he could manage, to find Leoba and bring her to him.

Stephen was sitting at his writing desk about half an hour later when Leoba knocked at the door of his chambers. He told her to come in. She was distraught; she didn't know why Stephen had reacted so strongly in the church, but she was conscious of her own wrong-doing, and she launched into an apology before Stephen even spoke. "Your Holiness, I beg your forgiveness for my gross misbehavior," she said. "I showed disrespect for the words of the Holy Gospel, and—"

"Read this," said Stephen, handing her Paul's letter. As she scanned the first words, all the blood drained from her face and she staggered and almost fell, but she managed to save herself. She continued reading, while thinking furiously about how to rescue the situation.

"Your Holiness," she said at last, "this letter is as shocking to me as it must be to you. Deacon Paul and I spent a great deal of time together during my stay in Rome, but that time was spent entirely in scholarly discourse and spiritual contemplation. Nothing such as is suggested here transpired between us—I can assure Your Holiness of that. I see from his letter that Deacon Paul's feelings toward me have been very different from what I imagined. However, when he seems to speak of carnal intimacy between us, that must be the product of his fantasy, perhaps fueled by loneliness, I don't know. It has nothing to do with what actually—"

"Enough!" said Stephen. "You're a brazen whore. We invited you to stay on at the Lateran palace, after Fulrad left, simply out of pity for your sickness. But we were clutching a snake to our breast, as I now realize."

"It wasn't the—" Leoba began, tears starting down her cheeks. But Stephen wasn't to be deflected. "You were sent by the Devil with the purpose of leading my brother into temptation," he went on. "And you succeeded in poisoning him with your wiles. Boniface told me that all women who come to Francia from Britain are whores, the one exception being yourself—but now I see that he was deceived even in that. There can be no—"

"Your Holiness," Leoba broke in again, "Your Holiness speaks as if anything that transpired between us—and nothing did transpire—you speak as if it was the result of my sinfulness alone. I am indeed a sinner, but I didn't cause those things to happen—which I can assure you didn't happen. Your Holiness's brother isn't some innocent child who—"

"Silence!" Stephen roared, sparing Leoba from further entanglement. "Your guilt is self-evident—your own words condemn you. Here's my verdict: Leave here immediately and return to Boniface. Confess your sins to him and accept whatever penance he deems proper. Don't attempt to contact Deacon Paul by any means, direct or indirect, don't speak to anyone of this, except in confession, and don't show your face in Rome as long as you live."

"Your Holiness—"

"*Silence!* We've spoken—now leave our presence."

32

Marcus and his family made only slow progress northward. Both Sibyl and Lenora became footsore. Rarely were they able to get rides on carts or wagons, because the poor condition of the roads forced most travelers to transport their goods with pack animals. The short winter days and inclement weather also hampered them. After a couple of weeks they had only made it as far as the southern part of Tuscany.

Some of the southbound travelers they met along the way spoke of troop movements in central Tuscany. This news added to Marcus's anxiety, and he and Sibyl debated whether they should continue toward Lucca. They decided to go as far as Siena and stay there if the situation in the countryside became too risky. But one afternoon, as they were making a long climb on the Cassian Way, a group of armed men emerged from the woods at the side of the road.

"Where are you coming from?" one of the men demanded.

"From Rome," said Marcus. "Who are you?"

"And where are you heading?"

"To Lucca. Why are you stopping us?"

"From Rome to Lucca, at this time of year? For what reason?"

"We're from Lucca, but we lived in Rome for the last seven years. Now we're returning home."

"Why?"

"Homesick, I suppose. We want to be with our parents."

"Homesick? That's what suddenly sent you out on the road in February, after seven years? What's your occupation?"

"Miller."

"There's work for you in Lucca?"

"I hope so. Why, what's the problem?"

"Spies are the problem."

"Spies?" asked Marcus. "You think I'm a spy? Would I bring my wife and daughter with me if I was a spy?"

"Very possibly. Whose side are you on?"

"Whose side? Is there a war?"

"There will be."

"We're Tuscans—citizens of Lucca."

The man who was questioning them turned to his companions. After they talked for while, he turned back to Marcus. "You must come with us," he said.

"Where to?"

"To meet our commander. Follow us."

The armed men led them down a footpath to a clearing where a larger group of men were camped. After some discussion among the men, four of them told Marcus and his family to go with them, and they walked northward on the Cassian Way for an hour, along with another couple of travelers who had also been detained on their journey northward. Eventually they reached a much larger encampment by a river. This camp looked like it could accommodate several thousand people. Hundreds of men were engaged in a variety of activities such as practicing the use of weapons and exercising horses, and women fetched firewood and cooked at open fires.

Marcus and his family were taken by their captors to a large tent, where several officers were meeting. The captors talked with one of the officers, who then turned to Marcus. "I understand that you're Tuscans, living in Rome?" he said.

"We've been living in Rome, but now we're returning to Lucca, our home," said Marcus.

"Tuscany and Rome are at war," said the officer. "Travelers from Rome are likely to be spies."

"We're not spies. We haven't heard anything about this war. What's the reason for it?"

"The Pope in Rome is threatening the King of the Lombards. Who sent you here?"

"Ourselves. No one sent us."

"So you're walking from Rome to Lucca, in this season, carrying so little?"

"We had to leave," said Marcus. "The Pope's men would have killed us." He briefly explained what had happened.

"So you have no love for Rome?"

"Not for Rome's rulers. Because of what happened before we left, but also for other reasons. They executed the grain-master, Gaius, because our ship-mills were destroyed in a flood, but it wasn't his fault. I feared for my own life if something like that should happen again."

"Ship-mills? What are they?"

"Mills that float on the Tiber."

"We need men who know Rome. Especially the

defenses."

"There's going to be a siege, then?"

"Most probably. Unless they agree to our terms."

"How could your army besiege Rome? The walls are twelve miles around."

"Three other armies will join us."

"The walls are very strong," said Marcus, "but there are weak spots."

The officer looked interested. "Such as?" he asked.

"At our mill on the Janiculum Hill, there's an opening, where the aqueduct used to come through." Lenora kicked her father in the shin as if to stop him talking, but he ignored her. He explained how the loss of the ship-mills forced them to reopen the mills on Trajan's aqueduct, and how the Janiculum mills were abandoned again after the ship-mills were rebuilt. "The opening we made was never closed up. We were there the day we left Rome—the hole was still open."

"Maybe they'll close it up, once a siege begins?"

"That's possible, but I don't think so. The hole is in the basement of the mill, which has been abandoned. No one would think to look there. And it's not visible from outside the wall either—it's hidden by the roof of the aqueduct. You'd really have to know about it."

"How large is it—the opening?"

"Large enough for one man at a time, that's all. But they could gather in the mill and not be seen. And the mill's right by St. Pancras Gate."

"All right," said the officer. "Wait outside." He turned to confer with his colleagues. The men who had brought Marcus and his family to the camp led them out of the tent and told them to wait until they were called back in.

"Why did you say all that?" Lenora asked her father in an angry whisper.

"Say all what?"

"About the gap in the wall. Do you want the Lombards to take Rome?"

"The Tuscans, not the Lombards. We're Tuscans. And I had to say something to prove that we're on their side. Do you want me to be killed as a spy—or all three of us maybe?"

"You didn't have to say that—did he, Mama?"

"I think it was all right," said Sibyl. "Rome isn't our home anymore. We're going back home to Lucca."

"How can you say that?" protested Lenora. "We've lived in Rome for years—most of my life. Everyone I know lives in Rome. Do you want the Lombards to break in and kill everyone we know, including Zaid—my future husband?"

"Zaid?" said Marcus. "He's not even in Rome."

"He will be. He's coming—"

"Stop this future husband nonsense. And it's the Tuscans—our people—not the Lombards."

"No! You heard him—the Pope is threatening the Lombards—that's the reason they're going to attack Rome. With three other armies, he said. That's the armies from Lombardy and Spoleto, and Benevento—isn't it, Mama? The Lombards and their servants, basically."

"She's kind of right," said Sibyl. "The Duke of Tuscany— Desiderius—he's a Lombard. This is Aistulf's war."

"All the more reason to say what I said," Marcus retorted. "There's no way Rome can resist a siege from all those armies. The city will fall, sooner or later. So do you want there to be a two-year siege, with half the population starved to death and a bloodbath at the end to finish off the rest, like what happened at Ravenna? Let's get it over quickly, have them come in quietly with the least bloodshed, let them take over the city from those damned priests, take some gold from the Lateran palace, and everyone can get on with their lives."

"The Pope is trying to—" Lenora had to stop talking as they were called back into the tent. The officer turned to Marcus again. "Very well," he said. "Come with us to Rome. We need millers. And your wife and daughter can work with the other women. If there's a siege, we'll need more information from you. If what you tell us is true, you'll be well recompensed and you can go home to Lucca. If not, you'll be killed. And your wife and daughter—well, let's not even talk about that."

33

Over the course of a month, a community of forty thousand souls had sprung up on the quiet banks of the Aisne river, a few miles west of the Neustrian city of Soissons. Its inhabitants had ridden or walked from every corner of the Frankish realm: wealthy horsemen in glittering armor from the Loire Valley, carrying their colorful standards; dour Swabians from the forests east of the Rhine, with their axes and staves; stubby fisher-folk from the Channel coast of Neustria, fat sleepy Burgundian farmers, and tall blond peasants from Frisia. Cavalrymen, foot-soldiers, archers, slingers, artillerymen, engineers, sappers, armorers, carpenters, bowyers, fletchers, trainers, farriers, iron-workers, butchers, bakers, cooks, draymen, mule-drivers, surgeons, and priests—all gathered together in the service of Pepin's planned campaign against the Lombards. While these contingents were accommodated in an extensive array of tents and other temporary shelters, Pepin and his Roman visitors enjoyed greater comfort a mile away at one of his residences, the royal villa of Brennacum.

A large training ground had been cleared on the right bank of the river, and part of this area was devoted to cavalry exercises. In one exercise, two hundred horsemen lined up at each end of the field, and then headed directly for each other. The horsemen advanced in three ranks, and within each rank the horses rode in precise formation, stride for stride, with the riders so close to each other that the legs of neighbors almost touched. Each rider wore full armor and carried a round shield in his left hand—with which he also held his horse's reins. His right hand held a spear, which he kept pointed at the enemy. He vibrated the spear as he rode to isolate it from the motions of his horse. Besides these weapons, each rider carried a short sword tied to his back.

As the two squadrons approached each other a tremendous noise arose. This came from the war cries of the combatants, as well as from the spectators, whose role was to imitate the cacophony of a real battle. Among the spectators were Zaid and Titus, who banged horseshoes against iron pots and screamed at the tops of their voices.

Soon the two squadrons collided with each other. Because the lethal iron tips of the riders' spears had been removed, no one was killed. Nevertheless, quite a few riders were knocked from their horses and some of these appeared to be hurt or dazed; those who could do so unsheathed their training swords and continued the mock battle on foot.

After the conclusion of these exercises the horsemen practiced their skills individually. They spent most of their time mounting and dismounting their steeds, which they did at great speed from the horse's right side, from its left side, and from the rear—all while wearing full armor and carrying their weapons. They even practiced mounting and dismounting at speed while holding their razor-sharp battle swords in their right hands. The idea was to be able to continue hand-to-hand fighting while making the transition between cavalryman and foot-soldier or the reverse, because losing one's horse, or finding another horse that was riderless, were frequent events during close combat.

Zaid marveled at the skills shown by the riders in these exercises, and he longed to attempt them himself—particular when he saw that Pepin's son Charles, a youth of his own age, was among those participating. But Titus reminded Zaid that they needed to get back to the stables to prepare the Pope's horses for departure, because Stephen and his party were about to set out on their long homeward journey.

As they walked back towards the royal residence, they passed other training fields where archers and slingers were practicing. Zaid had long experience of using a sling for hunting small game, and he couldn't resist approaching a group of slingers and asking them if he could try their weapons. They didn't speak Latin, but they understood Zaid's gestures and offered him a sling. This Frankish war-sling was much larger than the rope sling he was used to; it was a long wooden rod with a joint in the middle, like a threshing flail. Zaid had a hard time with it: the stone would hurtle skyward or smash into the ground rather than fly toward the target. The slingers laughed good-naturedly and demonstrated the proper technique. They looked as if they had been practicing their art since birth, because their bodies—especially their right shoulders—were enormously muscular, and they hurled their stones with great force and precision. What's more, they accomplished this with just a single revolution of the sling, and they followed one shot immediately with another, so that they might have more than one stone hurtling toward the enemy at any moment. The target posts were quickly reduced to splinters by this barrage. Zaid handed back his sling with a rueful grin.

Closer to the royal residence, artillerymen were practicing the use of siege engines. There were light artillery pieces, such as onagers, wagon-mounted crossbows, and mechanical slings and spear-launchers. But the pride of the Frankish artillerymen were the huge new trebuchets, whose design they had recently learned from the Byzantines. As Zaid and Titus watched, the men used one of the trebuchets to fire a small boulder at a wall that had been specifically constructed to resemble those built by the Lombards. The boulder struck the wall with a thrilling crash and sent bits of masonry flying in all directions. Given time, such a machine would be able to breach even the twenty-foot thick walls of Pavia. The trebuchets were far too big and heavy to transport across the Alps, however; Pepin's men would transport just the iron fittings, and they would assemble the entire engines at the site of the siege, using local trees for their massive beams.

As Zaid and Titus entered the village of Brennacum, they passed numerous workshops whose owners had been pressed into the war effort. In one, fletchers used pedal-powered lathes to turn perfectly straight arrow shafts; other workers fitted these shafts with feathers, cut a notch at the back end of each arrow for the drawstring, and fixed sharp iron broadheads to the other end. All this was done with such speed that new arrows piled up rapidly in the bins, until they were gathered and packed away for the long journey.

There was an entire row of workshops in which smiths were melting down scrap iron to produce a variety of metal objects: arrowheads, horseshoes, and the iron balls that some of the siege engines used as ammunition. Other workshops were devoted to the manufacture of leather goods, such as bridles and reins.

The street on which Zaid and Titus walked was thick with people—soldiers, laborers, horsemen, and carters transporting wood, grain, and other supplies. The air was laden with smoke from nearby bakeries and forges, and it carried the odors of food and excrement in about equal proportions. People were cursing and shouting at each other to get out of the way. There was a general air of excitement as Pepin's people got ready for another season of campaigning in distant lands.

At the royal villa, workers were packing supplies onto the carts that would accompany the pope on his southward journey. Zaid dropped into the kitchens to return the pots that he and Titus had been using as noise-makers, and then went over to the stables, where other grooms were already well along in the process of getting the horses ready for departure. Zaid joined them in their work. Not long after, they received word to bring the animals to the royal villa, where Stephen's party was ready to leave.

Stephen, it turned out, had learned that the Mont Cenis pass was open, and he was anxious to set out that very day, even though it was already noon. He had exchanged formal farewells with Pepin earlier in the day; Charles would accompany the party for a few days, as he had done on the way to Ponthion.

Compared with the Mons Jovis pass, which had caused them so much difficulty on their northward journey, the Mont Cenis pass was significantly lower and easier. In addition, Stephen recalled that Constantine had led his army over Mont Cenis in his campaign against Maxentius—the campaign that ended with victory at the Milvian Bridge. This seemed to augur well for himself and for Pepin, who planned to use the same pass to lead his Frankish army into Lombardy.

After the travelers assembled in the courtyard of the villa, joined by a large crowd of Frankish onlookers, Stephen led prayers for their safe return to Rome and for the success of Pepin's upcoming campaign. The prayers completed, nothing seemed to stand in the way of their departure, but Stephen signaled for Zaid to come to him. Zaid did so, fearing some public reprimand, perhaps in connection with his refusal to be baptized.

"Zaid," said Stephen, "I've received word from Rome—there was some irregularity in the circumstances of your enslavement. The letter recommends that you be manumitted—which is to say, freed."

Zaid gasped but said nothing. "The decision lies in my hands," Stephen went on, "and I've decided to agree to the request. You've worked hard and behaved yourself, and you've been of direct assistance to myself on several occasions, most especially during the crossing of the Alps."

Although Stephen didn't mention this, another factor influenced his decision—the story that Zaid recounted during those hours of darkness on Jove's Mountain—the story about his namesake, Zaid ibn Harithah. Over the ensuing weeks Stephen had mulled over this story on many occasions. Surely, for His own mysterious reasons, God had chosen this heathen youth to deliver an important message to the successor of Peter. If not by ministry and lovingkindness, He seemed to be saying, then by the sword. This was how Muhammad had secured his faith and carried it to all corners of the Earth, and Christ's representative must do likewise. Ostentatious vulnerability was all very well for the early Christians—a band of zealots bent on martyrdom before the imminent Second Coming of Christ. And even in Stephen's beloved predecessor, Zachary, his love of peace had sufficed to preserve a fragile papacy and the even more fragile city of Rome. But the world was changing rapidly; Rome was in acute danger of destruction at the hands of a monster in Christian garb. Paul had been right: the Pope must become a ruler—a Western Emperor, if necessary, just as Constantine had authorized.

Did not Christ Himself send Constantine a sign, before the battle at the Milvian Bridge? *In hoc signo vinces—Under this sign you shall be victorious.* Those were the words that Constantine saw written in the sky: Christ promised Constantine victory in battle. That, Stephen now realized, was the reason the blessed Paul carried a sword in every statue and fresco and mosaic in Rome, including in his own basilica on the Ostian Way. That sword was not the instrument of his martyrdom—it was the weapon that would defend the faith and the city of Peter.

With these thoughts in his mind, Stephen called Zaid to approach, and he touched the boy on his head with a staff. No *vindicta*—the official rod of manumission—was to hand, so his regular walking staff had to serve. "You are free," he said simply.

Zaid threw himself headlong on the ground, as he had seen Pepin do, and Stephen had to help him up. "You're free to go your own way, if you wish," he said, "but I expect that you'll want to return with us to Rome. I hope that you'll do so—I'll need your help again. If you do, your pay will be increased a little."

"Yes," said Zaid, "I would like to return to Rome with Your Holiness. I want to rejoin my father, who needs me. And I want to see the girl that I hope to marry. But what about this?" Zaid touched his right hand to his left shoulder.

"We can't get rid of that, I'm afraid," said Stephen. "We can overbrand it if that's what you want." Zaid visibly winced at the thought, and Stephen quickly went on to other ideas. "When we reach Rome we'll give you a letter attesting to your manumission, as well as the freedman's cap. So you may do whatever you wish. If you want to work for your father again, you may do so. But if you want to stay in our employment, we'll make sure there's work for you. When you've reached full adulthood, you may petition for citizenship. Now, help get us started on our journey—the day's far gone already."

34

*B*iscofesheimi supra Tauberim fluvium abbatissa—*The abbess of Bischofsheim on the Tauber River sends eternal greetings in the Lord to Paul, most honorable Deacon and, in the absence of the most holy and blessed Pope, Guardian of the Throne of the Blessed Peter.*

With copious tears and a heavy heart I must report to you the death by martyrdom of Boniface, Archbishop of Mainz and tireless missionary to the Germans, in the seventy-first year of his life. According to messengers who have just arrived from the north, this sad event took place one month prior to this date at the town of Dokkum in Frisia, where the Archbishop had gone with several followers to preach redemption by the Blood of Jesus Christ our Savior. They indeed succeeded in baptizing a great multitude of the Frisians, but the Archbishop and his followers were set upon by a band of armed men who, inspired by Satan, slew them all for their faith. His body has been carried to Utrecht, where several miraculous cures have already been attested among those who venerate it.

My uncle's death was a matter of—

"My uncle?" Deacon Paul, who had been perusing his correspondence without a great deal of interest, was suddenly jerked to full attention. So this letter was written by—Leoba? Yes, now he looked more carefully, this was Leoba's handwriting, no doubt about it. Those bosomy 'M's were unmistakable. A painful twinge of memory took him back to that sunny afternoon when Leoba had tried to teach him her fine uncial script.

Leoba was at Bischofsheim-on-Tauber? And she was abbess? However had that happened? Wasn't she on the road back to Rome with Stephen? Paul read on, more in fear of what he was about to find out than with joy at finally hearing from his beloved.

My uncle's death was a matter of deep personal grief to me. My only consolation is that he was full of years and beloved of God, and that he himself considered martyrdom the most wished-for end to a life spent in the service of the Lord, as he told me on several occasions.

I deeply regret that I did not have the opportunity to see him during the last four years, since the time when I left Francia with Burghard and Fulrad on our journey to Rome. When I finally returned to Francia with the Holy Father, I foolishly lingered too long at Pepin's court, being anxious to witness his coronation. Then I received my uncle's summons to Bischofsheim, but the journey took three weeks, and by the time I arrived he had already departed on his mission to Frisia.

I am full of guilt at my failure to obey my uncle's many requests that I should return to my duties with him. I hope to go personally to Utrecht to seek forgiveness at his tomb. Perhaps I will be able to oversee the removal of his remains to Mainz, or to one of the monasteries he founded, any of which would be a more fitting resting place than Utrecht, where no-one has any connection to him. However, I will have to discuss this matter with my cousins, Williband and Winnebald and Walburga, who labor at Heidenheim for the greater glory of God, and who have not yet heard of the Archbishop's death.

Because the Archbishop, in his last letter to me, gave me specific instructions to take over the governance of this monastery, I am obliged to do so, even though this undertaking will prevent me from returning to Rome as I had intended. Your brother, the Holy Father, instructed me in the same fashion, and with great emphasis.

Don't be angry with your brother for that, I beg you. His words, and Boniface's letter, helped me make the right choice for the remainder of my life. The friendship between you and me is something that I will always remember and value, not only for the personal reward that it conferred on me, but also because we accomplished together some work of lasting value to the Church. Nevertheless, a continuation of our friendship would have created a problem for yourself, for a close relationship between a man and a woman, no matter how innocent, is always liable to be interpreted as sin. And our relationship was not innocent. Indeed, when I think how Boniface would have judged me, or my beloved Abbess Tetta at Wimborne, if they had known of what passed between you and me, I am filled with guilt and remorse.

You are the only man among the Pope's counselors who has a clear vision of what needs to be done to save Rome from its present dangers, or of the direction that the Church must take to ensure its survival and the expansion of its influence. Already, even as a mere Deacon, your counsel has made possible the new alliance between Rome and Pepin, which I expect will soon lead to the utter destruction of Aistulf's forces. If so, you will have effectively saved Rome from her present enemies. But even more important work remains for you to accomplish in the future, if the papal tiara should at some point alight on your head. Of course, I hope and pray that your brother, the Holy Father, will enjoy a long and productive life. Still, he is significantly older than yourself and, I must warn you, he has shown some signs of ill-health as a result of his arduous journey to Francia. No doubt the return journey to Rome will also take its toll. When God finally calls him, it is of the utmost importance that his office goes to you, and not to some other counselor whose vision might be more limited or backward. Therefore I ask you to put considerations of personal gratification aside, as I do, and to devote yourself single-mindedly to the service of the True Church.

Paul lifted his eyes from Leoba's letter and stared unseeingly at the window of the papal writing-chamber. An inexpressible pain welled up in his heart, along with anger— at his brother, at Boniface, even at Leoba herself. What good would she do, running some hen-house of illiterate Germans? How could Stephen have thought that a suitable position for her? Wasn't it more likely that he wanted to keep her away from Rome, away from himself? He slammed his fist down on the writing desk. At that moment, however, the chamberlain knocked on the door. Paul tried to collect himself and called for the chamberlain to enter.

"The counselors are assembled, sir."

"Very well, lead me there," said Paul, and he rose from his desk, after stuffing Leoba's letter into a drawer. They descended the stairs to the reception hall, where Leo, Marcellus, Philip, Tullius, a Deputy First Notary, and several others were waiting. Paul conducted the usual prayers, then quickly got down to business.

"I have good news from Francia," he said. "The Holy Father has left Soissons and is on his way back to Rome. He is coming by way of Vienne and the Mont Cenis pass. In fact, by this time he should be in the neighborhood of the pass, or over it already, God willing."

"So he'll have to come through Lombardy and Tuscany?" asked Marcellus.

"Yes, unfortunately," said Paul. "But this is still safer than traveling by sea. Aistulf gave him a safe conduct. We hope that Desiderius will respect that and let him travel through Tuscany unhindered."

"That was before the Holy Father got together with Pepin, which is not going to make Aistulf—"

"Aistulf would make many enemies if he were to harm or hinder the Holy Father. Especially among the Lombard bishops. Not to mention the punishment that it would earn him in the hereafter."

"Can Satan add anything to what he already has in store for that sinner?" asked Philip. "Can hellfire burn more fiercely? Can the wheel break him more thoroughly, or the pains of hunger and thirst gnaw at him more deeply, or for longer than an eternity?"

"Probably not," said Paul, smiling at Philip's colorful imaginings. Then he remembered his charitable duty as temporary head of the Roman Church. "Let's hope that true repentance and atonement may yet save his soul from that terrible fate, through Christ's mercy," he said.

"Certainly," added another voice. "But if he came to me for absolution, I would have him hand over his kingdom and walk to Jerusalem with rocks in his shoes. Great sin calls for great penance."

"What about Pepin?" asked Marcellus.

"His army is assembling at Soissons. It will set out in a few weeks, according to the messages I've received," said Paul.

"In a few weeks? I thought the Franks began their campaigns in March. Has the Holy Father explained to him how urgent the situation has—"

"Yes, of course," said Paul, "but the coronation caused a

delay, and then the nobles had to agree to Pepin's plan for a campaign against the Lombards. Which they did only after Pepin showed them Constantine's Donation. There was a great deal of discussion and bargaining, it seems. Pepin's son, Charles, in spite of his youth, had an important influence on their decision—he's more popular among the nobles than his father, it's said."

"Perhaps Charles hopes to expand the Frankish realm into Italy," said Marcellus.

"What? Haven't we had this discussion before?" asked Paul in an irritated tone.

"Well, it's an issue worth discussing."

"No doubt you would like us to make a fresh appeal to the Emperor in Constantinople. 'We'll smash all our sacred images if Your Serenity will just come and save us from Aistulf.'"

"Images don't come into it," said Marcellus sharply.

"Marcellus, a Tuscan army is advancing on Rome. The Lombards, the Beneventans, and the Spoletans are getting ready to join them. The only question is whether Pepin will reach Italy in time before Aistulf and his allies knock down our walls, or some traitor throws open the gates to them. And you discuss whether or not Pepin is welcome! Should we perhaps send him an embassy: 'Most noble King, circumstances have changed, we're suspicious of your motives, why don't you campaign in Saxony instead—we're very confident that the Emperor will come to our rescue, and he is so much more respectful of our territorial claims than you are.' What nonsense is that, Marcellus?"

"I never mentioned the Emperor," retorted the Treasurer.

"No, but that's all you think of," said Paul. "You and Theophylact."

"Theophylact? You may have noticed that he's been absent from our deliberations this last half year, because your brother took him to Francia."

"My brother? If you mean the Holy Father, then please refer to him by that name."

"The Holy Father then," said Marcellus. "He took Theo on this extraordinary and arduous journey—a journey that's already taken the life of our beloved First Notary—and for no real reason other than to keep him away from Rome during his absence. To deprive us of his counsel."

"How can you say that? Theophylact took part in the discussions with Aistulf. And if he's been idle at Pepin's court, it's his own decision. He could have helped promote the Holy Father's plans, but he chose not to, according to what I've heard."

"A wise choice."

"A wise choice?" Paul's anger was now rapidly getting out of control. "So you consider the Holy Father's plans unwise?"

"The Holy Father's plans? Those are *your* plans, Deacon Paul, that the Holy Father's been persuaded to follow, against his better judgment. The Holy Father was schooled by our beloved Zachary to reject—"

Philip tried to cool the atmosphere. "Treasurer Marcellus, Deacon Paul, shouldn't we be considering the military—"

Paul wasn't to be deflected. "You're so brave as to insult the Holy Father while he is hundreds of miles away from this chamber, Treasurer—while he's on a mission to save our city from destruction. Let me see you do the same in his

306

presence, after he returns. 'Your Holiness is a mere puppet in the hands of your evil brother—you're so weak-minded as to let him lead you down his ungodly path.' Something like that? Let me hear you say it to his face! Then I will call you courageous."

"I never said that—"

"Better you never spoke. What do you know about matters of state? Stick to money-bags and taxes. Which, by the way, you've so mishandled that the Treasury stands near empty at a time when we most need funds. Defer to your betters on matters that you know nothing—"

"Defer to my betters?" said Marcellus. "There speaks a lowly Deacon who never failed to contradict and insult his own Archdeacon, and who doubtless engineered—"

"Deacon I am," said Paul, "but also Deputy to the Holy Father, empowered during his absence to make or unmake any official of the Lateran Palace, including yourself. So if you value your position, keep silent."

"Very well, I shall," said Marcellus. "And perhaps Your Serenity would prefer to put an end to these meetings altogether, so that you won't have to listen to any opinions other than your own."

"*Silence!*" roared Paul. There followed a good half minute in which no one spoke. During this interval Paul had time to regret his intemperate language. Marcellus was a dangerous fool, certainly, but Paul's attack had harmed himself more than the Treasurer—that was clear from the expressions of the men around the table. Leoba's letter, much more than Marcellus's words, was the cause of his outburst—this much Paul quickly realized. For a moment, he felt that he was about to break down into tears. With a great deal of effort he collected himself and attempted to repair some of the damage he had caused.

"Forgive my language," he said finally. "I value the counsel of each one of you, including yours, Treasurer Marcellus, and I urge you to express yourselves freely." He turned to the scribe who was taking notes of the meeting. "Notary, please delete everything that has been spoken up to now. Now, let me ask the Commander of the Militia—Leo, tell us how the situation stands with regard to the safety of our city?"

"Sir, the Tuscan army under Desiderius is advancing southward toward Viterbo. It could be here within a week. At that point we'll have to close our gates. However, his army is not large enough to fully invest the city: they won't be able to blockade all the gates or halt traffic on the Tiber. The Holy Father, when he returns, should have no difficulty entering the city, and we'll still be able to bring in supplies and men. What's more, Desiderius lacks heavy siege engines. We should be able to hold him off indefinitely. But the situation will change when the other armies arrive, particularly the Lombards under Aistulf."

"Where is Aistulf's army now?" asked Philip.

"Well," said Leo, "when our latest messengers left Pavia, Aistulf's army was nearly ready to set out. That was two weeks ago. If they set out right after our messengers left, they could be approaching Lucca, assuming that they move at ten miles a day, which is usual. I'm speaking of the main army—Aistulf might send cavalry units ahead, of course, if they were supported by the Tuscans. I expect we will hear more shortly."

"And what about the city's defenses?" asked Paul.

"I'm more confident on this score than I was six months ago," said Leo. "We now have about sixteen thousand men capable of defending the walls, thanks to all the country people who've taken refuge in the city, and their servants and slaves. But only the people of quality are trained for pitched battle. So, even if Desiderius should show up with a mere ten thousand men, we dare not face him in the field, even though it would be very tempting to give battle before Aistulf arrives."

"So long as Pepin is on his way to help us, I don't see any point in risking an engagement," said Paul. "So I agree with you. The main thing is that the walls are secure."

"Yes, well, even sixteen thousand men are not really enough—not for a long siege. But we have made some improvements, as you know—for example at the Pyramid of Cestius, by the Ostian Gate. That wasn't a good idea of Aurelian, or his engineers, to incorporate the pyramid into the wall. It saved them some expense, but it's a weak spot. Attackers can gather on the south side of the pyramid and use it as a shelter. So we've widened the parapet there to allow for more defenders, and we've put in some extra ballistas and a great supply of boulders. And similarly, where the walls come down to the Tiber, we've—"

"Yes, thank you, Leo, I've reviewed these new defenses with you and I'm very satisfied. I'm more concerned about treachery, as a matter of fact. Aistulf has placed many agents among the refugees, I'm sure."

"That's true," Philip put in. "And even some of our own citizens sympathize with him. Those whose wives are from Tuscany or Lombardy or wherever—or they have some grudge against us. How can we keep watch on those people?"

"We can't," said Leo. "But I've taken steps to reduce the danger. For example, I've had the locksmiths make many new locks for the city gates. Once the siege begins, we'll replace the locks every two weeks, or even more often if it seems necessary. The gate-keepers themselves will be changed frequently, and the passwords every night of course."

"What about grain?"

"We've been able to increase the size of our stores. But the number of mouths to be fed has also increased, on account of the refugees. So we stand about where we did six months ago: we only have grain for about six months."

"Aistulf can sustain a year's siege, or more," said Paul. "He proved that at Ravenna. So our fate will be in Pepin's hands—otherwise it will be starvation or surrender."

35

On the thirteenth of July, exactly nine months after his departure, Pope Stephen and his companions returned to Rome. Stephen had heard that the Tuscan army under Desiderius was already encamped on the Aurelian Way, to the west of the city. To avoid any contact with the Tuscans he chose a route far to the east, along the foot of the mountains, and circled around the city to the Asinarian Gate. Through this gate, two centuries earlier, Belisarius had led his Imperial army in triumph, bringing the Goths' sixty-year occupation of Rome to an inglorious end. Now Stephen, bedraggled and weary from the long journey and the summer heat, led his fifteen companions through the same portal into the city. The gatekeepers quickly closed the gate behind them, fearful of any concealed enemy forces who might attempt to force their way through.

The Lateran Palace stood just yards away. But if Stephen chose that gate with the hope of making a quick and inconspicuous entry into his palace, he was disappointed. "*Revenit Papa!—The Pope's back!*" shouted the gate-keepers excitedly. Others nearby took up the cry—"The Pope's back! The Pope's back!"—and some ran over to the palace to spread the news. Soon the bells of the Lateran Basilica were ringing, and then those of other nearby churches, and then the bells of all the churches across the city. Even at the church of St. Mary, in Transtiber, the three under-sacristans applied themselves lustily to the bell-ropes—not knowing for what reason, except that something important must have happened. They just hoped that it was good news, and not a breach of the walls or any such disaster.

People came running from all directions, but especially from out of the Lateran Palace, to see the Pope. Stephen and his companions were quickly surrounded by a crowd of excited men, women, and children. Some helped Stephen to dismount from his horse, and they marveled at his stirrups—a gift from Pepin. Others cheered, begged for Stephen's blessing, or for news, or they simply struggled to touch him. The guards around the gate tried to keep order, but without much success. Zaid and Titus used their horses to force open a space ahead of Stephen, so that he and his companions could move forward.

Now Paul and several other counselors emerged from the palace. They were equally excited, but they felt obliged to maintain some dignity, so they walked at a measured pace towards the crowd, surrounded by militiamen. Soon the soldiers had to push their way through the mass of onlookers. Paul began to wonder whether he would have done better to wait for Stephen inside the palace, but there was no turning back at this point.

Finally, the efforts of the militiamen brought Paul and the other counselors to Stephen and his traveling companions. After the two groups merged, the militiamen were able to force the crowd back a little way, allowing the officials some breathing room.

As the two men approached, Paul prepared to grasp Stephen's hand and give a formal bow, but Stephen forestalled his gesture and embraced him in a style more appropriate between brothers. There followed a disorganized series of greetings as the individual travelers and the officials who had remained behind sought each other out and exchanged words. Marcellus greeted Theophylact with particular warmth, and they started an earnest discussion.

Paul tried to lead Stephen toward the palace, but Stephen said, "I should say something—to the people." He turned to the crowd. "Romans—dear brothers and sisters in Christ," he began. But the crowd was so large by now, most of the onlookers didn't even know that the Pope was speaking, and the shouting and cheering went on, drowning out his words.

"Help me to get up here," Stephen said, pointing to a statue whose plinth rose five feet or so above the cobbled pavement. Paul was doubtful, but with considerable effort several militiamen were able to lift Stephen up to the plinth. He now stood in front of the legs of a colossal statue of a Roman emperor. It was probably not Constantine, but it was thought to be so, and therefore it had been saved from destruction over many centuries. Stephen held on to the statue's right knee for balance. Gazing up at his brother, Paul noticed how much older and sicker he looked than when he had left the city the previous autumn. Nevertheless, Stephen seemed to be enjoying the moment.

"Romans—dear brothers and sisters in Christ," he said, "we give thanks to the Almighty for our safe return to the city of Peter. And we pray for—" Stephen began to cough.

"Louder—can't hear you!" came the shouts from the

back of the crowd, which was growing larger by the minute. Stephen wasn't able to raise his voice much above a conversational level, so it seemed as if his speech was going to be more of a dumbshow than anything. But by good luck Stephen's crier appeared on the scene, and he was lifted up to stand next to Stephen and to repeat his words.

"Romans—dear brothers and sisters in Christ," Stephen began yet again.

"*Romans—dear brothers and sisters in Christ!*" bellowed the crier. His strident diction was strangely at odds with the pastoral meaning of the words, but they echoed between the palace and the Aurelian Wall, bringing the crowd to silence at last, though the ringing of the bells continued.

"We give thanks to the Almighty for our safe return to the city of Peter."

"*We give thanks to the Almighty for our safe return to the city of Peter.*" A burst of "amens" and cheers greeted the remark.

Stephen's address to the crowd continued in the same fashion, with each phrase or sentence repeated by the crier. The pauses allowed Stephen to cough and recover his breath. "We pray for the soul of our beloved First Notary, Ambrose, whom God took to his bosom at the abbey of St. Maurice in Burgundy, on our way to the court of Pepin. It is my intent that his remains be transported back to Rome, when conditions allow, so that he may rest in appropriate surroundings and receive the honor that is well merited by his lengthy service to the Church and the city.

"Now, I bring good news! Pepin, who was crowned King of the Franks by our own hand, has sworn on his knees before us to restore and defend the patrimony of the blessed Peter against all enemies. This he has undertaken in obedience to the Supreme Pontiff, and to seek favor in the eyes of the Almighty. Pepin is now leading his army southward against the Lombards and their allies. It may still be many weeks before he arrives in Italy. During this time, we must work together to defend our city, for as we've been told, the Tuscans are already at our western gates, and Aistulf's army, and those of his allies, are approaching.

"There will be days of fear and anguish, you may be sure of that. But have courage! Obey your commanders, those of you who serve in the defense of the city. And every one of you, join us in rites of thanksgiving, and penance, and supplication, so that our voices may be heard even in the halls of Heaven. As we follow the paths of righteousness, so God will come to our aid. Hearing our entreaties, He will protect the tomb of the blessed Peter and destroy our enemies."

Thunderous cheers greeted the conclusion of Stephen's brief address. The militiamen helped him down from the plinth and started ushering the entire party toward the Lateran Palace. As they moved off in an irregular group, Marcellus found himself next to Stephen. "Your Holiness's words are very heartening," he said. "This undertaking on the part of Pepin, of which Your Holiness spoke—to defend and restore our patrimony—was that given in spoken words alone, or was it attested in a formal document?"

"A document, dear Treasurer, a document. I will show it to you all tomorrow, when we meet. Pepin signed it in the presence of his nobles, when they met at the Marchfield."

"So, may I ask Your Holiness, does it list the regions that will be restored?"

"It does, and you may see them written down. Besides his

undertaking to protect Rome itself, he promises to restore all the territories unjustly seized by Aistulf, both those in Latium, and those beyond—Perugia, Narni, Ravenna, the Five Cities, and many others. Always assuming that he is victorious over the Lombards, of course, which by God's grace he will be."

"Ravenna—and the Five Cities? Are they part of our patrimony? Don't they belong to the Emperor, Your Holiness?"

Paul, who was walking on Stephen's other side, groaned inwardly to hear the same topic brought up that had been the source of so much conflict among the Lateran counselors. "We can discuss these issues at our meeting tomorrow, Marcellus," he said. "The Holy Father deserves rest at this moment, not interrogation."

"Let me answer the Treasurer's question," said Stephen, as the group entered the gates of the Lateran Palace and the crowd of cheering onlookers was held back. "In brief, the See of Peter is entitled to Ravenna for three reasons. First, the Emperor has effectively ceded ownership of the city by failing to prevent its capture by the Lombards, and by doing nothing to regain it in the three years since then." The group came to a halt in the forecourt of the palace, as the counselors clustered around Stephen to hear his words. Meanwhile, Zaid and Titus led the horses off to the Lateran stables.

"Didn't our beloved Zachary say, 'Let him who holds the power be called King,'" Stephen continued. "So it will be with Ravenna. The Emperor no longer exerts any power in Italy, except in Sicily, so he doesn't deserve to be respected as the rightful ruler of Ravenna. Second, the Donation of

Constantine—the deed that Providence revealed to us last year by the hand of the blessed Sylvester—the Donation gives the Supreme Pontiff the right to dispose of lands in Italy as he sees fit. And third, it will be necessary for Rome to control a port on the Adriatic for the future defense and expansion of our territories. Why take back the towns of the Flaminian Way, if the road beyond them leads to a dead end—to a Lombard city, or one ruled by some new governor that the Emperor chooses to send? No, Ravenna belongs to the Republic of St. Peter."

What on earth is this "Republic of St. Peter," Marcellus wondered. He was astonished by Stephen's remarks—not so much by their content, but by their tone. In the course of his journey, evidently, Stephen had developed a far more confident, even aggressive view of the Church's place in the world, and of his own role as a statesman. Marcellus said nothing, beyond thanking Stephen for his response, but he looked toward Theophylact as if seeking moral support. Theophylact said nothing, but he resolved to challenge the direction of Stephen's policies, once the military threat to Rome had passed.

The group moved on into the palace, accompanied by numerous well-wishers from the Lateran bureaucracy who had come out to greet them. Stephen took the time to express his gratitude to each of the men who had accompanied him on the journey, and he arranged a time for the meeting of his counselors the next morning. Then, accompanied by his brother and a few attendants, he wearily climbed the long stairway to the papal chambers. After the attendants helped him remove his traveling cloak, he and Paul were finally left together.

"My dear brother," said Stephen, embracing him again, "everything happened as you predicted. I think we can count on Pepin's full support. He convinced his nobles to join him against Aistulf, thanks to Constantine's Donation, which made a great impression on them—as it should."

"That's good," said Paul, "because we'll certainly need his help. When do you think he will arrive?"

"I don't know. Haven't you received news of his progress?"

"The last we heard, he was in Vienne, waiting for reinforcements."

"What's the situation here—with Desiderius?"

"Well, he arrived a month ago, but he hasn't done much. He seems satisfied to wait for Aistulf and the others. There have been a few small skirmishes, and of course he has done some damage to the land he controls."

"What about the Basilica of Peter?"

"He's respected it, as well as our people there. We moved everything valuable into the city—from the Basilica of Peter, and the Basilica of Paul, and several other churches outside the walls. But we couldn't move the tombs, of course. We were afraid that they'd be desecrated, or that the relics of the martyrs would be stolen, but that hasn't happened so far, according to people who've been out there."

"When we have the means, we should extend the walls to protect them," said Stephen. "The Basilica of the blessed Peter, at least."

"Perhaps we could do that—there's still plenty of stone and concrete in the Flavian Amphitheater. But the problem is the manpower. The longer the wall, the more men we need to defend it, and we don't have enough as it is."

"The city's population will grow again, once our territories expand."

"I hope so," said Paul.

"I wasn't happy with what I saw of the Frankish clergy," said Stephen, changing the subject. "Boniface has done a lot, but he needs to do much more, I told him that he needs to exert his influence on Pepin to root out—"

"Boniface?"

"Yes, he's the only—"

"Boniface is dead—you didn't know?"

"Boniface is dead?" said Stephen in a shocked voice. "No, I didn't know. What happened?"

"He was martyred, during a mission to the Frisians."

"God rest his soul," said Stephen. "Who did you hear this from?"

"From—let me see—from one of his monasteries. Fulda—or was it Heidenheim? I don't quite remember."

"He'll be greatly missed. By us, and also by Pepin, who depended on him with regard to the Germans."

"Indeed."

"Those British missionaries, they've saved many souls in Germany. Not just Boniface. Also the younger generation—Willibald and Winnebald, and their sister Walburga. And now Leoba."

"Leoba?"

The atmosphere between the two brothers suddenly became awkward. Stephen moved to the window, and he seemed to talk to the spaces outside of it. "You must have been expecting her return with me," he said.

"I—" Paul couldn't think of what to say.

"She wanted to come back," said Stephen.

"She did? And why didn't she, then?"

"It was thought better that she devote herself to missionary work, given her facility with the language of the Germans. Our Latin speakers have difficulty—"

"Well then, that's a good thing," said Paul. "And now Boniface is dead, she will be needed all the more."

"I thought it a good thing that she return to Germany," said Stephen, turning to look directly at Paul. "A good thing for everyone."

What does he know, thought Paul. *What is he trying to say?* It sounded like Stephen was the one who had forced Leoba to go to Bischofsheim, more than Boniface. A rage against his brother welled up inside him. But there was nothing he could say, unless he wished to spill out the entire story of their illicit affair.

"You're right," he said at last. "Leoba wasn't really accomplishing much in Rome, in spite of her many good qualities."

"Exactly," said Stephen. "We'll all be better without her, you'll see."

36

Zaid and Titus were greeted with excitement by the other stable-hands and peppered with questions about their journey, which they described as well as they could while they watered, fed, and groomed the traveling party's horses. Zaid was eager to get back to Silversmiths' Street, but by the time he had finished his work the paymaster's office was closed, so he stayed over that night at the stable.

The next morning he and Titus went early to the office to collect their wages for the trip. Zaid was pleased to see that he was paid the same as Titus, even though he had been a slave for the first half of the journey: the Pope must have arranged for all his back pay to be calculated at the freeman's rate. The paymaster also knew about the manumission; he told Zaid that the document certifying his freedom would be ready for him within a day or two. He urged Zaid to continue working at the stables, but Zaid was having none of it—he was free, and he was going to take advantage of that and return to his old life in Transtiber.

Zaid said goodbye to Titus. With his purse full of coins, he set off down the hill toward the Colosseum. After he passed the Basilica of the Four Crowned Martyrs, he stopped off at a bakery to buy some bread. He was surprised to see that the prices were much higher than they had been when he left Rome. The shopkeeper told him that it was on account of the siege, which had already cut off supplies from Ostia.

Eating the bread as he walked, Zaid noticed other changes. There were few men in the streets: they were manning the walls, he was told. And of those he did see, many were carrying weapons, which had not been customary before. He wondered whether he should get a weapon himself, and how to do so.

As he approached the river, he started to feel anxious. He tried to rehearse what he would say to his father, but the truth was, he had no idea how his father would react to his return. Would he welcome home his errant son, or would he reject him? He had to beg for his father's forgiveness, that much was clear. Perhaps the fact that he had taken part in such an important journey—one that might be the saving of Rome—and had earned a purseful of money in the process, would sway his father's feelings. He tried to imagine how it would be to see Lenora again. Would everything be the same? Would Lenora still love him? Or might she have given up on him and taken up with someone else?

Lost in these thoughts, Zaid missed the most direct way home, which would have taken him over the Aemilian Bridge. He found himself a little farther north, so he crossed the Jews' Bridge to Tiber Island, and from there by way of Gratian's Bridge to Transtiber. As he stood on the crest of Gratian's Bridge, he could see the new ship-mills tied up at the same location as their long-gone predecessors, just upstream of the island on the west bank of the river, where the current was strongest. The mills' wheels were turning steadily, and Zaid could see a carter unloading sacks of grain at one of the mills.

Aside from the mills there were no boats on the river, and looking northward he could see the reason: a chain had been drawn across the entire width of the stream. Zaid couldn't tell whether the chain had been put there to protect the mills from floating logs, or to prevent the movement of enemy ships along the river. Either way, it was an effective bar to river traffic north of Tiber Island.

Having reached the west bank of the river, Zaid cut through side streets to the Aurelian Way and soon reached Silversmiths' Street. Sibyl's store was no longer fronted with a bead curtain; instead, a peasant woman sat next to some piles of sad-looking vegetables. And Omar's store was deserted—a quick look made it clear to Zaid that no one had occupied the place for some time. All the relics and tools were gone. Zaid went upstairs, and here too everything of value had been removed. In the corner where he used to sleep, Zaid found a couple of his carved animals, but that was all.

Obviously his father had left, but when? And where had he gone? Zaid went next door and asked the peasant woman, but she seemed to know nothing about Omar or about Lenora and her parents. In fact, she obviously disliked being questioned. Perhaps she was a squatter and feared being evicted.

Zaid returned to the street, looking for a familiar face. He was suddenly very lonely. He walked back to the Aurelian Way, which was as busy as usual, and looked indecisively in both directions. At that moment he heard a voice yelling

"Zaid!" and his friend Antonius grabbed him.

"Zaid, you're back!" said Antonius, hugging his friend.

"Tonius!"

"Zaid—I can't believe it! How tall you've grown—and what about this?" Antonius ruffled the beginnings of a beard that had sprouted from Zaid's cheeks. "You're a man suddenly!"

"Tonius—where's my father? And Lenora?"

"Your father? He—Zaid, I'm sorry!"

"Sorry what? *What?*"

"He—he died."

"He died?"

"I'm sorry, Zaid."

"When?"

"During the winter."

"What happened?"

"He—he was killed."

"Killed—who by?"

"Robbers, apparently. One of them was killed too. It happened at night—in your home."

Zaid sat down on a low wall and buried his face in his hands. After a while he said "My father—what happened to him—his body? Was it buried?"

"Yes, one of your people—the spice merchant—don't cry, Zaid."

"Rasheed?"

"Rasheed, yes, I think so. But he's left Rome since then. He did everything properly."

"And he's buried—?"

"Where your people are buried—on the Appian Way."

"I must go there, right now. Will you come with me?"

"I suppose so, yes. I just got off duty. You should have someone with you, if you're going outside of the walls."

"Off duty?" Zaid finally noticed that Antonius was carrying a sling—a large wooden sling similar to the one Zaid had tried out at Brennacum. "You joined the militia?"

"Yes, they need everyone—for when the siege gets serious. Besides, I couldn't keep going with my pastry cart: the flour is rationed now."

"Has there been fighting, then?"

"No, not yet. We just man the parapets and keep watch, and practice our marksmanship."

As the two youths crossed the river and headed toward the Appian Gate, Antonius told Zaid everything he knew about Omar's death. And he explained how Lenora and her parents had left Rome that same night and hadn't been heard from since. Then he asked Zaid to tell him about his journey to Francia. Zaid told him what he could, but his heart wasn't in it—he was consumed by grief for his father, and by guilt at the fact that he hadn't been present to defend him, or to perform the obligatory rites for the deceased.

The animosity between himself and his father—that had always seemed to Zaid like a temporary aberration. He had imagined how he and his father would one day look back at what had happened, as they sat by a campfire in some eastern wilderness, and laugh over it. But now everything was frozen, permanent, irresolvable. At least the last time they saw each other, outside the stables, when Omar came to claim him, Zaid had acknowledged that Omar was indeed his father. What if he'd said, "No, I never saw this man before," as he'd been tempted to? That would have been unbearable.

A good *jinni* had put better words into his mouth.

At the gate, the watchmen warned Antonius and Zaid to keep an eye open for marauders from the Tuscan army, but the Appian Way was quiet. A few carts were bringing supplies into the city—some of the larger ones, carrying grain, had a few soldiers riding with them. Mostly, though, the road was empty, and the loudest sound was the noise of their boots on the stone paving.

The cemetery lay down a dusty side-lane behind the church that guarded the entry to the Catacomb of St. Callixtus. It was a small plot, with a few dozen graves, each marked by five or six feet of raised earth, and a few by stone markers. An olive tree offered some shade in one corner of the graveyard. A goat nibbled the dry grass.

An old woman, dressed in black, was tidying one of the graves, brushing off the dead vegetation with a birch broom and cleaning the headstone. She seemed oblivious to the summer heat. Zaid recognized her as the mother of Rasheed, the spice merchant. Her husband had died a couple of years earlier. Zaid wondered how she came to be there, and how she looked after herself, now that her son had left Rome. He greeted her respectfully, and asked where Omar was buried. The woman pointed out one of the graves. It had no marker, but it was clearly the one that had been dug most recently.

"Because you weren't here, Rasheed took on the obligation," she said. "He washed Omar's body three times according to custom, using camphor the third time. He had to clean away a great deal of—" She cut herself off and began again. "I wanted to help, and so did my daughter-in-law, but Rasheed said it could only be done by a man. And he obtained the *kafan*, made of three sheets of cloth, which he sprinkled with perfume from his store. After he wrapped and tied your father's body, it was brought here for burial, in the grave which Rasheed dug, with help from your friend." She nodded toward Antonius, who had remained standing at the entrance to the cemetery.

"He lies on his right side, facing toward the Qiblah, as is proper," the woman went on. "Rasheed untied the ropes around his *kafan* and placed some stones behind him and on top of him, so that he would not fall onto his back, and then he filled the grave. There were only the three of us here, Rasheed and his wife and myself, but we recited the *Sura Al-Fatiha* and the *Tashahhud*, and we spoke *dua* for your father and for all the dead. It's good that you've come."

As he listened to the old woman's description of his father's burial, Zaid gave way to an overwhelming grief. Sobbing, he clung to her as if to his long-dead mother. "Say the *dua*," she said. "Allah will comfort you."

Zaid stood on the northwest side of the grave, so that his tear-streaked face gazed across the grave in the direction of the Qiblah. But he wasn't sure of what words to use. "Help me, please," he said to the old woman.

"*Allahum maghfirlahu*," she began. "Allah, forgive him and have mercy on him and give him strength and pardon him."

"Allah, forgive him," Zaid repeated, "and have mercy on him and give him strength and pardon him."

"Be generous to him and cause his entrance to be wide, and wash him with water and snow."

"Be generous to him and cause his entrance to be wide, and wash him with water and snow."

"Cleanse him of his transgressions, as white cloth is cleansed of stains."

"Cleanse him of his transgressions, as white cloth is cleansed of stains."

"Give him an abode better than his home, and a family better than his family, and a wife better than his wife."

"Give him an abode better than his home, and a family better than his family, and a wife better than his wife—" Zaid hesitated, and went on "—and a son better than his son."

The woman looked up at Zaid, but she continued. "Take him into Paradise, and protect him from the punishment of the grave and the fire."

"Take him into Paradise, and protect him from the punishment of the grave and the fire."

"*Allahum maghfir lihayyina*—Allah, forgive our living, and our dead, those who are with us and those who are absent, our young and our old, our men and our women."

"Allah, forgive our living, and our dead, those who are with us and those who are absent, our young and our old, our men and our women."

The prayer completed, Zaid did indeed feel somewhat consoled. He turned and thanked the old woman. "I have money," he said, "Let me pay you for the burial."

"It's not necessary," she answered. "We sold some of your father's tools, and that covered it all. In fact, there's some money left over, which I'll give you. I'm sorry if you wanted the tools, but we thought you were gone."

"I don't need them—I'm not going to follow his business. Keep the money."

Zaid rejoined Antonius. "You didn't tell me you helped dig the grave," he said.

"They paid me," Antonius explained simply. "What are

you going to do now?" he added, as they turned to head back.

"I need to find Lenora. They must have gone to Lucca. I met her grandparents there, when we were traveling north, but we came back a different way."

"You can't go to Lucca now. Wait till the war is over. Join us at the wall—they need everyone they can get. Can you use one of these?" Antonius pointed to his sling.

"I tried, in Francia. It was harder than I thought."

"Let me show you," said Antonius. At the two youths walked back toward the city, Antonius gave Zaid an impromptu lesson with his weapon, picking up stones and small rocks from the side of the road to send them hurtling towards trees and other targets. Zaid tried to imitate his action, and he gradually began to get the hang of it. At one point, a large rabbit emerged from the undergrowth about twenty yards in front of them and paused by the roadside. "Watch," whispered Antonius. He picked up a rock, spun the sling, and the rabbit was sent flying into the air. It landed, lifeless, about ten feet beyond where it had been sitting. "Dinner," said Antonius, as he picked up the rabbit by its ears.

"The son of the King of Francia, he's our age," said Zaid. "He rides on a full-size warhorse, and wears armor and carries a lance and a sword, and practices with the other horsemen."

"Perhaps we'll see him," said Antonius, "if Pepin comes to Rome. Maybe there'll be a battle between the armies of Pepin and Aistulf, which we can watch from the walls."

"I think Pepin will attack Pavia," said Zaid. "Pavia is very small. Pepin could take it much more easily than Aistulf could take Rome. So Aistulf would have to go back to defend it."

"That would be a pity," said Antonius. "I'd like to see them go head to head—the Franks and the Lombards."

"That would be something to watch."

The gatekeepers remembered Zaid and Antonius from earlier, and let them through without questioning. "A good day's hunting, I see," said one of them, as he pointed to the rabbit that Antonius was carrying.

"Yes, he put up a fight," said Antonius with a smile, "but I was able to bag him in the end, at some risk to my life."

37

"Romans, defenders of the See of Peter, have courage!"

While his herald repeated his words, Stephen coughed and fought to regain his breath. On this late-August morning the sultry, dust-laden air irritated his throat. Even though he was sitting on his portable throne, he felt as if he needed to lie down. He wished he'd left this speech to Leo, or to Paul. He turned to look at his brother, who stood expressionless at his right side. But I'm Pope, after all, he thought. Whose duty is it to inspire our soldiers, except mine?

Stephen's throne had been set up on the Salarian Way, fifty yards inside the Salarian Gate. A few thousand armed men stood listening to him. They spilled off the road onto the ruined Gardens of Sallust. Aurelian's Wall ranged up behind them, blocking any view outside of the city. Behind Stephen ranged several groups of priests, deacons, and acolytes, each group clustering around one of the city's most sacred relics. Peter's chains had been brought from the Basilica of Eudoxia. From the Basilica of St. Peter's came a fragment of the True Cross—it had been brought into the city for safe keeping before the siege began. From the

Basilica of St. Mary came part of the crib in which the infant Jesus once lay. Glancing at that relic, Stephen was reminded of the miraculous snow that fell in August, four centuries earlier, as the plan of the basilica was being marked out. What blessed relief a little snowfall would be at this moment, he thought.

The herald turned to Stephen, reminding him that it was his turn to speak. "Have courage," he continued. "Aistulf faces us with a large army, much larger than ours, but we have two advantages that will bring us victory, have no doubt about it. First, we have the protection of an impregnable wall, which Aistulf may attack as many times as he wishes, but each attack will cost the lives of thousands of his soldiers, and each attack will fail. He may try again and again until not a single one of his soldiers is left standing, but the wall will not yield, not when it is defended by men such as you. Second—"

An impregnable wall—what nonsense is that, thought Paul, as he squinted at the fifty-foot barrier. What nonsense was that? Had Stephen forgotten how the Goths smashed through the wall—yes, through this very section of the wall by the Salarian Gate? Didn't he recall how they had torched the Garden of Sallust, on this exact spot where they now stood, before going on to commit much worse atrocities within the city? Didn't the blessed Jerome, in his hermit's cell by Bethlehem—didn't Jerome weep for Rome when he heard the news, and the blessed Augustine too, as he preached under the African sun? And that assault was on this very August day, three hundred and forty-four years before. Surely it was for that reason that Aistulf had chosen this particular date to amass his forces after weeks of preparation. Didn't Stephen care about the truth? Then Paul remembered how little he was entitled to fault his brother on that score, and a frown crossed his face.

Stephen continued with his speech, pausing for every sentence to be repeated by his herald. "Second, Aistulf and his soldiers are waging war far from home, for no other purpose than for worldly gain," he said, "which is a grievous crime against the Christian Law. They are fighting for gold, for land, for slaves. They offended the Almighty and all the blessed martyrs by their unspeakable acts against the city of Ravenna, a city which God's word has promised to the Republic of St. Peter. They violated the sanctity of the holiest and most ancient churches of that city, raping and murdering thousands of innocent women and children. By those impious deeds they set the councils of Heaven against them, so that they shall surely perish and lie with the wicked in the nethermost fires of Hell. They shall suffer the everlasting torment that awaits all those who turn away from the path of righteousness.

"But you, dear Romans and brothers in Christ, you're not fighting for worldly gain. You're fighting for your wives, your children, your homes, your own lives. You're fighting for these sacred relics, and the ancient churches that house them. You're fighting for the tomb of Peter, and the true Catholic faith itself. You're fighting for God."

Stephen paused while his listener absorbed his words, and he was seized by yet another fit of coughing. "Have no fear," he went on at last. "He who hands himself over to the service of God will be saved. Follow God's law, and Christ's angel and the shield of piety will defend you. The reward for the soldier's labor is to receive eternal life with the Lord, and he will rest in peace in Paradise with the righteous.

"Now, to your stations! Fight for God, brave Romans, and God will fight for you!"

A raucous cheer erupted from the ranks of Stephen's listeners. Then, weapon in hand, each man made his way toward his allotted section of the wall, but not before stopping by one of the fifty priests who stood ready to hear his confession. Sins little and large came pouring out, and every sinner repented and was absolved. Some of the men were not sure whether they had been properly baptized, and for them a font had been set up in which they could stand while a priest hurriedly poured holy water over them—a bishop being unnecessary on account of the emergency. Thus fortified equally for battle and for the afterlife, the men ascended the stairs to the top of the wall, or to the defensive chambers within the bastions, where they joined their comrades who already stood on guard there.

The view that greeted them was terrifying. Ranged at a distance of about a quarter-mile from the wall, and stretching from the western to the eastern horizon, was an immense mass of angry humanity. Those within view surely amounted to fifty thousand men. How many more lay out of sight could only be guessed. Besides the soldiers, great numbers of horses, wagons, siege towers, and other engines of war could be seen. Simply by being wheeled toward the city these engines had caused considerable damage to the cemeteries that fringed the Salarian Way.

Aistulf was no longer planning a lengthy siege—that much was clear. Whether on account of the lateness of the season, or the difficulty of provisioning such a multitude, or perhaps for fear of Pepin's advance, he was obviously hoping to settle the matter in a single assault, by throwing one overwhelming mass of soldiery at the city's defenses, no matter what the cost.

The Lombards were poised to attack, but they did not do so. They remained out of bowshot for an hour, while the men on the wall stood watching and waiting. As the sun rose higher in the sky, the heat became insufferable, and a few men who were wearing heavy chain mail collapsed and had to be carried back down to the base of the wall, where they were revived with watered-down wine.

Finally there was movement, but not of the whole Lombard army. Instead, just one little covered cart rolled slowly forward along the Salarian Way toward the gate. As it came closer, the defenders could see that it was not a cart at all, but a 'tortoise'—a mobile shelter pushed by about twenty men. Within the shelter walked one tall man in flashing armor. Who could it be but Aistulf himself?

"Don't shoot," the commanders on the parapets ordered their archers, as the tortoise came within about two hundred yards of the gate. It continued on, and finally came to a stop about seventy-five yards away, within easy bowshot. Aistulf stepped a few feet from the tortoise's sheltering roof into the glare of the sun, and he faced the Salarian Gate.

"Romans!" he shouted. A dead silence fell among the defenders. "Romans! My name is Aistulf, King of the Christian and God-beloved nation of the Lombards."

Hearing what was happening, Stephen had himself carried forward to the gate. He peered through a spyhole at the man with whom he had exchanged angry words at Pavia, nine months before.

"Romans!" Aistulf went on. "I come with a great army,

undefeated in battle. You're surrounded. We Lombards have stopped up this Salarian Gate, and all the northern gates. The Tuscan army sits at your western walls, and the armies of Benevento and Spoleto block the Ostian and Asinarian gates and all the other gates to the south and east. You're cut off. You can't escape, and no army can come to your aid. Come out and do battle outside the walls, and we'll destroy you. Stay where you are and resist, and we'll smash this wall—or else you'll languish in famine until you're forced to gnaw at the corpses of your own children.

"But Aistulf is a Christian king, and God instructs him to offer you Christ's mercy. Listen to my words. Open this gate. Deliver your wicked leader to me, this Stephen, this enemy of God who has placed the sacred tiara of Peter on his own impious head. He who should have devoted his office to preaching God's word and ministering to the faithful—instead, he has traveled about distant lands, busying himself in the affairs of other nations, stirring up wars, and claiming territories, for no purpose other than his own aggrandizement. This is against God's law for any man, and most certainly for a Pope. Yes, he even demands that cities and lands be handed over to him that never belonged to Rome and never shall. He shall be punished according to his crimes, but don't allow yourselves to be punished along with him, for you've done nothing to deserve it.

"Deliver this man to me. Elect another Pope—one who respects the ancient traditions of that sacred office. I'll leave you unharmed, and your wives and your daughters unharmed, and your houses and goods unharmed. All I ask for is a proper remuneration for the expenses of this campaign, and the acknowledgement of the legitimacy of all

Lombard possessions and claims in Italy. Then I'll leave you in peace and prosperity, and friendship will blossom between the people of Rome and the nation of the Lombards. Do those things now, and you'll suffer nothing. Refuse, and the punishment and the guilt will be on your heads."

The defenders on the walls looked at each other. Some, no doubt, were tempted to agree to Aistulf's demands, for a substantial party of Romans still revered Zachary and believed that Stephen was leading the city in a new and dangerous direction. But if so, they were given no chance to express their views, for Stephen too had heard Aistulf's words. He was incensed by the Lombard's personal attack on himself, and also by Aistulf's effort to negotiate with common soldiers—to encourage a mutiny, in fact. Didn't he know how to call a truce and exchange words with the Roman leaders, as the Christian Law demanded? "Drive him off," Stephen said to Leo, who stood a few yards away, and Leo signaled up to the parapet.

Within seconds, a volley of arrows converged on Aistulf, forcing him to duck back under the shelter of the tortoise. Many of the arrows struck the tortoise, but they failed to penetrate it. A second volley followed, which included many fire arrows, but they were quickly extinguished by the wet hides that covered the tortoise's roof. The tortoise and the men inside it moved back until, after a few minutes, they were out of range. The formalities over, Aistulf signaled for the assault to begin.

The Lombard engineers had realized as soon as they reached Rome that scaling ladders would be useless against the city's fifty-foot walls, for scaling a wall of this height required a sixty-foot ladder. A ladder of this length was prone to break under the weight of the men climbing it, and it therefore had to be constructed of massive oaken beams. This made it too cumbersome to be set in place and climbed before the defenders destroyed it. Even so, Aistulf had ordered dozens of such ladders to be constructed, knowing that a scaling assault—though sure to fail—would force the defenders to expose themselves on the parapet. Once in this vulnerable position, they could be attacked by Aistulf's main means of assault—siege towers.

Aistulf's carpenters had spent the previous weeks building mobile towers up to seventy-five feet high. Now the defenders saw a fearsome array of such towers—thirty or more in total—moving toward them. They were hauled by teams of oxen, each team in a single line so as to lessen their exposure to the defenders' arrows and missiles. In addition, the animals were draped with thick felt blankets that had been soaked in water for added protection.

Some of the towers carried twenty or thirty archers and slingers, along with small siege engines such as floor-mounted cross-bows. The role of the men on these towers was to drive the defenders from the walls. A second set of towers were equipped with drawbridges. These towers carried armored swordsmen whose role would be to cross onto the wall, fight their way down into the city, and open the gates from the inside. Behind each tower a crowd of a few hundred men moved forward, using the tower as a giant shield. These included the groups of men who were carrying the scaling ladders.

Only Aistulf's Lombard army advanced against the wall. Under Aistulf's orders, the Tuscans, Beneventans, and Spoletans remained in their positions to the west, south, and east of the city. This was at the request of Aistulf's own soldiers, who didn't want to divide the spoils of conquest with the non-Lombard forces. Still, just by standing in battle order near the walls, Aistulf's allies made his task easier, because they forced the defenders to remain at their stations round the city's entire perimeter, and thus prevented them from reinforcing the defense against Aistulf's assault on the northern wall. Zaid and Antonius, for example, had to hold their station on the wall near the Aurelian Gate, facing Desiderius's troops, and since those troops stayed just out of range there was nothing for the two youths to do except anxiously watch and wait. It was eerily quiet: they could neither hear nor see anything of the battle being joined two miles away at the northern wall.

Various obstacles impeded the advance of the siege towers: these included natural irregularities in the ground as well as gravestones, small boulders, tree branches, and other objects that had been placed there as a first line of defense. For the most part, the drivers of the ox-teams were able to negotiate around these obstacles, but sometimes they had to halt for a minute or so while men with axes or other tools ran forward to clear the way. Thus different towers progressed at different speeds; by the time they entered the range of the defenders' missiles the line of towers had become quite ragged, and those closest to the wall attracted the heaviest bombardment. To keep up their courage, the men in and behind the towers took up their battle song, shouted encouragement to each other, and hurled obscenities at the defenders. Drums, trumpets, and battle horns added to the noise.

As the first tower got to within about one hundred yards

of the wall, the lead animal in its ox-team was hit by a crossbow bolt that penetrated its felt blanket and entered its spine. The animal bellowed in pain and tried to tear itself out of its yoke, but with its hind-quarters paralyzed it could only drag itself ineffectually a yard or so, and then the whole team came to a halt. Men had to run forward and cut this animal loose, and the defenders launched a blizzard of arrows in their direction, hitting one in the shoulder. The first human casualty of the battle, he screamed but was able to run back into cover behind the tower.

Gradually, more and more towers entered the killing field immediately in front of the wall. As the number of close-by towers increased, so the archers on the walls had to divide their attention among them, which made it easier for the towers to get even nearer. The oxen, however, now offered easy targets, and animal after animal was cut down, causing panic among those that were still uninjured. It was time to dispense with the oxen altogether; their drivers cut them loose, and they ran bellowing across the field of battle until they were brought down by arrows or escaped to the rear.

The Lombards themselves now had to continue the labor of advancing the towers. Men grasped the poles where the animals had been attached, while others put their shoulders to the sides and rear of the towers. They tried as best they could to protect themselves by draping their shields over their heads or backs, but many of them were hit by arrows that found unprotected spots, or by crossbow bolts that penetrated their shields. Some of the men were killed, or wounded so severely that they fell immobile where they had been hit, and they too had to be dragged out of the way of the advancing towers.

The Lombards now had only one goal in mind—to reach the wall as quickly as possible, before they were all cut down. With scores of men frantically pushing at each tower, they advanced much faster than before, but with less control. The right-side wheels of one of the towers ran into a ditch, and the whole tower canted over, ready to capsize. A crowd of men tried to right the tower with ropes, but they immediately attracted the attention of the defenders, and many of them were hit by arrows or missiles. The tower had to be abandoned, and the men inside climbed down and joined the ground-level attack.

As the towers advanced to fifty, forty, and then thirty yards from the wall, they became more and more vulnerable to attack. The onagers and other engines on the walls smashed the fronts of some of the towers, and archers and slingers were able to shoot obliquely into the towers' unprotected sides. Thus many men within the towers were killed or injured. Two of the towers were set alight by fire arrows; one of the fires was quickly doused with jars of vinegar that had been brought along for this purpose, but the other raged out of control, forcing the men within that tower to abandon it. The smoke rising from the burning tower was the first sign of the battle that was visible to Zaid and Antonius over on the Janiculum hill, though they had been hearing the noise of it for some time.

Up to this point, the defenders on the walls had been spared any casualties, for the attackers had been focused solely on getting the towers close to the wall. Now, however, several of the towers were brought to a halt, and archers atop the towers began shooting at the defenders. These archers were not very numerous—only about ten archers could operate from the top of each tower, along with others from lower levels. Still, the Lombard archers were more skilled and accurate than the Romans, and their elevation about ten feet above the top of the wall gave them a distinct advantage. Many of the defenders were hit, and others were driven to seek cover behind the parapet. The defenders within the bastions, who shot at the Lombards through arrow-slits, were immune to attack, but the small number of these slits, the restricted range of view they offered, and their location below the top of the wall, all conspired to limit the amount of damage that these defenders could inflict.

Aistulf, who was standing immediately to the rear of the attackers, now gave a signal to his officers, and they in turn ordered the scaling ladders to be brought into action. A ladder emerged from behind each siege tower, carried by a team of twenty men, who ran with it toward the wall.

The defenders knew that these were the first Lombards with the capacity to get into the city, and they attacked these men and the ladders they were carrying with the utmost energy. At least one quarter were hit by arrows, bolts, or sling-stones before they reached the wall, leaving their surviving companions to accomplish an even more arduous task without them. Once the teams reached the wall, they had to erect their ladders, a difficult task involving ropes and poles that left the men completely exposed to the defenders immediately above them. Several ladders were destroyed with well-aimed rocks. At other locations, so many of the attackers were hit that too few remained to raise the ladders. Thus only about half the ladders were maneuvered into place, and even those had insufficient men to form an effective scaling force, leaving only ten ladders available for the actual assault.

The men who started up the ladders knew well the danger they were facing, but they were determined to avenge their dead comrades, and they were encouraged by the rewards that Aistulf offered to the first men to reach the top of the wall. Besides, any show of cowardice would earn summary execution. So, shouting curses and threats at the defenders, they climbed from rung to rung until they reached a dizzying height, almost within grasp of the parapet.

They never reached it, however. Some of the ladders were destroyed with rocks even as the men climbed them. The remaining ladders were too heavy to push away from the wall, but at some locations the defenders were able to insert heavy poles between the uppermost rungs; by levering these poles sideways they succeeded in twisting the ladders around, so that the attackers found themselves climbing up the underside of the ladders, from which position they could not get onto the parapet. These men were soon hit by some missile, or they fell of their own accord. Where neither of these defenses seemed likely to work, the defenders poured heated sand onto the attackers. The sand got in between the men's armor and their bodies, causing searing burns. Within ten or fifteen minutes, all the ladder attacks had been repelled, and a pile of dead and dying men littered the ground at the base of the wall.

As Aistulf had envisaged, however, the scaling assault also took a terrible toll on the defenders. During the assault, the defenders' attention was wholly devoted to the men on the ladders, and the archers and slingers on the siege towers were able to shoot down onto the walls without any risk to themselves. Thus the defenders were cut down almost as effectively as were the men on the ladders. A few fell to the ground in front of the wall where, if they still showed any sign of life, they were immediately dispatched with the stroke of a Lombard sword or spear. Most remained lying atop the wall itself, however, and these had to be carried back down into the city, where their appearance caused a great deal of wailing among the onlookers. The same priests who had absolved the defenders of their sins earlier in the day were now kept busy administering last rites to the dying, and new contingents of defenders were sent up the winding stairways to replace those who had fallen.

The ladder assault at an end, Aistulf ordered the next stage of the attack to begin, and the second set of siege towers were pushed forward. These were the towers from which armed men hoped to cross directly to the parapet of the wall. Because the drawbridges were only about fifteen feet long, and because both the wall and the towers tapered slightly with height, the towers had to be pushed almost into direct contact with the base of the wall. This exposed them to attack from three directions: from the wall itself and from the bastions to the left and right of them. On the tops of the bastions, artillerymen used the engines emplaced there— rock-throwing onagers and spear-throwing ballistae—to batter the sides of the siege towers, and they succeeded in a few cases to stove in the sides and kill most of the soldiers within.

Meanwhile, the defenders on the walls prepared to repulse the assault. Once a siege tower was in place against the wall, the defenders knew where the tower's drawbridge would be lowered onto the parapet, and they gathered near that spot. Some used axes to hack at the bridge as soon as it was in place, which others greeted the assailants with a hail of missiles when they emerged, killing most of them. The few who got near to the parapet were impaled with spears or simply pushed off the drawbridge. Thus the defense was mostly successful, but extremely costly, because archers in other towers fired into the concentrated mass of defenders and killed many.

For a long time, not a single Lombard soldier made it all the way across a drawbridge onto the wall. But this suddenly changed on account of an unfortunate accident. The artillerymen atop one bastion misaimed an onager: instead of hitting a siege tower the rock swept through the mass of defenders who were facing the tower, killing or injuring more than half of them. Those who were not hit fell back in shock, and the attackers took advantage of the situation to rush across the drawbridge and leap onto the wall. They savagely attacked those defenders who were on their feet, killing or severely injuring all of them. Suddenly ten Lombard soldiers were in full possession of the hundred-foot stretch of wall between two bastions. They signaled for other attackers to join them and then rushed for the stairways, but the doors guarding them were immediately slammed shut and bolted. The attackers took a look over the inner side of the wall, but one glance was enough to tell them that they could not survive a jump down into the city, so they yelled down for their colleagues to bring rope ladders.

Seeing the critical situation, defenders on the bastions directed every weapon they had at the Lombards on the wall and the siege tower they had used to get there. Before long, several well-aimed fire arrows had set light to the tower about halfway up its height. Although twenty more attackers made it across the drawbridge, the tower was soon in flames, cutting off the men's retreat and preventing anyone else from joining them. Now archers on the bastions began to pick the men off one by one: whoever sought cover from arrows shot from one bastion exposed himself to those fired from the other. Seeing that they had no future atop the wall, the leader of the group of Lombards urged his men to climb down the inside of the wall into the city. This proved to be an equally fatal choice, however: most fell before they had descended more than a few feet, because the wall offered little in the way of handholds. Those who didn't fall of their own accord were quickly picked off by archers stationed on the ground.

The assault was now running out of energy. Rather than see more of his valuable siege towers destroyed, Aistulf decided that it was better to withdraw his forces and prepare for a second assault on a later day. Once he gave the order, his men pushed the still-intact towers back the way they had come. The defenders let out a deafening chorus of cheers and taunts. Meanwhile, archers hit a good number of the men who were pushing the towers, and the Romans mocked these unfortunates for taking arrows in their backs, a sure sign of cowardice.

Within ten minutes, most of the surviving Lombards were out of range. As the fighters on both sides fell silent, another sound could be heard—the groaning of the injured, who lay among heaps of the dead, broken armaments, spent arrows, and the smoking remains of several siege towers. A similar sound came from those still lying on the top of the wall and those who had been carried down into the city. The dreadful sounds continued into the evening and through the night, as packs of roaming dogs began to investigate the human detritus of the day's fighting.

38

———

"*In paradisum deducant vos angeli*—May angels lead you into Paradise; may the martyrs receive you and lead you to the holy city of Jerusalem. *Chorus angelorum—*" Stephen stopped to catch his breath, and broke into a fit of coughing. The noise echoed and re-echoed around the Pope's private chapel, but luckily no one was there to hear it except his brother.

"Finish it, please," Stephen whispered.

"*Chorus angelorum vos suscipiat,*" intoned Paul. "May the company of angels receive you, and with the pauper Lazarus may you have eternal rest."

After a short pause Stephen said: "I should write the letter, it must go out during the hours of darkness. Have them take me upstairs, and send for my notary. We'll complete our prayers later." Paul called for Stephen's bearers, who carried him in his chair up the long staircase to the papal chambers.

Paul walked alongside his brother. "Theo is blaming this on us," he said.

Stephen said nothing, so Paul went on. "Maybe it *is* our fault."

"It's Aistulf's fault," said Stephen. "He'll pay for it, in this world or the next."

"Yes, but perhaps our plan was wrong."

"Paul, despondency won't help us."

"Despondency? I'm just being realistic. You heard Leo's figures: three hundred and seventy dead, nearly two thousand wounded, many of them not expected to survive."

"We drove Aistulf off," said Stephen. "It was a victory for us."

"A victory?" asked Paul. "How many more such victories can we endure? Aistulf withdrew in good order. Give him a day or two to repair his towers, and he'll be back. And this time it won't just be the Lombards—it'll be his allies too."

"Well, that's why we must try to hurry Pepin up."

"If he's even on his way at all."

"He's on his way, believe me. You're talking like Marcellus or Theo now. What do you want me to do—appeal to the Emperor?"

"No, no," said Paul. "I'm sorry—today has been the worst day of my life—all this bloodshed. But Pepin's our only hope now, that's clear. We've cast our dice."

The notary was already waiting when Stephen and Paul entered the papal chambers. Stephen immediately started dictating the letter. His frequent pauses for breath gave the notary plenty of time to take his words down in shorthand.

"Petrus vocatus apostolus a Jesu Christo," Stephen began. *"From Peter, called by Jesus Christ, Son of the Living God, to be his Apostle, to those most excellent kings, Pepin, Charles, and Carloman, and their most holy bishops, abbots, and monks, and all the dukes, counts, armies, and people dwelling in Francia—"*

Paul broke in. "From the apostle himself?" he asked.

"The blessed Peter himself wrote this letter? Is Pepin going to believe that?"

"Probably," said Stephen. "And even if not, he'll still recognize my right to invoke—"

"I'm not comfortable with this. Such a presumption could earn us—"

"Paul, I know what's right here. As the successor to Peter I have the right—the obligation—to give voice to his thoughts. I'm certain that he shares our suffering. I'm sure he desires as strongly as we do that Pepin come to our aid. I've already written to Pepin several times in my own name; now, only the words of the apostle himself can move him. So let me go on, please.

"*Ferocissimi Langobardi,*" he continued, "The most ferocious and God-despised Lombards have laid waste the lands of the Romans with fire and the sword. They have burned the churches and cast the images of the saints into the fire. They have devoured the consecrated bread and wine at their gluttonous feasts, and stripped the altars of their altar-cloths and other adornments. They have carried off and violated the nuns and beaten the monks. They have driven off the cattle, cut down the vines, and trampled down the harvests. They have even dug up and carried away the bones of the blessed martyrs.

"And now the Lombards under their evil king, Aistulf, lay siege to my holy city of Rome itself, and in a most merciless and wicked assault have slaughtered many hundreds of the brave Roman citizens. The Lombards taunt the Romans in their rage and fury, saying 'Now we have surrounded you— let the Franks come if they can and deliver you from our hands!'

"On you alone depend the lives of all the Romans. If they perish, all the nations of the earth will ask, 'Why did the Romans place their confidence and trust in the kings and the nation of the Franks?' More than that, the sin of their ruin will lie on your soul, and in the last great day of judgment, when the Lord shall sit surrounded by all the Apostles to judge by fire every one of this world's potentates, He will harden His heart against you. He will say to you—O God forbid that it should be so—'I know you not, because you did not help the Church of God, and because you took no care to deliver his people when they were in peril.'"

Paul was lost in anxious thought. Over the preceding weeks he had begun to feel more and more guilt about his role in the creation of Constantine's letter, the macabre trick he had used to bring it to light, and the false arguments he had used to fool his brother and his fellow counselors into accepting it. Earlier, Leoba had been able to overcome his doubts; the whole thing was her idea, after all. It did seem at that time that the deception was justified by the situation. But now Leoba was gone, and Paul was facing the reality of Aistulf's siege and the terrible cost of today's assault.

Might not this be punishment for what they had done, Paul wondered. Punishment for taking the name of the blessed Sylvester in vain, for defiling his bones, and for corrupting with falsehoods the mind of the Supreme Pontiff? But how could he undo what was done without bringing down shame on himself, embarrassment on Stephen, and further destruction on Rome? There seemed to be no way out. Yet the more qualms he had about the whole affair, the more certain was his brother that they were on the right path.

Stephen continued with his dictation. *"Currite, currite!* Hasten, hasten! By the living and true God I exhort and summon you, hasten to help, before your spiritual mother, the Holy Church of God, through which you hope to receive eternal life, be foully ravished by impious men. I speak on behalf of that city of Rome in which the Lord ordained that my body should rest. Liberate that city and its people, who are your brethren, and do not allow it to be destroyed by the nation of the Lombards. Let me not be separated from my Roman people, so that you in turn may not be separated from the kingdom of God and the life eternal.

"I conjure you, my best beloved ones, by the living God, do not permit the city of Rome or the people that dwell within to be tortured any longer by the nation of the Lombards, lest your own bodies and souls be tortured in the eternal and unquenchable fire of Tartarus with the devil and his pestilential angels. Do not allow the sheep of the Lord's flock—the Roman people—to be scattered abroad, lest the Lord scatter you and cast you forth as He did the people of Israel."

"That's the whole thing," said Stephen to the notary. "Add the usual formalities. Have it written out as quickly as possible—don't worry about how it looks. Give it to Leo, his messengers are waiting."

"How will they get it out of the city?" asked Paul.

"By the river."

"And how will they find Pepin?"

"Believe me, that won't be hard. When an army moves, the whole world hears about it."

39

Zaid was shaking with fear. He was standing on top of the Aurelian Wall, just north of St. Pancras Gate, along with Antonius and several other slingers and archers. In front of him a row of siege towers, crowded with archers and armored swordsmen, were advancing on the wall. Within minutes, it seemed, the battle was likely to turn into a bloody fight on the parapet. Zaid, with no armor and a weapon that was useless for hand-to-hand combat, would be among the first to die.

It was three days since Aistulf's first attempt to take the city, and as Paul had predicted, he had now ordered a combined assault by all four of the armies that were besieging Rome. Zaid knew that if Desiderius's Tuscan forces got the upper hand at St. Pancras Gate, there would be little chance of assistance from defenders stationed elsewhere around the city's perimeter, because the ranks of the defenders had been thinned by the losses they had already suffered. Most likely, Leo would order his forces to abandon Transtiber entirely and set up a new line of defense at the Tiber bridges, even though that would mean giving up the ship mills and the granaries on the west bank.

The area of the wall where Zaid stood was particularly likely to be overrun, because this was where it doubled back after its excursion to the top of the Janiculum Hill. The sharp west-facing corner was vulnerable to attack from several different directions at once. St. Pancras Gate, with its huge flanking bastions, was located immediately south of the corner, so it faced to the southwest, but Zaid, who was stationed just a few yards away around the corner, faced to the north. Over his left shoulder he could see the gate and, stretching away from it to the west, the Aurelian Way and Trajan's aqueduct. To his right, the wall descended rapidly toward the river, with the urban portion of the Aurelian Way just inside it. In front of Zaid, just a few hundred yards of clear ground lay between the wall and the nearby woods. It was across this open space that the Tuscans were advancing toward the wall.

The men on the siege towers shouted curses and taunts and brandished their weapons at the defenders as the towers approached. Arrows were flying in both directions, but the towers were still out of slingshot range, so Zaid and Antonius tried to protect themselves by crouching behind the parapet. At their feet lay a pile of ammunition: river pebbles that had been wrapped in lead to make heavy, fist-sized missiles.

"If you live, take this," said Zaid to Antonius, showing him the locket around his neck. "So that if you ever see Lenora, you could give it to her, and tell her—"

"You're not going to die—"

"Tell her what happened. And that I—I was thinking about her."

"I will, but let's not talk about that. Get ready." An

officer yelled at the slingers to stand up and join the battle, because the nearest tower was only about fifty yards distant. Both Antonius and Zaid got up, put stones in their slings, and hurled them toward the tower. Zaid's stone missed its target completely; the one fired by Antonius hit the front of the tower and bounced off without doing any damage. The two youths continued firing off stones as the tower came even closer. Zaid felt better now he was taking an active part in the defense.

"I got him!" yelled Antonius after a while. One of his stones had hit an armored soldier in the chest and sent him reeling, although the man seemed only winded. Zaid completed his own shot, which hit one of the beams supporting the tower, and then turned to congratulate Antonius, but his friend wasn't there. Looking down, Zaid saw that Antonius was lying flat on his back, with an arrow in his throat.

"Tonius!" Zaid screamed. He knelt down at his friend's side. "Tonius! Are you all right? Are you there? Tonius! Don't die! Don't die!" But Antonius had died instantly—with only a fine trickle of blood staining his neck.

"Tonius!" Zaid screamed again. But an officer yelled at Zaid: "Back into action! There's time for crying later. Shoot, shoot, or we're all dead!"

Zaid stood up again, placed a stone in his sling, and whirled it with all his energy and rage. He aimed at an archer who was leaning out of the siege tower and pulling an arrow from his quiver. The man was tall and fair-haired, with an excited smile on his youthful face. The stone caught him on the side of his head, which exploded in a spray of blood and brains. He fell fifty feet, but he was dead before his body hit the ground.

Nausea and panic seized Zaid. Throwing down his sling, he ran blindly for the stairway. "After him!" shouted the officer. "Get him back, get him back!" Reaching the ground, Zaid darted between houses and came to the Aurelian Way. As he crossed the street he glanced to his right: he saw that the defenders on the left side of the gate were shooting at another siege tower close to the wall. He ran on, zig-zagging his way among more buildings. Then, in front him, he saw the abandoned mill. A quick shove forced open the door. He slammed it behind him and collapsed onto a bench in the milling chamber. He was seized with a fit of retching, made all the worse because his stomach was empty.

A whirlwind of emotions—grief, guilt, anger, and fear—raged in Zaid's head. Antonius—this boy who was just a seller of pastries, who had fed Zaid and his homeless companions from his little cart—Antonius, just snuffed out like a candle, gone in an instant, never even knowing that his end had come! And he, Zaid—he in turn had taken another life. Was it the man who had shot Antonius, or someone else? There was no way to tell. But it didn't matter; it was a horror beyond anything Zaid could have imagined, to have been responsible for that. In those few seconds, war had become real for him.

Burying his head in his hands, Zaid wept and wept. And when he had done weeping, he just sat there in numb silence, staring at the abandoned machinery of the mill. What could he do? To return to the wall meant death, he knew that—death for desertion, or death at the hands of the enemy.

Now one emotion above all seized him—loneliness.

Those others on the wall, he thought—they have their priests to absolve their sins and administer their last rites. They have their families to bury them, their angels to wing their souls heavenward, and their saints and martyrs to welcome them to eternal rest. Perhaps they were blessed martyrs themselves, dying as they did in defense of their holy city. But he, Zaid, who did he have? Who would forgive him? Who would bury him? Who would make *dua* for him? Who would pray for his soul? And what would Allah say to him after death—a man who had killed in a battle of Christians against Christians? Such a deed was not permitted by his faith, Zaid knew. Why then had he allowed himself to join the militia? Why had he stayed in Rome at all? Why had he ever been born?

Zaid leaned against the masonry wall of the mill. He wanted to pray. There was no water to wash himself, and no way to tell the direction of the Qiblah. Exhaustion and despair prevented him even from rising from the bench onto which he had thrown himself. *"Rabbana faghfir lana dhunubana wa kaffir,"* he recited in a toneless whisper. "Our Lord, forgive us our sins, and take away our evil deeds, and allow us to die the death of the righteous."

40

———

The Tuscan encampment was located to the south of the Aurelian Way, half a mile or so from the city walls. Around midday, Lenora and her parents were sitting in front of their tent, sharing a simple meal that Lenora and her mother had brought from the camp kitchens, where they worked. Marcus was covered in his familiar coating of flour; he had spent the morning operating a portable horse-powered mill.

"Don't look, Nora," said Marcus. Orderlies were carrying several injured men on stretchers past their tent on the way to a medical post. Some of the wounded men were silent and motionless, but others thrashed about and groaned or screamed in pain.

"Thank God you don't have to fight," said Sibyl.

"Thank God indeed. And let's hope the assault succeeds this time. The longer we sit here, the more likely that the Romans will come out and attack the camp. Then we'll all be fighting—me, you, and Lenora here."

"Don't speak of that," said Sibyl. "I hope this will soon be over and we can get home to Lucca. We should never have moved to Rome in the first place."

"Then I wouldn't have met Zaid," said Lenora.

"Zaid!" said Marcus. "When we get home to Lucca, there'll be a young man for you."

"Papa! This is my home—here in Rome. This is where I grew up, where my friends are, where Zaid is."

"Don't keep on about—"

"Let her be, Marcus," said Sibyl.

"Let her be? This has gone on for—"

The family argument was cut off by the arrival of a half-dozen armed soldiers led by an officer, who walked up to their tent. "Miller Marcus," the officer said, "I'm told you have information about a way into the city—through the aqueduct?"

"I do," Marcus replied. "You just need to get into the channel of the aqueduct and follow it to the city."

"So there's a passage through the wall?"

"Yes."

"It hasn't been closed off?"

"Not when I was there. It was closed off long ago, but we opened it up again to let water through for the mills. I can't be certain that it's still open, but I'm guessing that it is. If it's closed off, you'd just have to turn round and come back—or else you could take tools and try to break through—they might have placed some blocks of masonry there."

"We'll be taking tools anyway—in case we need to force the locks on the gate. But how big is the passageway?"

"You can walk upright in the aqueduct, even where it goes through the wall, but then there's a low arch, just as the aqueduct comes out on the inside of the wall. You'd have to duck under the arch, or maybe you'd have to go through on hands and knees, but it's big enough, I'm sure of it."

"Just one person at a time?"

"One at a time, yes," said Marcus.

"That's not good," said another soldier. "They'll just kill each of us in turn as we come through."

"Perhaps we could do it at night," added a third man.

"We can't wait until night," said the officer.

"It doesn't come out into the street," said Marcus. "It opens directly into the first mill—into the basement of the mill where the water-wheels are. No one will see you in there. You could gather in the mill, and from there you could reach the gate in a few moments—as you come out of the mill you turn to your left, you can see it right in front of you."

"How do we get into the aqueduct?" asked the officer.

"That I'm not sure about, but there must be access holes in the roof. You'd have to look for them."

"And it's dry?"

"Yes," said Marcus. "The water was diverted north, to St. Peter's and the baths around there. The take-off point is just a little west of here. You could check to see if the fountains are running there."

"They are," said one of the soldiers.

"Then the aqueduct is still diverted," said Marcus. "So from here down to the city should be dry."

The officer turned to one of his men. "Go to Desiderius, explain the situation. Tell him we're ready to go ahead. If he wants us to do it, he needs have men ready to storm the gate once we get it open."

The man ran off, and the officer turned back to Marcus. "You'll be rewarded, miller, if this succeeds," he said. "If not—well, I won't be around to say anything about it." He led his men away.

"I hate you!" said Lenora to Marcus.

"Don't speak to your father like that!" said Sibyl sharply. "The spirits will punish you."

"I'm not going to sit here and argue," said Marcus, getting up. "I have to get back to work." He picked up some tools and walked toward his mill.

"We need to get back too," said Sibyl. She and Lenora walked to the camp kitchen. The supervisor told Lenora and several other women to fetch water, so they took jars and headed to the well. The camp was half-deserted, because most of the soldiers were engaged in the assault. At the well, a line of women were waiting in the hot sun to draw water. "It's nearly dry," said one woman to Lenora. "If you want, you can try the other well—it's just outside the camp on the north side."

Lenora and her companions walked to the camp gate. A few women with water jars were coming and going. A guard at the gate pointed Lenora in the direction of the well, two hundred yards away. He warned her to keep her eyes open and hurry back if there was any sign of the enemy.

A few minutes' walk took them to the well on the south side of the Aurelian Way. The aqueduct ran along the other side of the road on high arches. There was a line at this well too, and the women had to wait their turn. In the distance Lenora could hear the noise of battle. It seemed so strange to be going through the motions of daily life while men fought and died less than half a mile away.

As the women were standing there, the same group of armed men who had spoken with Marcus passed by on the road, walking away from the city. They were grim-faced, carrying crowbars and other implements in addition to their weapons.

"I need to pee, can you hold my jar?" said Lenora to the woman next to her. She crossed the road; as she did so she looked to her left and saw that the men were walking up an incline. Because the aqueduct needed to maintain a level course, it became shorter and shorter as the road ascended. Obviously the men were looking for a place where they could get into the channel of the aqueduct without scaling any great heights.

Having crossed the road, Lenora walked under an arch of the aqueduct and entered the woods beyond. She turned left, trying to follow the men inconspicuously. They had climbed atop of the aqueduct, which was only about six feet above the road surface at this point. She heard them talking to each other.

"Look for a hole," said one. The men walked in opposite directions looking for a way into the covered water channel.

"This could be it," one of them shouted. He had found a pyramid-shaped stone that might be the lid of an access hole. The other men joined him, and they pried up the stone with crowbars.

"We've got it," Lenora heard one of them say. They moved the stone to one side and, after peering in, they disappeared one by one into the hole.

Lenora waited a minute, then went up to the spot where the men had climbed onto the aqueduct. It was an easy scramble. From the top she could see the open access hole just thirty feet away. She walked up to it and looked down. The floor of the channel was perhaps six feet below the opening. Two or three iron hoops had been cemented into the inside wall as a kind of ladder. Lenora placed a foot on the first hoop, and then cautiously lowered herself into the dark space. A few moments later she was standing in the watercourse. She could just hear the voices of the men receding into the distance.

Lenora looked around. The channel wasn't completely dry: a scant half-inch of water wet its floor. Evidently the diversion wasn't completely watertight. Some kind of slimy material lay underfoot, making the channel very slippery. The lower portions of the sides of the channel were covered with a marble-like material, made of minerals that been deposited from centuries' worth of flowing water. It didn't look like any maintenance work had been done on the aqueduct in a long time.

Lenora's first impulse was to follow the men, with the idea of interfering with their activities in some way. But what could she do? How could she, an unarmed girl, stop six armed soldiers from gaining access to the mill? She looked the other way. Not far in that direction, her father had said, lay the take-off point where the water had been diverted to St. Peter's. She started cautiously walking in that direction.

The tunnel was dark, but not totally so. Chinks in the masonry of the aqueduct and breaks in its roof allowed a little light to percolate through. She kept her hands in contact with the two sides of the tunnel and proceeded slowly. Eventually, Lenora heard the sound of flowing water. Soon after, she could make out a blockage ahead of her. As she got close, she saw that it was a heavy timber sluice-board sitting in the floor of the channel and blocking the tunnel's lower half.

Luckily, the roof was more or less open at this point, so

that there was much more light here than elsewhere in the tunnel. Perhaps the workmen had made the hole in the process of working on the diversion. Peering over the sluice-board, Lenora could see the rushing water. It came up against the board, and then turned northward into the openings of several large pipes that had been crudely cemented into the aqueduct's northern side-wall, near its base. Lenora could even see that someone had scratched letters into the cement above each pipe. She made out "SP" over one of them. Lenora could not read, but she knew her letters and she guessed that these stood for 'Sancti Petri.' Evidently these were labels to indicate the destination of each pipe.

Lenora knew that opening the sluice gate would send a torrent of water down toward the city. If the water reached the wall before the men did, it might well prevent them from getting into the mill. She saw that the sluice gate could be raised with an iron crank that worked a kind of screw mechanism. But what would happen to her once the water started flowing? She would be swept away or else left clinging to the board without any hope of rescue. The water, after all, would never stop flowing.

Lenora looked around, and then up. Yes, there was a crude set of iron hoops, similar to the ones she had used to get into the tunnel. She climbed up a few of them to make sure she could get out, and even stuck her head out of the hole at the top. This seemed to be a practical escape route. Reassured, she climbed down again, and applied herself to the crank, but rust or minerals from the water had locked it in place.

Looking around again, Lenora saw a few cobble-size

stones on the floor of the channel. They must have fallen out of the masonry. Grasping the largest one as a hammer, she struck the crank repeatedly. Eventually it began to give, and the sluice-board rose almost imperceptibly. A little more water ran into the channel than had been getting through before. Encouraged, Lenora kept on working at the crank, which began to move a little more easily. Now there was a half-inch gap below the board, through which a narrow jet of water spurted. Before long, the gap had increased to an inch, then two inches. Lenora could see the stream of water running away down the aqueduct, but still it was not nearly enough to hamper the soldiers' efforts to get into the mill.

Suddenly, there was a loud crack, as of splintering timber, and the entire sluice-board gave way. An immense mass of water erupted through the gap, filling the tunnel to half its height, a great wave heading toward the city. Lenora grabbed the crank with both hands, but there was no way that she could pull herself out of the water as the rushing torrent tore at the lower half of her body. For several minutes she managed to stay where she was, but her arms and her spirit began to fail her. At last she lost her grip with one hand, and then the other. She found herself hurtling down the aqueduct in a roiling wave of water, tumbling and colliding with the walls, trying to take a breath when she could, but more often choking on the water that she inhaled.

41

The felucca eased its way up the Nile, its sail filled by a gentle breeze out of the north. It was a cool night, and the crescent moon, like a silver galleon, drifted on its own river of stars toward the western horizon. Under the sheepskin blanket that covered the young lovers, Zaid reached for Lenora's warm body and drew her to him. A passion rose once again in his loins. As he turned to fulfill his desire, however, he was distracted by a scratching or knocking on the hull of the boat, as if the steersman had carelessly guided it onto a shoal. "Be careful, you're carrying a precious cargo," Zaid said to the man, indicating his young bride. But the steersman didn't reply, and the strange sounds became louder—

Zaid jerked awake. He had no idea how long he had been asleep, but the rough planks of the bench had left him sore and stiff all down his left side. The events that had brought him to the mill came back to him in a rush of horrific memories.

Something was happening in the basement of the mill. Zaid peered quietly over the unprotected edge of the upper deck. Directly below him, an armed man was standing in the channel of the aqueduct, between the two mill-races. He was stooping down to assist a second man, who was trying to work his way under the archway that marked the entry of the aqueduct into the mill.

"Here, give me your hand, it's just this last part that's narrow," whispered the standing man.

"All right," said the other. "But don't pull too hard—no, let go, let go, let me get through on my own—I'm fatter than you!"

Both men spoke with a Tuscan accent. Zaid realized immediately that they were attempting a covert entry into the city, probably with the aim of opening St. Pancras Gate. Zaid had no idea how the battle was going outside on the wall, but the Tuscans must not have made it across yet, if they were resorting to this kind of tactic. To Zaid, what the men were doing seemed to violate a basic code of warfare: they were employing underhand deceit and trickery rather facing the enemy in a fair battle.

"What's this water?" said the man under the arch. Earlier, the channel had been just slightly damp, but now there was now an inch or so of water running down it. A sluice-gate guided the water into the south mill-race, but the water level wasn't high enough to turn the large wheel that was suspended in the race.

"Help me!" the man said urgently, and the first man stooped again to pull him through.

The danger of the situation banished Zaid's qualms and despair. But how could he stop these armed men? If he ran for help, he'd be seized and maybe killed on the spot as a deserter. He looked around. A spare millstone was propped up against the wall, just an arm's length from where he was crouching. Without taking a moment to think about it, Zaid grasped the stone and rolled it across a couple of feet of the deck and then over the edge. Alerted by the noise, the man looked up, but too late. The falling millstone crushed his back, killing him in an instant.

Zaid dashed down the stairway. He saw that the water was now several inches deep, and the wheel in the south race was beginning to turn. The wheel, and the long-abandoned machinery connected to it, were protesting the sudden resumption of service with loud creaks and bangs. But Zaid paid no attention to the wheel, for the second man was now almost through the arch and was about to get to his feet. Zaid pulled the sword from the scabbard that was still attached to the dead man's belt. It took a strong tug to get the sword out, because both it and the scabbard had been slightly bent by the impact of the millstone. Once the sword was in his hand, however, Zaid drove it into the neck of the second man. A spurt of blood jetted from a severed artery and mixed with the flowing water of the aqueduct, coloring it with bright red streaks. The man staggered and tried to cry out, but he fell dead alongside his companion in the main channel of the aqueduct.

Now the water was a foot deep or more as it flowed into the mill. Zaid heard a voice at the other end of the tunnel—the man seemed to be asking a companion what he should do. "Go, go!" another voice said. A moment later a man appeared under the arch—he was more or less swimming in the flowing water. Zaid stabbed him in the back, but the stroke didn't kill him. Bleeding profusely, he tried to get up out of the water; he managed to lift his body over the sluice board into the main channel, but Zaid kept stabbing him, and eventually he stopped moving.

While this was happening, yet another man came under the archway, but he didn't seem fully conscious: he was swept along by the current, which carried him into the south mill-race. The paddles of the large water-wheel, now turning at a brisk pace, caught the man and crushed him. The wheel juddered to a halt with the man's body jammed between it and the floor of the race. With the race partially blocked, the surging water spilled over into the main channel, rinsing away some of the blood that had collected there.

The water in the aqueduct had risen almost to the top of the archway by the time a fifth intruder appeared there. Zaid struck at him immediately with the sword, but the man was wearing a helmet and chainmail hauberk, and Zaid's stroke failed to penetrate the armor. Though he was underwater, the man was conscious, and he grasped Zaid's leg. Zaid felt himself being pulled down and he grabbed at a projecting hook that was cemented into the masonry above the archway. Then he placed his free foot on the man's head. Pressed down by Zaid, and by the weight of his armor, the man was unable to raise his head out of the water or to get his body out from under the archway. After struggling for a while, he stopped moving. Zaid lifted his foot and the man's body slid forward into the mill-race, where it came to rest against the body of his companion lodged under the wheel. No motion or breath came from the submerged body.

Although Zaid was nearing exhaustion, he heard more noise coming from within the archway. A man was cursing and splashing: although caught by the flow of water, he had been able to keep from entering the mill by jamming himself against the upstream face of the archway. He seemed to know that his companions had met a lethal reception and was fighting to avoid the same fate. But he could not hold out for long: while he still held on to the masonry with both hands, his body slipped feet-first through the arch, and Zaid stabbed him in the groin and then the stomach. He bled profusely as he struggled to pull back against the flowing water, but he was carried through into the mill; he was already dead as his body was swept into the mill-race.

Zaid waited by the archway, breathing heavily and still in a frenzy of excitement, but no one else came through, alive or dead. He sat down on the stairway, keeping a tight grip on the sword. The basement of the mill resembled some vision of Hell, with the bodies of the six intruders lying in contorted poses, their wounds still oozing blood. Zaid had only been sitting for a minute or so, however, when he heard the noise of something bumping against the inside of the archway. He jumped up and prepared to stab the seventh soldier. A body, unconscious or already dead, was carried head first into the mill. Zaid raised his sword to stab the intruder, but then he saw that it wasn't a soldier at all—it was a young woman.

As Lenora's body was swept into the mill-race, Zaid grasped her and lifted her out into the main channel. He looked into her face, but failed to recognize her, dirt-caked and bruised and bloodied as she was. Still, he knew that she could not be a combatant, and he shook her by the shoulders to see if there was any life left in her. Lenora was roused enough to provoke a fit of coughing and vomiting that cleared rivers of water out of her lungs and stomach. After a while she blearily opened her eyes, staring straight in front of her. She saw a familiar locket.

A hundred yards away, a group of soldiers was hurrying up the Aurelian Way to assist the defenders stationed at St. Pancras Gate, for the battle was raging at the wall with the outcome still in doubt. A woman standing in a doorway yelled at them as they passed: "The fountain—look, it's bleeding! It's bleeding!"

The leader of the soldiers glanced across to where the woman was pointing. In a little market square, a long-dry fountain was now gushing water tinged a pinkish-purple color, as though it was indeed mixed with blood.

"They've started the aqueduct!" said the leader of the soldiers.

"Why?" asked another. "What good is that to them?"

"I don't know. Go to the mill—there, by the wall—the aqueduct comes in there. Find out what's going on."

Leo was roused from sleep an hour or two after midnight. He had been up very late, supervising the recovery of bodies and making sure the night watches were properly set. After a day of ferocious fighting, Aistulf had pulled his forces back once more, and the city seemed safe for the moment. Still, it had been another day of terrible losses—at least two thousand men were killed or severely injured. With their ranks so weakened, Leo doubted that the defenders could withstand another such assault. But his duties done for the moment, he had decided to take some sleep in a cot near the Salarian Gate, rather than returning to his headquarters. After the failed intrusion through the aqueduct, it was clear that the besiegers might attempt another surreptitious attack, very possibly at night, and Leo wanted to be ready to jump back into action at a moment's notice. Sure enough, after what seemed like just a few moments of sleep a soldier was shaking his shoulder. "Sir!" he said, "sir!"

Leo sat up quickly. "What is it?" he asked.

"There's a fire out there, sir," the soldier said.

"Out where?"

"In the Lombard lines!"

"A campfire?"

"No, sir, a big fire."

Leo jumped up, ran to a stairway, and climbed to the top of the wall. Several men were standing there looking out to the north. It was a very dark night and there was little to see, except directly ahead of them where some kind of large beacon was burning.

"It's a siege tower," Leo said. "It must be a fire attack. Alert all the northern gates."

Runners took off for several nearby gates to make sure that defenders were ready to fend off the impending attack, but it seemed most likely that it would be directed at the Salarian Gate, right by where they were standing. The gate was covered with iron sheets to protect against fire, but Leo knew that determined attackers could pry the sheets away. In fact, if the fire burned hot enough, it could ignite the gate's timbers even with the metal cladding still in place.

"It strange, though, isn't it, sir?" asked one of the men, "Strange that they would set fire to the tower so soon? They've still got to move it three hundred yards."

"Maybe they started it too early by mistake. That would be a lucky stroke for us—it gave us good warning."

"Look, sir, another tower!" A second beacon flared up, off to the left. Then another, and a few minutes later a fourth tower was in flames. Now more and more defenders, woken from their slumbers, were joining the night watch atop the wall.

"They're not moving," said Leo. "I don't know what they're up to. We didn't send anyone out there, did we?"

"Not that I know of, sir," said an officer. "Those orders come only from you. And the towers are well guarded, that's for certain. If our men were doing this, we'd hear the fighting."

"Well, whoever started these fires is doing us a huge favor. Look, there must be twenty towers burning now—that's all of them, more or less. Smell the smoke!"

The Romans stared hypnotically at the burning towers. After an hour, the flames started to subside. After two hours, nothing but a few glowing piles of embers remained visible, and complete darkness returned. But messengers arrived with the news that siege towers were burning at many other locations around the city.

At first light, the defenders on the walls saw nothing but ash-strewn wreckage where the tall towers had once stood. No Lombards were to be seen. Leo sent scouts to investigate: he watched as they cautiously crossed yesterday's killing ground and then stepped among the remains of the towers and other siege equipment. Then they walked further into the distance and were lost to sight. An hour later they returned. The Lombard camp was empty, they told Leo; Aistulf was gone.

42

——

Pepin's army stretched out like a fifteen-mile long serpent over the winding descent of the Mont Cenis pass. Ahead of the main body of troops, scouts inspected the road itself as well as the steep terrain to either side, checking every crag, cave, or defile that might offer concealment for an ambush. Behind them, forming the army's vanguard, strode eight hundred of Pepin's best-trained troops, armed with spears and short steel swords, helmeted, clothed in chainmail from neck to thigh, with their round wooden shields on their backs. A contingent of archers accompanied them. To the extent that the difficult road allowed, these troops marched in strict step like a Roman legion of old, singing marching songs that dated back to the time of Scipio. Their leader carried a standard: it bore the image of a cross on a white ground, for Pepin waged war in the name of the Christian God.

The vanguard was followed by a thousand horsemen, each of them a Frankish landowner rich enough to outfit himself with steed, armor, and steel weapons. Pepin himself, surrounded by his personal bodyguard and several high officers, rode at the rear of the cavalry, where he could best stay in touch with the entire length of the moving column. Close behind Pepin rode several bishops, who brought with them a casket containing St. Martin's cloak, the relic most effective in ensuring Frankish victory in war. The bishops were followed by fifty chaplains; another hundred chaplains were scattered throughout the advancing army in case of urgent need.

Behind the religious men came a much larger contingent of foot soldiers—perhaps thirty thousand men in total. These were less affluent men equipped with iron swords and little or no armor, as well as archers and slingers. They were followed by artillerymen shepherding their equipment on carts and wagons. Behind them came the baggage train. Mules, packhorses, and heavy ox-drawn wagons carried everything that an army might conceivably need on a campaign into unknown territory: slingshot and arrows by the tens of thousands; equipment for bridging streams and rivers; siege engines, or the metal parts needed to construct them; thousands of spades, pickaxes, and other tools for digging fortifications and erecting palisades; cooking equipment, surgical instruments and supplies, portable altars, and food—enough grain and fodder to sustain men and animals until they could forage in the Italian lowlands. The grain alone filled two hundred wagons. At the end of the baggage train, a small body of horsemen formed the rearguard.

While those horsemen were still negotiating the chilly, treeless heights of the pass, Pepin's group was passing through forests of black poplar and aspen, which were at the height of their autumn color. And the men in the vanguard were already approaching the grassy, oak-studded expanses of the Susa Valley. As they descended toward the valley, a strong hot wind blew at their backs, helping to speed them on their way. Rounding a rocky spur, they finally caught sight of the fortified town of Susa, which lay a few miles away but still well beneath them.

Susa, like Aosta on the road to Mons Jovis, had a Frankish garrison: its role was to guard the Mont Cenis pass from Lombard incursions. Pepin's men had looked forward to setting up camp next to the town for the night, so that they would enjoy an extra measure of protection. But when the scouts descended another half-mile toward the valley, they saw that a large army was stationed between them and the town. The Lombards, it appeared, were determined to stop Pepin's army before it could emerge from the pass onto the open spaces of the valley.

Pepin had expected to encounter Aistulf at the summit of the pass, if not earlier, because there were many locations on the rocky heights where a defensive force could have enjoyed a great advantage over an advancing column, with or without the benefit of concealment. But Aistulf had not been able to reach Mont Cenis in time, even though he abandoned the siege of Rome at the very instant that he got news of Pepin's southward advance. He therefore stationed his army at the southern end of the pass, hoping to force the Franks into combat before they could establish their proper battle lines. A smaller contingent remained behind the main Lombard army, to protect it in case the Susa garrison was tempted to rush out and attack their rear.

As soon as the Frankish vanguard reached the lowermost slopes of the pass, they saw the Lombards advancing toward them. They had a minute or so to gather round the chaplain, who made a quick appeal to St. Peter for victory. Then the Frankish soldiers formed a dense, stationary phalanx and prepared to receive the assault. The first act of hostility was a wave of arrows launched toward the Franks while the Lombards were still about two hundred yards away. Momentarily, the arrows darkened the sky, and the Franks quickly raised their shields into the overlapping pattern that provided them with a continuous protective roof. The arrows had been launched in a high, arcing trajectory so as to increase the speed of their descent and their penetrating power. As a result, however, the swirling headwind caught many of the arrows and caused them to fall short. Some did reach the Franks but failed to penetrate the thick wooden shields.

A few moments later, the first line of Lombard soldiers closed on the Frankish phalanx, screaming their war-cries and brandishing spears and swords. In preparation for the onslaught, the Franks held their spears in front of them, presenting a wall of razor-sharp spear-points to the onrushing Lombards. The impact caused many casualties on both sides, and the screams of the wounded and dying mixed with the yells and curses of those still able to fight.

So close-packed was the Frankish phalanx that the wounded soldiers were not able to fall out of place. In fact, even some of the dead soldiers remained propped up between their living companions. In those places where casualties did fall out of line, the Franks quickly closed their ranks, keeping the same impenetrable wall of spear-tips facing toward the enemy. The Lombard soldiers in the front line, or those of them who were still alive, lost courage and moved back a little, but they were quickly replaced by other troops from the rear, so that the Franks faced an almost continuous attack.

While the Frankish vanguard was holding its position, the horsemen behind them hurried down to join the battle, and they gradually assembled a large enough force to challenge the Lombards. These horsemen tried to get around the location of the ongoing battle in order to attack the Lombard infantry from the side or the rear. The north side was blocked by a small river that descended from the pass, but to the south lay an open grassy landscape, and the Frankish horsemen moved into this area. They immediately saw that the Lombard cavalry had gathered here and formed a close line, with the aim of blocking any flanking attack.

The Franks charged the Lombard line, running into it with an impact that killed or injured dozens of men and animals on both sides. Many riders were unhorsed and had to fight on foot with their short swords, which they used to stab the bellies of their enemies' horses. Riderless horses were quickly commandeered by fighters who had lost their own. Broken spears and shields, the flailing bodies of injured horses, along with the human casualties, turned the ground into a treacherous obstacle course, but those who could do so continued to stab and hack at each other in noisy, bloody chaos. Some riders were able to unhorse their opponents by ramming into them with their shields. Neither side gained the upper hand, but the superior numbers of the Lombards began to favor them, as the fallen horsemen were replaced with fresh combatants from the rear. Although many individual Lombards were put out of action, the line itself showed no sign of disintegrating.

A trumpet blew, and then, as if abandoning any hope of success, the Frankish horsemen wheeled away and fled in disorder toward the south. Sensing victory, and not waiting for orders from their commanders, the Lombards urged their horses forward in hot pursuit. Farther and farther fled the Franks, and farther and farther the Lombards went after them, losing all cohesion in the process. They managed to catch and cut down a few of the Franks. But then, at the sound of a second trumpet, the Franks wheeled around once more. The retreat had been a feint, and it had succeeded in causing the solid Lombard line to disintegrate into isolated chase groups separated by widening gaps. As they had practiced many times on the training ground at Brennacum, the Frankish horsemen re-established their close order and charged into the gaps the Lombards had left, attacking them from the sides and rear.

The ploy was a complete success. Soon not a single organized group of Lombard horsemen remained; instead, each man found himself fighting for his life against spears and swords directed at him from every side. The carnage was soon over, as the Lombards who were still able to do so dashed pell-mell eastward, away from the battle.

The Frankish horsemen let them go, turning instead on the lines of Lombard foot-soldiers, who were still engaged in close combat with the troops of the Frankish vanguard. Charging the Lombards from the south, the horsemen immediately broke into their ranks and sent hundreds of them into chaotic retreat. This allowed the southern flank of the Frankish vanguard to rush forward and strike down many of the fleeing Lombards.

Still, the larger northern portion of the Lombard infantry

held firm and continued to do battle both with the Frankish vanguard to their west and the horsemen to their south. Reinforcements were able to reach them, and with the main Frankish infantry still far up the pass, the weight of numbers favored the Lombards.

At this point Frankish officers realized that the strong wind blowing on their backs could be put to their service. They ordered their troops to retreat slightly, and at the same time they had archers shoot fire arrows into the open ground between the two lines of combatants. The long dry grass quickly ignited; within a minute or so a single long line of fire was racing eastward faster than a man could run. The Lombards retreated, first slowly and then in a panicked rush. Many were caught by the flames. Others escaped by dashing into the river, where most of them were picked off by the Frankish archers.

By the time Pepin himself arrived on the scene, the opposing army no longer existed as a fighting force. He sent his cavalry onward to pursue the fleeing Lombards, who abandoned not just the battlefield but also their camp with all its supplies and equipment. After waiting for the main section of his army to descend from the pass, Pepin moved on to Susa where he set up his own camp. The road to Pavia lay open before him.

43

"The Pope really wanted me to stay," said Zaid, as he guided a horse-drawn cart northward toward the Flaminian Gate. "He offered me employment—as deputy stable-master, if you can believe it. The old deputy died in the siege. He begged me, actually—but I said no."

"Maybe you should have taken it. I hope you didn't refuse for my sake," said Lenora.

"Well, for our sake, let's say. We need to go to Lucca if we're ever going to find your parents. And Rome means nothing to me anymore. My father's dead; I have no friends or family here."

"But to have the Pope for your protector, your patron—how many people can say that?"

"Not many, that's true," said Zaid. "But he can't last long—everyone says that. I mean, I wish him well, he's been very kind to me, but he's so feeble, he can hardly stand up. When I spoke with him, it was difficult even to understand what he was saying. And once he's gone, everything might change, so it's not really something we could rely on. Anyway, here's the gate—it's too late to change our minds now." The Flaminian Gate stood open, and Zaid steered the little cart through the narrow cobbled passageway.

The horse and cart were presents from the Pope, along with a small sum of money to help Zaid and Lenora on their way to Lucca. Stephen had seen Zaid's action at the mill as yet another sign that the young man had been sent by God. Zaid's desertion had long been forgiven or forgotten. In fact, the story had somehow got around that St. Peter himself had called Zaid away from his position for the specific purpose of repelling the covert assault.

Zaid had barely gotten the cart through the gate when a group of mounted soldiers came toward them at considerable speed. They were escorting someone who looked like an official messenger or legate. Zaid pulled the cart sharply to the side of the road, allowing the riders to dash through the gate and into the city. Then he and Lenora continued on their way, past the cemeteries, over the Milvian Bridge, and up the slopes of the Cassian Way toward the rolling upland landscape north of the city. The broken road surface presented so many obstacles that they could have made faster progress on foot, but the horse and cart were too valuable to abandon.

At the summit of the first climb Zaid stopped to rest the horse, and Lenora brought out a small loaf of bread and divided it between them. "When we get to Lucca, I'm going to find work in a bakery," she said. "It's the only work I know how to do."

"Fine," said Zaid, "but remember, we'll be traveling soon. I'm going to be a trader like my father—you know that."

"Won't you need money to get set up? You could work for my grandfather in the meantime. He must be quite old, so he could use help, probably."

"Soap-boiling?" said Zaid.

"Yes. He could get you into the guild, couldn't he?"

"Soap-boiling—that's disgusting work, my people don't do that. Besides, I have money already—look." Zaid reached into his purse and pulled out some gold coins.

"Solidi? Four, eight, ten—twenty solidi?" said Lenora in astonishment. "How did you get so much money? From the Pope?"

"No, I found it in our home. My father had a hiding place, behind a wall upstairs, where he kept money, and I looked to see if anything was left there. But I didn't expect to find this much."

"They're new."

"Yes, it must have been a single payment, and from a wealthy man. I wonder what he got for that—I don't ever remember my father selling something for so much."

"Don't new coins come from the Lateran Palace? Maybe it was the Pope who bought something."

"No, the Pope wasn't even there—he was traveling with me."

"Or someone else at the palace?"

"Maybe—who knows?"

"Listen, Zaid," said Lenora after a pause. "there's something I haven't told you."

"What?"

"Omar, before he died—my father asked him who had attacked him. He said—" Lenora hesitated.

"He said what—*what?*"

"He said 'Deacon Paul'—he said Deacon Paul sent those men."

"What?" Zaid exclaimed. "Deacon Paul? Why didn't you

tell me this before?"

"I'm sorry. I was afraid of what you'd do. I planned to tell you, but after we got to Lucca."

"You should have told me."

"I was afraid you'd—you'd try to get revenge, and then you'd get killed too. And anyway, maybe your father was wrong. How would he know it was Deacon Paul's men, and—"

"Maybe they told him."

"--and why would Paul want to kill Omar? He didn't even know him, did he?"

Zaid was seething. "You should have told me," he said. "We need to go back." He began to turn the cart around.

"*No!*" said Lenora, and she tried to grab the horse's traces. "We're going to Lucca. If we go back now, you'll get yourself killed."

"It must have been Paul's money. And he sent those men to get it back."

"They didn't even look for any money. They just ran downstairs."

"Because they heard you coming—you and your father."

"Zaid, this doesn't make any sense. If they wanted the money back, they wouldn't have just killed Omar, they'd have forced him to give them the coins. And all for twenty solidi? That's a lot for us—but it's nothing for the Lateran."

Zaid wasn't listening. "This is blood money," he said, looking down at the coins that were still in his hand. Then he hurled them in the direction of Rome. The coins sailed in a long arc, flashing in the sun, then bounced with a tinkling sound off the paving stones and lost themselves in the grass on either side of the road.

"*Zaid!*" cried Lenora, who was now equally angry. "We're going to Lucca. And we need the money. Whatever you want to do about Paul—you can do it later." She jumped off the cart, ran toward where the coins had landed, and starting searching for them. "Come on," she shouted, "Come and help me, if you want us to be together," she shouted.

Zaid stayed on the cart for a while, then he got down and reluctantly started helping Lenora find the coins. As they searched, he calmed down a little. Yes, he thought, I have to avenge my father, but it doesn't have to be right now. And the money could help me when it comes to the time.

After a long search they found nineteen of the coins, and then they resumed their journey northward. An hour or so later, Zaid noticed that the sun was beginning its downward path. He stopped the cart once more in order to perform the *salah* appointed for this time of day. Unrolling his prayer mat under a tree, he faced toward the south-east and began his prayer.

Meanwhile, Lenora gazed out over the autumn landscape. In spite of what Stephen wrote in his final appeal to Pepin, the Lombards had done little damage to the villages and farms around Rome—they had not had enough time. Peasants were back on their plots, hastening to gather in what they could of their neglected crops. Lenora recited her own private prayer, invoking God's protection on her parents and grandparents, and asking that she find them safe in Lucca.

Zaid raised his head from the mat and remained for a while on his knees. He kept his left foot tucked under his body, his right heel raised, and his hands on his knees, as his father had taught him. "*Allaahumma salli 'alaa Muhammadin,*" he said. "*O Allah, bless our Muhammad and the people of Muhammad, as you have blessed Abraham and the people of Abraham. Surely you are the Praiseworthy, the Glorious. O Allah, be gracious unto Muhammad and the people of Muhammad, as you were gracious unto Abraham and the people of Abraham. Surely you are the Praiseworthy, the Glorious.*"

Zaid looked over his right shoulder, toward the angel who was recording his good deeds. "*As salaamu 'alaikum wa rahmatulaah,*" he said. "*Peace and blessings of Allah be upon you.*"

Then he looked over his left shoulder, toward the angel who was recording his sins. "*As salaamu'alaikum wa rahmatulaah,*" he said again. "*Peace and blessings of Allah be upon you.*"

44

In the papal chambers, Stephen was doing his best to urinate into a glass flask. Having done so without too much spillage, he handed the flask to his personal physician and lifted his bloated legs back onto the couch. The physician in turn handed the flask to two uroscopists, who had been summoned to consult on Stephen's illness. One of them was an old man who was deformed by an unnatural stoop and who walked with the help of a cane; the other was a younger man who might have been his son.

The uroscopists took the flask and left the chamber. They peered at the urine against the whitewashed wall of a corridor. Then they went out to a balcony, where there was direct sunlight, and held the flask up to the sky. There was only a small amount of urine, and it had a murky yellow-brown hue. The older man held up a grubby sheet of parchment on which a circle of about twenty small flasks had been painted. Each flask contained urine of a different color, and next to each was a description of the corresponding ailment and its treatment. The two men consulted the parchment, looked at the urine, swirled the flask gently, looked back at the card again, pulled long faces, and had a lengthy discussion in Greek. Then they returned to the papal chamber and took the physician aside.

"Let me hear, let me hear," said Stephen. "It's my piss, isn't it?"

"Very well, of course, Your Holiness," said the older uroscopist, and the three men moved over to Stephen's couch. "We were telling this learned physician what we have been able to deduce from an examination of Your Holiness's water. From its color and consistency, and its warmth, we are able to conclude that Your Holiness is afflicted by a temporary overheating of the liver, which is affecting the production of venous blood. This has led in turn to an excess of the substance from which venous blood is made, which is to say lymph, whose particles are clouding the urine. Certainly, by God's grace and with appropriate treatment from your excellent physician, this condition will be righted. Your Holiness may expect a return to full health and vigor, or such vigor as is to be expected in a person of Your Holiness's seniority."

"Why can't I breathe, then?"

Stephen's physician stepped in. "The excess lymph is collecting in Your Holiness's chest. We hear it on auscultation. As we are now in autumn, the season of black bile, we don't expect this to worsen, but it will be important to alleviate the condition before the season of phlegm commences."

"Show me that card, and the flask," said Stephen. Reluctantly, the uroscopists handed the two items over to Stephen, who peered at the urine, then at the card, and then at the urine once more. After a brief fit of coughing, he said: "This one is the right color: what does it signify? Here—

what does this writing say? I'm too old to read this tiny scrawl, and my Greek was never good."

The uroscopists were not pleased by Stephen's effort to participate in the diagnostic process. They looked at each other, and the younger one said at last: "Well, Your Holiness, this corresponds to a failure of the—"

"But the colors on this parchment have faded, Your Holiness," broke in the old man. "It was made by a very ancient and trustworthy authority and given to my grandfather when he lived in Smyrna. The proper match is with this one here, where it says, 'ΗΠΑΤΟΣ ΠΝΕΥΜΑΤΑ ΤΑΡΑΞΟΝΤΑΙ—*the humors of the liver are disturbed, which may be treated by cutting.*"

"By cutting? Cutting what?"

"I will recommend that Your Holiness permit me to make small incisions—painless incisions—where the excess lymph has collected, which is to say in Your Holiness's legs," said his physician. "And perhaps also in the region between Your Holiness's legs and Your Holiness's back—I mean the nether cheeks, forgive me. This will permit the lymph to drain out, which will also help Your Holiness to breathe more easily."

There was a quiet knock at the door, and Stephen's chamberlain let himself in. "Your Holiness will excuse me," he said, "but messengers have arrived with a letter from King Pepin. I thought Your Holiness should know right away."

Stephen was excited by the news. "Thank you, thank you," he said. "We should read it with my counselors. Have them assemble in the—no, have them come up here, it's easier. And thank you too, learned gentlemen, for your wisdom. Concerning the treatment, I'll speak with you about it later. In the meantime, send someone to the Sacred Way—have them collect water from where the apostles knelt. I have more faith in that than in all your cutting."

The uroscopists and the physician bowed and left. After a while, Stephen heard his counselors begin to gather in an anteroom. Once they were all together they knocked and filed in. Attendants brought some chairs and arranged them around the couch on which Stephen was reclining.

Stephen led a prayer for good news, and then told the herald to hand the letter to Tullius, the Librarian, who unsealed it and began to read. "'*Vir illustrissimus Pippinus, Dei gratia rex Francorum—The most illustrious Pepin, by God's grace King of the Franks, sends eternal good wishes to the most revered and excellent Bishop of Rome, High Priest of the Roman Sanctuaries, Vicar of the Son of God, Holy Father, Successor of the Apostle, Holder of the Keys, Servant of the Servants of the Lord, Universal Pope and Patriarch, and Father of the Republic of St. Peter. Eighteen days ago—*'"

"Father of the Republic of St. Peter?" interjected Theophylact in feigned perplexity. "What is this Republic of St. Peter? I've never heard of such a thing—or such a place, if it is a place. Is it a city? Is it a nation? Or perhaps it's a duchy of the Heavenly Kingdom? And who chose its father?"

"Why don't we let Tullius get to the news that Pepin has for us?" said Paul. "It must be something of considerable—"

Theophylact ignored Paul's interjection. "If I recall the words of the Profession that Your Holiness attested to on the day of your anointing," he went on, "Your Holiness promised 'not to change or lessen one word of what has been handed down from my most worthy predecessors, nor to add anything new,' but Your Holiness will forgive me for thinking that this is a new papal title—one that no Pope until now has—"

"What Pepin chooses to write, you may lay to his charge, not mine," said Stephen. "Keep reading, Tullius."

"Yes, Your Holiness. Where was I? Ah yes: *Eighteen days ago, we wrote to Your Holiness concerning the magnificent victory granted by the Almighty to the Frankish army at the city of Susa, through the intercession of the blessed Peter and the blessed Martin. The King of the Franks, Aistulf, was himself injured in the head during the battle, but the Devil bound up his wounds and he survived. But in his haste to escape from the battlefield he threw away his own armor, which was a most shameful act. Many of his officers and princes were killed, as were two Archbishops who were rash enough to support Aistulf in his wicked endeavor.'"*

"Peace be on their souls," said Stephen. "Continue."

"*'After that most glorious event, and pausing only to destroy the camp of the Lombards and to collect the treasure that they left there, we hastened on to their capital at Pavia, hoping to prevent their King's entry into his own city. In that aim we were not successful, even though we abandoned our supply train and reached the city in only five days. We found the gates closed against us.*

"*Not wishing to undertake a three-year siege, such as the Lombards themselves undertook when they seized the city from King Alboin, we ordered the construction of an encircling earthen wall and ditch, facing the city and three hundred yards distant from it. We emplaced a palisade on top of this wall, so that neither man nor beast could leave the city. And we constructed a second wall and ditch, facing away from the city and five hundred yards distant from it, so that no army could approach or offer relief to the Lombards. For the armies of some of their allies are still in the field. And the city of Pavia being quite small, and having forty-five thousand men at our disposal, we were able to complete the circumvallation as well as the contravallation in just nine days.*

"While we undertook this work, there arrived two legates from the court of the Emperor, their names being John and George. They said that they been directed by messengers from your Treasurer, Marcellus, to find us here. These legates—"

"You told them to go to Pepin?" asked Paul incredulously, staring at Marcellus.

"No—not really," Marcellus stammered. "I had representatives at Perugia who were discussing the taxes that were due from some estates there. And these two Greeks arrived from the coast and asked about the state of the war, so my men told them about the battle at Susa, and the likelihood that Pepin would attack Pavia—which after all they could have found out from any fishwife, because the news was talked about everywhere. Never did my men urge them to go there, nor did they instruct them what to do or say if they met with Pepin."

"But you knew that the Emperor's agents were on their way to Pepin?"

"I—"

"This may all be irrelevant, if the news is what I hope for," said Stephen. "Go on, Tullius."

"Yes, Your Holiness. *These legates said that, when we had forced Aistulf to our will, we should demand that he give up possession of Ravenna and the other cities. We told them that this was indeed our intent. And the legates said, 'The Emperor requests that you instruct Aistulf to hand these cities back to His Serenity, who is their rightful ruler.' But we replied—'"*

"Exactly what I suspected," said Paul. "So this was a plot to restore those cities to the Emperor, in which Marcellus was a participant—an unwitting one, perhaps."

"That is not at all how I—" began Marcellus.

"Silence, please," said Stephen. "Let Tullius complete his reading without interruption."

"Thank you, Your Holiness. '*But we replied that the Donation of Constantine required us to hand those cities and territories to the Republic of St. Peter, and that we had given our solemn oath to do so. We said that we undertook this campaign for the benefit of no man, but for St. Peter and for the good of our own soul. So the legates went away unsatisfied, and they were not able to enter Pavia or speak with Aistulf.*

"*Having completed our investment of the city, we constructed engines of the largest kind and placed them before the walls, and with these engines we began to batter the walls of the city.*

"*Seeing what we had accomplished, King Aistulf sent his Archbishop out to us, asking for terms of surrender. We said that, if Aistulf opened his gates immediately, we would spare his life and his royal office and realm, and the lives of his citizens. If he refused, however, and forced us to continue the siege or to take the city by storm, then we would treat him and his people with the same mercy that he showed to the governor and people of Ravenna.*

"*The Archbishop well understood the meaning of our words. The next day Aistulf opened the gates of the city, and we laid down the conditions of submission, to which Aistulf agreed. By this agreement, he will pay recompense in the amount of one-third of his treasury, and shall surrender two hundred hostages, being the sons and daughters of his nobles, including his own son, and shall pay a yearly tribute of three thousand solidi. And the twenty-one cities promised to the Republic of St. Peter will be handed over: We have sent Fulrad, Abbot of St. Denis, who accompanies our army, to collect the keys of those cities and bring them to Your Holiness.*

"Thus by God's grace we have been empowered to fulfill the obligations to Your Holiness that we undertook on behalf of the blessed martyr and Apostle. It would have been my wish to come myself to the Holy City and pray at the tomb of the blessed Peter. We dearly desire with our own hands to place the keys of those cities on the Apostle's tomb, and to do obeisance once more to Your Holiness, Our Savior's one true representative on Earth. But the lateness of the season compels us to return to Francia, and then, as soon as the spring floods on the Loire have subsided, we must lead our army to Aquitaine, whose fractious Duke needs instruction in the modes of penitence. Thus it is not likely that we will be able to renew our personal intercourse with Your Holiness. Even so, my eldest son Charles, who accompanies us on the present campaign, has become enchanted by the beauty and abundance of Italy. He has told me that his heart's desire is to travel to Rome, and I am sure that he will do so once he has reached his majority, in order to kneel at Your Holiness's throne and to pray with the martyrs. That—"

"Or in order to expand the Frankish empire south of the Alps," commented Theophylact.

Finding himself near the end, Tullius dared to ignore Theophylact's remark and continue on. "*'That Your Holiness has crowned him King, along with his brother,'*" he read, "*'is a richer and more consequential gift than our own coronation. Until the time of his visit, may the Almighty preserve Your Holiness in full health of body and mind, so that the Catholic Church in the entire world may continue to enjoy your wise and sacred governance. Farewell. Pray for us, that our many grievous sins be not counted against us.'*"

In spite of Theophylact's reservations, there was general rejoicing among the counselors at the happy outcome of Pepin's campaign. "There must be a joyful celebration, right away, in which all our citizens can participate," said Stephen. "Will you see to that, dear Paul? And then, when those keys are delivered, there must be a rite of thanksgiving, an event so glorious that Romans will speak of for centuries to come. For the moment, though, I am a little tired."

The counselors took the hint, bowed, and hurried out, eager to spread the good news throughout the Lateran Palace and to the entire city.

Stephen turned to his chamberlain. "Please call the doctors back in."

45

———

It was an exceptionally cold day, even for January, but nearly the entire population of Rome had turned out for the procession to the Basilica of St. Peter. Merchants with their families and slaves; carpenters, turners, and blacksmiths; tanners and cobblers; day-laborers, fishermen, wagon-drivers, and tillers of the soil with their barefoot children; millers and bakers; clerics and civil functionaries from every district and church of the city, and from the other cities and towns of Latium; notaries and scribes by the hundred from the Lateran Palace; monks and nuns, some released by special disposition from their cloisters; coffin-makers and grave-diggers; pilgrims and idlers and whores. Among the various groups of citizens walked choirs singing hymns of praise and thanksgiving.

The procession was supposed to take a leisurely, winding course around the city, stopping at some of the holiest churches for prayer and the veneration of relics. But the bitter weather, and the Pope's extreme ill-health, forced a change of plans. From the Lateran Palace the celebrants headed directly down the hill, past the Basilica of the Four Crowned Martyrs and the Colosseum, around the north side of the Capitoline Hill, and through the residential streets of the Campus Martius to the Bridge of the Blessed Angel.

Near the tail end of the procession, Stephen was being carried on something that resembled a bier more than a throne; he was leaning far back, almost lying down, but with his shoulders and head propped up by pillows. He was covered in many layers of blankets, with his papal vestments laid out across the top of them. Occasionally he raised an arm slightly to acknowledge the crowd, and then an attendant quickly helped him cover himself. The many incisions in his legs, each propped open with a tiny sliver of cork, oozed edematous fluids, and the seepage gradually soaked the bandages in which his legs were wrapped, making them feel even colder than they were before.

Abbot Fulrad walked with some of the Lateran counselors in front of the Pope, and just behind the bearers of the holy books. Fulrad was shocked by the worsening of Stephen's physical condition since they last met in France. He, like Paul and the other counselors, urged Stephen to send a deputy to the ceremony, or to hold it at the Lateran Basilica, adjacent to the Lateran Palace, rather than all the way across the city at St. Peter's. But Stephen was not to be dissuaded. "The ceremony must be held at the tomb of the Apostle," he said, "and the Pope must be there to see it completed."

As the procession crossed the bridge, a slight flurry of snow added to the chill—the flakes were drifting almost sideways up the river, and they caught the marchers on every patch of exposed skin. Stephen himself, though well covered on most of his body, could feel the ice crystals sting his cheeks. Snow was not very common in Rome, and Stephen was reminded of the miraculous snowfall that had accompanied the foundation of the Basilica of St. Mary Major. But that snowfall was in summer, in the season of yellow bile, and it had offered a welcome relief from the heat. Now, in the season of phlegm, it just increased his discomfort.

Treasurer Marcellus was not in the group of counselors; instead, he was farther forward in the procession, amongst a large number of senators and nobles, some of whom had made a rare trip to the city from their country estates.

"We pray for the restoration of his health and a long life, of course," Marcellus was saying to some gentlemen who were bundled up in furs. "Even so, we must be prepared in case the Lord should call him to his rest, which could happen at any time. And then his successor will have to be chosen."

"Isn't his brother the likely choice—Deacon Paul?" asked one man. "He's in the Pope's favor, isn't he?"

"The Pope may favor Deacon Paul," said Marcellus, "but only because he's his brother, I'm afraid, not for any qualities that make him worthy of consideration. I've had many opportunities to observe the Pope's favoritism."

"Really?" said another man. "But didn't Paul play a role in the events that we're celebrating? I heard it was his idea to bring the Franks into the war. Without them, wouldn't Rome still be under siege, or laid waste already?"

"Paul's scheming was what led to Aistulf's anger against us in the first place," explained Marcellus. "If the Pope had followed the advice of Archdeacon Theophylact—if he had confined himself to his role as spiritual leader here in Rome—then none of these tragic events would have happened. Many Romans would be alive and well today who now lie dead in the cemeteries, or who limp around on stumps and crutches, like that man over there. But no, at Paul's instigation, he adopted a policy of confrontation, insulting the Emperor, challenging Aistulf to his face, demanding lands and cities that Rome has never claimed a right to before now. And Aistulf will be back as soon as the Franks are gone, believe me, so long as Paul continues to— mind your step!"

The senator barely avoided treading in a pile of horse dung. "When the time comes, Archdeacon Theophylact will be a worthier candidate," Marcellus went on. "He was a loyal disciple of our beloved Zachary. He respects the traditions of the Church and the teachings of our forefathers. He'll reestablish good relations with the Emperor. And he'll restore the ancient privileges of the nobility."

That aroused some interest. "Which privileges do you mean?" one man asked, as they continued on toward St. Peter's.

"Well, first and foremost, the right to elect the Pope," said Marcellus. "We've seen too many irregular elections in recent times, with Popes chosen by a clamoring mob, or by a secret cabal of clerics. This isn't good. We've seen Popes consecrated who never should have been chosen and who aren't in God's favor—who weren't in God's favor, I mean. You senators and nobles, you should have a voice in choosing the Pope—the leading voice."

"That's right," said one man, a landowner from Sutri. "*Qui omnibus praeesse debet ab omnibus eligatur*—let the ruler of all be chosen by all. It's the Pope who rules us now, not the Duke or the Emperor. The Pope orders us to feed Rome and defend Rome—it's our peasants and slaves who died in the siege—so we are the ones who should choose him."

"Exactly," said Marcellus. "But Stephen has refused to make it so. And I can tell you the reason: he knows that his brother would be passed over, because Paul favors the clergy."

"I supported Theophylact at the last election," said a senator. "He's a good man. But Deacon Paul also has good qualities."

"Maybe so," said Marcellus, "but Theophylact would restore other privileges too, such as exemption from military service for those who can pay for a substitute. This was always permitted until recent times."

"Yes, I heard that from my father," agreed a senator.

"And regarding the treatment of slaves," Marcellus went on, "no person of quality should have to answer for the death of a slave, according to the ancient authorities—it's an insult to his honor and position—but Paul wants to give the slaves of senators and nobles the same rights as those of the clergy—even slaves who are pagans! What nonsense is that? And what about dress? This Paul struts in finery richer than the Pope's—look, you can see him back there at the bridge—but he wants to stop senators from wearing the time-honored tokens of their rank, except at meetings of the Senate—which never take place, as you know. According to the rumors that I've heard, he's planning to abolish the rank of senator altogether. This man is not your friend."

Paul walked up the steps of the basilica next to his brother. Entering the basilica's open courtyard, he saw that both the courtyard and the flanking cloisters were packed with thousands of men and women who had not been able to get into the basilica itself. People were even standing directly on the graves of former popes and martyrs, Paul noticed in disgust. He himself had ordered many of these relics to be brought to St. Peter's from the catacombs, in order to save them from depredation, and it pained him to see them being defiled by the shoes and bare feet of the common people. He turned to Notary Christopher, who was walking near him in the procession, accompanied by his teenage son Sergius. "Have those people moved," he said.

Christopher, who had risen a step or two in the Lateran hierarchy since returning from Francia, bristled at being addressed like a servant. But he said "Yes, certainly," and he waved his son in the direction of the offending onlookers. Then he added, "Constantine's Donation has brought us to this triumphal day. You must be very proud." Paul gave him a piercing look, but Christopher returned an innocent smile. "I mean, your policies turned out to be the right ones, and the Donation proved it." Paul said nothing and turned his attention back to his brother.

The central door of the basilica stood open, and Stephen's bearers brought him through into the nave, with Paul still at his side. The crowded mass of celebrants, who had been talking and laughing loudly enough to drown the singing of the choir, fell suddenly silent, as they saw their Pope and understood for the first time the grave condition he was in.

Stephen gazed down the nave, past the forty-two immense columns that supported the ornately painted timber roof. At the far end, he saw the altar, guarded by the twisted columns that Constantine was said to have brought from

Solomon's Temple in Jerusalem. Behind and above the altar, the apse mosaic showed the risen Christ, with St. Peter and Constantine, who offered their Savior a little model of the basilica. In the light of thousands of lamps and candles, the three solemn figures seemed to stand forward from a background of shimmering gold.

Once inside the basilica, Stephen's bearers brought him to his allotted place and lifted him onto his throne. Thanks to the thousands of people jammed into the nave and the four side-aisles, it was noticeably less cold than it was outside the basilica, but attendants had placed several charcoal braziers next to Stephen's throne. Once Stephen was sitting more upright, he could breathe a little more easily, but his legs quickly became more congested and began to ache more severely than before.

Stephen had handed over all his liturgical responsibilities to others, and so he only had to sit on his throne and watch the proceedings, wrapped in his blankets, with his brother on one side and two doctors on the other. The mass dragged on for a long time, for many extra elements had been added to lend weight and pomp to the occasion.

At long last the all-important final portion of the ceremony began. As the congregation stood watching, a pair of strangers entered the church. They were dressed in linens and silks cut in the fashion of the Five Cities: they were clearly nobles, and they carried between them a silver platter covered with a white linen napkin, on which lay a pair of large iron keys. They walked slowly and solemnly to the altar, as a single voice from the back of the apse chanted God's praises. The men crossed themselves and bowed to the altar, and then descended to the Confession of St. Peter. They kissed the rim of the tomb and then stood in silence.

After a moment, the basilica's largest and most deep-toned bell rang out, filling the vast chamber with sound and compelling the congregation's absolute silence. When the echoes had died away, the men declaimed in loud voices: *"Beatissime Petre, claves civitatis Arimini apportamus—Most blessed Peter, we bring the keys of the city of Rimini, in acknowledgment of your great glory and the glory of your Republic, by God's mercy."* They offered the platter to a priest, who took the keys and placed them on the tomb. The two men stood aside, the chorister sang again, and another pair of noblemen took their place. The great bell rang out once more.

"Most blessed Peter, we bring the keys of the city of Cesena."

In succession, the ambassadors of Urbino and Gubbio and Narni and many other cities surrendered their keys.

Stephen watched the proceedings with deep satisfaction, but as the thirteenth or fourteenth set of keys was handed over, he slumped forward and seemed to lose any sense of where he was. As Paul and the doctor reached to help him, he recovered himself, and with their help he was able to regain a normal sitting posture. "Stephen, are you all right?" Paul whispered, as the attention of the congregation turned toward them and the line of ambassadors halted its forward shuffle.

"I'm all right," said Stephen in a weak voice. "Perhaps I nodded off for a moment, I don't know."

"You don't look all right. Shall we take you to the sacristy? You can lie down there. We can tell them to make a pause."

"No, no, keep going," Stephen insisted. "I'll be fine.

Keep going, we're nearly done."

Paul signaled for the ceremony to resume, and the line of ambassadors began to move forward again. "Most blessed Peter, we bring the keys of the city of Pesaro—the city of Jesi—the city of Sarsina—the city of Comacchio." With each new pair of ambassadors, the bell rang out and the keys were placed on the tomb.

At last the ambassadors of the twenty-third and final city entered the Confession, carrying a platter of gold. The bell rang for the twenty-third time. "Most blessed Peter, we bring the keys of the city of Ravenna, in acknowledgment of your great glory and the glory of your Republic, by God's mercy."

"God's mercy—by God's mercy," Paul repeated to himself, lost in his own self-torturing thoughts, as all the bells of the basilica rang out, joined quickly by those of nearby churches. "May God's mercy descend on me," he prayed, "and cleanse me of my evil deeds, through the intercession of the saints and blessed martyrs, and by the blood of our Savior Jesus Christ, through whom all sinners may be redeemed."

Soon, the bells of the entire city rang out in jubilant discord.

46

'*Per istam sanctam unctionem—Through this holy unction and His own most tender mercy, may the Lord pardon you for whatever sins you have committed by sight.*" The priest touched the holy oil to Stephen's forehead, above his left and right eyes. Stephen's eyes were open, but he didn't seem to register what was going on. A small group of clerics, doctors, and other attendants watched in silence.

Paul, who stood next to Stephen with his head bowed in prayer, spoke the "Amen" on behalf of his brother.

"Through this holy unction and His own most tender mercy, may the Lord pardon you for whatever sins you have committed by hearing." The priest touched the oil to Stephen's ears, but the Pope lay silent and unresponsive, and again Paul responded for him.

The priest proceeded to anoint Stephen's nose, then his lips, his hands, and his feet, which were as cold as those of a man already dead. Finally the blanket that covered him was lifted aside by an attendant, and the priest touched the oil to Stephen's genitals. "Through this holy unction and His own most tender mercy," he said, "may the Lord pardon you for whatever sins you have committed by carnal delectation."

The covers were replaced.

"Amen," said Paul, and he raised his head from prayer. "Thank you, I'll sit with him," he went on. "You may leave us." The priest and the other attendants bowed and left the papal chambers.

Paul watched his brother, who seemed to hover indecisively between life and death. From time to time he stopped breathing altogether, making Paul think that he had already passed. Then he would notice some slight movements of Stephen's chest, which gradually built up to a climax of rapid heaves, as if he were making up for the breaths that he had missed. Then they would weaken and die away again. Stephen's spirit, Paul thought, was like a newly-fledged bird that struggled to take wing, then rested, then struggled again, as if it longed to quit the outworn nest of his body and soar freely into the endless spaces of the sky.

It was very quiet. The church bells, which had filled the city with joyful noise a month earlier, now hung muffled and silent, as if time itself had been ordered to stand still. Outside the palace, watchmen diverted the occasional noisy cart, and they urged passers-by to restrain their children's shouts and laughter. Only the birds in the Lateran gardens kept up their usual chatter. Rome waited.

Paul's thoughts turned to his childhood and youth. Always, it seemed, his older brother had been there by his side—his playmate and protector. Rarely, Paul thought, had two people spent so much of their lives together. How would it feel when he was alone? Yes, he might well be chosen as Stephen's successor, but what joy would that bring him? He was popular with the people, but within the Lateran Palace he had few friends. Who would give him good advice? Who would he share his hopes and fears with? Who would grin at him, as they stood at the top of the long stairway with its shiny balustrade, and say, "I dare you to slide down?"

Yes, he would have power. He could do good for many, and that was worth a great deal. But what good could he do for himself? Paul had a vision in which, sitting on the papal throne, he commanded his minions: 'Send to the monastery of Bischofsheim-on-Tauber; have the abbess come to Rome, where she shall found a hostel for the British pilgrims. Or better, she shall teach me her language, or that of the Germans. Or she shall return to her studies here in the Lateran Palace, and she shall be my secret concubine—"

"Aistulf," came a barely audible whisper.

What was that? Paul tore himself away from his unworthy fantasy. Had someone spoken? Unless it was a spirit, it could only have been his brother. Paul hovered over Stephen's face, looking for some sign of awareness.

"Aistulf," Stephen whispered again.

"Aistulf?" Paul asked. "Aistulf is dead."

"Dead?"

"Yes, we heard three weeks ago. We told you, don't you—"

"Dead?"

"Yes, he fell during a hunt. He lingered unconscious for three days, and then he died. The Devil has him now."

"Repented—?"

"He didn't get much chance."

"So, who—" Stephen's words were cut off by a fit of coughing.

"Who is king, you mean?"

"Yes."

Paul was amazed at his brother's return to lucidity. He wondered whether the Extreme Unction had something to do with it. "Ratchis, Aistulf's predecessor," he said, "whom our beloved Zachary persuaded to give up his throne. When he heard the news, he left his monastery and hurried to Monza. He seized the Iron Crown and placed it on his own head. But Desiderius has raised an army against him. They will fight it out, and by God's grace they will destroy each other, and the Lombard Kingdom too."

Stephen was silent, and Paul wondered whether he had lost consciousness again. But then his brother murmured: "I'm ready."

"Ready? For— "

"For the—the anointing."

"Oh. I—they performed it already. A few minutes ago, when you were sleeping, or—we thought—well, shall I have them come and perform it again?"

One of Stephen's hands strayed across to the other, and felt the oil. "No, that's sufficient," he said.

There was a silence. Then Paul asked, "Is there anything I can get you, or do for you?"

"Not for me—the Church."

"Which is what? Do what?"

"Go seek—people who'll speak—who'll support you. Like Theo is doing—isn't he?"

"He is."

"Don't let him win."

"Stephen, there'll be time for that, when the day comes. So long as the Pope lives, no man shall canvass for his successor—isn't that the law?"

"You *must* be my—my—" Stephen whispered.

"I will be. But let me sit with you for now."

Another, longer silence followed. Once more, the twittering of the birds in the garden was the loudest sound to be heard. Stephen's bouts of effortful breathing weakened, and the pauses between them lengthened.

This is my last chance with him, Paul thought. With the Holder of the Keys. My last chance to wipe the slate clean.

"Stephen," he said.

"Yes."

"Stephen, I want to confess—to three mortal sins, and to seek absolution."

"Yes."

"Shall I begin?"

"Yes."

Paul kneeled at the side of his brother's bed. *"Ignosce mihi, Pater, quia peccavi,"* he recited. "I've sinned—carnally."

"With a woman or a man—or a child?"

"With a woman."

"Was any issue born of—born of that union?"

"No, no—no issue."

"Did she or you—" Stephen tailed off, seeming to lose track of what he was trying to say.

"Stephen?" asked Paul urgently.

"Did she or you, by means of any herb or poison—" Stephen tailed off again, and took a few halting breaths. "— Or by any incantation or black art, prevent—prevent— pre—"

"—Prevent the birth of any child already ensouled and quickened? No, Holy Father, no."

"And are you truly contrite?"

"I am truly contrite."

"And not merely—"

"—Not merely for the sake of my own soul's salvation."

"I absolve you of your sin—in the Holy Name of Jesus. Thirty days' penance."

"Thank you, Holy Father," said Paul. "And I wished a man dead, who then was killed on my behalf."

"Are you truly—?"

"I'm truly contrite, and not merely for the sake of my own soul's salvation."

"Did that man have a wife or children—who are still living?"

"He had a son, who I believe is still living."

"I absolve you of your sin. Do sixty—" Stephen paused to cough and regain his breath. "In the Holy Name of Jesus. Sixty—sixty—"

"Sixty days' penance? Thank you, Holy Father."

"Seek out that—that man's son. Make restitution to him."

"I will. Thank you, Holy Father."

There was another silence. Stephen seemed to lose any engagement with his surroundings, but then he murmured, almost inaudibly, "A third—?"

"A third sin? Yes." Paul was sweating and shaking with anxiety, even terror.

"Speak."

Paul remained silent. Then he realized that Stephen was slipping away again, and he determined not to lose his chance. "Constantine's letter—the Donation—" he began, and then halted again.

"The Donation?"

"Yes."

"What about it?"

"I—I wrote it."

"Wrote?"

"I wrote it—I invented it," Paul stuttered. "To provide a reason for—it was with a good intention, and the result was what—but I lied to you about it, Stephen—Holy Father."

Stephen had been lying motionless on the bed, but now he began to writhe slightly, and he tried to raise his arms in front of his head, as if warding off demons. He seemed to speak a little, but Paul caught only one word: "Sylvester?"

"Sylvester? I placed it in his sarcophagus—in his hand— so that you would find it—"

Stephen turned his head slightly toward his brother, but didn't say anything intelligible. He seemed to be engaged in a physical struggle, though whether against Paul or against his own oncoming death, Paul couldn't tell.

"I'm truly contrite," Paul said, "and not merely for the sake of my own soul's salvation."

Stephen still said nothing. His eyes darted from side to side, as if following invisible creatures that swirled around him. Ropes of frothy saliva, tinged pink with blood, drooled from his mouth.

"Am I absolved?" Paul asked urgently.

Stephen didn't speak. His breaths, which had been losing what little strength they had, gave way to great retching heaves that raised his whole trunk momentarily from the bed.

"I'm contrite," Paul said again, more forcefully. "I'm contrite."

Finally Stephen was able to get a few words out. He was staring at the window of the chamber, and he cried out with a stronger voice that he had been capable of up until now: "The star! I see it!"

"The star? What star? It's daytime," said Paul. "Am I absolved?"

But Stephen was far away. "The falling star!" he cried out. "I see it!"

"Stephen—Holy Father—I'm truly contrite—I beg for absolution!"

"The falling star!" Stephen cried out again, oblivious to his brother's words. "From the north—to Rome—bringing great evil!"

As Stephen took leave of his senses, so also did Paul. He reached down and grasped his brother by both shoulders, lifting his trunk and shaking him violently.

"Am I absolved?" he shouted directly into Stephens face. "Tell me—am I absolved?" Stephen didn't speak, nor did he take a breath.

"Am I absolved?" Paul screamed one more time. Then he let his brother fall lifeless back onto the bed.

Alarmed by the clamor, doctors and priests rushed into the chamber.

AFTERWORD

This book is a historical novel, meaning that it is a mixture of truth and fiction. For readers interested in disentangling the two, the following is an attempt to spell out the historical context of the novel and the extent to which its characters and events are based in reality.

Aside from the "little people"—Omar, Zaid, Marcus, Sibylla, and Lenora—the main characters of the book are actual historical figures. Pope Stephen II reigned from 752 to 757—he is referred to as Stephen III by those who believe that his predecessor should be included in the Apostolic Succession in spite of having died before his consecration. After Stephen's death, the succession was contested between Stephen's younger brother Paul, who was a Deacon during Stephen's papacy, and Archdeacon Theophylact, but Paul was chosen and held the office until his own death in 767.

Other historical figures include First Notary Ambrose, Governor (or Exarch) Eutychius, the Lombard King Aistulf, the Frankish King Pepin (Pepin III or Pepin the Short), his wife Bertrada and their sons Charles (the future Charlemagne) and Carloman, Leoba (later canonized as Saint Leoba or Lioba), Abbot Fulrad, Bishop Chrodegang, Duke Autchar, and the roving heretic Aldebert. Historical characters who play off-stage roles in the story include Archbishop Boniface (now Germany's patron saint) and the Emperor in Constantinople. The Emperor is not named in the novel, but it was another Constantine: Constantine V, nicknamed Constantine Copronymus ('Constantine Whose Name is Shit') because he supposedly soiled his baptismal font.

Stephen's papacy, though it only lasted five years, was quite significant in the historical development of the Catholic Church. Readers unfamiliar with European history may imagine that popes from St. Peter to the present day have formed an unbroken succession of spiritual guides devoted exclusively to the saving of souls. The reality, of course, has been very different: starting in late classical times, popes took on the role of civil administrators in Rome, and also began to accumulate estates (or patrimonies) scattered throughout Italy. These estates were mostly deeded to the Church by landowners concerned for the welfare of their souls, and they became important sources of income and grain for Rome.

Nevertheless, by Stephen's time, Rome was a shadow of its former Imperial self, greatly reduced in population, and politically and economically insignificant. The city was alternately harassed and abandoned by its supposed rulers, the Eastern Emperors, who attempted to govern Italy from their power base at Ravenna. A succession of mostly Greek-speaking Popes, ending with Zachary, had tried to maintain some kind of accommodation with Constantinople, but this was made difficult by the doctrinal dispute over sacred images (icons). At the same time, they struggled to fend off threats from the Lombards and other potential invaders.

Lacking an effective army, the Popes used bribes, threats of hellfire, or simple persuasion to do so. Many of the patrimonies were lost to the Lombards or their allies, or to Constantinople, so that Rome became increasingly impoverished. The fall of Ravenna to the Lombards in 751, shortly before Stephen's accession, seemed to portend a similar fate for Rome.

Yet Stephen initiated a process of re-expansion that enabled the Catholic Church to play a central role in European politics for over a thousand years. By his alliance with Pepin he acquired territories in Italy that became the Papal States. In addition, by crowning Pepin King of the Franks, he established an authority over Europe's civil rulers that led, forty-five years later, to Charlemagne's coronation as Emperor of the Romans by Pope Leo III, and later to the Holy Roman Empire. Though marred by many vicissitudes and inglorious episodes, the papacy maintained itself as a political force until 1870, when it finally lost possession of the Papal States. In fact, the very concept of "Europe," by which parts of the ancient Mediterranean world acquired a shared identity with lands north of the Alps, takes its origin in considerable measure from Stephen's papacy.

Perhaps inevitably, this expansion of the Church's role was accompanied by a change in thinking. In earlier years, most practical decisions and moral judgments were reached by reference to prior authority—the authority of the gospels, the writings of the Fathers of the Church, or the pronouncements of earlier Popes. A new Pope's primary duty, as laid out in his sworn Profession, was to adhere to the beliefs and practices of his predecessors. As the Church developed a political role, a more pragmatic, even

Machiavellian style of thinking came to predominate. Now prior authority, if it was lacking, could be invented. And as the Church slid from its godfearing principles toward the moral nadir of the tenth-century "Pornocracy," the forging of documents became a small industry.

The main events of Stephen's papacy—the Lombard threat, the journey to Pavia and Francia, Aistulf's siege of Rome, Pepin's invasion of Lombardy, and the handing over of the twenty-three Italian cities to the Pope, took place more or less as described in this book. I have compressed the story somewhat, however. For example, it actually took two campaigns by Pepin, in two successive years, before Aistulf was finally brought to heel, rather than the single campaign that I describe.

The detailed episodes within this larger story are a mix of fact and fiction. The episode in which Stephen's party is terrified by a falling star, for example, is historically attested; the snowstorm on the Mons Jovis pass, on the other hand, is not.

The historical personage with whom I've taken the greatest liberties is Leoba. She was indeed an English missionary, and she was called to Germany by Boniface and appointed abbess of Tauberbischofsheim. But she is not known to have visited Rome, nor to have met Paul.

With regard to people who were already historical in the eighth century, such as the early Christian martyrs, I've stayed fairly close to accounts that were in circulation in Stephen's time. The story of St. Peter's daughter Petronilla was told in the Apocryphal *Acts of Peter*, which was current in the eighth century (see M.R. James in Sources); her supposed sarcophagus and body were moved from a catacomb (not the Catacomb of Priscilla, actually) to St. Peter's by Paul after his accession to the Papacy (see Dorothy Verkerk in Sources).

My accounts of relics and their provenance are based mostly on stories that were accepted as true—the Holy Face of Lucca's miraculous journey to Italy is an example. Omar's relics were of course fakes, but fakes that would have been believable to many. Stephen did not give Pepin Jesus' foreskin, but he plausibly might have done, since there were several exemplars of this relic in circulation. One of them, in Antwerp, was still dripping blood more than a thousand years after Jesus' birth.

What about the Donation of Constantine? This is an actual historical document that exists in several ancient copies. The version that Tullius reads in chapter 17 is an abridged version of the text, in a 1910 translation by Ernest Henderson (see Sources), with a few modifications.

The origin of the Donation is somewhat mysterious. There is a general consensus that it was produced by someone in the papal chancellery, given that the text of the Donation is so obviously devoted to the furtherance of papal interests. Some historians have named Paul as the prime suspect, in part because Paul is known to have had a special interest in Pope Sylvester. In addition, certain passages in the Donation are said to resemble those found in extant letters written by Paul.

If Paul was the perpetrator, he could have written it (or had it written) while he was Stephen's deacon, or during his own pontificate. With regard to the date of production, most experts have pointed to the mid-eighth century or slightly later, based on linguistic peculiarities of the text. As to the purpose of the forgery, some writers have concluded that it was produced to strengthen Stephen's hand with Pepin (the interpretation followed in this book), while others believe that it was produced with the idea of influencing Charlemagne and others during the turbulent decades that followed Stephen's papacy. Less plausibly, it has been suggested that the Donation was a mere literary exercise with no political significance.

Whoever produced the Donation used existing legends about Constantine as a starting point. The development of these legends was traced by Christopher Bush Coleman (see Sources, below). The earliest known versions cropped up in the East (Mesopotamia and Armenia) in the fifth century. These legends may have been created by grafting Constantine's name onto earlier legends in which Eastern monarchs, such as King Abgar of Odessa, were cured of leprosy by conversion to Christianity. In the following century the legend was Romanized by the naming of Pope Sylvester as the person who cured and baptized the Emperor. This version, known as the *Vita Silvestri*, was fleshed out with many local details such as the story of the dragon under the Tarpeian Rock. Thus, all that the producer of the Donation had to do was to select the most relevant material from the *Vita*, add the material relating to the primacy of the Roman See, the privileges relating to liturgical dress, and the territorial donation to the Papacy, and put the whole thing into the form of a letter from Constantine to Sylvester and his successors.

For many centuries after its creation, the Donation was almost universally accepted as authentic. Some details did raise concern, certainly. Most notable was the discrepancy between its account of Constantine's baptism in Rome and his historically attested baptism by Eusebius in Nicomedia, near Constantinople, shortly before his death. This discrepancy was resolved by medieval writers in a variety of ways: the Roman baptism was judged heretical and had to be repeated, the Constantine baptized in Nicomedia was a different person from the one baptized in Rome, the Nicomedian baptism was a myth resulting from a confusion of names (Eusebius of Nicomedia versus a Roman bishop of the same name), and so on. What's more, Christian writers had difficulty accepting that Constantine delayed his baptism until the end of his life, because that would have meant that he presided over the all-important First Ecumenical Council (the Council of Nicaea) without having being baptized into the Christian faith.

During the Middle Ages, the disappearance of ancient texts and the general forgetting of classical history allowed many errors in the Donation to go unchallenged. It would have been difficult, for example, for anyone before the Rennaissance to check whether Gallicanus was co-consul during the fourth consulate of Constantine, as the Donation states. (He wasn't.) Nor would anyone have known whether Constantine wore a tiara (he didn't) or whether his attendants were called "satraps." (They weren't.)

At least ten Popes cited the Donation as authority for a variety of worldly claims. In the twelfth century, for example, Pope Adrian IV used it as justification for his donation of Ireland to England's King Henry II. (It may not be a coincidence that Adrian, born Nicholas Breakspear, was the one and only English Pope.) This laid the groundwork for the Anglo-Irish conflict that has persisted until very recent years.

Medieval law-books cited the Donation extensively. Writers and artists also accepted its veracity. Dante Alighieri assumed the truth of the Donation while lamenting its evil consequences (see the epigraph at the beginning of this book). A remarkable series of eleven frescoes in the Roman Basilica dei Santi Quattro Coronati, probably dating from the late thirteenth century, illustrate episodes in the story of the Donation: a detail from one of these frescoes is shown on the cover of this book. Raphael (or his assistants) also painted the Donation. Raphael's work fails to capture the spirit of fourth-century Rome—or eighth-century Rome, for that matter—but it does offer a valuable interior view of the old St. Peter's Basilica before it was torn down to make way for the present church. Raphael's painting is the basis for my description of the basilica in chapter 42.

One of the first writers to attack the authenticity of the Donation was the German cardinal and philosopher Nicholas of Cusa, who presented a number of arguments for its fraudulent nature in his book *De Concordantia catholica* (1432-1435). A much more thorough job, however, was done a few years later by Lorenzo Valla, secretary to King Alfonso V of Aragon. Valla was a leading humanist, in the Renaissance sense of the word—that is, a scholar who devoted himself to the unearthing of Classical texts and the revival of learning. His *Discourse on the Forgery of the Alleged Donation of Constantine* (1440) attacked the Donation on many fronts. Most interesting and compelling, perhaps, was his use of textual and linguistic analysis to show that the Donation could not have been written in the age of Constantine. The book has earned Valla a reputation as the father of textual criticism. Nevertheless, his book was also highly polemical, because his patron Alfonso was locked in a war with Pope Eugene IV. Thus both the doing and the undoing of the Donation were politically motivated.

The first printed edition of Valla's work appeared in 1517, and may have contributed to the anti-papal fervor of the Reformation. Thus Martin Luther, after reading it, expressed his violent reaction in the letter to his friend Georg Spalatin (February 24, 1520):

> *I have at hand Lorenzo Valla's proof ... that the Donation of Constantine is a forgery. Good heavens! What a darkness and wickedness is at Rome! You wonder at the judgment of God that such unauthentic, crass, impudent lies not only lived but prevailed for so many centuries, that they were incorporated in the Canon Law, and (that no degree of horror might be wanting) that they became as articles of faith. I am in such a passion that I scarcely doubt that the Pope is the Antichrist expected by the world, so closely do their acts, lives, sayings, and laws agree.*

Contemporary historians, however, are less interested in the Donation as evidence for the wickedness of an individual forger or of the Papacy as a whole; rather, they see it as a window into the thought processes of people who lived at that time. Thus Boston University historian Clifford Backman writes: "To the early medieval mind, the genuineness of a document lay in its contents, not its form. If what a document said was true, in other words, it did not matter if the document itself was counterfeit." (see Sources,

Backman, p. 137). The arguments used by Leoba to justify the forgery are intended, to some extent, to reflect this point of view. If that was a general attitude, it may make Paul's eventual pangs of remorse one of the less plausible aspects of my story.

Regarding names, I mostly use the forms of names that are readily comprehensible to English-speaking readers. Sometimes that wasn't appropriate: I refer to the Great St. Bernard Pass by its ancient name of Jove's Mountain, for example, because St. Bernard was not yet born at the time of this story. And I use Francia as the name of Pepin's kingdom, because its borders did not correspond to those of present-day France.

SOURCES

The following are some of the main sources I used in writing this novel. Please bear in mind, however, that I am not a historian and that this book is first and foremost a work of fiction.

Atchley, E.G. Cuthbert F. (1905). *Ordo Romanus Primus.* London: Alexander Moring, Ltd. (Available at http://www.archive.org/details/ordoromanusprimu00atchu oft).

Bachrach, Bernard S. (2001). *Early Carolingian Warfare: Prelude to Empire.* Philadelphia: University of Pennsylvania Press.

Backman, Clifford R. (2009). *The Worlds of Medieval Europe (2nd. ed.).* New York: Oxford University Press.

Canadian Society of Muslims (no date). *How to Perform Salaat, the Islamic Ritual Prayer.* (Available at: http://muslim-canada.org/salaat.html).

Coleman, Christopher Bush (1914). *Constantine the Great and Christianity: Three Phases: The Historical, the Legendary, and the Spurious.* New York: Columbia University Press.

Coleman, Christopher Bush (1922/2000). *The Treatise of Lorenzo Valla on the Donation of Constantine.* University of

Toronto Press.

Gager, John G. (1999). *Curse Tablets and Binding Spells from the Ancient World*. New York: Oxford University Press.

Halsall, Paul (translator)(1997) *Rudolf of Fulda's Life of Leoba*. (Available at Medieval Sourcebook, http://www.fordham.edu/halsall/basis/leoba.html).

Halsall, Paul (translator) (2000). *Huneberc of Heidenheim: The Hodoeporican of St. Willibald*. (Available at Medieval Sourcebook, http://www.fordham.edu/halsall/basis/willibald.html.)

Henderson, Ernest F. (1896). *Select Historical Documents of the Middle Ages*. London: G. Bell.

Herrin, Judith (1987). *The Formation of Christendom*. Princeton: Princeton University Press.

Hodgkin, Thomas (1899). *Italy and Her Invaders. Book VIII: 744-774 Frankish Invasions*. Oxford: Clarendon Press.

James, M.R. (translator) (1924). The Acts of Peter. In: *The Apocryphal New Testament*. Oxford: Clarendon Press. (Available at: http://www.earlychristianwritings.com/text/actspeter.html).

Noble, Thomas F.X. (1984). *The Republic of St. Peter: The Birth of the Papal State, 680-825*.Philadelphia: University of Pennsylvania Press.

Poole, Reginald L. (1915). *Lectures on the History of the Papal Chancery Down to the Time of Innocent III*. Cambridge, England: Cambridge University Press.

Richards, Jeffrey (1979). *The Popes and the Papacy in the Early Middle Ages, 476-752*. London: Routledge and Kegan Paul.

Rinne, Katherine Wentworth (no date). *Aqua Urbis Romae:*

The Waters of the City of Rome. (Available at http://www3.iath.virginia.edu/waters/first.html).

Smith, Julia M.H. (2005). *Europe After Rome: A New Cultural History 500-1000.* New York: Oxford University Press.

Smith, Preserved (1914) *The Life and Letters of Martin Luther.* Boston, New York: Houghton Mifflin.

Verkerk, Dorothy (2007). Life After Death: The Afterlife of Sarcophagi in Medieval Rome and Ravenna. In: Éamonn Ó Carragáin, Carol L. Neuman de Vegvar (Eds.): *Roma Felix: Formation and Reflections of Medieval Rome.* Aldershot, England: Ashgate (pp. 139-158).

Wallace-Hadrill, J.M. (translator) (1960) *The Fourth Book of the Chronicle of Fredegar With its Continuation.* Connecticut: Greenwood Press. (Available at: http://www.bu.edu/english/levine/grch4+5.htm)